CARTOUCHE,
THE FRENCH JACK SHEPPARD.

SOME BLOWS FELL FAST ON THE UNHAPPY FUGITIVE.

NO. 1

CARTOUCHE!

THE FRENCH JACK SHEPPARD.

CHAPTER I.

THE ASTROLOGER'S PREDICTION.

IN one of the lowest quarters of the gay city of Paris there dwelt, in the year 1695, a man named Stephen Cartouche. Stephen was a cooper by trade, and laboured honestly at his calling. Being rather stingy, he was reputed wealthy for a man in his position.

Stephen Cartouche was refreshing himself in a wine-shop one winter evening, when a woman, a neighbour of his, entered.

"Ah, Monsieur Cartouche, let me congratulate you," she exclaimed. "Such a fine boy!"

"Eh! Another boy? Well, boys are more useful than girls."

"Depends! But surely you will call in the wise man, Maroquin, and let him draw the child's horoscope, so that we may know what fortune the stars foretell for him."

"Yes, we will do that. Did you note the exact time?"

"To a minute, by the church bell."

"Good! Then, Madame Lafarge, if you will do me the favour to drink this glass of wine to the health of my new son, we will seek Father Maroquin at once."

The woman—one of those hags who always contrive to be present at births and deaths (they are not so welcome at weddings)—drank the liquor Stephen Cartouche offered her, and then he went off to have his first look at the infant who is to be the hero of this tale.

Madame Lafarge, for her part, undertook to bring the wise man—the astrologer Maroquin—in order that the career of the new-born infant might be decided by a reference to the heavenly bodies at the time of his birth.

"And he shall be named Louis Dominique Cartouche, which is the name of my brother, the wealthy merchant at Rouen," the cooper remarked, after having a good look at the little lump of humanity.

"Pray Heaven he may not disgrace the name," sighed the mother.

"Madame! do you think disgrace can ever attach itself to the name of Cartouche? If you were not——"

"No violence, Stephen."

"I will use no violence; but you injure the innocent child by your base suspicions."

"Hush! here comes Pere Maroquin."

There was a tap at the outer door, and in response to the cooper's invitation to enter, the astrologer walked into the apartment and gravely saluted those present in a style which was generally thought to be imitated from the Arabians, but certainly was not French.

Pere (Father) Maroquin, as the man was called, was an elderly man, dressed in a robe of dark brown, confined at the waist by a belt of light blue, on which various strange figures were embroidered. On his head was a tall fur cap.

"Peace to you all," said he, as he seated himself on a chair. "You desire my counsel and advice?"

Stephen Cartouche, the father, nodded, and told the astrologer why. Maroquin then produced paper, pencil, and rule, made some mystic signs on the paper like those on his girdle, and finally pronounced—

"This boy will be renowned——"

"Huzza!" shouted Stephen Cartouche, and his wife feebly echoed the cry.

The astrologer waved his hand to command silence, and all were quiet except the baby, who at that moment set up a feeble, fitful cry, as though protesting against having his fortune told at such an early age. Madame Lafarge took the mite of humanity and held it over the table upon which Maroquin had spread his paper; and then the wise man went on—

"For what will he be renowned? Of a truth I cannot yet say; but, Master Stephen, place a piece of silver here where my first finger is—now another where my thumb rests, and now yet another piece where my last finger touches the paper. That is right—now wait a few minutes.

Stephen Cartouche knew that the fee of Pere Maroquin was three pieces of silver when artisans consulted him, while from the rich he took as much gold as he could get; so he put down the coins as directed, and then, while the astrologer was casting up some figures on the margin of his paper, he bent over the table, staring with all his eyes upon the queer diagram Maroquin had drawn. So did Madame Lafarge, holding the infant in her arms.

"Mercury, in conjunction with Venus at the hour of nativity, and both planets in the ascendant. That is a great sign!"

"Sign of what, Pere Maroquin?" demanded Madame Lafarge.

"That the boy will be great at acquiring wealth; the influence of the planet Mercury renders that certain."

"But will he keep it? Will he use it as a

brave Frenchman and good citizen should?" Stephen Cartouche inquired.

"Alas!"

"Why do you sigh, Pere Maroquin?"

"The planet Venus also rules him, and I fear that his gains will be lost through his devotion to the fair sex. And if he should be lucky enough to escape hanging—oh, murder!"

The sudden change in the astrologer's voice was caused by the action of Madame Lafarge, who dealt Pere Maroquin a sounding slap on the cheek, and demanded how he dared defame an innocent infant. Stephen Cartouche also assumed a threatening look, as he pointed to the door, and intimated that Maroquin had better put himself the other side of it.

"Be it so. I depart, but I leave no blessing behind——"

"It would do little good—beware, though, how you curse."

"I curse not—but I prophesy that you, Madame Lafarge, will die a violent death. Why, where is the coin?—did you not put three upon the table, Monsieur Cartouche?"

"Yes; three pieces, your usual fee in such cases. Take them and begone, Pere Maroquin."

"But there are only two pieces—one has vanished."

"I put down three. Did you not see me, Madame?"

"I did, and I'll take my oath I did not touch them."

"Then I'll take the two and depart," said Maroquin, as he stood in the doorway. "But though you have cheated me you will not be able to cheat Fate. Madame Lafarge——"

"Away brute, dolt, idiot!"

"You will die a violent death, madame."

At this juncture anyone in an ordinary frame of mind could have heard the tramp of a file of soldiers ascending the stairs. But neither Maroquin, Cartouche, nor Madame Lafarge heard it, and the astrologer went on—

"A violent and shameful death, Madame Lafarge; and for you, Stephen Cartouche, it is written in the Book of Fate that your son shall become a great robber and a companion of notorious women—and that book never lies."

"And for you it is written about ten years at the galleys I should fancy," said a deep, harsh voice—that of a corporal—who at the same moment seized Maroquin by the arm. "The robber of the Countess De Sevigne's diamonds cannot, surely, have less than ten years chained to the oar."

Maroquin said nothing, but turned very pale, and seemed on the point of fainting as the soldiers led him away. It may here be said that the corporal proved a true prophet, for the astrologer, being found guilty of stealing the jewels of a titled lady who consulted him, was condemned to serve ten years as a galley-slave.

"Put the child back with his mother, Madame Lafarge," said Stephen Cartouche, when the echoing tramp of the soldiers could no longer be heard. "But what is that he has in his little hand?"

Examination proved that it was the missing piece of silver. As Madame Lafarge bent down over the table those little fingers clutched upon the coin and held it fast.

"Are the words of Pere Maroquin coming true so early?" said Stephen Cartouche.

And Madame Lafarge shook her head with an air of most intense wisdom.

CHAPTER II.

IN THE TOILS.

LOUIS DOMINIQUE, as he was christened, grew and thrived, and by all except a few the prognostication of Maroquin was quite forgotten.

But Cartouche senior could not help noticing that his second son (for Louis had an elder brother) was extremely adroit in acquiring the toys, fruit, and cakes of his playfellows without much reference to their ideas or wishes. And those playfellows for the most part were younger and weaker than himself.

"Dominique shall go to school," said the cooper to his wife.

"What school will you send him to?" asked she.

"The Jesuits' school at Clermont."

"Nay—that is far beyond our means and above the station he will hold in life."

"Wife, no one knows what station our son, Louis Dominique, may hold, nor how exalted he may be."

The woman, who knew the tricks and ways of her boy better than his father, could not help thinking that the young scapegrace might perhaps be exalted to the gallows, for in France, as in this country at that time, people were hanged for very slight offences.

However, she kept her thoughts to herself, and listened to what more her husband might have to say.

"As to its being beyond our means, why the good Father Renard, the reverend superior, promised me six months ago that my son should be admitted when he was ten years of age."

"And he was ten yesterday."

"And to school he goes to-morrow, so see that everything is in readiness for his journey."

And Cartouche went to school accordingly.

The Jesuits' school was a large, old-fashioned building, standing in its own grounds, which were surrounded by a high wall, on the top of which was a formidable row of spikes.

Louis Dominique found his companions in the school were for the most part sons of aristocrats; young barons and counts were plentiful enough, but the cooper's son soon made himself at home with them. He was sufficiently subservient without cringing, and being very quick-witted and amusing in his conversation he became tolerably popular.

One thing, though, annoyed the boy.

His companions were mostly well-dressed, had plenty of money in their pockets, and had lots of dainties to eat and drink in addition to the ordinary school fare, which, though sufficient, was not very luxurious.

"This shall be altered," thought he

The Jesuits gave their pupils plenty of liberty to go outside the school grounds on certain days. When they were not allowed out several sellers of cakes, fruit, and so forth, were admitted.

One day, while a number of boys were clustered round these humble merchants, young Cartouche found a first-rate opportunity of transferring several very fine apples to his pockets. Emboldened by his success he next tried his hand on the basket of a cake seller, and managed the affair without being detected.

At least he thought so then and for some time after.

One day, however, walking through one of the poorest streets of the place, he was saluted by the cry of—

"Ho! come hither, little Jesuit!"

Young Cartouche looked around, and saw that the speaker was one of the apple women who did business at the school—the particular woman, in fact, on whose stock-in-trade he had first exercised his dexterity.

"What would you have with me, mother?" he asked.

"Have with you? why the honour of your company for an hour at my humble abode."

Cartouche hesitated.

"Some trick," thought he.

But then he considered that he was scarcely worth either robbing or killing, so he thought he might venture.

"Some of her stock-in-trade must be in her house, and if she does not invite me to have any I can surely help myself," was the result of his meditation.

"My daughter Louise will be so glad to see you; she is so pretty, such a good figure, such fine black hair and eyes, such delicate skin!" the woman continued.

That settled the business.

Young as he was Cartouche had begun to show a decided partiality for the opposite sex. His companions, the young aristocrats, many of them boasted openly of their amours, and why should he not follow their example?

"I will go with you, mother," said he.

"I am called Madame Lafarge," the woman remarked.

"Pardon, madame, a thousand pardons," exclaimed young Cartouche, pulling off his hat and making a polite bow.

Madame Lafarge led the way.

"How old is Louise?" Cartouche replied.

"She is just two years older than yourself, and you will be twelve to-morrow."

"That is true; but how should you know my age?"

"I was present when you were born."

Louis Dominique Cartouche thought that strange, and he was still silently thinking about it when they they reached the dwelling of Madame Lafarge, who said—

"And here is Louise."

She was in truth as pretty a girl as Madame had represented, but her beauty was rather spoilt by an air of impudence mingled with cunning. Cartouche saluted her with all the politeness he was capable of, but she only laughed in his face and cried—

"So, mother, you have trapped the little Jesuit!"

"He is safe enough," the woman replied, as she locked the door and put the key into her pocket.

Cartouche had a certain amount of courage in his composition, but at that time it was not developed, and to tell the truth he felt rather frightened, as was very evident from his pale face and trembling limbs.

"Sit down," said Madame, and Cartouche obeyed.

"So!" she continued, "we have often heard that the fathers bring up their pupils to be liars, but is it possible they make thieves of them also?"

"Impossible!" Cartouche began.

"Nothing is impossible to the boy who can rob a poor apple-woman's basket so cleverly as you did. Ha! you thought you were not seen, but my eyes are good, and I allowed you to go on because I knew I should want you."

"What do you want of me?" Cartouche faltered.

"Money!" was the fierce reply of Madame Lafarge.

"I have none—my father is poor."

"The fathers of the college are rich. Father Renard has a good store of gold—and I must have some. If you cannot find his, try some of your young aristocratic friends. The Marquis de Loisy has a well-filled purse."

That was true, and Cartouche had more than once thought of helping himself to some of the young noble's crowns, but had not seen his way to doing so safely.

"If I do that I shall be a thief!" muttered Louis Dominique.

"You must be, you are, you cannot help it! The wise astrologer consulted the heavenly bodies at the time of your birth, and the stars foretold that you were to be the greatest rogue that ever dwelt in France. You cannot fight against Fate."

"If you find plenty of money you shall take me to the fair of St. Germains next week," Louise whispered, as she put her arm round the youth's neck and pressed her warm rosy cheek against Cartouche's face.

"We will go to the fair!" he exclaimed, "and you, madame, shall have gold—plenty of it."

"That is well, but do not disappoint me. If I tell old André, the one-legged soldier, who it is steals his cakes, he will not be so merciful as I have been; he has no pretty daughter, but he has a thick cudgel—aye, and a sharp dagger, too, which he will not hesitate to use when provoked."

Madame Lafarge, as she spoke, drew an ugly-looking blade from her dress, to let Cartouche see that she too was not without a weapon to use if occasion arose.

"You will take me to the fair, dear?" Louise whispered, drawing her arm closer round the youth.

"That I will. I swear it."

"That is brave!" said Madame. "Now let us be merry."

She put some of her best fruit on the table, with wine and brandy, and Cartouche set to work.

He saw that all immediate danger was at an end, and resolved to enjoy himself while he could. At last the hour came when he must return to the school, so he rose, and, with the best grace he could assume, wished Madame good-day.

"Beware, if you fail me!" she said in low tones.

"You *must* take me to the fair," Louise whispered.

"I will not fail," he replied, making the one answer to both.

Cartouche looked back as he turned the corner of the street. He saw Madame Lafarge playing with the handle of her dagger, while the impudent Louise kissed her hand to him.

"I am in for it now," Cartouche thought.

And in a very meditative frame of mind he walked back to the old school, inwardly wishing that he had never seen the place.

"But I must worm out of my father all he knows about this Madame Lafarge and the astrologer. As she says, it is useless attempting to fight against Fate."

The bell, the signal for closing the gate, was ringing as young Cartouche entered the school-grounds, and he hastened to the common hall to take his place at the supper table. But what with Madame Lafarge's wine, fruit, cakes, and threats, he had not much appetite for the meal.

"Come to my rooms presently, Cartouche," the young Marquis de Loisy whispered.

For this young aristocrat, and many more of noble rank, had private apartments and his own servant to attend on him.

Cartouche accordingly went to the rooms of the marquis. He went very quietly and paused for a few seconds outside the door, for he heard the young noble speaking to his servant.

"You have received the money, Pierre?"

"Yes, my lord, one hundred golden crowns."

"Good, and where did you put them?"

"In the little trunk over the cupboard, my loi "

"Good, and now set out the wine, for I expect young Cartouche and two or three friends here soon."

"Pardon, my lord," said the servant, who was an old family favourite, "but may I presume to offer advice?"

"Bah! but I suppose I must listen. What is it?"

"May I recommend you not to be too familiar with one so far beneath you in birth and breeding. No good can possibly come of it."

"I am not familiar with the fellow, Pierre, but he amuses me and my friends."

"Mark me, my lord, no good will come of it."

"Silence, old croaker, and set glasses on the table."

The man said no more, but busied himself about his work. Cartouche retreated half a dozen paces noiselessly, and then walked up to the door, so that he might be heard. A few seconds later four other pupils arrived, and a jolly time was the result.

Cartouche kept his eyes and ears open, but he could not see the little trunk, nor did the marquis make any allusion to it, although they had a game or two of cards and De Loisy lost. He was obliged to retire that night without effecting his object, and so it chanced next day and the next, till there were only two nights more before the fair at St. Germains, and then it chanced that Cartouche sat beside the young marquis in class, and his fingers chanced to come in contact with the outside of De Loisy's coat pocket, in which there was something hard.

It was a key—the key of De Loisy's chamber, and in a twinkling Cartouche transferred it to his own pocket.

"Now we shall see," thought he, "if good will come of it. For, good or evil, the deed must be done."

CHAPTER III.

THE ESCAPE FROM SCHOOL.

THAT evening the young Marquis de Loisy went out of school, grumbling much at the carelessness of his servant, who had left his door unfastened.

As soon as Cartouche saw the gates closed upon his aristocratic friend he hastened to the room and entered, not needing the key.

In an inner room, where the marquis slept, was a tall, large, old-fashioned cupboard, reaching nearly to the ceiling. On that, no doubt, was the trunk which Master Dominique wished to see the inside of. So he first put the key of the door on the chimney-piece, and then climbed up.

There, sure enough, was a small black trunk; it was locked, but Cartouche, with an implement he had brought with him from his father's workshop, soon overcame that weak fastening, and was rewarded for his trouble by finding two bags inside, which were marked as containing fifty crowns each.

He lost no time in conveying them to his pockets, and was about to descend, when he heard footsteps, and began to tremble with the apprehension of being discovered.

It was old Pierre, the servant of the marquis.

Cartouche coiled himself up in as small a space as possible, while the old man busied himself putting the chamber in order.

For three whole hours old Pierre worked and grumbled as he worked; then he went away to his own little slip of a room.

Of course Cartouche lost no time in descending and quitting the apartment. All the other pupils were, a couple of hours since, in bed. Now was the time to escape.

He crept stealthily along the corridor, down the stairs, and passed out at the doorway.

No one heard him, at least, so he thought,

but therein Master Louis Dominique was greatly mistaken.

He surveyed the spike-surmounted wall he had to scale, and decided that he must escape close by the great gates, the hinges of which would assist him to climb up. To be sure, the said gates were opposite the window of Father Renard, the superior, but then, doubtless, the reverend gentleman would be asleep, or at his prayers in the oratory.

So Cartouche, after a glance up at the windows, where no lights were visible, crept rapidly across the grounds to the gates.

Now it happened that Father Renard was neither sleeping nor praying at the time, and he distinctly saw the youth's figure.

"Ha! one of my pupils breaking out of bounds," he exclaimed. "This must be put a stop to."

Father Renard had once been in the habit of scourging his fellows in the monastery where he was brought up and of being scourged by them in expiation of sin. The implement used was a whip with seven stout knotted thongs, and this he had brought with him to Clermont for use upon the bodies of the pupils if occasion required.

Grasping it in his hand, he rushed out and nearly reached the wall just as Cartouche threw one leg over it between two of the spikes.

"Ho! come down, rascal!" he shouted.

To emphasise his command he swung the scourge over his head and brought down the thongs upon the most prominent part of young Cartouche's person, just where his breeches were strained rather tightly.

Louis Dominique shrieked with pain and turned his head to see who it was.

"Ah, it is you, villain!" thundered the superior. "Take that, and that, and come to my study for more."

And more blows fell upon the unhappy wall-climber, who, however, struggled on.

At the expense of a big rent in his garments the youth contrived to get both legs and his body over the wall, and to drop safely on the outer side. Just as he was scrambling to his feet again he heard the superior exclaim—

"Now I wonder which of my pupils that was, and if there are any more of them out? Ho! Joseph! Joseph! hasten hither with the keys. Quick, man!"

Joseph was the porter of the establishment, a very powerful man and active on his legs. Cartouche knew well enough that if he fell into Joseph's hands he would be very quickly dragged back to the school, when, of course, everything would be discovered, so he started off at his best pace, congratulating himself on the fact that Father Renard had not seen his face.

Up one street, down another, and then through some narrow passages, he ran at full speed, and soon was beyond fear of capture that night, at all events.

How matters would be in the morning he could not guess; the morrow must take care of itself.

It was long past midnight when he ventured to give a quiet tap at the door of Madame Lafarge, in whose window a light was still burning.

"Ah! you have done the deed, then?" said that worthy woman, as she looked at Cartouche's damaged dress and flurried face.

"I have. I would do anything for Louise."

"And Louise herself shall thank you. How much did you *borrow*, my son?"

"Fifty crowns," replied Louis Dominique Cartouche.

Madame Lafarge held out her hand, and the youth shook it.

"No foolery!" the woman exclaimed, her eyes flashing with indignation. "Give me the crowns."

Cartouche sulkily drew one of the bags from his pocket and handed it to the woman, who saw by the wax seal on the string that fastened its mouth that it had not been tampered with.

'Was it from Father Renard that you borrowed this?" she asked.

"No, the Marquis de Loisy."

"Then you can yet borrow from the father when you go back?"

"I thought I was to go to the fair with Louise."

"True—you shall go. You will not receive much extra punishment for playing the truant two days instead of one."

Cartouche had very little intention of going back. He knew the marquis would rebuke old Pierre, and that would probably lead to the discovery that a robbery had been committed— and who so likely to be the thief as the absentee.

However, he said nothing to Madame Lafarge on that subject, but gently hinted that he was much in need of rest and refreshment, being both thirsty and weary.

"True, I had forgotten," said she.

Madame Lafarge placed bread, cheese, and wine, upon the table, and bade him eat; then she pointed to some sacks in a corner of the room, and told him that when he felt tired he might rest there in safety.

Cartouche obeyed her, and just as he stretched himself upon his rude couch the candle flickered and went out.

Artful though, young Louis Dominique quietly removed the other bag of gold from his breeches pocket and placed it at the foot of his bed.

He knew by this time quite enough of Madame Lafarge to imagine that she might search his clothes. In fact, before he fell asleep he felt her hands, or someone's, investigating the pockets of his breeches and other garments, and about his rough pillow; but those hands found little for their pains. Presently Cartouche heard light footsteps crossing to the inner room where Louise and her mother slept, and then he knew that he might close his eyes in safety.

But he did not sleep long.

The strange place, the exciting events of the evening, and Madame Lafarge's wine had set his brain in such a whirl that he was not able to take a good rest, and about an hour after the break of day he sat up.

The first action of Cartouche was to restore the bag of gold to its proper place—at least what he considered its proper place—to wit, his breeches pocket.

" What shall I do now ?" thought he.

For some few seconds he was firmly resolved to return at once to the school and submit to whatever punishment might be inflicted ; but then the bag of gold which he had risked so much to obtain would certainly be discovered in his possession, and that would render him liable to at least a dozen years labour as a galley-slave.

And then there was Louise—the pretty, enchanting Louise, whom he had promised to take to the fair at St. Germains.

Any wavering ideas that had found an entrance into his mind were dispelled by hearing her voice in the next room, and soon she came into the apartment where he was, looking as fresh and impudent as ever, rather more so perhaps.

" So you are going to take me to the fair, Louis ?" she said, putting her hand on his shoulder.

" Yes, at least, I thought so yesterday, but——"

" Surely you are not going to refuse. Well, there is Gribichon—he will be glad to take me."

" Who is Gribichon ?"

" He is much bigger than you and far more amiable, Master Louis Dominique Cartouche."

" Confound Gribichon !"

" And then there is Red Judas. He would go down on his knees and kiss my feet if he thought that would persuade me to go with him to the fair at St. Germains."

" May the fiend fly away with Red Judas ! I thought last night to go to the fair with you, but——"

" Well, go on."

" Your mother took all my money——"

" Borrowed it, you mean," said Louise, sternly.

" Well, borrowed it ; and it is no use going to the fair unless we have some money."

" I daresay my mother will lend you some."

" Of course I will," said Madame Lafarge, who entered the room just at that moment. She had evidently been listening.

" Of course I will lend you some money, my children," she repeated, but tapping Cartouche on the shoulder, she added—

" You must pay me back, though, with interest. You can easily *get* money at the fair, and I must have ten crowns for these five."

" You shall have them," Cartouche replied.

He had no intention of stealing any more, but he thought it would be easy enough to give Madame Lafarge ten pieces out of the fifty he had so adroitly kept.

So after breakfasting and spending some time in decorating themselves, Louis Dominique Cartouche and Louise Lafarge set off towards St. Germains Fair.

There were plenty of carriages to be hired, so, to save themselves the disagreeableness of a walk along the dusty road, Cartouche engaged seats in one of these vehicles for himself and his inamorata.

And the young couple thoroughly enjoyed themselves. There were wild beast shows, horse riding, theatres, dancing booths, swings, tents, where wine and other refreshments were sold, and Louis Dominique Cartouche took Louise Lafarge into everyone of them ; they ate, they drank, they danced, they swung, they fed the wild beasts, they applauded the tumblers ; and if there was anything Louise did not see it was her own fault, for Cartouche was able and willing to pay for all the fun of the fair.

They were both careless for the future, and therefore able to make the utmost enjoyment out of the present.

At last the youth thought it was high time to take his companion back to Paris, for, to tell the truth, Louise began to show symptoms of having taken quite as much wine as her head could stand.

So Cartouche tumbled her into one of the waggons about to return to Paris, and she very soon fell asleep.

On went the vehicle, and Cartouche, having no one to talk to, fell a thinking. How should he face the Jesuit fathers, how should he meet his own parent, and, above all, what would happen when he encountered the terrible Madame Lafarge.

Presently he resolved to cut and run.

" No matter what happens I shall be out of the power of that woman," said he, " and that will be a fine thing."

Acting on the impulse he quietly dropped from the vehicle without the driver or Louise being aware of it, and stood close up to the fence, watching till his late companion had disappeared. Then he began to consider what he should do.

Night was coming on, and the hour would soon arrive when the gates of the city would be closed. Should he remain in the country or enter Paris ?

He soon decided on the latter course, and resolved also to see his father before venturing back to the school.

But he had not gone far when he became aware that some one was following him. A person was stealthily following, stopping when he stopped, going on when he proceeded, and at the same time avoiding being seen as much as possible.

" Whoever it is he shall have *this* if he interferes with me," Cartouche muttered.

And he drew from the breast of his coat a long broad-bladed knife, which he had bought from a travelling dealer at the fair, and clutching it firmly in his hand, waited for the approach of the spy, who stopped.

Cartouche hastened on a few paces and then slipped into a deep dark doorway.

The follower paused, looked carefully about, and then continued his progress, though with more caution.

"I will stab him to the heart!" gasped Cartouche, his own breast heaving with a tumult of emotions at the idea of shedding blood.

On came the spy—at least, so Cartouche considered him—till he was within two yards of the doorway.

Then out jumped the truant from Clermont, with his weapon upraised, to strike a deadly blow.

But the other was quick of eye and hand.

Cartouche's arm was arrested in its descent, and, whilst a vice-like grip held his wrist, a voice whispered—

"Hold! Would you kill me, Louis Dominique? Do you not recognise Alphonse?"

"What?"

"Alphonse, your brother!"

Louis Dominique Cartouche looked sullenly at his brother for some few seconds and then asked—

"And why are you following me, Alphonse?"

"I have been looking for you all day to warn you of danger—great danger, indeed."

"Explain."

"Your absence from Clermont is known to our father. The principal of the college has been to our house, and he says that the Marquis De Loisy is determined to prosecute you to the utmost."

CHAPTER IV.

FRESH COMPANIONS AND STRANGE ONES.

"FOR what will the marquis prosecute me?" said Louis Dominique Cartouche.

"For the robbery from his chamber of one hundred crowns in two bags, each containing fifty crowns," replied Alphonse Cartouche.

"I know nothing of De Loisy's money," said Louis Dominique.

"That is a mistake—Madame Lafarge has betrayed you."

"Curse Madame Lafarge!"

"If you are innocent of the robbery you need not curse her. But she has betrayed you—has handed over to the marquis a bag of crowns which she says you gave her to take charge of."

"She robbed me of them, the she-demon?"

"Then you robbed the marquis—and if you are caught, Louis, you will certainly be sent to the galleys."

"But how does that vile woman clear herself?"

"She said that you gave her a bag of gold to take charge of; that after you had left her house, doubting whether it could have been obtained honestly, she closely examined the bag, on which she found the coat-of-arms of the marquis plainly impressed, and his seal on the wax that held together the string round the bag's mouth. Then thinking that the bag must certainly belong to the Marquis de Loisy she took it to him, and explained how it came into her possession."

"She is the greatest liar that ever uttered a word in the French language," Louis Dominique Cartouche exclaimed.

"Can you disprove her lies?"

Cartouche shook his head, knowing well that the tale was true.

He considered for a minute, then said—

"Alphonse, do not tell our father that I am guilty. Farewell, brother, you will never see me again."

And before his elder brother could stop him he turned round, darted down a narrow thoroughfare, and was lost to sight in a few seconds.

The die was cast. Louis Dominique Cartouche had cut himself adrift from home and kindred.

All that night he skulked about the lowest quarters of Paris, snatching a few minutes' rest at times in some unusually quiet street, and then starting off, with guilty terror urging him on, when he heard the tramp of the patrol.

By sunrise the youth had made his way to that side of the city which lay exactly opposite the gate by which he entered the previous night, and at the earliest possible moment he passed out into the country.

Which way should he go?

A few seconds' reflection convinced him that all roads were alike, so that they led him away from Paris and not too near St. Germains.

He walked on till hunger began to tell on him, when he entered a little roadside inn and breakfasted.

"Are you going far?" asked a little old man who was sitting in the house.

"No," responded Cartouche.

"Ah! you are lucky. I have a long way to travel, and I fear it will rain, and my coat it is too thin to keep out the moisture."

"Mine is thick enough."

"Yes. I wish I had such a coat!"

"What will you give me to exchange with you?"

"Give? My brave youth, I am poor."

"So am I," rejoined Cartouche; "but I am better able to put up with bad weather than you, so if you will give me a little money I will take yours and you shall have mine."

"I have no money."

"Then, my father, how will you pay for your breakfast?"

"That is an impertinent question; but I will answer it. You will pay for it."

"Ha, ha, ha! you must be mad, old man."

"I am not mad, and I think you will pay for my breakfast. My sister, Madame Lafarge——"

"The devil!"

"She is a devil when her temper is roused. Well, as I was about to say, she told me that if ever I met Louis Dominique Cartouche he would be polite and hospitable to me for her sake."

And the old rascal finished his speech by sweeping the floor with his ragged cap as he made a very low bow. Cartouche was so rude as to swear. However, he paid for the old man's breakfast, and then once more made some allusion to an exchange of garments.

"With pleasure," said the old man, at once taking off his coat; "and I shall not be displeased if you leave a few sous in your pockets."

Cartouche took the hint, and left some loose coins jingling in the coat he gave to the old man. He was too anxious to get away from Madame Lafarge's brother, or anyone connected with that woman, to argue the question.

"She is a nice girl, my niece Louise—eh, you young dog?" the old reprobate said, thrusting his thumb into Cartouche's ribs. "You will be back to see her soon, no doubt."

"No doubt at all, Monsieur Lafarge——"

"That is not my name, but no matter; you will not be able to keep from her long."

"Within two days I shall be back in the Rue Courtelle, Monsieur——"

"Never mind my name. Well, adieu, my young friend, and may you keep out of the clutches of the Jesuit Fathers and the Marquis De Loisy."

With these words the old man began to walk in the direction of Paris, and young Cartouche at once hastened on—of course, taking the opposite way. He proceeded more than a league, and according to his computation it wanted two hours to noon, when, feeling sleepy, he turned into a field, and, first hiding his bag of crowns that he might not be robbed, took three hours' sleep.

Then up and on again. He had another meal at a village he passed through, and purchased a loaf to carry with him, lest he should feel the pangs of hunger during the night. For now that he had left Paris some distance behind him villages were few and far between, and, therefore, food could not be so readily procured.

But by sunset fatigue began to tell upon Cartouche.

There was no house near that he could see, and the road led across a wide, open heath, upon which were a few scattered bushes and little clumps of trees.

Here, then, Cartouche determined to lodge for the night.

He withdrew himself some five hundred yards or so from the road, and creeping into a thick bush, which promised him shelter in case of rain, he curled himself up like a dog, and soon slept like one.

How long he slept Cartouche knew not, but when he awoke it was night, and the stars thickly studded the sky.

There was a fire, too, burning close by, and round it were seated the most grotesque set of beings Louis Dominique Cartouche had ever set eyes upon.

"Were they mortal?" was the youth's first thought, and as he looked at them by the fitful light of the fire he could scarcely believe they were beings of this earth.

There were at least a dozen of them, male and female Cartouche judged by their dress, seated round the fire, over which a cauldron was suspended. But such men—such women! Dark as Moors from Africa, arrayed in most grotesque garments, and chattering as fast as they could in a language which was unknown to Cartouche, they seemed more like fiends from hell, or the witches he had heard of, than ordinary mortals.

"Heaven preserve me! Holy Virgin protect me!" thought Cartouche, as from his leafy covert he watched the motley group.

They ate, they drank, they laughed, they sang, did these strange beings, and as their outlandish mirth grew more riotous so did the terrors of Cartouche increase.

The youth heard the midnight hour chime from the belfry of some far-distant church, but the weird crew he was watching heeded it not. Daybreak began to streak the eastern horizon with bars of light, but still the revel went on, till in very bitterness of spirit the youth groaned aloud—

"The saints have forsaken me—I am given over to the powers of hell!"

Instantly the outlandish noise was hushed and all eyes were directed towards the bush whence the voice proceeded.

A minute—which to Cartouche seemed an hour—elapsed, then a woman, stepping forward, exclaimed—

"A spy! There is a spy in yonder bush—drag him out."

In an instant a dozen of them surrounded Cartouche's hiding-place, and he was dragged out into the fire-light. Fierce faces were all around him, and more than one swarthy hand brandished a glittering dagger.

"What is your name?" demanded the woman.

"Dominique Louis," responded Cartouche, who did not like to tell the *whole* truth, though he was afraid to utter an entire lie.

"And what were you doing in the bush—were you playing the spy upon us?"

"I went there to sleep."

"And why? You are not one of our people. You have a home—where is your home?"

"In Paris."

"Ah! I can see you are a truant from school—is it not so?"

Cartouche nodded.

"It is well that you admit it, for you cannot deceive the gipsies. We Egyptians read the stars, and we know whether people speak truth or falsehood. What school did you run from?"

"You will not betray me—will not give me up to those tyrants of masters?"

"Bah! we will not betray you."

Stimulated by this promise Cartouche confessed that he had taken an unauthorised departure from Clermont.

"And what money have you about you?—see to him, Ishmael."

Half a dozen pairs of nimble hands at once executed such a strict search that not a coin Cartouche had about him escaped notice—the bag of fifty crowns which he had saved from Madame Lafarge was hailed with shouts of delight.

"This cannot have been honestly come by,

"You stole this, little Jesuit," said the chieftainess of the party.

"Shall we hang him for theft, Queen Judith?" asked a red-haired fellow, the only one of the party who was not as swarthy as a Moor.

"No, Judas," was the response. "The money is forfeited, of course."

"Had I not better silence him?" demanded Ishmael.

"No—that would perhaps get us a hanging."

"Let me join your company and be one of you," said Cartouche.

He had got over his first idea that these were witches or fiends, and comprehended that he was in the company of a gang of gipsies, a people of whom he had heard much. He had never before met any of them, for they were proscribed by law and therefore seldom ventured near a town.

"You *shall* be one of us," Queen Judith responded. "We could not have a better recruit."

The whole band then grouped themselves round Cartouche and Queen Judith, two long daggers were put together cross fashion, and on that emblem Louis Dominique, who now told them his family name, was sworn to be a faithful member of the band and obey all its laws and customs, with the assurance that if he failed to keep his oath one of those blades would soon be sheathed between his ribs.

"And now, Judas, we hand him over to your care," said the queen; "teach him all you know, and that, with what he has already learnt, will make him a credit to the Egyptian race."

"I doubt not he will make a good and willing pupil."

"Come then, let us after our fashion celebrate the arrival of a recruit by passing round the wine cup."

Cartouche drank and the gipsies drank, then they sat round the fire and devoured the contents of the cauldron, and then the wine cup again circulated.

So strong was the liquor that under its influence Cartouche became a living exemplification of the proverb, "In wine there is truth," for he told the gipsies his whole history.

Then he fell back upon the turf and soon began to snore, oblivious of what was going on around him.

CHAPTER V.

A GREAT CRIME.

When Cartouche awoke he thought for a few seconds, from the utter stillness around him, that the events of the previous night were all a dream.

He looked around, but the smouldering fire, the bones and other relics of the feast convinced him that there was some reality in the business; besides, he had too vivid a recollection of the taking of the bag of crowns, to have any doubts on that matter. No, it must have been real, but where were the gipsies?

Cartouche thought of the oath he had taken,

and certainly thought it strange that after swearing him to be true to them they should go off and leave him. He must have spoken his thoughts audibly, for a gruff voice said—

"Don't think they have left you, young fellow. You were too sound asleep to be disturbed, so they told me to look after you."

The speaker was Judas—Red Judas as he was commonly called on account of his hair and complexion.

"Where are we going?" Cartouche asked.

"Over to that other clump of bushes. We will have a good long rest there, for we must travel most of the night."

"But whither?"

"In good time you shall know; but come away now, for the villagers will be soon prowling about our camp, and it would not do for them to know that we were left behind."

Cartouche himself was not willing to be seen, so he silently followed Judas to some other bushes about a thousand yards from the camp, in the midst of which they were quite secure from observation.

"Now, young fellow, I must change your looks a bit—alter you so that your mother would not know you."

"What for?"

"You don't want to be captured, do you?"

Cartouche shuddered at the thought and said he didn't.

"You may depend on it the Marquis De Loisy will send all over the country to hunt you down. Your description has been circulated."

"I will do anything rather than be captured."

"That is right; then I will begin by painting your face so that you will be as black-looking a fellow as Ishmael himself. Your features will suit that sort of complexion first-rate."

Red Judas drew a large bundle from under some dried ferns and branches, and took out of it a bottle, with the contents of which he stained Cartouche's face, neck, hands, and arms a walnut colour. Then he gave the youth breeches and waistcoat utterly unlike those in which he left Paris, and another coat instead of that he had obtained from the old man calling himself Madame Lafarge's brother. When the change was completed Cartouche looked a very different fellow from what he appeared when the gipsies dragged him out of the bush.

"What next?" demanded he of Red Judas.

"Eat and drink," was the laconic response, and the red-haired gipsy produced a huge parcel of bread and meat and a flask of wine.

"Now have a good rest," said Judas, when the repast was finished. "We must start at sunset."

Cartouche began to think over affairs again. He was tall for his age, and might easily pass for a year or two older than he really was. The gipsies had him in their power, and really the best thing he could do, in his opinion, was to throw his lot in with theirs.

So he went on with Judas, when the sun set,

and by midnight they had come up with the main party.

"But why did not we travel by daylight, Cartouche?" asked Judas.

"Because the villagers would likely enough assault two of us when they be in fear of the whole band, so our Queen Judith gave orders that we were to remain in hiding till night, and travel when the peasants were snug in their beds."

"Why do they call her queen?"

"Because she *is* queen, and you had better obey her in everything, or you may chance to feel one of those daggers between your ribs."

The hint was enough for Cartouche, who resolved that he would not be guilty of disobedience or disrespect to her majesty.

* * * * * *

For more than four years Cartouche remained with the gipsy band. One or two of the crew died during that period, and a few others who chanced to fall into the hands of the authorities passed away to end their lives in prison or on board those slave ships the galleys. Cartouche had, however, the good fortune to escape such mishap, so did Ishmael, Red Judas, Queen Judith, and all the clever members of the gang. Ishmael, in fact, often said that the only ones who got captured were those who deserved it for their clumsiness or cowardice.

"I should have been taken more than once if I had allowed the fellows to hold me when they clutched me; but I drove my blade into their hearts, and so escaped," Ishmael remarked.

Cartouche up to this time had not shed human blood, but he had heard some of the elders of the band speak as if killing was not unknown to them. He resolved that if ever he ran the risk of capture he would follow the example of Ishmael rather than undergo the horrible slavery of being chained to the oar of a galley.

The course of their wanderings brought the gipsy band into the neighbourhood of Bordeaux, and about ten miles from that beautiful city they pitched their camp for a time.

The women told fortunes, and sold baskets and such trifles, as gipsy women have done ever since European writers knew anything of them. The men lounged about, and apparently did nothing, but the farmyards suffered severely, and the cauldron in the gipsies' camp was never without two or three fat hens simmering down into a savoury broth.

"My children," said Queen Judith, one night when they were all assembled round the aforesaid cauldron, "you all know the village of Pitron."

"Yes," was the general response. There was not a village or house or hamlet for many miles round with which they were not acquainted.

"And you know the house where the good curate lives?"

Ishmael muttered a curse.

"He's no good! He really *is* poor, and can't give us anything."

"Ishmael, you are too hasty. The good curate is poor, but he is a very learned man. And he has taken into his house a very rich youth who has brought with him a trunk full of gold pieces. The ostler at the Golden Lion who helped to unload the postchaise told me about it."

"My cursed luck!" exclaimed Ishmael. "I could have cut that trunk from the back of the chaise; but as the postilion said he was going to a priest's house, I guessed it only held books and saint's toe-nails, and such-like rubbish."

"It was full of gold, my son. Now think over the matter all of you, and consider how that gold may become ours."

A trunk full of gold!

It was certainly a big stake to play for.

"We will have that money," said Cartouche to his friend Red Judas. "We can get it."

"I should like to finger it, but I don't see how it can be done," responded he of the beet-root complexion.

"Nor I at present; but we have brains, and we can most assuredly devise some scheme for easing a fat-witted old country priest of that which his book teaches him to despise. Think it over."

Red Judas did think it over. He considered all the gipsy dodges and devices he had ever seen or heard of, but could not find anything to meet the case. Cartouche also thought it over, with this result—he said to Red Judas—

"Force is the only thing. We must take it by force."

"How do you mean?"

"Why, we cannot scheme any plan by which they will be led to put the gold in our hands, so the only thing is to burst open the door of the house, force the lid of the trunk, and take the gold; and woe betide any person who tries to stop us."

"I am with you."

"Then it shall be done."

Next day Cartouche, Red Judas, and a gipsy girl named Esther were very much about the village of Pitron. Without asking any direct questions they contrived to learn a great deal about the curate and his pupil-lodger. The latter was, according to all accounts, enormously rich, and had been sent by his father to study various abstruse sciences in which the curate was supposed to be specially learned. And the trunk was said to contain a vast amount of gold, the curate's fee for hammering wisdom into one who was not naturally quick-witted.

"We will have that gold," said Cartouche.

That same day the gipsy encampment was removed to a village some four or five leagues distant from Pitron.

But at the *auberge* or inn of this last-named place there arrived a couple of horsemen decently clad and well mounted. They were young men, and, according to their account, had lost their way whilst travelling; they would stay the night at Pitron if they could be provided with food and beds.

"Certainly," the host responded; "the Golden Eagle is noted for——"

"Bad liquor and beds infested with vermin," one of the travellers muttered. He did not intend his words to be overheard, but the landlord caught them, and replied—

"Noted for clean beds, plain, but wholesome fare, and sound wine made in the vineyards of this part of the country." And inaudibly he added—

"I know you, my fine fellow, and I am certain you are after no good. You are one of the gipsy tribe—but who is your friend and companion, I wonder?"

As a matter of fact the two travellers were Cartouche and Red Judas, who intended to make an attempt to carry off the gold the curate of Pitron was supposed to have received.

The French police was not well organised in those days, save in Paris and a few big cities, or the landlord of the Golden Eagle would have given information that two suspicious characters were at his house. He resolved, however, to watch.

Cartouche and Red Judas dined, and then called for pipes and tobacco. When the sun vanished beneath the horizon they went outside and sat upon a bench in front of the inn.

"A beautiful night," said Red Judas.

"Splendid, let us stroll a little way by the moonlight," Cartouche replied.

The host was listening, but his suspicions were almost quenched when Cartouche ordered a dish of eggs to be ready in an hour, when probably they would have a good appetite for supper.

The hostess, who knew of her husband's suspicions, would have it that these two gipsies were going to perform some very mysterious incantations by the light of the stars, when any venturesome person who intruded upon the ceremony would be struck blind.

So no one dared follow the pair as they strolled along the high-road for some yards, and then turned off on a footpath which led through a wood to the curate's house.

Not a light was visible in the old house. The people in that part of the country were very primitive in their habits, and retired to bed soon after sunset as a rule.

A dog gave a low growl as they approached, but Red Judas was ready with a piece of poisoned meat, which the faithful animal devoured—and then died.

"This shutter seems loose," whispered Cartouche; "and this is the window of the curate's dining-room."

"Let us in, then," said Judas.

The shutter was not fastened. Cartouche opened it, in less than a minute the window yielded to his attack, and in two minutes they were both inside. They had first disguised themselves by putting masks over the upper part of their features, so that even if they were seen at their work they might not be recognised.

Cartouche had a dark lantern with him, by the rays of which they took a stealthy look round the apartment.

It was a decently-furnished room, though of an old-fashioned type. On one side of the room was an ancient-looking trunk or chest.

"There is our prize," said Cartouche.

"Light the candles," whispered Red Judas. "We can do the business better by the light of a couple of candles than by this bull's-eye arrangement."

A couple of candles stood upon the table; Cartouche lighted them, and then extinguished his own lantern.

"This is the thing to open a lock when you don't happen to have the key," Louis Dominique whispered, handing to his companion a bent piece of iron. "Don't be afraid to put your strength out."

Red Judas exerted about half his strength and the lock of the trunk flew off.

"Now for the treasure!" said he.

Cartouche took one of the candles from the table and held it whilst Red Judas lifted the lid of the chest.

"Hell and furies!" the latter exclaimed.

"What is the matter?" Cartouche asked.

"A fraud—a vile fraud!"

"How is that?"

"The chest is empty!"

Cartouche swore as deep an oath as his accomplice.

But while they were swearing the two robbers did not notice that the door of the room had been quietly opened.

It was so, however. Young Monsieur Florian, the curate's pupil, had heard the very slight noise made by the robbers. The good curate himself had gone away, and would not be back till morn, so M. Florian deemed himself bound to protect the place. He therefore slipped on his breeches, and, grasping a pistol in his fist, stole down to the part of the house whence the noise seemed to proceed.

A single glance enlightened him as to the state of affairs.

"Surrender, villains!" he exclaimed, and through the half-opened door he aimed his weapon at the head of one of the robbers.

"Snap!"

Either the pistol was not properly primed or the flint was a bad one; at all events, no explosion followed the pulling of the trigger.

In an instant Florian saw that he must seek safety in flight till he could provide himself with other weapons. He had two more pistols in his own sleeping-room. With them in his hand he would certainly be a match for two robbers.

"After him," whispered Red Judas. "If he escapes we are utterly lost."

Cartouche at once followed.

Florian's room was on the floor above that which the robbers were ransacking when the alarm was given. The young man had reached the top of the staircase, and had his hand on the fastening of his room door, when he stumbled and fell.

"I take Ishmael's advice," exclaimed Cartouche.

And, drawing his knife—the same he had pur-

CARTOUCHE,
THE FRENCH JACK SHEPPARD.

"SURRENDER, VILLAINS!" THE YOUNG MAN EXCLAIMED, AS HE OPENED THE DOOR.

chased years before at St. Germains—he drove the weapon twice into the bosom of the unfortunate young gentleman. He then walked back to the room where he had left Red Judas, with the blood of poor young Florian still dripping from the point of his blade.

"You've done it," exclaimed Judas.

"I have. I worked on Ishmael's advice."

"We must be on."

"But what is in the chest?"

"Nothing save a few mouldy parchments; not a coin, not a spoon or a fork."

"There must be something of value in the house," said Cartouche.

"Then we must search in some other part for it," Red Judas responded. "It is not here."

The two ruffians were about to ascend the stairs to see if any money could be found in the upper part of the house, when other footsteps were heard. Our curate's housekeeper had detected some sounds that seemed to forbode danger; and she was up, lantern in hand, to discover the cause thereof.

Cartouche and his companion stood behind the door, whilst she peeped in timorously.

"Dead women are as dumb as dead men!" Cartouche whispered. "Go, silence her before she gives an alarm."

Judas nodded, then he pounced upon the poor woman; there was a struggle for a few seconds, followed by a half-choked cry for help; then Red Judas rejoined Cartouche, holding an ensanguined blade in his hand.

"Is there anyone else in the house?" Cartouche asked.

"I think not," replied Judas.

"There must be no one left to tell this tale, so let us make a good search."

They searched, but no living being could be found; they forced cupboards, boxes, and closets, but no treasure could be discovered.

"By my faith this is a sorry night's work!" said Cartouche.

"The night's work is of your planning," Red Judas growled by way of reply.

"It is a failure—except in the one matter. We have both fleshed our blades, and therefore shall not hesitate to strike again if need be," answered Cartouche.

"Let us get away."

They walked back to the inn, and burst open the stable door because the ostler seemed long in bringing out their cattle to them. Not waiting for the dish of eggs that the landlord had in readiness, they mounted and rode off at full speed. Many a wakeful villager heard the clatter of their horses' hoofs, but no one durst bid them stand, and at early morn the curate of Pitron, returning from his journey, was the first person to find his housekeeper and his lodger weltering in their gore.

CHAPTER VI.

HOW CARTOUCHE WENT TO THE PAWNSHOP AND SAW HIS UNCLE.

"It must have been the gipsies," was the verdict, most unanimous, of the villagers, when they heard of the deed of blood.

"But," thought some of them after a little while, "the gipsies left hours before the murders were done."

The landlord of the Golden Eagle agreed with both parties, and then promulgated his own idea that the foul deed was done by two disguised gipsies whom he described.

"But why should they murder our curate?" was the question asked by more than one villager.

"For money!" responded the innkeeper. "Our good curate had no gold, but some of you circulated a report that young Monsieur Florian had much, so I doubt not the poor padre has been slain by those who, believing him rich, aspired to the possession of his wealth."

"After the gipsies then! Away, brethren—away! Let us kill the murderers, the child-stealers, the midnight thieves!"

"Away after them!" was the response.

Now the track left by Queen Judith and her band was large and plain enough. The sand of the high road showed plainly enough where the wheels of the gipsy carts had passed, and also where the donkeys and ponies of the gipsies had strayed along—very leisurely said one who was accustomed to tracing out such work; but the sand of the highway showed no marks whatever of those two men.

However, there was a spirit invoked which boded little good for the gipsies. Queen Judith's gang was not the only band that had passed along, plundering whenever a chance offered them, and now murder had been added to all their other crimes. They must be punished.

So pursuit was made, and within forty-eight hours Ishmael, Judith, and all of them, except Judas and our young friend Cartouche, were fast by the heels.

The real murderers had escaped, but that mattered little, for there were a score of gipsies to hang, burn, or otherwise destroy, so the good people of Pitron were nearly as well satisfied as if they had captured the real culprits.

Cartouche did not long remain in the company of Judas after escaping from Pitron. The fiery complexion could not be entirely disguised, and Cartouche knew that a description of it would be circulated throughout the length and breadth of the land; his own features, on the other hand, could be more easily altered by the aid of a little art.

At the first stop they made after leaving Pitron Cartouche said—

"We must part company."

"Why?" demanded Red Judas.

"Because if we travel together we shall both be captured and hanged, if not broken alive on the wheel."

Red Judas shuddered at the thought.

"Therefore for our own safety we must separate."

"Which way do you propose to go, then?"

"See yonder where four roads meet? Let us spin a coin for choice, the winner to choose which road he will take, and the loser to go in exactly the opposite direction."

"Agreed," said Judas.

The coin was tossed up and Cartouche won.

"I take the right-hand road."

"Then I must go to the left," said Red Judas, sighing. But the rascal was inwardly pleased at the choice Cartouche had made, for he knew the country well, and was thoroughly alive to the fact that the right-hand road led, though in a roundabout way, back to Pitron.

Judas was not so artful as Cartouche, though, who, having gone some little distance, turned back and took the main road which led in a direct line from Pitron.

"Now for a change," said Cartouche as he reached a little wood through which a brook ran.

In the first place, by the aid of some acid he removed the dark tinge from his face, and appeared with a fairer skin and hair than he had shown for some years. Next, having a bottle of that stain in his pocket, he stained the four feet of his horse which were white, and also discoloured a white blaze upon the beast's forehead.

Having thus disguised himself and beast he set forward.

But before he reached any village a fierce thunderstorm came on.

Digging the spurs into his horse's sides he rode off at full speed towards a ruined building he had noticed, not doubting but some part of it would suffice to shelter him from the rain, which fell in torrents.

It was an old church, part of some abbey which had been destroyed.

Riding into it Cartouche fastened his horse to a broken column, and then seated himself where the altar had once stood.

"Why, what is this on my hand?" he said, aloud. "I washed it clean enough at the brook."

"Innocent blood!" exclaimed a voice.

Cartouche started up and looked round for the speaker, who was not to be seen. He had concealed in his bosom the blade with which he had recently done such fearful crime, and he now drew it from its sheath.

"If I could find the spy," he muttered, "I would serve him as——"

"As you served young Florian!" said the voice of the unseen one.

Cartouche was not superstitious—he had got over all fears of the supernatural—but he feared much that the voice was that of some person who was watching an opportunity to hand him over to the authorities.

"Come forth and show yourself," said he.

To this invitation there was no response, so Louis Dominique thought he would search the ruin and find out who was the unseen speaker. Whoever it was must be hiding close by, for no one at the far end of the building would be able to discern the few drops of blood which flowed from a scratch his hand received in riding through the forest.

First, thinking there might be some passage leading from the altar to other parts of the building, he sounded the wall, but everything thereabouts seemed solid, and the floor, too, gave no indication of having vaults underneath it.

Cartouche was about to give up the search, when he noticed that near the spot where he had quartered himself there were two tombs or monuments.

He kicked one of them heavily with the toe of his thick riding-boot.

Ha! there was a smothered exclamation as though someone was concealed within; but how to get at that person without overthrowing the ton or so of marble, of which the monument consisted, was a puzzle.

"I will try gunpowder," said he, speaking his thoughts aloud that the hidden person might hear. "It was lucky that I bought an extra quantity. Surely I have enough to blow this lump of marble to atoms."

"Hold!" said the voice, and this time there could be no doubt whatever that it came from within the tomb.

"Come out and show yourself, or I will blow you to the sky," exclaimed Cartouche.

"Wait a minute," said the voice.

Then came a sound as though some machinery was set in motion; the tombstone revolved, and disclosed an aperture which apparently led to some vaults beneath, and from that aperture came a woman.

A woman who in younger days had been beautiful, and even then had some traces of good looks on her weather-worn cheeks; a woman who once had been well-dressed—but now was scantily and coarsely clad—but who still had the fire of danger gleaming in her lustrous eyes.

But Cartouche, who once dreaded her, no longer stood in awe.

"Madame Lafarge, I believe," said he, raising his hat and bowing as only a Parisian could—or can.

"Yes—yes, assassin!"

"Ah! that is an ill name to bestow upon an old acquaintance, madame."

"But you are an assassin! You slew poor Florian!"

"Do you know that for a fact, madame?"

"I do," replied Madame Lafarge.

Cartouche walked close up to the woman and looked her in the face, as he said, in low but very distinct tones—

"Then if you know that I have taken one life you must know that I would not for a moment hesitate to take another—yours even—to preserve my own. Now, what are you doing in this very uncomfortable place of concealment, and what do you want with me?"

And as he spoke these words Cartouche sat jauntily on the tombstone.

Between his teeth he held the knife, on .the blade and handle of which some spots of poor Florian's blood still remained. In his hands he had a large pistol and the powder-horn and other apparatus for loading the weapon, so altogether he looked about as truculent a villain as one could meet.

"Now madame, I shall be glad to hear why you are in this part of France. Speak quickly, please, and when you have found your tongue, be pleased to tell me *all—all*, absolutely *all*, that you know about an unavoidable affair which you call a murder."

Madame Lafarge looked at him ; she saw that his physical strength had doubled since the night she had him in her power, and it needed not a second look into those cold grey eyes to perceive that there was in his nature a relentless determination to take care of himself to the very utmost. The words of Ishmael the gipsy had fallen on a very fruitful soil.

"Now, madame, I wait—but as the storm is passing away I cannot tarry much longer. Your answer, if you please, to my questions."

"You asked why am I in this part of France. I tell you I had to leave because I was so much persecuted by the police."

"It was rude of them ; did they give any reason for their ungentlemanly behaviour ?"

"They said that watches, snuff-boxes, and other trifles that had been lost by ladies and gentlemen were too often found at my house, or at the apartment of my brother——"

"Worthy old rascal !—how is he ?"

"As well as an old man can be who spends his time between the galley and the lazaretto."

"And Mademoiselle Louise ?"

"You have not been in Paris lately, monsieur ?"

"That is true, and I care not if I never set eyes upon the city again."

"If you had been in Paris lately you would have heard of—if you had not seen—La Belle Louise, the flower seller. She is usually to be found in front of the Louvre or the Palais Royal in the day."

"And this is the young lady I took to the fair at St. Germains. And now, madame, as I have finished loading my pistol, just be good enough to explain how much you know about the death of a certain young gentleman named Florian."

"I saw you and the red-haired gipsy leave the house ; then, when the alarm was given, I knew whose work it was."

"Why have you followed me hither ?" asked Cartouche, who during this conversation had kept the muzzle of his pistol pointed towards Madame Lafarge.

"Nay, it is you who have followed me. I was here an hour before you arrived."

"And how did you discover the mechanism of this little hiding-place ?"

"By accident. It was open when I arrived in the ruin."

Cartouche jumped down from his seat on the tomb and looked very carefully. He saw at once that the wheels which caused the stone to turn were frequently used—there was plenty of grease but no rust about them.

"Have you been down below ?" he asked.

"No—I was afraid."

"Then go at once, and return within five minutes with an exact report of what is to be seen in the vaults."

Cartouche would have gone down himself, but he feared to trust Madame Lafarge behind him, knowing well that if she had a dagger, and an opportunity of using it, she would not hesitate to strike him dead.

Down the steep, winding staircase went Madame Lafarge, whilst at the top stood Cartouche, pistol in hand, ready to send a bullet through the first foe that should show.

CHAPTER VII.

THE DROWNING OF RED JUDAS.

LEAVING Madame Lafarge to explore the vault while Cartouche waits for her, let us see how matters fared with Red Judas.

He, too, had a notion that it would be advisable to double on his pursuers, so he turned aside as soon as he had lost sight of Cartouche.

"Ho for Paris !" he exclaimed. "There is no hiding-place so good as a big city. In a village every tom-fool insists on knowing all about you, but in the town a stranger is not noticed. Most men are strangers to each other in a crowd."

Red Judas got so jovial at the bare idea of hiding safely in a densely-populated place that he forgot to take proper notice of the road he was travelling, and as a result he presently found himself riding through Pitron, the village he most of all wished to avoid.

"Hi ! stop !" shouted the sexton, who saw him coming up the street.

Judas drew a big pistol from the holster, and resolved that rather than be stopped the grave digger should need a grave for himself.

"Secure the murderer." screamed the fat landlord of the Golden Eagle, who recognised his late customer. "There he is ! stop him !"

Judas turned in the saddle, and uttering a savage oath discharged his weapon at mine host. The bullet pierced the man's hat, and so thoroughly convinced him of the danger of interfering that he rushed into his house, and was seen no more that day.

Most of the inhabitants of the village were away, hunting in a different direction for the man who thus boldly rode through the village, so there was no pursuit. Judas used his spurs in a cruel manner till the horse he was riding dropped beneath him ; then he stole another from a field by the roadside and continued his headlong career towards Paris.

But ride as he would he could not outstrip the news that had gone before him of the murder of poor young Florian. Wherever he halted suspicious glances were thrown at him, and men whispered to each other—

"That is one of the murderers."

It was early morning when the towers of Paris rose upon his view.

"This horse will betray me if I ride him into

the city," Judas thought to himself. So he dismounted, and with a cut of his whip sent the animal galloping back, whilst he walked on and passed through the gate soon after it was opened.

Red Judas knew the city quite as well as the country, and made his way to a quarter into which few would venture, and there sought a lodging.

The people of the house knew him, and had even heard of the crime in which he was a participator, but they would not betray him to the police.

"Who is this Cartouche?" asked Bérard, the landlord of the house in which Red Judas sought refuge.

"He is a devil!"

"And *where* is he, Master Judas?"

"Who can tell where last summer's swallows have gone? I know not where he is—but mark my words, Master Bérard, if that young man decides that his headquarters shall be in Paris he will lead the police a pretty life."

"Is he then so artful and daring?"

"More artful than Satan himself. But let me go to bed—I must have at least twenty-four hours' rest before I shall be fit for anything. Don't disturb me unless anything of great importance takes place."

"You may sleep as securely here as though you were in the Bastile itself," responded Bérard, who then conducted Red Judas to an apartment.

Fatigued by travel, the rascal slept soundly —how long he could not guess, but he was awakened by what sounded most uncommonly like a tapping at the casement.

Judas jumped up at once and looked out.

Night had drawn her sable mantle over the city of Paris; there were a few oil lamps here and there, but most of the close streets and alleys were in darkness. Still there was light enough to let Red Judas see that a cold drizzling rain was falling through the thick atmosphere, and that the few pedestrians abroad shivered as they hurried along, and wrapped their cloaks closely about them.

Red Judas, however, cared little about the state of the weather or the feelings of those compelled to be abroad; he wanted to know why that warning was given.

"Who is there?" he demanded in low tones.

No answer came from the darkness outside the casement.

Judas then tried the door.

"What is it?" he whispered.

"Danger," responded a voice in equally low and guarded tones, though the speaker was invisible.

That one word was enough. Red Judas gathered up his garments and prepared for instant flight.

"What is the danger?" he asked.

"The police are in the house, some are in the courtyard, others are stationed on the staircase, and they are breaking open the doors of rooms that are locked."

Red Judas waited to hear no more.

A terrible sentiment of dread seemed to overwhelm his soul, and every sense that was not deadened by fear seemed to be calling out—

"Fly! Fly for your life!"

But whither?

He had but little money in his pockets; the attack on the curate's house had been a miserable failure from a financial point of view, and the exchequer was in a wretched state.

He dashed down the staircase and rushed away with some vague idea that he could hear footsteps close behind him. He ran on, rejoicing in the darkness of the night, seeking remote parts of the town, where the streets were narrow and ill-lighted. When he saw a lamp burning he started and turned back into some other court or street where all was in darkness.

And yet as he sped along, far from becoming fatigued, his steps were swifter, but his thoughts were slower and more confused.

How to escape the danger that seemed ready to overwhelm him was more than Judas could imagine.

Presently his strength failed him, and cowering up in a doorway he sat down, and pressed his hands to his burning forehead in order to retain his scattered senses.

Judas was just beginning to doze when he heard—close to his elbow it seemed—the deep, hollow sound of the horn at that time carried by the Parisian police or watchmen.

The man was standing only a foot or two off, and the halbert, or partisan, he carried clattered against the pavement as the carrier of the weapon placed the shaft of it upon the pavement.

Judas crouched still closer, and although the sound might have cost him his life he could not repress a groan forced from him by very bitterness of spirit as he thought that here, too, there was no safety, but danger all around him.

The guardian of the night moved on, and Judas, as soon as possible, quitted his hiding-place. Whither should he go now?

Again he rushed forward along the narrow rows of houses to the only place of which he had any distinct recollection—that is, the house he had so recently left.

"The search will be over by this time, so I need have no fear," he muttered, as he sped back towards the narrow thoroughfare.

There was some irresistible attraction dragging him back to that last hiding-place. It was not that he thought it more secure, nor that he had much confidence in Monsieur Bérard, but something he could neither define nor describe impelled him to go back.

On approaching the lodging-house from which he had so abruptly fled only a few hours before, Red Judas perceived a dark shadow in the doorway. It was Bérard's usual waiting-place at night when any danger was apprehended, because then he could at once give a warning signal, which would cause any frequenter of the place to keep away. But was that Bérard's shadow?

The miserable Judas started back and then

drew nearer again, for he perceived that there was no one in the doorway.

There was a secret spring under the porch, known only to a few of the regular lodgers. Judas felt about for this, but being, in his confused state, unable to find it, he bethought him of a bunch of keys usually hanging in the entry, and succeeded in gaining possession of them. Thus equipped he hurried through the large hall to the gallery in which most of the sleeping-room doors were. But still it seemed that the shadowy form was flitting about, following every step he took.

It had a secret way—that old house—leading out on the river bank, and Judas resolved to make for it, in the belief that his foes would not be watching there. He took off his boots that he might glide with less noise along the various passages he had to traverse.

First of all there was a secret door to be opened and then a staircase to be descended. The rats which abounded in that dark underground retreat squeaked and scampered about, and seemed to have some thought of attacking the intruder.

At length Judas reached a second door, which led out into a kind of sewer communicating with the river, and by walking some little distance along the river, where the water would reach to his waist, he would arrive at a similar opening by which he could procure entrance to another house, the door of which was in a different street to that he had just left.

A violent shudder—the omen, as it seemed, of some disaster—shook the limbs of the red gipsy as he tottered step by step down the steep and slippery path leading to the river, and when he placed his foot in the water he heard what seemed a mournful groan.

There were some posts driven into the bed of the stream just thereabouts, and Judas caught hold of one of them to help himself on his perilous journey. As he did so he again heard that mournful groan, though now he discovered that it was nothing but his own breathing.

The water was deeper than when Judas was last there. It reached quite to his waist, but still he found the bottom, and stood in the cold rushing stream.

It was a gloomy, miserable night; the rain drizzled down through the thick heavy atmosphere, and a dense fog enveloped the quays, and stairs, and houses along the river bank.

It was only very indistinctly that a flight of steps could be discerned, leading down to the water's edge, or a supporting pillar, or the gable of an old house might be seen standing out against the grey sky.

"It will be a tough job to get round," Judas murmured.

The water running swiftly down towards the sea, dashed against the old piles and staircases and other projections with a harsh and monotonous sound; it was the only sound audible at that time of the night, but it seemed like thunder roaring upon the ears of Red

Judas, and he felt as though the heavens were conspiring to strike him dead or lead his pursuers to his hiding-place.

He set another foot forward in the water and groped along as well as he could in search of safety. He clung to the slippery wooden piles to prevent his sinking further into the bed of the river, and at last found himself at the bottom of the steps leading to the other house, through which he intended to make his exit into the back slums of Paris, and so evade the pursuers.

One swing of his body round the angle leading to the foot of the stairs and he would be safe—his feet would touch the steps, and he could ascend at his leisure.

Suddenly, as he was about to make that turn, Red Judas fell back powerless, and the foot he had raised sank into the dark chill water.

Before him, on the piles that bordered and stood above the stream, he beheld a dark bent form. He could distinguish the outlines in spite of the gloom; he could see an old hat and the ugly features of a face which he well knew—the face of Jasper, one of the most awful, and, therefore, most-to-be-dreaded, members of the Parisian police force.

Jasper knew Judas, and sat motionless on the top of one of those piles to which the red-haired gipsy was clinging so desperately.

Judas rubbed his hands in front of his eyes, and then waved them violently in front of him as though he would drive away the spectre that sat there mocking him. But it was no delusion; there sat Jasper, silent and still, on the top of the green, weed-covered post, only a few feet from the poor wretch who was within such a measurable distance of drowning.

Presently Jasper slightly moved and stretched out a long, bony-looking hand, as though to clutch the red gipsy by the throat.

Uttering a shriek Judas fell back—his foot slipped down the steep and muddy river bed, and in a moment he was up to his throat in the foul water of the Seine. For a minute he held firmly by one of the posts, while the stream rushed past him howling wildly and threateningly into his ears. He held up his hands again, but his eyes were still fixed upon that grim and goblin-like figure that sat on the green, moss-covered post.

The spectre, Jasper, approached still nearer, and again held up its hand in that threatening and warning manner.

Judas sprang, terror-stricken, further out into the stream—there was a splashing sound, a loud cry, and the short struggle of a drowning man. Then all was over—the river rolled towards the ocean, bearing upon its bosom a senseless and apparently lifeless body.

But immediately after the bank of the River Seine became animated; torches flitted to and fro on the brink of the dark water as the holders of them searched for something which evidently could not easily be found—the body of Red Judas.

CHAPTER VIII.

PARIS ONCE MORE.

MADAME LAFARGE as she descended into the vaults beneath the old abbey ruin had as little faith in Cartouche as he had in her. She believed that, if he had the chance, he would kill her, or betray her to the police; so she resolved to make the first stroke—if she found an opportunity.

Cartouche did not descend the staircase. Having mastered the secret method of moving and replacing the tomb, he thought that it would be an excellent thing if one person remaining above could safely imprison some other person who incautiously had ventured below. And he thought that Madame Lafarge was a very fit and proper subject for the experiment. If she was unable to get out, why so much the better for him—he could then continue his journey to Paris with less care on his mind than would be the case if she were at large and he knew not where.

He stood at the top of the steps, and called out—

"Madame! Hi, Madame Lafarge!"

"What is it, Louis?" she replied.

"Can you not find some passage or opening leading from that cellar?"

"There seems nothing but solid walls here. The masons did their work thoroughly, and I can see no way out except the stairs by which I descended."

"Look again, do not give up the search."

"Why not descend and examine the place for yourself, Monsieur Louis Dominique?"

"Because my horse is restive and I must attend to him, or he will break loose and bolt away."

"I will look again," said Madame Lafarge, "but I fear the search will be useless."

"I fear it will," responded Cartouche, as he silently rolled back the tomb, and then drove in a wedge of wood in such a manner as to prevent any exit from the vault till that wedge was removed.

"Now for a quiet smoke," said he.

He pulled from his pocket a clay pipe, a paper of tobacco, a flint, steel and tinder, and soon was in the full enjoyment of the American weed. Smoking was not a common habit in France in those days, and Cartouche, perhaps, enjoyed his pipe the more for its being out of the fashion.

He sat thus for about a quarter of an hour.

"The woman is devilish quiet," he thought. Either she has found a way out or she is gone off in a fit. But she is not one of the fainting sort, so I had better take a look round the vault myself, and see where this secret passage leads."

He first of all looked very carefully to his pistols, fresh primed them, saw that the flints were in good order, and the bullet rammed well down upon the powder; then, with his dagger in a place close to his hand, he went down the steps, and found himself in a narrow and remarkably crooked passage.

He could find nobody in the vault. Madame Lafarge had disappeared, and Cartouche could not discover the way by which she had made her exit.

But whilst searching about he found a treasury which she had evidently missed—a secret door, artfully contrived, opening into a chamber which, from the dust and cobwebs about it, seemed not to have been disturbed for some years.

But it was, nevertheless, and literally a treasury.

In one corner were some sacks of corn and beans, and other food; in another part of the place a cask of wine stood, with a chalk mark upon it denoting that it was set there half a dozen years before; on the walls were a score of pistols, all fit for service although a trifle rusty, and a dozen good swords, which also showed want of care upon their blades and hilts.

Cartouche took a mental inventory, and then set to work to master the method by which this chamber could be closed and opened, which did not occupy much time.

"Quite a little arsenal," said he to himself—"and it may come useful some time or other; but where is this woman?"

That he could not tell, but he closed the door carefully, once more ascended to the upper part of the building, and rode off.

"There he goes! stop him! that is Cartouche!" was the cry that greeted his ears as he spurred his horse through the wood.

He recognised the voice of Madame Lafarge, and at once comprehended that she knew some way of escaping from the vaults. Also it was pretty plain that she had brought down people from the neighbouring village to capture him.

He turned savagely in his saddle and drew a pistol from his holsters, resolved that if he could only get a fair aim at her she should never cross his path again. Only three men, however, were in sight, and a glance convinced Cartouche that he need not fear them. All he had to do was ride on and leave them behind, which he did.

He wondered what had become of Red Judas, but a few whispers that he heard at a place where he halted late at night were sufficient to inform him that the red-haired one had gone back towards Paris.

"He is a traitor, but no fool," Cartouche muttered. "And perhaps my best course is to make for the city."

So he, too, rode for the city, which he entered nearly at the time when men were searching for the body of Judas.

Leaving his horse at a hostelry near the gate Cartouche hastened on foot—whither?

He hardly knew which way to turn; he durst not go to his father's house or his brother's. But he considered that age had so altered his personal appearance that there was little chance of his being recognised, so he kept on till fate should bring him to some place which looked safe.

He was passing by a restaurant when he

heard one of two men walking in front of him say to the other—

"Here comes La Belle Louise !"

"Her smiles are more expensive than the bouquets she carries in her basket," was the reply.

Cartouche looked and recognised the daughter of Madame Lafarge standing outside the house.

The pretty girl had grown into a magnificent woman, but in her style there was not much change.

As her dark eyes rested upon Cartouche's face she recognised him at once, and cried—

"Ah ! you have just returned from the fair ?"

"Let there be peace between us, Louise."

"It will be a bad thing for you if war should chance to break out between us, Master Louis Dominique Cartouche. You travel quickly, but the news of the murder reached Paris before you. And so did Red Judas."

"What of him ? where is he ?"

"The police were hard on his track, and in trying to escape he fell into the river and was drowned."

"Drowned ! Red Judas drowned ?"

"Well, not exactly ; but he got very wet and muddy. Gribichon, who was trying to steal some brandy from a boat, found him as he was floating down the stream. You know Gribichon ?"

"I have heard of him—a young gentleman who would have taken you to the fair if I had not."

"Precisely, and would not have deserted me in such a very ungallant manner. But where are you going ?"

"I don't know—but tell me about Judas."

"Gribichon got him ashore, only about an hour ago, and took him to a safe place, where he is recovering from the effects of his bath, and where the police will have little chance of worrying him. And, by the way, you could not do better than put up at the same place ; Decade will be glad of such a recruit as you."

"And pray who is Decade ? what is he ?"

"I am thirsty—here is a wine-shop—let us sit down whilst I tell you."

There were no other customers in the drinking-house. Louise seemed well known there, and as she was evidently disposed to be friendly Cartouche sat at his ease.

"Decade is a soldier, he has fought for the French King, but now he wages war against the rich on his own account. He has several men serving under him."

"In fact, he is captain of a band of outlaws."

"You are right."

"I will go to him without delay."

"But where will you find him, Monsieur Cartouche ? The police would be glad enough to have an interview with him if they only knew where to meet him."

"Red Judas is with him, you say ?"

"Yes, through the kindness of Gribichon."

"Louise, what a charming woman you have become," said Cartouche.

The young man had learnt from the gipsies that the best way to get on with a female is to flatter her, and he now found the value of that learning.

"You want to see Red Judas ?" said Louise.

"Yes."

"And you will put yourself under the control of Captain Decade ?"

"Yes · I will do anything for you, Louise. But do you love this Captain Decade ?"

"I hate him ! I fear him ! I love only one man !"

"Gribichon or Red Judas ?"

"They are both detestable scamps," responded Louise, and there was something in her eyes which told him plainly that he was the man she preferred to all others. So, without any more fuss, he slipped his arm round her waist and had the satisfaction of knowing that he was not mistaken.

An hour later he was sitting in a strange room in a strange house, a regularly sworn member of the band of Decade. There were half a dozen young fellows there, and Red Judas could be heard alternately swearing and groaning in an adjacent apartment. Louise was there also, but it was clearly understood that Cartouche was her lover, so no one interfered except to pay her a few compliments.

CHAPTER IX.

THE MIDNIGHT ATTACK.

"AND now, gentlemen," said Decade, when a couple of bottles of wine had been emptied to the health of the new recruit, "it is time we arranged some business. Little has been done lately and the exchequer is in a bad state."

"Let the new hand show what he can do," said Gribichon, a young fellow some four or five years older than Cartouche, who at once responded—

"I am quite willing to show the metal I am made of. But what kind of adventure shall it be, gentlemen ; shall I rob the king as he rides along the street surrounded by his guards ?"

"That is too much," said Decade. "Listen. In the Rue de Noailles there lives a man who for many years past has oppressed his fellowmen by charging them enormous interest on trifling loans which their necessities compel them to borrow from him. Now I propose that we borrow all his money without even giving him a note of hand for it. Cartouche shall be entrusted with this task, choosing any two of the band to assist him."

"I shall not need more than one security to back the bill I shall present to this old miser. May I have the pleasure of your company, Monsieur Gribichon ?"

"Certainly—but I thought Red Judas——"

"He is not sufficiently recovered from drowning to run a chance of being hanged," said Decade.

"Then I am with you, Cartouche."

"And the sooner we do this business the better."

The preliminaries were soon arranged. Cartouche was to be the leader, and being equipped with all the necessary appliances they were about to start, when Louise beckoned to Cartouche, and whispered—

"I dwell at the sign of the Wolf on the other side of the road. Do not forget the address, and be sure that at any hour you will be a welcome visitor."

"I shall not forget," said he, pressing another kiss on her full ruddy lips.

Then, accompanied by Gribichon, he started out to attack the house of the old miser of the Rue de Noailles.

In those days this street was extremely narrow, and consisted of old-fashioned houses; public lamps were few and far between, only an occasional oil light being hung out to let the belated wayfarer know how dark it was.

One of these lamps hung close by the miser's house, and by its dim light Cartouche and Gribichon considered how they could best effect an entrance.

"These windows seem fast enough," Cartouche whispered.

"Too fast for us," rejoined Gribichon.

"I am not certain of that."

'If we force open the shutters there are thick iron bars to be removed before an entrance could be made."

"You seem to know the place, friend Gribichon."

'I have often had a look at the outside."

"Well, we will explore the interior to-night. Is there any back way?"

"None whatever."

"Then it seems we must go in by the door."

"There is a very strong bolt inside."

"Which, no doubt, will give way to persuasion."

Gribichon did not exactly understand what the new recruit meant, or how he intended acting; but as he had been placed under the orders of Cartouche he considered himself bound to give implicit obedience, to answer all questions, and to offer the best advice he was capable of.

"Why not try the upper windows?" said he. "They are not very high above the roadway."

"Anyone climbing up will be at a great disadvantage in case of resistance, so we will try the iron bar."

"As you like. Here it is."

"Then insert it here and give a good strong wrench."

Gribichon did so, but failed at the first effort to force the massive fastenings.

He made enough noise, however, to alarm the miser, who made his appearance at one of the upper windows and shouted loudly for the police.

And a couple of officers who were patrolling the district happening to hear the outcry came running to the place.

"Quick, Gribichon!" exclaimed Cartouche.

"Confound the door!" was the reply of the rascal, as he tried in vain to force its fastenings.

"Back! stand back for your lives!" Cartouche cried, as he fiercely confronted the officers with sword and pistol ready for immediate use.

"Surrender!" exclaimed the foremost.

"Never! Come along, Gribichon."

Cartouche as he spoke made a thrust at one man, who stepped back and avoided it. In an instant he knocked down the other with the butt of his pistol, being anxious to avoid firing, which would cause too great an alarm in the neighbourhood.

Gribichon, also starting to his feet, bestowed a blow in the stomach to the man who avoided Cartouche's thrust, and having for the time put both antagonists out of action they started off.

"Remove your mask," said Cartouche, when they had got a little way from the scene of their exploit, "and walk slowly."

"Are you not anxious to get away?"

"Certainly; but running will make people suspect us."

"True. Well, we must go back and report our failure."

"Don't be in a hurry about that either."

"What do you mean?"

"Why, in about half an hour we will have another try."

"It will be dangerous."

"All the more glorious if we succeed."

"The place will be watched."

"Not so, friend Gribichon. They will be scouring the other parts of Paris in search of us, but they won't dream of our going back again to complete the work we were disturbed at."

"Good. But by heaven we are pursued."

"To the right! Run for it!"

The two started off at full speed, followed by the officers, who had called to their assistance some three or four citizens who chanced to be abroad, and had been attracted to the spot by the clamour.

"To the right again," Cartouche whispered.

Gribichon obeyed.

But the noise behind them increased; others were joining in the pursuit.

They were running down a narrow street, much of the same type as the Rue de Noailles and parallel with it, when Cartouche noticed an open door.

It was the thought and work of but a second to catch Gribichon by the arm and swing him into the passage, follow himself, and then close the door. As he did so a soft female voice said—

"Who are you? What do you want here?"

"We mean no harm to you—we are escaping from a man to whom we owe money, and who means to send us to prison if he can catch us."

"I sympathise with you; my husband is now in a dungeon because he was unable to pay a loan for which he had made himself answerable."

"Then you will not betray us?"

"I will not; you are safe here as long as you please to stay."

The woman produced a candle from some back room, and, having thoroughly looked at the two unexpected visitors, said—

"Ascend, gentlemen, if you please, to my apartment."

She led the way to an upper room at the back of the house, where the first object that attracted the eyes of Cartouche and Gribichon was the form of a youth about fourteen years of age extended on a rude bed.

At first they were not certain whether it was a living being or a corpse. that lay there so quietly and looking so ghastly pale by the feeble light of the spluttering candle. But presently there was a slight movement, which convinced them there was still breath in the body.

"My son, gentlemen," said the woman.

"He is ill !" said Cartouche.

"He is dying. And when he goes heaven only knows what will become of me ?"

"What is his complaint ?"

The woman, who looked quite as ill as her son, turned a pair of glittering eyes upon Cartouche, and simply replied—

"Hunger !"

It needed no confirmation, that simple word ; everything about the place bore evidence of the poverty of the occupiers. The furniture was of the humblest kind, and probably would not have fetched the price of a loaf of bread if disposed of. The woman's clothing, too, was of the poorest kind, though, like her home, perfectly clean and neat.

"If he suffers from hunger I will prescribe— food."

"I have no money to buy it."

"Do you know where to buy it at this hour ?"

"Not very near here, but there are plenty of places in the city where food can be purchased at any hour."

"Then buy some," said Cartouche, putting a crown on the table.

"But my boy ?"

"We will watch and take care of him till you return."

"Heaven bless and reward you," said the woman, and then she swiftly darted from the room, leaving her sleeping son to the care of Cartouche and Gribichon.

"You are in a sentimental mood to-night," was the remark made by Gribichon, when he and Cartouche were alone with the slumbering invalid.

"Not a bit of it, my boy."

"Giving money away in that reckless way."

"Sound policy. I wanted to get the woman out of the way for a time, but did not care to pitch her through the window."

"There is nothing here worth having."

"Listen, Gribichon. Before I had been here five seconds I saw something which highly delighted me."

"What was that, pray ?"

Cartouche led his companion to the window and pointed out the wall of another house not five feet away. Through the windows of that other house they could see there was someone moving about and carrying a light from room to room.

"That is our old miser of the Rue de Noailles."

"No !"

"It is, though. I had a full view of his face as he stood at the window when we came in."

"Proceed," said Gribichon.

"We can easily get from this house to that. I can see that there are no bars to the window here."

"How do you propose to do it."

"I nearly fell over a builder's ladder as we came up the stairs of this house ; we will thrust it across from this window to the other, and so pass over."

"You are a man of genius."

"Then fetch the ladder quickly."

Gribichon did so. The youth who was lying on the bed did not stir or speak.

"It is a good sound sleep," Cartouche muttered.

"He is dead," responded Gribichon.

And so it proved. Whilst his mother was away for the purpose of procuring food the breath failed, and she would return to find her only hope gone.

But little did these two reckless ones care about that.

The ladder was put across the space between the two windows. Cartouche passed over. The miser's casement was fastened on the inside, but their useful crowbar soon gained them an entrance.

"Silence !" said Cartouche. "He is coming this way."

Two seconds later the restless old man, haunted by thoughts of robbers and the loss of his gold, came back into that room where the two were waiting to despoil him.

As he entered Cartouche's arm was pressed across the old man's mouth, whilst Gribichon quickly pinioned his hands behind him. As soon as that was done a twisted handkerchief was thrust into his mouth and fastened behind his head, and there he was bound and gagged— incapable of making any alarm.

"Better finish the job," said Gribichon.

"No. I want to finish this affair without any shedding of blood. Lend me a hand to carry him away."

They handled the old miser very roughly as they bore him down the stairs and put him in a back room.

"Now, if your money is in this room say so by nodding your head ; if it is not in this room shake your head."

The old man did neither, and Cartouche at once guessed that the money was in that apartment. There was a cupboard in one corner, and Cartouche walked towards it.

Down went the old man on his knees, trying hard, but in vain, to articulate a petition that they would spare him his little store, the savings of a long life. But Cartouche and Gribichon only laughed as by a dexterous use of the crowbar they forced the door of the cupboard.

"Here is the hoard. Look here, Cartouche."

And Gribichon hauled down from the top shelf a very strong and heavy wallet or portmanteau of leather.

"Your keys, friend," said Louis Dominique,

snatching them from the old man's coat-pocket. It took little time or trouble to find the right key; the valise was opened, and it was found to contain weighty bags of coin, one of which Cartouche opened.

"Gold!" he exclaimed. "This is something like business. But just guard our friend while I look into the other rooms and see if there is anything worth confiscating."

He searched in vain; the old usurer had no heavy silver plate—everything was of the plainest kind. However, they had a good booty, and Cartouche suggested that it was time they should be off.

"But first tie our old friend's legs together as well as his wrists, then he will not be able to give the alarm till we are far away and safe from pursuit."

This was quickly done; then they laid the miser on the floor with his face downwards, and, closing the room-door, decamped.

"Which way do we go now?" Gribichon asked.

"Back the way we came. He did not see how we got into the house and will be equally puzzled to know how we left it."

So they reascended the stairs and went back over the ladder to the room of the poor woman who had befriended them.

"I am sorry your son is dead," Cartouche wrote with pencil on a scrap of paper. "Here is something for the funeral."

He enclosed five gold pieces in the document, which he left on the table. Then they replaced the ladder, and carrying their booty between them walked out into the street.

"We had better get along as quickly as possible; there will be considerable excitement when this affair is known," said Cartouche.

"It will be a long time before the old man is able to give the alarm," Gribichon replied.

"The police will call there in the morning, and then if he does not respond to their knock they will force an entrance."

CHAPTER X.

THE DUEL.

"By the time the police call in the morning we shall have put on disguises that will enable us to pass freely, without fear of being recognised," said Gribichon. "But what will the captain say when he sees our booty?"

"He ought to be well satisfied with our night's work," returned Cartouche.

"He is a difficult man to satisfy," responded Gribichon.

Thus talking the two men made their way to the head quarters of the band, and entered without being observed. The captain professed himself well satisfied, bottles and glasses were put on the table, and there was a grand carouse in honour of the success of the new recruit.

"There is only one thing about it that I don't like," said Cartouche, when he had recounted all the circumstances. "What is that?" demanded the captain.

"Our friend Gribichon was indiscreet——"

"What is that you say?" demanded the individual mentioned, who sat opposite Cartouche.

"I said that you were indiscreet——"

"You teach me discretion, eh?"

"Order! order! no quarrelling. Explain yourself, Cartouche," said the captain."

"Gribichon was good enough to mention my name in the hearing of the old gentleman whose house we visited."

"That was certainly unwise."

Gribichon, who had been drinking deeply—swallowing glass after glass as rapidly as he could fill them—felt very much disposed to pick a quarrel with Cartouche or the captain. But some of the band got him away out of the room, and peace was restored.

Next morning, at a tolerably early hour, La Belle Louise went out to purchase the flowers which she would retail in the public places of Paris. Cartouche was ready to accompany her, and as he was attired in different garments, and disguised with a wig, there was no danger in his doing so.

All the band were anxious to know whether the police had any clue to the perpetrators of the previous night's outrage, and Louise, who sold flowers at the entrance to the chief office of the police, could easily find out from her customers.

She was very fond of vending her wares at that spot, and the police officials who laughed and joked with the handsome flower-girl little guessed they were talking to one of the most active members of the band they were so anxious to capture.

Having purchased the flowers Louise sat down on a doorstep to tie them up in small bunches for sale.

Cartouche stood near her, watching her nimble fingers and listening to her equally nimble tongue.

"You will have good luck to-day, Louise," said he.

"Why do you think so, Louis?"

"I don't know, but I feel convinced that such will be the case, and I shall have good luck."

A few minutes later a tall officer came swaggering past, and pushed rudely against Cartouche.

"Now, young fellow, if you don't want to buy you can make way for the favourite customer of La Belle Louise," said he. "Good-morning, sweetheart."

"Sir, you were very rude to me, and must apologise."

The officer stared at Cartouche and twisted his moustache.

"What have you in your basket, Louise?" he continued, not replying to the young man.

"You must apologise or fight," said Cartouche.

"Fight! with whom, pray?"

"With me."

"Pooh! some tradesman's apprentice out for a holiday in the dress of a gentleman. I am an officer of the Civic Guard, and I never fight with such."

"You, an officer of the Civic Guard, dare you insult me! I am the Baron St. Elmo and an officer in his Majesty's Bordeaux Regiment. You must answer for this insult, and I shall expect to find you in the Gardens of the Tuileries in a couple of hours."

"If you are the Baron St. Elmo, monsieur, I shall be glad to act as your second on this occasion," said a young dandy of the Court who happened to be passing.

"You are very kind, sir, and as I have only just arrived in Paris I will gladly accept your offer."

"I am the Count Cichini, well known at Court. Your father once did me a very great service, and I am happy to have an opportunity of making some slight return to his son. And this fellow of the Civic Guard ought to think himself honoured that two noblemen of birth and standing take notice of him."

"I shall be there," said the Civic Guardsman, "and my weapons are pistols; they do the work better than swords."

"Bring field pieces if you will," replied Cartouche, "it matters not to me; but do not fail to present yourself."

The Civic Guardsman growled an oath and walked away.

"There are few of us who care to fight with the Civic fellows," said the count; "they are such a low, vulgar set. But this man happens to belong to a good family, so you will not injure your reputation by going out with him."

"I always prefer to fight when insulted, even when the man is of a lower grade."

"Just so; but now, my dear baron, I must hasten away for an hour. I will not fail, however, to meet you at the gate of the gardens at an hour and a half from the present time."

And with a very grand bow the young count moved on.

Cartouche remained in the company of Louise.

"You are a good one to pass for a baron!" said she.

"Why not? I am as good-looking as some nobles, quite as brave, and perhaps as rich."

"But Cichini is really a count."

"He is a gentleman. But do you know him, Louise?"

"Yes; he often buys flowers of me, so does his wife. She is such a handsome woman, and dresses splendidly."

"Not handsomer than you, Louise. She cannot be!"

"Flatterer! go and be shot."

"I shall dine with you to-night, Louise, in spite of all the frowns and oaths of the Civic Guard fellow."

They chatted away till it was time for Cartouche to go and fight. At the gate of the Tuileries Gardens the Baron St. Elmo met the Count Cichini, and they entered together.

One part of the place was famous as the spot where Parisians were in the habit of settling their differences by an appeal to the sword, and as Cartouche and Count Cichini approached it they saw a gentleman being assisted into a carriage, while his late antagonist walked away with a contented smile upon his face.

"And here comes our man," said Cichini.

"I am ready for him."

"He is a good shot—are you?"

"Pretty good. That is to say I am very quick in taking aim. Do you know the man he has brought with him."

"By sight. He is a man to be avoided."

The combatants and their seconds saluted, and the terms of combat were quickly arranged.

The principals were to have one shot each, but if no damage was done then swords were to finish the combat. So the men were placed in position and the pistols handed to them.

"Listen, gentlemen," said Count Cichini, "you are not to raise your pistols till I count two, when the word 'three' is pronounced fire as quickly as you like, but not before then."

Placing himself back a little from the line of fire the young noble counted rather quickly "one, two, three."

Cartouche fired first, and his ball passed so near the head of the Captain of the Civic Guard that his aim was disturbed.

"Ten thousand curses on the luck," he growled, dashing his weapon to the ground on seeing that the sham Baron St Elmo still stood erect and uninjured.

"Your swords now, gentlemen, if you please," said the captain's second, unsheathing his own blade.

Cartouche and his adversary drew instantly; but it was noticed that the captain looked rather flurried. He had so thoroughly calculated on doing the business with his favourite weapon the pistol, that he felt rather put out at being compelled to fight it out with swords.

However, there was no help for it—so with coats thrown off the men confronted each other.

"On guard!" cried the captain's second, and the blades crossed each other with a ringing sound.

"Now I shall have you, Monsieur le Baron St. Elmo—you cannot escape," replied the Captain of the Civic Guard.

"Is that so?" laughed Cartouche, as he parried a thrust.

"You cannot escape my vengeance!" the captain growled.

"We shall see," answered Cartouche.

"I shall see—through the hole I shall bore in your cursed body."

"My friend, I am not easily perforated."

The captain tried to make a hole in the baron's shirt, but the thrust was easily put by. Then Cartouche saw his opportunity, and lunging over the captain's guard, split that gentleman's sword-arm from elbow to shoulder.

"You are satisfied, I trust," said Cartouche, saluting his disabled opponent and the gentleman who seconded him.

"Quite, for the present," was the response.

Then the wounded man was led from the field, and the successful duellist, turning to his second, said—

"And now, monsieur, thanking you for your

CARTOUCHE,

THE FRENCH JACK SHEPPARD.

"BACK! STAND BACK FOR YOUR LIVES!" CARTOUCHE CRIED, AS HE FIERCELY CONFRONTED THE OFFICERS WITH SWORD AND PISTOL.

kindness, I must hurry away, as I have other important business on hand."

"I am pleased and proud to be your friend, Baron St. Elmo."

Cartouche rushed off at full speed, and the Count Cichini was about to depart in a more leisurely manner, when he was tapped on the shoulder by a young swell, who asked—

"What did you call that fellow?"

"The Baron St. Elmo."

"Who introduced you to him?"

"As a matter of fact he introduced himself." And Cichini recounted the circumstances of his first meeting with Cartouche.

"And he told you he was the Baron St. Elmo?"

"Yes, my father's friend."

"He uttered the biggest lie that ever came from mortal lips. The Baron St. Elmo is now at the Hotel de la Reine, where you shall see him if you will honour me with your company," said the young swell, the Vicomte d'Arlincourt.

"Who, then, is this impostor whom I seconded?"

"I cannot guess."

"That was Cartouche," said a young ragamuffin who had witnessed the duel, and was now listening to the conversation.

D'Arlincourt caught the ragged youngster by the arm.

"Do you know him?" he asked.

"Yes, my lord."

"What is he—where does he live?"

"He is a thief, and I don't know where he lives."

Cichini twisted his moustache, and then, pointing to a printed bill posted against the gate of the gardens, said—

"Read that, you young rascal."

"I cannot read, my lord."

"You can eat and drink. Away with you, then, and spend this golden piece."

The youngster snatched the coin and bolted. The Count Cichini read the bill, which was an announcement that the Government would pay a reward of

ONE HUNDRED CROWNS
FOR THE APPREHENSION OF
LOUIS DOMINIQUE CARTOUCHE!!
DEAD OR ALIVE!!!

And then, in smaller type, the placard detailed the murder which caused our hero to take refuge in the French capital, the robbery of the old miser, and a few other things.

"He must be a noted thief," said the Vicomte D'Arlincourt.

"He is a good swordsman, and fought well," the Count Cichini responded.

"Well, my boy, when you seconded him you did so under a mistake, and as he fought fairly and well you have not lost anything by the adventure."

"No, but still——"

"Well, still, what?"

"Still it will not be pleasant to hear people laugh as they say that the Count Cichini was second to a robber."

"Bah! If they say it offensively you know what to do."

"And I shall do it."

The two friends then parted; but although they walked in different directions they both heard the name of Cartouche freely mentioned by all sorts of folks.

The placard had been well posted all over Paris, and the name of Louis Dominique Cartouche was famous.

CHAPTER XI.
WHO SHALL BE THE CAPTAIN?

AND this famous man, where was he?

After the duel he quitted his second, the Count Cichini, in a rather abrupt manner. That, however, was not from any want of courtesy, but is rather to be attributed to the fact that a police officer was staring at him in a rather offensive way.

This particular policeman had no personal knowledge of Cartouche, but he had just posted up that bill, and he could not help thinking that the description of Cartouche tallied to some extent with the personal appearance of the Count Cichini's friend. But the now famous robber did not feel called upon to enlighten the officer; he preferred to leave him in darkness.

Cartouche, in fact, thought it would be advisable to alter his personal appearance as much as possible, so he sought a barber and theatrical costumier, and with their assistance disguised himself so effectually that Louise did not know him when he went back to her.

But when she knew who it was she was indeed glad to see him alive and uninjured, for she had fallen deeply in love with the young scamp, and would have sold soul and body for him.

He told her what had happened.

"You must not go back to the head-quarters," she said.

"Why not, my charmer."

"Because I know the place is watched. The police have some notion of your haunts, and they are looking for you."

"Does our captain allow the police to know where he lives?"

"They have contrived to get some information."

"He is not fit, then, to be captain."

"I have long thought so," responded Louise. "But how can he be deposed?—who shall take his place?"

"Leave that to me."

"I know who *ought* to be captain," said Louise, giving him a very tender look.

"And I know who will be—unless fortune goes very much against him," Cartouche answered. "But if I cannot go back to the head-quarters I must let him know where I am in case he has need to communicate with me."

"That is easily done," said Louise.

She beckoned to a small ragged urchin who was standing near, and whispered something to him, at the same time slipping a small coin into his hand.

"Wait in the neighbourhood till he returns," said Louise, "but do not stay too much in my company, for most of the police come to chat with me, and one of them might recognise you."

Cartouche saw the value of her advice, so he walked about on the other side of the road, and had the pleasure of seeing a lot of fellows making love to his mistress, but he could not interfere lest the police should be down on him.

In about an hour the boy messenger returned.

Cartouche crossed over to where Louise was standing with her basket of flowers, and heard the youngster say—

"The captain desires that Monsieur Cartouche will not try to re-enter the head-quarters, lest he should be followed by the police."

"What am I to do then?"

The boy looked at Cartouche, whom he had not seen before, and then he cast a glance at Louise, who said—

"Say what you have to say. This is Monsieur Cartouche, and he may hear your message."

The French boy pulled off his cap and made a bow which many an English peer would have given a year's income to imitate successfully.

"Monsieur, the captain will be pleased to meet you at the Quai de la Mégasserie at the hour of midnight."

"I shall be there," responded Cartouche.

And after some more conversation with Louise he walked away to pass the time till he should meet the captain of this band of robbers with whom he had become associated.

"I will become captain myself," said Cartouche, as he strolled away leisurely.

The idea had occurred to him very soon after joining the band. Cartouche had an idea that he was a much better leader than follower, and he was not going to sit down and play second fiddle to anyone.

Gribichon—well, he seemed to be lieutenant now, and should be allowed to keep that position when he—Louis Dominique Cartouche—assumed the sceptre of authority over all the rascaldom of Paris; and then the Parisians would have their eyes opened just a little.

Cartouche went to a café and dined; then he played a game or two of billiards, winning just enough to pay for his dinner; after which, when the hands of the clock began to point to the hour of midnight, he strolled down towards the Quai de la Mégasserie to meet his captain.

The River Seine at Paris is not bordered by wharves and warehouses, but has on each side a broad terrace or roadway lined with houses. Some of these are of modern build, but the Quai de la Mégasserie is an ancient one, and has existed for five hundred years or more.

And there Cartouche met his captain, who complimented him on the dexterity with which he robbed the old miser, and also upon his success in the duel.

"When I die you will certainly be my successor in the command," said the captain.

"I am very young," replied Cartouche.

"What of that? Many of our greatest men made their success in youth."

"But our comrades would not have confidence in me," said Louis Dominique.

"Pshaw! your youth is in your favour. You will live all the longer to achieve renown."

"But I am not equal to many of them."

"In strength, bravery, and cunning, if you live to the age of Methuselah, you will not improve upon what you are now at the age of nineteen."

The captain was walking along thoughtlessly, and Cartouche now saw his opportunity.

"You are right, captain; I shall succeed you in the leadership of the band."

"Of course, when I am dead."

"That will not be long."

There was something in Cartouche's manner as he uttered the words that caused the captain to halt, and as he did so Cartouche plunged a dagger into his breast.

Cartouche had studied anatomy whilst with the Jesuits, and he had no need to repeat the blow. Down fell the captain—dead!

"Help! murder!" screamed a voice near at hand, and Cartouche, turning his head, caught a glimpse of a female form. "Here is Cartouche! Here is the monster you were to apprehend!"

The voice was that of a woman of whom the captain was enamoured, and she had that day consented to be his, but only on condition that he should betray Cartouche to the police and give her the money reward that was offered for his apprehension.

Cartouche had seen this woman and the captain conversing, and now her exclamation enlightened him as to the business they were discussing.

"You jade, you shall follow him!" he cried.

But in the distance he could hear the footsteps of the police, who were coming to arrest him, so there was no time to be lost.

With a mighty effort Cartouche plunged the body into the river and then started off at full speed.

In a minute he had distanced them—but now he had to consider what course he would take.

"The boldest course is often the safest. I will go back and assert my right to be captain of the band."

Cartouche rightly guessed that the police, having received instructions to arrest him on the Quai de la Mégasserie, would have relaxed their watch on the headquarters of the gang, and therefore he would be able to enter unobserved. In fact, it was not likely that the late captain had informed them all about the hiding-place of the band, for that would be putting his own liberty in their power.

So he sped through the dark streets, reached the house, gave the signal, and was admitted.

Cartouche thought, as he entered the room, that Red Judas started and turned pale.

"Can he have had a hand in this?" Cartouche thought. "If I can prove it his captain's death will be a very tame affair in comparison with what he will suffer. I will watch you closely, my good friend, Judas; but I will not betray you to the police, for I want to have the pleasure of punishing you myself if I find you are a traitor."

Louise welcomed her lover and had neither eyes nor ears for anyone else.

"Where did you leave the captain, Cartouche?" asked Gribichon.

"In the river."

As he spoke he rose from his chair, and taking Louise by the arm walked with her to the head of the table, where he installed himself in the seat usually reserved for the captain. Placing his lovely companion on his right hand he said—

"Listen to me, gentlemen."

Every voice was hushed at once, save that of Cartouche, who said—

"Gentlemen, from this time I am your captain."

"How is that?" asked one or two.

"Your late captain was a traitor to us all; he intended to hand me, you, all of us in fact, into the hands of the police. I discovered the treachery he meditated, and I prevented it by killing him; therefore this chair and the leadership of this assembly becomes mine by right of conquest. Does anyone dispute my title?"

Tomasso, one of the old hands, suggested that the question should be put to the vote.

"But for whom else will you vote? There is no competitor—I have no rival."

And Cartouche looked round the room as though he would very much like to see anyone setting up a claim against him. However, as no one did so, he was saved the trouble of quarrelling.

"Then it is agreed that I am your captain?" said he, after a pause of a few seconds.

The men paused also before there was a reply. Then Tomasso said—

"Yes, we cannot do better. So huzza, my boys, for our bold Captain Cartouche!"

"Huzza!" they shouted.

"Huzza!" whispered Louise, "and you will not have a more docile, obedient servant in the troop than the little girl whose waist your arm encircles."

"That I believe, and if ever you turn traitor I shall kill myself—not you."

"If you don't die till that happens you will live to a good old age, my Louis, my captain. But where is Lizette?"

"What, the captain's sweetheart?"

"The *late* captain's sweetheart. She went out two hours ago."

"She was close by when I thrust my dagger into his heart, and she knew what a foul traitor he was. Listen, comrades, if any of you see the girl Lizette show her no pity, for she was as much our common foe as her dead lover."

"Then of course she won't come here again," said Gribichon.

"She had better not," growled old Tomasso.

He was an old Corsican, familiar with blood-shedding from his infancy. It was a jest among his comrades that he had used his dagger so often that he could not count the lives he had taken—and from the way in which he played with the handle of that weapon it was pretty certain that Lizette's earthly career would be considerably abbreviated if he chanced to meet her.

"And now, comrades, the business being settled, there is nothing to be discussed but some bottles of wine which I shall have much pleasure in paying for. Wolf will fetch them, I know."

"Yes, captain," responded the youngster, who was known by the name of the Wolf.

"And keep your eyes open, both going and returning; see if there are any of the police loitering about the neighbourhood. You know most of them by sight."

"Better than their own chief, captain."

The Wolf departed with the coin furnished by Cartouche, and he soon returned with a basket of bottles. As he placed them on the table he whispered something to Louise.

"What does he say?" Cartouche demanded.

"He has seen my mother."

"What Madame Lafarge?"

"I have only one mother, you goose! That is the name by which you know her."

"Yes, but does she know this place?—does she come here?"

"I have never seen her here."

"Then she is not one of the gang?"

"No. She was a friend of Captain Decade, and she wished to marry him."

"And he did not respond to her advances?"

"No, the brute; he wanted me for his wife."

"Why do you hate him so much, Louise? Surely not because he wished to marry you?"

"He was a brute. He was cruel to that poor girl who drowned herself to escape from him. She, poor creature, could see no way of avoiding him but the river; but you were away from Paris—you know nothing of that."

"If he tormented any girl so that she drowned herself he is an accursed villain, and I am not sorry that I plunged my dagger into his bosom," Cartouche replied.

"And, knowing that I knew all about it, he wanted me to wed with him. Thank Heaven, he is gone."

"But your mother?"

"When she hears of his death she will do her best to hunt down the man who slew him."

"Does she know any of the other members of our band?"

"Red Judas and Gribichon."

"Gribichon is safe enough, but I believe Judas is like his namesake the priests talk about—he would betray anyone for thirty pieces of silver, or copper either. But he is also a terrible coward."

"That I know."

Louise beckoned the Wolf to her, and whispered—

"Do you think any of the others know that my mother has returned to Paris?"

"I should say not," replied the Wolf.

"You must not say a word to any of them about her. Especially you are to note whether Judas holds any communication with her. You will not fail?"

"You shall know everything."

* * * * * *

Madame Lafarge had returned to Paris.

The vault which Cartouche thought he had searched so thoroughly had a secret way of exit, by which one could pass out into a disused stone quarry, which was so thickly overgrown with bushes that few people were aware of its existence.

Madame Lafarge, however, knew many things.

We have seen her as one who encouraged roguery, and in that capacity she had become acquainted with Ishmael, Judith, and the rest of the gipsy band now doing penance on board the galleys, and from them had learnt the secret of the vault.

It was a secret not entrusted to all the gipsies; only a few of the old and trustworthy ones knew the way into that secret arsenal in the old ruined abbey. And it was a treasury as well as a magazine of arms.

Madame Lafarge, to avoid the consequence of some petty larceny business in which she was involved, had thought it necessary to leave Paris for a time and travel in the country.

CHAPTER XII.

THE POLICE OFFICE.

MADAME LAFARGE knew the route usually taken by Judith and her Egyptian band, and took the same direction, believing she would be safer in their society than away from it. Also, she could get some sort of pecuniary assistance from them.

But suddenly she heard of the murder and of the apprehension of the gipsy band save two—Cartouche and Red Judas. She knew that they could not remain in the country, that they were bound to go back to Paris; so she resolved to help herself from the secret treasury of the gipsies, and go back and denounce Cartouche, so earning her own pardon and a good reward.

She was in the vault helping herself to the coin—there was not much left—when Cartouche entered the building. She knew where the weapons and provisions were concealed, but she did not want anything in that line, so she did not disturb the door leading to it, which was covered with dust and cobwebs.

The money was in a hollow place in the tombstone itself, and, having secured it, Madame Lafarge was about to return to upper earth when she became aware that there was some one in the old ruin.

How she and Cartouche met each other has already been related.

But when she returned to the vault, and found that Cartouche had fastened her down, she slipped off through that secret way into the old quarry, and roused the villagers to come and secure the murderer who had made the neighbourhood so famous.

And then, when they just missed him, she resolved to follow on to Paris.

The bill on the gateway offering the reward for the apprehension of Cartouche was the first thing that attracted her attention, and she resolved that the crowns should be hers.

"If I could but meet Red Judas or Gribichon!" said she.

Both those scamps were old pupils of hers, and she knew they were members of the band of Monsieur Decade.

How to find Captain Decade was the thing that most puzzled Madame Lafarge.

She knew that the captain of the Parisian banditti had a big house in which he sheltered the rascals who owned his rule, but she could not tell where, although she had a pretty good idea of the locality. She was loitering about not far from the place she desired to discover when the Wolf saw her and reported the fact to Louise.

"When Decade marries me, as he must, he shall not keep this place a secret from me," Madame Lafarge thought to herself.

But she little guessed that the fishermen down the river were already dragging Decade's lifeless body to land, and that Cartouche had proclaimed himself chief of the most daring band of outlaws in the French metropolis.

So at a late hour at night, or an early hour in the morning, she retired to a lodging, not far from her old house, resolved that she would yet compass the death of Louis Dominique Cartouche, against whom she had formed a mortal enmity.

In the morning Madame Lafarge went out again.

The petty business for which she had been obliged to leave Paris was soon settled by payment of the value of the stolen property. She had the money from the gipsy treasury; and now with her name scratched off the list of those "wanted" by the police Madame Lafarge could boldly walk in any part of Paris.

And she chose to walk in the direction of the Police Office.

The chief of the police at that time was a certain Monsieur Peuchet, an elderly gentleman who had risen from a very subordinate position in the force. He was remarkably acute, and when once possessed of a clue seldom failed to run down the particular offender he was in search of.

He was also amorous though elderly, a fact that was sometimes taken advantage of by the female adventuresses of Paris, and Madame Lafarge, who was not more than forty years of age, and tolerably good-looking, thought she might try her luck with him.

She thought it would be a great joke to find out Cartouche through the agency of the police, and then get the reward through these same policemen.

So she presented herself at the door of the Police Office.

"What can we do for you, Madame Lafarge?" asked the man who admitted her.

"You know that my name is no longer on your list."

The man nodded, and after making another entry in his criminal account-book, said—

"Yes, you got off that business very well. But why are you here, Madame Lafarge?"

"Is the chief in his bureau?"

"He is."

"I wish to have a few words with him," said Madame Lafarge, quietly.

"You !—with the chief !"

"Yes, I, with Monsieur Peuchet, the chief of the police."

"And what do you want with Monsieur Peuchet?"

Madame Lafarge looked at the man quietly for a few seconds, and then answered—

"I daresay he will tell you—if he wishes you to know."

"I will inquire if he is in," said the man.

"You have already told me that he is in, so there is no need to make any inquiries. Let him know that I am here, and have some rather important news for him."

"I shall very likely get in trouble for doing so."

"The trouble will be greater if you do not."

The much-worried officer touched a bell, and a messenger appeared, to whom he said—

"Tell Monsieur Peuchet that there is a lady——"

"Madame Lafarge," the messenger said. He knew the woman's pedigree and record as well as she did herself, and no doubt could have reminded her of several little bits of petty larceny that she had forgotten. "Madame wishes to see the chief, I presume," he continued.

"Doubtless, or I should not be here."

"And equally without doubt monsieur will be delightful to see madame. He adores the fair sex, and I will hasten to let him know that one of them is waiting to see him."

"Go about your business, ass, but do it quickly."

The man hurried away, and soon returned with a message that Monsieur Peuchet would see Madame Lafarge if she would step into his private room. Madame had no objection; at the door of the private room she met the chief's private secretary, a withered old mummy, who was supposed to be full of secrets.

But Peuchet did not trust him to know everything that went on in his bureau, so when Madame Lafarge was announced he was sent out on some useless errand.

Peuchet rubbed his hands and smiled a very evil smile when the woman entered.

"So you have come to see me, madame," he said.

"Yes, monsieur," she replied.

"You cannot keep away from the police, eh? But pray be seated, madame."

Madame Lafarge placed herself on the chair indicated by Monsieur Peuchet, and spent some seconds in the consideration of how she should begin the business.

"It is not so easy to keep away from the police of Paris when they desire an interview with one," she said.

"Have any of my men told you to come here?"

"No, I came of my own accord, on a matter of business of a most important nature."

"It is a great pleasure to transact business with a fine handsome woman like you, Madame Lafarge," said he; and as he spoke he touched her cheek with his forefinger, which was about as long and bony as that of a skeleton.

"You are joking, monsieur."

"No, indeed; and if I were not married perhaps you would not remain long a widow. But as it is I must have a kiss."

"Nay, let us talk of the business first."

"And then——"

"And then, perhaps, Monsieur Peuchet.'

"Well, what is this business?" the chief demanded, seating himself at his desk, and assuming his official demeanour. "It must be something important to bring you to my office."

Madame Lafarge pointed to the wall against which was pinned a copy of the proclamation offering a reward for the apprehension of Cartouche.

"Oh! you know him then?" said Peuchet.

"The French police don't know everything; they don't know that I ever saw Cartouche," Madame thought to herself. "So I must not tell them too much."

"Yes, I know Cartouche. Years ago when I sold fruit at the Jesuit College at Clermont he robbed my basket."

"And he robbed one of his schoolfellows, the Marquis de Loisy."

"So I have heard, monsieur," responded Madame Lafarge.

But the artful woman did not tell the Chief of Police that she instigated the robbery and had most of the plunder.

"Well, you know him; can't you tell me where he is?"

"I cannot now, but I hope soon to know. He is in Paris."

"Our latest information is that he has left the city after a short stay."

"And I saw him this morning not far from this spot."

This was a stretch of imagination on the part of Madame Lafarge, but she did not always adhere closely to the truth, especially when any advantage was to be gained by the contrary.

"Where did you see him?"

"He was in the Rue Parthenope, which, as you know, is not a great distance from your office."

"Did he see you; did you speak?"

"He saw me, and, I am certain, recognised me; but when I taxed him with being Louis Dominique Cartouche he denied it very rudely."

"What name did he give, madame?"

WITH A MIGHTY EFFORT CARTOUCHE HURLED THE BODY INTO THE RIVER.

"None whatever."

"Well, when you discover his hiding-place let me know, and some small portion of the reward shall be yours."

Madame Lafarge shook her head and smiled, as she replied—

"No, no, monsieur, I want all, or nearly all, the reward, and you want a kiss."

"Many kisses, my dear madame."

"Then you must write me an order which shall be recognised and obeyed by any of your men to whom it may be shown, commanding them to assist me in the capture of this Cartouche, but that the capture is to be considered as effected by me, and the reward is mine. Of course, I shall give them something—say a fourth."

The chief of police laughed, but wrote what was desired; he read it to Madame Lafarge, who approved, and put it in her pouch. As she did so the remainder of the money taken from the gipsy treasury in the old abbey could be heard jingling.

"You wish to become wealthy, Madame Lafarge—but you are not absolutely without money now."

"A few copper coins, nothing worth speaking of."

"I know the sound of copper coins, and of silver, and of gold."

"But if I succeed in capturing Cartouche I shall be rich enough to set myself up in some respectable business, and so contrive for the future to keep out of the hands of your men."

"Preferring to come to the arms of their chief. Now for a taste of those ruddy lips!"

The amorous old official passed his arms round the waist of Madame Lafarge, kissed her once, and would have done so a second time, but she broke from him.

"Only one now. Wait till Cartouche is captured."

"And then——?"

"And then I can refuse you nothing."

With which words of farewell she darted from the room and down the stairs into the street.

"The old fool!" she exclaimed, wiping her lips as though she would rub off the kiss; "is he mad enough to think I could ever fancy a withered old ghost like him? I suppose next we shall have corpses rising from their graves to make love to us!"

CHAPTER XIII.

A STRANGE MEETING.

By the time Madame Lafarge had got a few yards from the Police Office she thought it advisable to stop and consider what her next move should be.

"How am I to find out and capture this Cartouche, who is as artful as Satan, as daring as a lion, and as bloodthirsty as a tiger. It must be done though, or my own life is not safe. Well I must have a drop of something to wash the taste of that old goat's kiss from my mouth, and then consider about it."

Madame Lafarge entered a little wine-shop, and, calling for the beverage she loved, seated herself at one of the tables.

Opposite her was a younger woman, and not a bad-looking one; but she appeared to be in some great trouble, and had been weeping bitterly about it.

At another table sat a man who wore what was not often seen in Paris at that period, namely, bushy whiskers and beard.

It struck Madame Lafarge that she had seen the young woman before, but she could not remember under what circumstances. But Madame knew that the wine-shop was often visited by the criminal classes who were no more able to keep from the neighbourhood of the Parisian Police Office than in London they can refrain from lounging in the neighbourhood of Bow-street.

"You have probably lost your husband or sweetheart," Madame thought to herself. "But you are not bad looking, and will have no difficulty in finding another in place of the fellow who has been snapped up by one of Monsieur Peuchet's men."

Madame sipped her wine for a few minutes, and then called for brandy, saying the weaker liquor was too cold for her stomach.

"And will you have some, my dear?" she added, addressing the weeping woman; "you appear to be in trouble, and a little drop won't hurt you. When you get to be my age you will know that it is a fine thing to keep up the spirits."

The weeping one nodded and the brandy was brought.

"You are very kind, Madame Lafarge," said she, with tearful eyes; "very kind—and I have no friend."

"You know me?"

"Yes, and your daughter, La Belle Louise, as they call her, and I should like to scratch her eyes out."

"Do it, and welcome, for all I care; she is a bad daughter to me, and I have given up troubling myself about what happens to her."

"I would if I did not feel so low-spirited."

"Drink plenty of this, my dear—it will give you courage for anything. But still, I should like to know what Louise has done to rouse your anger?"

"Her lover killed my lover. That is why I am weeping."

"You can soon find another. But tell me, who is her lover?"

"His name is Cartouche."

"Great Heavens!" exclaimed Madame Lafarge, starting from her chair, and then sitting down again abruptly. "And what was the name of your sweetheart, child?"

"Henri Decade—Captain Decade they called him."

Here was a pretty pass! Madame Lafarge had been speculating on marrying Decade herself, and now she found herself hearing that he was dead from the lips of one who styled herself his sweetheart.

"Tell me all about it, child," said Madame. She found that this young woman did not know how her own ambition had soared, and thought it best not to tell her.

The way in which Cartouche disposed of his captain need not be repeated. The young woman gave a fairly correct account of the affair, except the cause of the quarrel, and that she did not know.

"What is your name, child?" Madame asked.

"Lizette," responded the younger woman.

"And you wish to be revenged on this Cartouche?"

"Aye, that I do!"

"So do I, for he has injured me more than I can tell, and I will not be content till I have brought him to the scaffold."

The bearded man, although he made no outward sign, was listening very attentively to this conversation.

"Do you know the way of entering the house where Decade's men live?" Madame Lafarge asked.

"No, but I can find out from Red Judas," Lizette answered.

"But when will you see Judas?"

"I don't know, but I am pretty certain to meet him soon."

"And will you tell me as soon as you can?" Madame asked.

"Of course I will, but where can I see you?"

Madame Lafarge revealed her name and place of abode, and then went on to tell Lizette that the Chief of Police had promised her a *part* of the reward if she could get Cartouche into his power.

"I have seen Monsieur Peuchet this morning," she continued, "and—can you read, my dear?"

Lizette's education had been neglected, and she owned it.

"You know the great seal they stamp on all the police proclamations? Well, here it is, and this is an order for the police all through the city to assist me, and for me to receive part of the reward."

She showed the document to Lizette, and the keen eyes of the bearded man caught sight of the official stamp, so he knew there was some truth in the statement made by Madame Lafarge.

Lizette nodded, as though to say that she recognised the official mark.

"I will do anything to help you catch that villain Cartouche," she said.

"Then work with me, let me know anything you can find out about him, and before long we will see him executed—and you shall have half the money. And now I must be off."

Madame Lafarge departed, and Lizette followed soon.

As soon as they had both gone the bearded man rose from his seat and walked out. As he passed the doorway he bent down, and when he stood erect his beard and whiskers had disappeared.

It was Cartouche himself!

"The devil is in all women," he muttered. "However it is pretty plain from their talk that Louise has nothing to do with this affair. She loves me, I believe."

He stood thinking for a few minutes.

The band must be warned of their danger and the old home abandoned for a time—that was absolutely necessary. That useful young rascal, the Wolf, happened to be in the neighbourhood, so Cartouche scribbled a few lines to Gribichon warning him of the danger, recommending the dispersal of the men for a few days, and ordering that a strict watch should be kept on the doings of Judas.

Off went the Wolf with the missive, delighted at being high in the favour of the new captain.

"And now for an interview with the Chief of Police," said Cartouche. "It is pretty evident from the description of me on the bills that Monsieur Peuchet and his men are not personally acquainted with me, so I will pay a visit to the office. By all the saints, the Parisians will laugh when they hear of it."

A minute later he walked boldly up to the office of the Chief of Police, and desired to see Monsieur Peuchet.

"Certainly, monsieur, what name shall I announce?" said the officer.

"The Baron St. Elmo."

The police-officer in charge of the door bowed and sent word by his messenger that the baron was waiting, and in a very short time Cartouche was ushered into the presence of the man all other French rogues wished to avoid.

Cartouche took a rapid but comprehensive view of the room and of the man he had to deal with.

"What can I do for you, monsieur?" Peuchet asked.

By way of answer Cartouche drew his dagger and said—

"Do me the favour to look at this weapon, monsieur."

Peuchet looked at it. There was nothing very peculiar to be observed about it, and he said so.

"I came here to show you this dagger, monsieur," Cartouche continued; "but before I explain how it came into my possession permit me to remark that the point is very near your face."

Peuchet smiled.

"And that it is poisoned. The least prick of it would be certain and speedy death to any man."

"Good Heavens!" exclaimed Peuchet, removing his countenance from too close an investigation of the dagger.

Although there was no sign of joking on his visitor's face, the Chief of Police could not help saying—

"You don't mean that, do you?"

"I do indeed, Monsieur Peuchet. There is no remedy for the poison with which this blade is smeared."

"It is very dangerous."

"Undoubtedly it is," responded the visitor, and in a harsh whisper he continued, "and if you do not instantly lay yourself flat upon the floor, with your face towards it and your hands crossed behind your back, or if you make the slightest noise or cry, I will stick the poisoned dagger between your ribs, as sure as my name is Cartouche!"

The police chief hesitated only for a couple of seconds, then, seeing that the deadly blade was held within an inch or two of him, he incontinently placed himself on his stomach in the position commanded by Cartouche, and submitted to have his hands bound and a gag put in his mouth.

"That is a good bit of work. Now for the money."

Cartouche then opened the official cabinet and took from it a large bag of gold, which had just been brought to the office to pay a section of the men. Next he took a sheet of paper and wrote upon it—

"*Monsieur Peuchet has been bound, gagged, and relieved of his money by Cartouche.*"

"And now I leave you, Monsieur Peuchet," said he. "When next you offer a reward for Cartouche be certain that you are able to hold him when he presents himself at your office. Adieu, monsieur."

And Cartouche tripped lightly down the stairs. Passing through the hall he said to the janitor—

"Monsieur Peuchet wishes not to be disturbed for a little while, but if he does not ring his bell before the expiration of a quarter of an hour you are then to go up to him in his room."

The official bowed and pocketed the coin given him by the noble, generous Baron St. Elmo, and Cartouche hastened off.

He was to meet Gribichon and learn what had become of his men. He had also to appoint a rendezvous where he could meet them and communicate from time to time; also a fresh lodging for himself and Louise must be looked out and taken possession of.

All these things would take some time.

: "And then," said he, "when I have plenty of leisure, I will punish those traitors—Madame Lafarge, Lizette, and Red Judas."

Walking a little way on he came to the spot where Louise was selling her flowers.

"You shall not do that any longer," said he. "No more work—no more exposure to the weather for you, Louise."

"But think, Louis, how useful I can be. I gain much information when I am selling these. The police, the citizens, the courtiers, they all stop to chat, and I gain something worth knowing from nearly everyone," she answered.

"I am jealous of those swell courtiers when I see them talking to you."

"You need not be, for I shall be true to you, although I let my tongue run for their amusement."

"Well, be it so, then—for a time. But one of these days, with our purses well lined, we will bid adieu to France—to Europe, and seek a home in this new world out in the western ocean—America, I mean. What say you?"

"I will go anywhere with you, Louis. But here comes the Wolf, and Tomasso with him."

"What news?" demanded he, as the old Corsican came up.

"Judas has met with an accident. He stumbled on the stairs and sprained his leg this morning, so he cannot move. But Captain Gribichon told me and several others the purport of the note you sent, and we don't think it is such a desperate case. Two hundred crowns, the amount of the reward offered, if they were quietly slipped into the hands of the Chief of Police, would procure you liberty to walk about the streets of Paris as much as you please."

"I don't think so," replied Cartouche.

And then he related to Louise and the Corsican how he had robbed the Chief of Police in his own office, and left him bound and gagged upon the floor.

"You are a devil, captain!" the Corsican exclaimed.

Louise at once saw the danger. The Chief of Police, naturally unable to extricate himself from the difficulty in which Cartouche left him, must be assisted by some of his men, and that would render him ridiculous in the eyes of his underlings, a thing he would never forgive.

"Come, Louis, come, Tomasso; let us go to some quiet place and discuss what is to be done," she said.

They at once adjourned to a wine shop, leaving the Wolf outside with strict orders to be close at hand in case he was wanted to run with any messages.

The young Parisian arab promised strict obedience, and, with some coins Cartouche had given him, procured a gorgeous meal of three different kinds of sausage, which he devoured sitting on a neighbouring doorstep.

Cartouche, Louise, and Tomasso found no other customer in the wine shop, and they at once began their discussion.

"It will be unsafe to remain in Paris," said Tomasso. "I did not think there was a devil in the city would go and rob the Chief of Police in his own office."

"However, I have done it."

"And, in consequence, will have to leave Paris," said Louise, in a very mournful way.

"You don't want to leave town?" Cartouche asked.

"I will if you go," she replied.

"But I don't intend to go. In the country everyone sees a stranger, and points him out to others; in town all are strangers except the most intimate friends."

"But we should be able to hide in a forest where we should never see one of the police corps," Louise urged.

"And we should never see a shop where we could buy a bottle of wine or a loaf of bread we should never see a house with a roof on it to shelter us from the rain."

"That would be bad indeed," said Louise; "but is forest life so very bad, Tomasso?"

"I have gone through a lot of it; I remember twenty years ago, in consequence of the vendetta, there were six of our family had to be up in the mountain forests for nearly a year. It was quite as much as I could stand, and I am sure you could not endure it. The climate of Corsica, too, is better than that of Fontainebleau or whatever French forest you think of taking your picnic in. I was in England once, in a forest called Epping, but that was very damp, so don't go there."

"What, then, shall we do?" asked Louise; who was for the most part anxious about Cartouche—not for herself.

"Do as the chief says—remain in Paris. A thickly-peopled town is a better hiding-place than a barren mountain-side," replied Tomasso.

"So say I. And you, Louise, if you keep in the flower business, may learn a lot of things that will be good for us to know," said Cartouche.

"I would I knew where my mother was living," replied Louise.

"So do I," said Cartouche; adding, under his breath, "She would not *live* there very long."

"Well, the best thing for you, captain, is to get an apartment for yourself and Madame Louise—in one of the poor quarters of Paris, because the poor always hate the police, and never will help them. Then Madame can sell her flowers as usual, and pick up any news the police drop; and the Wolf can bring messages to Monsieur Cartouche, or convey orders from him to the remainder of the band."

Thus spoke Tomasso.

"Your advice is good," quoth Cartouche; "but where will you live, my veteran."

"At the old place," replied the Corsican.

"But the police will be down upon you."

"No. If they thought the place was empty hey would burst the door; but if they see a few of us passing in and out they won't interfere. I will stay there with Gribichon and Leon."

"And Red Judas?"

"If he attempts to move an inch from the room where he now is I will blow his brains out—of course, with your permission, Captain Cartouche."

"You have my permission to blow out his brains, if he has any, on the slightest appearance of treason."

"And I will do it, too, or cut his throat. I don't care much about pistols, they are noisy weapons, and miss fire sometimes, which the dagger never does."

"But only on good proof of treason, mind," said Louise.

"If you keep him in that room, and don't allow him to see anyone from the outside, he can't play the traitor," Cartouche remarked.

To which Tomasso replied—

"Then we must not allow him to receive any message from without or send any."

"You are right. Keep him apart from the rest of the world like a leper or a plague-stricken person."

"I should poison people of that sort, captain," Tomasso growled.

"Perhaps you will be called upon to do so before very long. Well, then, the old house is your place of rendezvous, and the Wolf can always hear of you and Gribichon there?"

"That is so, captain."

"The Wolf is to be trusted, you think?"

"Why, captain, I would trust him with my money," exclaimed Tomasso.

"Or your life?" said Cartouche.

"Pooh! I don't value that over-much, but I generally keep it in my own hands."

"Good; then the Wolf shall remain about here till Louise and I have found a suitable apartment, and then he shall let you know where we are."

"And here is the address of a man who can make you both safe and comfortable."

Tomasso handed Cartouche a card on which was inscribed the name of "Gustave Arnaud, Rue Pelayo. Apartments"

"And he is a merchant captain," continued old Tomasso. "If you have more jewellery than you wish to wear he will buy it, and never ask whether it was your uncle or your grandmother who gave you the article in question."

"A useful man to know. Come then, Louise, let us see Monsieur Gustave Arnaud, and arrange for our lodging. You will hear from us very soon, my good friend, Signor Tomasso."

* * * * * *

The Rue Pelayo—I do not know if it exists now—was a narrow and rather ill-smelling thoroughfare, which might be compared with our Drury-lane, or Great St. Andrew-street, or Kent-street in the Borough of Southwark.

It contained lots of small shops inhabited by vendors of cheap food, second-hand clothes, drink and tobacco, and there were some houses where you could scarcely tell if they sold anything, although there seemed to be a great deal of business transacted in them.

Cartouche and his Louise made their way down the street till they came to the house inhabited by Gustave Arnaud, whose name was over the door, though there was nothing in the window except a thick blind.

CHAPTER XIV.

DANGER AHEAD.

"MONSIEUR ARNAUD!" exclaimed Cartouche, as he hammered at the supposed captain's door, there being neither bell nor knocker attached to the house.

"At your service, monsieur."

Out came a little dried-up old man, who took off his cap and bowed politely.

"What can I have the pleasure of doing for you, monsieur?" he asked. "I have little to sell except potatoes."

"My wife and I require an apartment."

"What! La Belle Louise married! Allow

me to congratulate you, madame, the bride ! And you want an apartment ?"

"We do. One where we can be safe from prying eyes and inquisitive tongues."

"I have just the place to suit you. Will it please your worship to look at it ?"

"Yes—show us."

"The apartment is near the roof, but that is an advantage to one so much sought by the police as you are, Monsieur Cartouche," the old man said, as he tripped up the stairs quite nimbly for one of his years.

"Who told you my name ?" the robber captain asked, as he clutched the old man fiercely by the arm.

"I think it was Madame Lafarge—in fact, I am sure it was," the old man replied.

"You know her, then ?"

"As I told you some years ago, about the time you made your escape from the Jesuit seminary, I am her brother."

"You !" exclaimed Louise.

"I am your uncle—your mother is my sister."

Louise stared, so did Cartouche ; but Cartouche now recognised the little old man whom he had encountered just after leaving Clermont.

"Yes, Louise, your mother is my sister—may all the fiends of hell conspire together to drag her off to perdition ! Pardon my cursing your parent, child," he added, turning to Louise, and then launching out a string of the foulest oaths the French language contains. And the French can swear when they give their minds to it.

Louise, who had long ceased to feel any love or regard for her mother, readily pardoned her uncle ; but she could not help asking—

"What has that mother of mine done that you dislike her so very much ?"

The little old man, Monsieur Arnaud, paused for a space on the landing of the stairs, and, throwing open his shirt, pointed to a tattooed mark on his breast.

"That is what she did, or caused to be done ! May Satan take her, &c., &c."

After a pause for breath he said—

"You know the mark, Monsieur Cartouche ?"

Yes, Cartouche had seen several of them, although he had been lucky enough to keep his own skin from such disfigurement. It was the brand put by the French Government upon all criminals condemned to do hard labour in the galleys or in the convict prisons of the country —as our own country used to brand soldiers who quitted the army without permission.

"But how ?" demanded Louise.

She had some very slight recollection of this uncle, but had lost sight of him—in fact, had not thought of him for many years past.

"How did your mother get me condemned to the galleys ?" said Monsieur Arnaud. "Did she not boast of it to you ?"

"I never heard her speak of it."

"Well, here is the apartment I propose to rent to you. Sit down and I will tell you."

Cartouche, Louise, and the old man entered a room just under the roof, and, having seated themselves, the old man began his story. And if the number of oaths with which he garnished his narrative is any proof of the intensity of his hatred—well, he certainly disliked Madame Lafarge.

"And how did my good mother put you away, uncle ?" said Louise, as she settled herself down on a chair in the room. "What was the offence you were charged with ?"

"She said I robbed her."

"Well, if she had anything worth taking, uncle, she must have stolen it from someone.'

"Of course ! This affair happened soon after I first had the honour of meeting you, Monsieur Cartouche. I went back to Paris to say that I had met you. Madame Lafarge swore that when I had been a little time in the room she missed some money, and the police-officer swore that he found a coin in my pocket which Madame Lafarge swore she had marked—the Prefect of Police said that I was a rogue and must go to the galleys at Toulon, and I say that she——"

It doesn't matter what Monsieur Arnaud said about his sister ; the language he used would scarcely bear repetition. But still it showed that he did not love her.

Cartouche himself did not listen very attentively to the tale told by Monsieur Arnaud. He was busy looking over the room and taking note of what means of escape there were if the police should be in possession of the staircase.

There was a way out on the roof, and he could very well scramble along the tops of several houses, trusting to chance to show him some way of escape down a chimney or through an attic window, and that would be a great thing.

"Well, monsieur, well, my niece, how does this sort of apartment suit your ideas ?" the old man asked.

"I think it will do," said Cartouche.

"And I think so," said Louise, who had been looking at it from a housewife's point of view.

"And the rent is only five francs a week."

"That is cheap," Louise remarked.

"But it must be paid in advance always," said the old man, holding out his hand.

"We are your tenants for a month," replied Cartouche, dropping twenty coins into Arnaud's hand. "But I trust you will not think it necessary to tell the neighbours anything about your new lodgers."

"Certainly not."

"If you do I shall make things very unpleasant for you, old boy."

"At my time of life I want things to go pleasantly."

"Then keep your mouth shut about me."

"You shall be obeyed, my Lord Cartouche."

"If you do well in this matter I shall be a good tenant. If you cause me any annoyance I have a pair of pistols and a dagger which would quite settle you."

Monsieur Arnaud looked at his lodger.

Cartouche was sitting quietly on a chair near the window, Louise was examining the fireplace, the cupboards, and all the other affairs

CARTOUCHE,

THE FRENCH JACK SHEPPARD.

THE CHIEF OF POLICE SUBMITTED TO BE BOUND BY CARTOUCHE.

NO. 4.

with the eye of a good housewife, when there was heard a thundering knock at the door of the house, and a moment later Monsieur Arnaud's housekeeper came rushing up, exclaiming—

"The police ! the police !"

Cartouche jumped up and drew one of his pistols.

"What of the police, child ?" Arnaud asked.

"They are outside the door."

"Let them remain there."

"But they swear they will break the door down unless it is opened. They say that Cartouche, the awful robber and murderer, of whom all Paris is talking, has been traced hither, and they will not go away without him."

"Go downstairs, girl," said Cartouche.

Monsieur Arnaud's housekeeper was young—not much older than Louise—and fairly good-looking. She did not at that moment know who the new lodger was, and seemed rather surprised at the very commanding air he assumed.

"Go downstairs, child, and keep the door bolted."

"But the police will break it in !"

"Then they will have to deal with your master. Say nothing, you, but keep the door fast."

The girlish-looking housekeeper descended.

"What shall I do—or say?" Arnaud asked. "I will swear this business is none of my doing."

"I believe you. Go and talk to them through the keyhole till they burst the door open ; then things must take their course."

Old Arnaud toddled down as well as his stiff joints and gouty feet would permit.

"What shall I do, Louis?" Louise asked. "Give me your dagger and I will defend the doorway while you get off by the roof."

Cartouche hugged the flower-girl in his arms for a few seconds, and whispered—

"Stay where you are, and remember that when the police ask the question you have never even heard of me. By the time they get into the room I shall be away, and you will be quietly seated at your knitting or sewing."

"I will fight for you if you like."

"You can aid me better by keeping quiet in the way I have said. Trust me, I can take care of myself and you, too ; so now, one kiss, my beauty—a good one, as if you really loved me, and look for my return in four or five days time.

Louise gave him the kiss, and Cartouche went out by the attic window just about the moment that a sound of crashing timber proclaimed that the police had broken in the door.

He took just one brief glance round, and the situation was not very cheering.

He saw by glancing over the parapet that the road below was filled with soldiers and police ; he knew that some of them were ascending the stairs of Monsieur Arnaud's house, and from the excited exclamations of the crowd it seemed pretty certain that other houses were being

entered with the idea of stopping him if he attempted to escape over the roofs.

"But the fools are looking to this side of the street only," Cartouche muttered. "It is not too wide for a jump, I think."

He made a mental calculation, and then gave a big spring just as a woman appeared at the opposite window and beckoned to him. He just managed to cross, and narrowly escaped a pistol shot which was fired at him from below.

"Be quick," said the woman, whose face seemed not unknown to him. "The back door of the house is open, and you can escape into the next street, through the narrow court, long before they can get in here."

"I shall not forget you," said Cartouche, as he threw a piece of gold on the table ; and then he dashed down the stairs.

Out in the court, and in the back street he was free, for the police had quite forgotten the possibility of his taking that desperate leap. And an hour later he was out of Paris.

The police found Louise knitting a stocking, and demanded of her—

"Where is Cartouche ?"

"How should I know ?"

"He is your lover, and he was here with you a very few minutes ago."

"I have a lover who was here a few minutes ago, and made his escape through that window."

"And that was Cartouche."

"You are mistaken, monsieur," Louise replied. "My lover is a German, and his name Herr Von Slammingen."

"And why did he cut away like that?"

"Didn't want to see you. He has artistic tastes, and doesn't care to look at ugly things."

The policeman swore and then asked—

"When is the Herr Von What-the-devil-is-his-name coming back again ? You can answer that question, Louise."

"As soon as possible after you have gone. So if you want Herr Von Slammingen to return to the arms of his loving Louise you had better go away and clear all your men away out of the street."

"What has this German—if he is anyone but Cartouche—been doing that he should fear to face the French police ?"

"He has been making love to me and has won my heart—and that is why you jealous ones want to lock him up in one of your dirty prisons. Bah ! go away."

The police-officer had been taking a good look round the apartment, and he knew that Cartouche really had escaped. He also knew that he had not sufficient evidence to convict Louise of any participation in the crimes Cartouche was said to have committed, so he took that lively young lady's advice and went away.

Also, he withdrew his men, leaving only two of the keenest of them to watch the street and keep Louise in sight.

The woman at the opposite house was questioned, but she only knew that a man had jumped across the street, had forced his way cross her apartment and down the stairs, she being unable to prevent him.

CHAPTER XV.

DIVIDING THE PLUNDER.

CARTOUCHE did not intend to go far from Paris or remain long away from that city.

He guessed that there would be a very strict search in the town for a few days, but that afterwards the country would be searched in every direction.

He resolved to remain in the neighbourhood, not doubting that in a few days he would be able to communicate with Louise, Tomasso Gribichon, and the others.

"As for Red Judas, I am bound to kill him. It is only a question of time," Cartouche muttered.

Two hours' walk beyond the walls brought him to the edge of a forest. He was tired, hungry, and thirsty. There was a roadside inn, close by, but Louis Dominique Cartouche suddenly remembered that he had no money to purchase refreshment with. The coin he threw to the woman through whose window he escaped was his last, all the rest being left with Louise.

"How would it be to rob the inn?" thought he.

But just then a couple of very powerful men, evidently the proprietor and his son, with a couple of very powerful dogs of the wolf-hound breed, made their appearance at the doorway, so Cartouche thought he would postpone the attempt.

He was strolling along, not on the road, but keeping close by the side of it, when he heard the sound of wheels.

At the same moment almost he became aware of a couple of rough-looking fellows, who, like himself, were keeping under the screen of bushes by the roadside.

They were rude-looking fellows, dressed in thick wooden shoes and coarse blouses; poachers, or perhaps worse than that.

Cartouche stepped along almost as noiselessly as a cat, and came close up behind them without attracting their attention.

The two ruffians were calculating the possibility of robbing a coach which was coming along.

"Two servants besides the driver and a gentleman inside! The odds are against us, Henri," said one.

"I should like to try, though, Jean," replied the other.

"Let me help you. Three of us can manage the business."

The two men started, and turning, beheld our hero.

"I want money, so do you. I have no doubt they have plenty in that coach—we will take it and share."

"Who the devil are you?" Henri asked.

"My name is Cartouche."

"The devil!"

"No. But we will rob that coach, though,"

The two ruffians thought it a high honour to be associated with such a renowned robber as Cartouche, and at once agreed to put themselves under his directions.

"Remember, there must be no killing. I am not the bloodthirsty wretch the police falsely represent me," he said.

"Right, Monsieur Cartouche," they replied.

The coach came on slowly, one of the horses being so lame that he could scarcely keep on his legs.

"You, Henri, must tackle the two footmen. You, Jean, will attend to the driver and horses. Have you any pistols to frighten the people with?" said Cartouche.

Yes, they both had pistols.

"I will deal with the persons inside, and collect the toll which we have a right to collect from all travellers who pass along this road."

They nodded.

Presently the coach came near enough, and Cartouche gave the signal agreed upon.

Out sprang the three ruffians, the traces were cut, the servants knocked down, and Cartouche, pistol in hand, presented himself at the window.

"I will thank you for a little money, sir," he said, "I and my friends are very poor, and you will have to be charitable."

"This is robbery."

"No—only asking alms. But you, doubtless, are highly educated, and will remember the saying of the old Latin poet, 'He gives twice who gives quickly.'"

"Who the devil are you?"

"I am Cartouche, and I shall take the liberty of blowing out your brains unless you hand over all your money in less than two seconds?"

The name was sufficient. The gentleman, a wealthy merchant, produced a goodly sum of gold. The servants were told to mend the traces and go on their journey—a command which Henri enforced by firing a couple of shots from his pistols over their heads.

Then the three men went into the forest to divide the plunder, which they did in the following fashion.

The three seated themselves on the grass, and the coin was turned out on a napkin.

"Who is to count it?" Cartouche asked.

"I will," said Henri.

"All right."

Henri got on his knees to begin the task of counting the gold. Cartouche whispered to the other fellow, Jean—

"If you were to send a bullet through his brains we could halve the money."

This appeared such an excellent proposition that Jean at once caught up one of his pistols and shot his fellow-ruffian in the head.

"Give him the other barrel. There is nothing like making sure in a business of this kind."

Jean was a good pupil; he at once discharged his second pistol, and there could be no doubt that poor Henri was dead as any mutton.

And Cartouche alone had loaded pistols.

Assuming a magisterial air and grasping his weapons, he said—

"Jean, you are a scoundrel of the worst kind to murder your comrade in that cold-blooded way. If I could have you properly tried and executed by the civil authorities of the realm I would do so; but, as I cannot do that, I must take the law into my own hands."

"What do you mean, monsieur?" Jean gasped.

"I mean that I appoint myself both judge and jury, and find you guilty—on the evidence of my own eyes—of a most atrocious murder. Little remains now but to pronounce sentence, which is death!"

"You are jesting, monsieur."

"Certainly I am not."

Cartouche slipped his loaded pistols into his coat pocket and drew his dagger.

"I pronounce sentence of death, and as the hangman is not in the neighbourhood I execute the decree of the Court thus."

And he drove his dagger into the poor fellow's heart, exclaiming—

"That is a much better way than wasting powder, which makes a noise. Now I will divide this money with myself."

He wiped his dagger on the fellow's blouse, gathered up the money, and walked off. He did not approach the roadside inn he had noticed, but walked away along the edge of the forest till he came to a peasant's cottage, where he obtained food and drink.

All that day and the next he wandered about, but the third day he went to a place where the members of the band were accustomed to spend some of their leisure time and spare cash.

This was a comfortable inn about a league from Paris, with a nice garden attached to it.

He knew that Louise would be anxious about him, and he thought it very likely she would try to communicate with him there.

Cartouche was not mistaken.

He had just finished a good meal, and was seated at a bow window which commanded a good view of the road, when he saw a peasant lad coming along from town.

At least the youth was dressed like a peasant, but his style was certainly that of the street arab.

Cartouche recognised him.

"The Wolf!" he muttered. "Louise is certainly a very clever girl."

He went out and met the boy in the roadway.

"What news, Wolf?"

"Madame Louise is well, but the police are watching her so closely that it was some time before she could get a chance of telling me to come out here and look for you."

"Tell her I shall be back within twenty-four hours. How about Gribichon and the others—have any of them been arrested?"

"No one, monsieur."

"Tell them to meet me at the Pont Neuf at twelve to-night. Now drink a glass of wine, and hurry back. Be very careful."

CHAPTER XVI.

THE FORTY THIEVES OF PARIS.

PARIS at the time of which we write could compare with its present magnificence; what it lacked in that respect was, to the ar[t] at all events, more than made up by its unus[ual] picturesqueness.

Tortuous, narrow, and ill-lighted streets gabled and turreted houses surrounded most the great churches and public buildings.

Two of the leading bridges in the centre the city were of wood, but the bridge on whi[ch] the present scene is laid, the Pont Neuf, was handsome erection of stone.

It had been commenced in the reign Henri III. and completed by the greatest ki[ng] France ever knew—Henri IV.

Those of our readers who have visited the g[ay] capital of France will remember the fine eque[s]trian statue of that king which now adorns t[he] bridge.

Many of the bridges were, like our old Londo[n] bridge, lined with houses, a narrow street run[s] ning between them, but the Pont Neuf was a[n] exception.

Hence, at night it was more suitable for deed[s] of villainy than the other bridges with thei[r] inhabited houses, and the solitary wayfarer wh[o] was out late at night always crossed it as rapidl[y] as he knew how, or crept under the shadow of it[s] low and crumbling walls.

This being the case, it was often the midnigh[t] meeting-place of the robbers and cut-throats o[f] Paris, when they wanted quietly to concoct some new scheme for enriching themselves at the expense of their fellow-creatures, for the bridge was nearly always deserted.

The night was calm and clear, the moon throwing a glamour over the scene, as it lighted up the ripples of the Seine; even the very mud itself looked quite attractive as it reflected the few lights from the old buildings on its banks.

Red Judas and the Wolf met by previous arrangement this night, cautiously approaching each other, and coming from different quarters of the city.

They had stationed the Ferret and a younger hand who had just joined the band on the bridge itself, to give the alarm in case of danger or the possible advent of a victim.

They themselves retreated under one of the ornamented arches, which formed gateways at either end of the Pont Neuf.

"Is all right?" asked Red Judas, in a subdued but clear, hard tone of voice.

"The coast is perfectly clear," answered the Wolf. "Where's our noble captain?"

"Oh, after the girls, I expect. He's really spoony on that last young lady from the country. Bah! he's too sentimental altogether for business men like ourselves."

"And where's Gribichon?"

"Prowling round the hen-coops or robbing some old woman's apple-stall—it's about all he's fit for! A precious pair, by all that's blue!"

"You are always grumbling. You had better not let the captain hear you."

"Bah! listen to me. I've a plan to make all our fortunes."

"Well, what is it?"

"A banker's house to break into."

"Is the captain to join us?"

"No," answered Red Judas, seriously; "I shan't trust him—this is my affair."

"Beware," replied the Wolf, even more seriously; "beware how you work without his orders. His rules are strict, and strictly he enforces them. But hark! what's that?"

"I hear nothing. The Ferret will warn us if there's any risk."

"Who goes there?"

It was only Gribichon, who came up to them in a devil-may-care style a few moments later.

"What's up, my Trojans?"

"Nothing," answered Red Judas; "in fact, we're all confoundedly down in our luck; not a franc as yet. Where have you been prowling?"

"I've been in the country for the benefit of my health."

"Ah! imitating our noble captain's example," said Judas, with a sneer.

"My friend Judas," responded Gribichon, "let me advise you in a perfectly friendly way not to put your nose into other people's affairs, more especially our captain's, or, depend upon it, he will do himself the pleasure of cutting your throat!"

"Bah! let him try it."

"He's very likely to do so; but who is this coming? Boys, to your holes at once; this looks like a little bit of business."

The stranger who was approaching had pretty evidently lost his way.

It was François Cariol, who had at last come to town in search of his foster-sister, Louise, and he was muttering away to himself—

"This is a pretty state of things. Here am I something uncommonly like a green countryman, I don't mind admitting to myself—lost in this big city; I don't like it a bit. Hallo, what's that?"

"Hallo there!"

"This is getting warm, I'm afraid; it seemed to me that there were several voices a little way off. I wonder whether it's good enough to ask them the way to the Rue De Temple—I don't half like to. Well, I'll risk it, after I've stowed away my pocket-book in my inside pocket. Three hundred francs is a pile of money. Gentlemen, I want to find my way——"

"To the devil? Here, fork out; we just want the loan of that three hundred francs you were muttering about."

"Would you rob me?"

"My dear sir, you are evidently a young man from the country, and don't understand the language of polite society; we only appropriate. Be quick, for I've a most particular appointment with the bishop."

"Aye! hurry up, my fine fellow, and shell out, or you'll get a foot and a half or so of cold steel in your carcase," said Judas, producing a long dagger from his belt.

The Ferret and his companion now came running up, and the whole five of them set on the unfortunate Cariol.

Cariol had nothing but a stick, while all the rest were fully armed, but he kept them well at bay for two or three minutes.

The countryman's sturdy arm was more than a match for, say a couple of them, but five were rather too much of a good thing.

However, he slashed away with his good oak stick, slowly retreating before the band of ruffians.

They, on the other hand, did not care to fire, and so bring the guard upon them, while it had been decided in a few hurried words that it was not worth making a murder of it with their knives or daggers. Three hundred francs, when divided, was hardly a big enough thing for which to run so much risk.

So they mauled him about with their fists, and got a good many sore knuckles themselves from his good old stick.

Cariol was, however, fatigued by his long journey, and was fast weakening, when an unexpected arrival on the scene changed the aspect of affairs very materially.

It was Cartouche!

The five ruffians drew off momentarily.

"How now," said the captain, angrily; "is this your style—five upon one? Back, you curs! Is this the way you obey my orders? Shame on you for attacking this poor lad—can't you fly at higher game than a green countryman, with but a few paltry francs about him?"

Red Judas muttered between his teeth, an ugly frown on his hang-dog looking visage—

"You always interfere when there's a chance of making money."

"Dog! hound!" retorted Cartouche, his temper thoroughly up. "Do you dare to dictate to me? Another word and I'll cripple you? But hark! boys, the patrol is coming—make yourselves scarce."

They separated in different directions, and were soon lost to sight, Cariol rejoicing that so far he hadn't lost his three hundred francs, which to him seemed like a small fortune.

Cartouche and Gribichon alone stood their ground, and awaited the arrival of the guard.

The times were troublous, and the Colonel of Musqueteers, Count D'Aubarne, with M. Bobilet, of the Civic Guard, and a number of soldiers, were patrolling the streets on the look-out for such customers as had just quitted the scene.

"How now, fellow," said the colonel, addressing Gribichon; "who are you, and what are you doing here at this time of night?"

Gribichon was never at a loss for a little ruse, and he thought the best thing he could do was to pretend to be intoxicated. So he answered in a drunken kind of manner—

"Who am I? Well, I like that. It is not everyone who would stand such—such—confounded—confounded, I say—impertinence. Who am I? Well, this is a joke. Why, sir, I'm the best-known man in Paris — I'm the Marquis of Vieux-Chateau d'Espagne, while only the other day my dear old aunt, the Grand Duchess of Gerolstein, left me an estate fifteen feet by six—I mean miles. Yes—miles, sir. I've just come—I don't mind telling you," and here Gribichon lurched against the colonel and nearly knocked him over.

The Count D'Aubarne, a man of good family, drew himself up to his full six feet of dignity, and was about to make an empty protest, when he bethought himself that it was hardly the thing for a man of his position to quarrel with this drunken vagabond, so he simply said—

"Well?"

"I've just come from an assignation with the lovely wife of a stupid donkey of a wine merchant, one of the Civic Guard."

Bobilet pricked up his ears ; *he* was a wine merchant, and also one of the Guard.

"And pray," said he, " who is the fair lady ?"

"Her Eupho—eupho—euphonious name is Madame Bobilet."

"Madame Bobilet—my wife—I will not believe my ears ?"

"You'd much better ; that's the name of the lady, anyhow."

"She's my wife, I tell you !"

"Why, then, you must be her husband, my dear fellow. I pity you—I pity you from the bottom of my heart. I sincerely sympathise with your misfortune, but it can't be helped."

"Oh, curse your sympathy !"

"Madame Bobi—Bobi—what the deuce is the rest of her lovely name?—you see is a woman of taste, and, very properly, prefers me to you. *I* don't wonder at it !"

"But then I am her husband—her lawful protector !"

"Why don't you protect her a little better, then ?"

"Because I'm obliged to be out late at night protecting those wretched citizens of Paris. But I'll go at once to Madame Bobilet and——"

The count had been listening to all this, and was much amused thereby, so he said, with a smile—

"You forget, Monsieur Bobilet, that you are on duty."

"Duty be——"

"Eh ?"

"I forgot, Count. If I'm on duty of course I can't do my duty."

"I'll go for you, old fellow, and tell Madame what a rage you are in," said Gribichon, as he lurched away into the darkness, amid the laughter of the soldiers and of the Count himself.

"Attention ! Forward !"

The order for marching was just about to be given, when Cartouche, who had stood in the shadow of a wall, came forward.

"Pardon me, monsieur ; but have I not the honour of addressing the Count D'Aubarne, Colonel of Musqueteers ?" said he with a polite bow.

"You are right, sir. And may I be favoured with your name ?"

"I am the Baron Von Pumpernickel, from Holland, a stranger in Paris, though not to the fame of your distinguished name."

"Really, sir, you are very good to say so."

"A most gentlemanly man of the highest breeding, evidently," thought the Count. "Will you honour me, Baron ?" and so saying he offered Cartouche his gold snuff-box, which glittered with several brilliants let into the lid.

Cartouche's eyes glittered also as he answered—

"With pleasure, count. I am not usually addicted to these small vices, but since you are so pressing, so very pressing, I will accept your kindness," and he put the box into his pocket.

Meantime Bobilet had just remembered that one of his duties that night was to affix a placard to the walls, which, printed in big capitals, read—

1,000 FRANCS FOR

CARTOUCHE,

DEAD OR ALIVE.

This was followed by a description of the murderer and robber who was so much "wanted."

Bobilet just at that moment called the attention of the count to the placard.

Cartouche saw in this an opportunity for puzzling them and disguising the fact that he had kept the gold snuff-box, so he asked, hurriedly—

"And who, pray—who is this Cartouche ?"

"Is it possible that you have never heard of him—of the most notorious thief in all France ?"

"A thief, you say? No, indeed, I have not the honour of knowing any thieves. And you have not been able to catch this fellow ?"

"Confound him, no. I have not encountered him as yet, but when I *do* get near him——"

"You flatter yourself that you will capture him? My dear count, don't trouble yourself ; you'll never be nearer to him than you are at this moment. What a very handsome ring !"

"Ah, you admire it? Superb, is it not? A present to my father from the king," answered the count, taking off the ring and handing it to Cartouche for inspection.

"It is evidently of great value as well as beauty."

"Ten thousand francs or so," said the count, shrugging his shoulders as though that sum was a mere bagatelle.

"I have no doubt that rascal Cartouche would like to get hold of it," said the sham baron.

The count was a man rather vain of his wealth, and in the present instance it was rather unfortunate for him.

Drawing Cartouche, whom he regarded as a distinguished foreign baron, aside, he whispered in his ear—

"Ha, ha ! no doubt ; but I have something here which I think he'd rather have—a draft on

JEAN AT ONCE CAUGHT UP ONE OF HIS PISTOLS AND SHOT HIS FELLOW-RUFFIAN.

the Bank of France for a hundred thousand francs. Won it at cards last night, and have not cashed it yet," and he held out the paper to Cartouche.

"Dear me," said that gentleman, looking at the draft, and then placing it in his pocket, "is it possible so small a piece of paper can be worth such a lot of money? Colonel, I have the honour to wish you a very good evening, and am delighted to have made your acquaintance."

At this moment there was a sharp whistle heard outside.

"Ah," said Cartouche to himself, "the coast is clear, and my merry boys will be here directly."

The count began to feel a bit mystified.

Barons of distinction do not usually pocket the snuff-boxes, rings, or cheques of their acquaintances.

He was getting uneasy. What did that low, sharp whistle, too, in the distance mean?

"Excuse me, baron, but—but——"

"You are very good, I am sure, to a stranger, and I shall never forget your noble liberality," said Cartouche, laughingly.

"But you have forgotten to return——"

"Eh?"

"My snuff-box—my ring—my——"

"Well?"

"My order on the bank——"

"Don't trouble yourself about remembering such trifles, my dear count; I couldn't think of returning them."

"What, surely——"

"I have made up my mind to keep them in memory of you."

"This is some dreadful mistake—am I dreaming? I thought that fellow a little while ago was drunk, but surely it is I who am feeling the effects of my wine."

"I assure you that it is no mistake, my dear sir. We take, but we never mistake."

"Is this a joke?" demanded the poor count, in a dolorous tone of voice.

"You will find it no joke, although you will get over it easily enough in time. There is nothing like time for assuaging grief."

"Then, who in the name of Satan are you?"

"Why, my dear sir, a harmless, inoffensive creature named Cartouche!"

The effect of this announcement on the brave colonel was, for the time, overpowering.

The soldiers fled just as Cartouche's gang, including Gribichon, Red Judas, the Wolf, the Ferret, and several others of the gang, arrived on the scene.

Gribichon, seeing Bobilet standing with his mouth wide open and a very white face, could not help having his little joke.

"Bobilet," said he, "my excellent wine and vinegar merchant—principally vinegar, my brave guard—go home at once to your wife and give her my love!"

This was adding insult to injury with a vengeance. Nevertheless, Bobilet went.

Meantime the Count D'Aubarne, who was in reality a brave man, though he had been so thoroughly flabbergasted by the loss of his property and the sudden appearance of the gang, recovered somewhat from his despair.

"Villain, coward!" said he at last, between his clenched teeth, "I'll live to be even with you!"

"Coward!" said Cartouche, "that is a word I never took yet from man without having satisfaction. Count, your sword!"

"Do you think I will cross swords with a notorious robber?"

"If not I shall do myself the honour of running you through the body."

With this he made a lunge, and the count was obliged to fight.

He was a good swordsman, as most men of his rank and standing are in France.

But the events of the night, and especially his losses, had first unnerved him, and then rendered him furious.

He fought with more vigour than care or skill, and after a very few passes his sword fell from his hand.

Cartouche disdained to take any advantage of his adversary.

"So, count," said he, "my honour is satisfied, but I regret that the exigencies of the case must oblige me to keep you in custody until I have cashed that draft at the bank. Fear nothing; you shall be well treated, and only detained just as long as I deem absolutely necessary. Away with him, Gribby; give him the best room in our den, and then, as soon as it is daylight, order in a breakfast for all of us worth eating, and plenty of wine."

"Captain, excuse me, but are you going mad? Where's the money to come from?"

"Don't worry yourself; I think there will still be a little change left out of this," and he showed Gribichon and the rest the draft for a hundred thousand francs, which the reader doubtless knows is the equivalent of four thousand pounds.

"Don't you think this is better than robbing a poor countryman of his last few hundred francs?" asked Cartouche of Red Judas.

And Red Judas was obliged to admit that business on a wholesale scale was better than on a retail one.

It was now early morning and the dawn was breaking.

After Cartouche had despatched the Count d'Aubarne, the Colonel of Musqueteers, in charge of Gribichon—having ordered him to be kept in their den until he had cashed the order on the Bank of France, which he had obtained from the count—and the others had left him, he was walking along musing, when he saw two female figures approaching.

They were conversing in a friendly way, and one of them looked uncommonly like Louise.

It proved to be that young person. The other he did not know.

Wishing to find out whether she was faithful to him or no he retired into the shadow of an archway, and as they were merely sauntering along could hear all they had to say.

Louise uttered the first words he heard.

"And do you really compare your made-up perfumes to the delicious fresh odour of these flowers, Can-can?"

It must be explained that Louise, who still kept up her old trade of flower-seller more as a blind, and so that she could pick up information in all parts of Paris which might be important to Cartouche, than for the sake of the few francs she might gain by it, had just come from the Central Flower Market.

She had met her friend Marie Dupont, a vendor of perfumes and little nick-nacks of various kinds, whom she, as we have just seen, playfully addressed as Can-can.

There was a reason for this nickname; Marie was one of the best dancers at the Jardin Mabille, or the various other dancing-saloons and casinos of the gay city, and could do the can-can to perfection. She was so light on her limbs that she could whisk a fly off her partner's nose with the toe of one of her neatly made shoes without otherwise interrupting the performance.

She was a good-hearted girl, though, as this might indicate, a little frisky.

"What are your perfumes compared to mine? The fragrance of the flowers you sell soon dies, while my scents last for months. A bottle of my otto of roses is worth all the roses in the city!"

"Nonsense, my dear, you're jealous!"

The two girls were simply fencing, the real subject of their conversation, like the postscript to most female letters, had to come, and was the most important part of it.

"My ducky, I'm not a bit jealous; why should I be? Or inquisitive, either; you know well, Louise, that I never was. No woman is, my dear."

"No woman is, my dear," answered Louise, with a comical shrug, which meant volumes.

"But I should like to know, dear Louie"—this to show the truth of her assertions in regard to inquisitiveness and jealousy, we suppose—"I should like to know who is the young man you meet so often near the Pont Neuf. What's his name?"

"I don't know."

"His profession?"

"I can't tell. How should I know?"

"His residence?"

"Is unknown to me."

"My dear, you know nothing about the Great Unknown! Do you know, my love, I don't quite believe you!"

"I'm sorry for that; but——"

"Oh, it's all right. I believe in faithfulness myself."

"And so do I," thought Cartouche, who, perfectly satisfied that Louise would not betray his secrets, that the poor girl was more true to him than he expected to be to her, quitted his hiding-place and walked homewards, being also somewhat ashamed that he had doubted her, and therefore anxious to get away unobserved.

"Well," said Can-can, "your young man seems something like mine. I hardly know whether I can call him mine, though. He had a beautiful name—Adolphus Adrien Eugène Victor Maximilien Jean Thomas——"

"I wonder you can remember it all, my dear!"

"Oh, love improves the memory—although I'm not quite certain that I do care for him now."

"Why?"

"He came twice or three times to my stall and made the most violent love to me almost from the very first. On the first occasion he got as far as 'darling,' which was pretty good for a beginning, wasn't it?"

"I should say so; my sweetheart hasn't wasted much of that kind of thing on me. Nor do I want it, indeed! But go on, Can-can, you interest me."

"Well, next time he called me an 'angel,' and the third time, wanting to make a change I suppose, addressed me as Venus. After that he borrowed three francs, saying that he had left his purse on his dressing-room table."

"Still he came back and returned it, of course, and brought you a bouquet?"

"I've never seen him since."

"Then you've lost your sweetheart?"

"I don't know, and am not quite sure that I ought to consider him as one."

"Don't you care one way or the other?"

"Well, perhaps I do. I feel sure that I shall meet him some day, and discover who and what he is. He told me that he was very highly connected and very rich, but——"

"But what, dear?"

"Well, he wore a shocking bad hat and an awfully seedy suit of clothes, but that might have been his eccentricity merely. You know many millionaires do the same, my dear Louise."

"Not as a rule when they're young, Marie."

"Louise, you're unkind."

"Marie, I think you're a little goose!"

"And you too! It seems as though you don't even know the name of your fellow, while——"

"Fellow, indeed!"

"While Adolphus Adrien Eugène Victor Maximilien Jean Thomas gave me his card."

"With no address on it."

"Louise, I'll never speak to you again."

"Marie, save yourself the trouble by all means. I will not answer if you do."

And so the girls parted, as have many others under similar circumstances, doubtless to make it up again at the earliest possible opportunity, each having a sweetheart and a secret.

"Can-can"—Marie Dupont—was not, however, to reach home without an adventure, for rounding a corner, she nearly walked into the arms of—M. Bobilet!

We left that worthy wine merchant and member of the Civic Guard on the way home to give his wife a severe talking to. He had listened to Gribichon's boasts about his conquests till his mind had become thoroughly poisoned.

On the way, however—for he rather feared Madame, with all his talk—he had determined to get a little refreshment to give him courage.

And to get that refreshment he had—at that hour of the night, or rather early morning—to seek the neighbourhood of the Central Market, just as belated wanderers in London, nowadays, go to the neighbourhood of Covent Garden, or the region of big printing establishments, to order drinks intended for practical market-gardeners or printers, salesmen or editors.

Having found his own particular wine-shop he entered and ordered some cognac—fine champagne—and as he was known to be a member of the Civic Guard there is some possibility that he got that brand—that much-abused brand.

The host, knowing him, came forward, and was asked to sit down and have a brandy himself.

The latter, somewhat flattered, and wishing to be on good terms with the Civic Guard, readily consented, and when the glasses were emptied offered M. Bobilet to refill them as his treat.

Bobilet did not yet quite feel valiant enough to encounter Madame in the early morning, and so readily enough consented.

Several marketmen came in and out shortly afterwards, some of whom temporarily joined the host and M. Bobilet, and as these gentlemen, from the very exigencies of their business, were rapid drinkers, the worthy wine merchant, who remained seated, smoking and drinking, treating and being treated, began to get a little muddled, and he had sense enough to think it time to leave.

So bidding adieu to the host and such of the marketmen who remained he toddled, or rather rolled, out, and the cool morning air brought back to his memory the errand on which he was bent.

"So," said he to himself, "now I feel all right"—he didn't quite look it—"now for Madame Bobilet! Who could have suspected such atrocity, such wickedness, such depravity? Who would have believed that the wife of my bosom, the wife of a respected citizen and member of the Civic Guard could or would——"

At this moment the encounter with Can-can at the corner of the street took place.

"Hullo!" said Bobilet, still to himself, but half-aloud, "that's a very pretty girl—I'll make love to her, and be revenged on Madame Bobilet! My dear!"

"Did you address me, you old fright?"

"Old fright! that's not very encouraging, but nevertheless, here goes; she can't have noticed me. My charming darling!"

"Just the way Adolphus Adrien Eugéne Victor Maximilien Jean Thomas began. But I will be true to him—if he prove only a memory."

"My adorable angel!"

"Again like Adolphus Adrien Eugène—— But no, this old man shall have no encouragement from me. Go home, bear, to your wife, if you have one. If you have I pity her. If you have not, look elsewhere; don't bother me."

"Behold me at your feet, angelic Venus, disdainful beauty."

"Oh, bother!"

"How very unromantic," said poor Bobilet, who, having gone down on his knees, found considerable difficulty in rising again.

The course of true love never did run smooth, and that of the more or less fictitious kind is apt, sometimes, to cut up very rough indeed.

The truth of this was shown in the present instance, for, before Bobilet could struggle to his feet again, Madame Bobilet, who had become anxious at his long absence, and had come out to search for him, came round the corner.

"On his knees to a woman!" feebly shrieked poor Madame. "Oh, the wretch!"

"Who are you?" coolly inquired Can-can.

"His poor injured wife."

"Then take better care of him!" and with this parting shot Marie, who had her code of honour, such as it was, hastily ran down the street, and was soon lost to view.

Now occurred a somewhat funny incident.

Old Bobilet was more than a little short-sighted, a little deaf, and a good deal drunk.

Hence these quick transactions and Marie's abrupt departure had not been noticed by him, and he continued making love, as though she were present.

"Adorable perfume-vendor, give me thy soft and delicate hand."

"Take it," came forth in stentorian tones from the injured lady, as she boxed his ears.

"My wife—the devil! The cockatrice!"

"What do you mean by cockatrice, you monster?"

"Go to your bottle-nosed adorer—you antediluvian donkey!"

This was meant for Gribichon. Madame was equal to the occasion.

"What do I want with a donkey when I've got you?"

"I'm a public functionary, Madame B——. I'm a member of the Civic Guard, please remember."

"You're a public scandal! Don't you run after all the girls?"

"And don't all the men run after you?"

"That appears to me much more natural."

"You're a disgrace to Paris. I'll be divorced at once."

"Only too happy," and so forth.

There is no telling how long this "family affair" would have continued but for the reappearance of several of the fraternity on the scene—Gribichon and Red Judas among the number.

"Stand!"

"Stand!"

It was all very well to say "Stand," but both the wine-merchant and his wife felt and looked more like falling.

They might almost as well have been told to "fly!"

"Oh, dear," gasped Bobilet at length; "it's my bottle-nosed rival! He has brought his ruffians to drag my wife from me."

"My charming Madame Bobilet," said Gribichon, winking at the rest.

"Go away, you wretch! I don't know you!"

"Didn't you promise me this gold chain? You know you did!" replied Gribichon, following with action the word, as he removed it from her neck.

"And didn't you order us to take charge of your husband's gold watch and purse?" said Red Judas; "well, if you didn't, you ought to have done."

And watch and purse left their original owner, no more to return.

"Now, good people, both of you go home, and remember that late hours are neither good for constitution or pocket," said Gribichon, in a lofty moral tone.

Bobilet and his wife were glad to get off with their lives, and ran off, faster than they had ever been known to run before, although there was no fear of the band committing murder when it was so very easy to do without it.

Besides, Cartouche had walked quietly up while the row was going on and had told them not to commit any violence, although he considered that the wine merchant and his wife, both rich people—she having property in her own right—were quite fair game for anything else.

Furthermore, though Bobilet, as a man, was a wretched creature, he happened to be one of the Civic Guard, who would resent any serious outrage on one of their number, though they would never even know of these robberies, for the simple reason that neither Bobilet nor his wife would ever inform them or the police.

He would have had to explain what he was doing out, half-intoxicated, at that early hour, while Madame would have to make herself more or less of a laughing-stock if she told of her jealousy, and of her meeting with poor Can-can, her early morning search, and what came of it. Silence was better policy.

But Red Judas—always the Judas of the party—did not approve of letting off rich people so easily; he would have detained them for a ransom, or, failing that, cared nothing what else was done.

Again, therefore, though, after the various warnings he had already received, he might have known better, he approached the captain in an insolent manner and said—

"If the others hesitate to speak, captain, I don't. First of all, this love-making of yours is wasting a lot of valuable time; secondly, when we have a grand chance of enriching ourselves you interfere; thirdly——"

"Thirdly!" said Cartouche; "if you go on to thirdly you'll probably never reach fourthly. What do you mean, ruffian? Rebellion?"

"That we've endured your rule long enough —I'm tired of it!"

"You, you rebellious cur—you're tired of it, are you? Are you tired also of your life? Do

you defy me? It is your last chance! Do you dare——"

"No," growled Judas, "but——"

"I'm quite as tired of you," retorted Cartouche, with an angry gleam in his eyes, "as you can possibly be of me. You have long endeavoured to breed discontent in the band, but I'm glad to say with little success. Am I right, boys?"

A ringing cheer of "Long live the captain!" came from the band in response, and Judas, feeling that he was nowhere among his companions, once more slunk away.

"Boys," said Cartouche, "I am grateful for your confidence. Let us get home and drink to our union—that union which nothing shall break!"

"Brave captain! We will live and die with you!" and in the enthusiasm of the moment they probably all, or nearly all, meant it.

CHAPTER XVII.

MADAME LAFARGE HAS ANOTHER INTERVIEW WITH MONSIEUR PEUCHET.

WE left Monsieur Peuchet lying bound on the floor of his own private room in the police-office, and a furious man was he.

There he lay for some hours till his secretary, returning, and knocking twice without receiving any answer, ventured to open the door and look in.

For once in his life that secretary was indiscreet.

Instead of releasing his chief and saying nothing about the affair, he called for help, and three or four underlings came rushing in, thinking the house was on fire. So the murder was out, and there was the Chief of Police lying upon the floor bound and gagged by Cartouche the robber.

It was some time before Peuchet could recover his breath and overcome his indignation sufficient to permit of his speaking.

When he was able to articulate, however, he first of all vented some score of the fiercest French imprecations on the man who had left him in such a condition.

"Where are those other fellows?" he asked, after a pause.

"What fellows does monsieur mean?" the secretary humbly asked.

"Why, those who helped you unbind me."

"I sent them to fetch doctors, monsieur. I was much afraid that you would die."

"Fool! now I shall be talked of all over Paris."

"But, monsieur, you looked so ill."

"I shall look worse when I am made ridiculous. But, by Heaven! if they talk about me they shall repent."

The mischief, however, was done. The two men sent for doctors returned, but not until each had been into his favourite wine-shop and retailed the joke, so that Peuchet was not wrong when he prophesied that he would be the laughing-stock of Paris.

The doctors having ascertained that the chief of police was not scratched with the poisoned dagger, pronounced his life in no immediate danger. He should keep quiet and avoid any work that involved mental exertion or excitement.

"But what a rogue this Cartouche must be to venture on such a trick," said one of them.

"You, then, have heard of it?"

"Aye, a joke soon spreads in Paris."

"The villain shall suffer for it. And listen, Monsieur Doctor, do not say too much about this matter yourself. I hate to be talked about, and can make things very unpleasant for those who cause me annoyance."

The doctor shuddered. He had often seen the outside of the Bastile, and he had no wish to become acquainted with the interior. And Monsieur Peuchet doubtless had the power to consign him to that grim prison.

"I will not say a word. I did not see you bound, and I am not obliged to believe all the silly rumours that may be circulated by your servants, or by people who have even less chance of knowing what has taken place," said the doctor.

"It will be well for you to be silent. So now good-night."

The doctor departed. The other had gone before Peuchet commenced his very brief lecture on the virtue of silence.

Then the Chief of Police called his secretary.

"I am here at your disposal, monsieur," the old man replied, as he shuffled into the room.

"I repeat that it was very indiscreet of you to call for assistance before you had removed all traces of that ruffian's outrage on me. Do not be so thoughtless again——"

"I trust you do not apprehend a repetition of the attack, monsieur?"

"I do not. Now call in those fellows—those who came when you called for help—you know them, I suppose?"

"Doubtless, monsieur."

And forthwith he called them. Brief yet stern was the lecture he gave them upon the impropriety of spreading any rumour which might be detrimental to their superior; if they ever did so again they would be severely punished with imprisonment and other pains and penalties.

"And now, go find me out this woman, Madame Lafarge," said the Chief of Police. "Bid her come to me at once."

The poor trembling rascals of policemen departed on their errand.

Not having Madame Lafarge's address given them, they had some difficulty in finding the abode of the woman, who, of course, had her own reasons for not advertising her whereabouts.

After a time they found her—but not in a fit state for an interview with Monsieur Peuchet.

Madame Lafarge, we grieve to say, was rather addicted to the consumption of intoxicating liquors, and brandy was what she loved best. She had made an attempt to capture Cartouche, and, failing, deemed it best to drown her sorrows in flowing bowls of her favourite beverage.

So when the police spies arrived they found her so thoroughly intoxicated that she was unable to walk or even speak.

"What is to be done?" said one of the men.

"I will stay and keep her in view so that she does not escape, while you go back and tell the chief what a state she is in."

"How she stinks of brandy!"

"I should like a drop myself. I wonder if she has a bottle in the room?"

"Not a bad notion. Let us look."

A very slight search revealed to them Madame Lafarge's bottle standing in a little recess at the head of the bed she was lying upon.

The flask contained about half a pint, English measure, and the two policemen quickly disposed of it. Then one remained in charge of the woman, while the other went back to report to the chief on the state in which he had found Madame Lafarge.

"Let watch be kept over her, and as soon as she is in a fit state let her come to me. If she objects bring her by force, if she is so ill that she requires medical aid you know how to procure it."

Such was the mandate of the Chief of Police, and the officer departed to execute it.

It was twenty-four hours before Madame Lafarge was in a fit state to appear at the office of the police. The fact that the two policemen had abstracted the contents of her brandy flask may have facilitated her recovery—but that is merely guess.

Two hours before she started for the police-office, the man in charge of Madame Lafarge allowed her to have a bowl of good strong soup, with a small quantity of brandy in it, and that did her good. The man had often had a hard carouse himself, and knew what was good to take when recovering.

And then Madame Lafarge appeared before Monsieur Peuchet.

"So Madame, you have not captured Cartouche yet," said he.

"No, but if what I hear is true, he succeeded in capturing you."

"Woman, this is no joking matter."

"Monsieur could not have found it very pleasant. Ha, ha! but Cartouche is a merry lad."

"I begin to think that you must be in league with him. Beware how you play me false."

"Monsieur was more affable a short time ago, when last I had the honour to visit him."

"I am enraged! If I find that you have been playing any tricks with me you shall be punished. Women have been broken on the wheel before now."

"Monsieur was far more amiable when last we met," said Madame.

Monsieur would have been more amiable then had he not posted his secretary in a private cabinet, with orders to take down in writing all that was said by the woman, and it

CARTOUCHE,

THE FRENCH JACK SHEPPARD.

"HA! HA! CARTOUCHE!" HE YELLED, "YOU WILL REACH THE STREET SOONER THAN YOU EXPECTED!"

would not do to say anything about the love-making.

So Monsieur Peuchet judged it expedient to change his tone a little. He reflected for a few moments, and then said, quietly—

"Well, understand, Madame Lafarge, the questions I have now to ask you refer solely to Cartouche, and have nothing to do with any other matter that may have been spoken of when you were here before."

"I perfectly understand, monsieur."

"Then answer me, madame, when did you last see this demon, Cartouche?"

"Not since the time I told you of when I last saw you, Monsieur Peuchet."

"Ha! but you have heard?"

"A little. For instance, I have heard that he has left Paris."

"Aye! I sent in search of him the instant I was released from my very unpleasant predicament, but he contrived to evade me. Have you heard nothing more?"

"Nothing that I can tell you now. I have a clue, but I will not even tell you until I am able to deliver him into your hands. I believe some of your men are in league with him."

"So do I," said Peuchet.

"And if one of them knew what your moves are there would be no chance of capturing Cartouche."

"What men do you suspect of being his friends—men of the police, I mean?"

"I cannot name one. I have only a general suspicion that he gets information from some of them."

"When will you know?"

"I cannot say, monsieur. But you may depend upon it I will capture Cartouche as soon as I can. I see, by the way, there is another bill issued."

"Yes. The higher reward will be yours if you succeed."

"Then I will succeed, for I hate Cartouche and I love money."

"Let me know the instant you hear anything of importance."

"I will not fail to do so."

"Find out, if you can, what women he consorts with, for they can often be led to give information. A little money will often do a great deal."

Madame Lafarge thought that a little jealousy would in most cases do more than coin, but she did not say so. She promised the police official to obey faithfully all his instructions, and then departed.

She knew not how or where to find Cartouche; but she was destined to meet him much sooner than she expected.

*　　*　　*　　*　　*

It has already been recorded how Cartouche came back to Paris, and met his companions at the Pont Neuf; also how he prevented their injuring the poor youth from the country; how he fought a duel, and how the whole band dispersed at the alarm that a police patrol was approaching.

Louise had been quick-witted enough to provide another lodging, but Cartouche insisted on going back to the house the police had driven him from. He felt certain that having routed him out of the place they would not be looking for him there.

The old man was rather shy of admitting him, but at length consented, on the condition that he and Louise should not be seen coming into the place or going out of it in company.

But he was not in the house long after Louise went out the next morning.

He knew where she was to be at various times of the day, and more than once passed by to see how she was getting on—that she was not annoyed or persecuted by the police, or too much bothered by the young swells who crowded round to pay her silly compliments.

It was about three in the afternoon when he called at one of the places where Louise was sure to stand for an hour or two.

It was a narrow street, never much frequented at the best of times, except by a few swells from the Louvre, who found it a convenient cut from the palace to an hotel which they much frequented.

The day was uncomfortably hot, and there were few people about. Louise was there, however, and there was a young officer of the Archer Guards.

Louise saw her lover approach, and the swell did not, because his back was towards Cartouche, who also had a habit of walking very quietly when he did not wish to attract attention. And in order that he might progress in this cat-like fashion with the greater ease his spurs were without rowels, and his boots often had extra soles of thick cloth, doubled and quilted, fixed to them. He was wearing those soles now.

A quick gesture from Louise warned Cartouche not to approach too near. He slipped aside into a deep, dark doorway, and listened very attentively.

The first word he heard was his own name.

"What can they have to say about me?" he thought.

"And pray what, Cartouche?" Louise asked.

"As much as all the rest of Paris. Everyone talks of him, you know."

Louise nodded, knowing well that he was the talk of the whole city.

"You have seen him, of course?" said the officer.

"How should I see him, silly man?"

"You get about the town so much, and mix with such a curious lot of people, that I thought it likely you would have met him."

"A great mistake. I never set eyes on him in my life."

"Very soon you will have a chance of doing so He will be captured in an hour or two. The police have ascertained that he has had the audacity to go back to the place where they nearly took him a few days ago, and they will take care he does not escape this time, clever as he is."

"I shall believe the police are very clever when they catch him," Louise replied.

"We shall see. Well, I must be off."

The officer took a flower, paid for it handsomely, and was walking away, when Louise said, carelessly—

"I wonder how the police heard that Cartouche had gone back to his old lodging?"

"A woman named Lafarge told them. I think she heard it from one of his gang. I shall see you to-morrow. I'll wager you a louis against the best flower you have in your basket that Cartouche will be captured by that time."

"Done!" cried Louise.

And the officer walked away.

As soon as he was out of hearing Cartouche emerged from his hiding-place.

"You are a clever girl, Louise," he said. "Listen. You must go to the new lodging. I have kept possession of it, and here is the key. You will find food and wine there, and I will join you soon; but first I must find out what the police are about."

Cartouche turned his head aside and slipped on the false beard and whiskers before mentioned.

"I don't think they will know me now, Louise?"

"I should think not. But hasten away, my good boy; do not run any risks."

Cartouche obeyed, and in a very short space of time was snug in the new lodging, no one, as he thought, having seen him enter the house.

In this, however, Cartouche was much mistaken, for in the house next that was a man who saw him plainly from behind a window-curtain, on the ground floor. This man was of the underlings of Peuchet's force, and the previous night he had been at the theatre where some of the actors disguised themselves in false beards, and it struck the fellow that this person who had entered the neighbouring dwelling was also disguised.

"A man who walks the street disguised in the daytime must be a criminal wishing to escape detection," he argued. "Who knows but it may be Cartouche!"

He resolved to signalise himself, and at once rushed into the next house.

"You have a new lodger?" said he to the woman in charge.

"Yes: Monsieur Steinitz from Germany. Fourth floor."

The man hurried up the staircase noiselessly.

On the second floor landing he saw an axe which he appropriated to break the door down if the German gentleman should refuse to open on demand being made.

The fourth floor was at the top of the house and the door had a large hole, formerly the key-hole, but the lock was now removed a few inches.

Peeping through this hole the police spy saw the supposed German seated on a chair. Then he saw the foreigner remove that beard and whiskers, and in another instant he recognised the features of the French Jack Sheppard.

"Cartouche! open the door! Surrender in the name of the King—I command you!" he yelled.

"To the devil with you!" exclaimed Cartouche, as he discharged a pistol, the shot from which passed through the door very close to the police-officer's head.

Gerault, the policeman, drew back for a moment, and Cartouche at once hung a cloak over the door, so that his future proceedings could not be discerned by anyone who was not actually in the room.

"It is a tight fix—but I can get away yet," said he.

Louise, when she took the room, had a good look round to see what ways there were of escaping if the police should track herself and her lover to the spot.

"No exit except by the staircase," was the conclusion she arrived at, for she saw that the street was too wide for Cartouche to clear at a leap, as he had done just before, and she had no doubt that if the police did track him they would carefully occupy all the neighbouring houses before presenting themselves at his lodging.

An expedient at once suggested itself. She walked out quietly and purchased a rope of sufficient length, as she guessed, to reach from the window, where there was a stout iron ring to which it could be fastened, to the street.

"In case of fire—there have been several bad fires lately in which the staircases were burnt and those living in the upper storeys perished," she explained to the woman of the house, who replied—

"You are very prudent, madame."

Cartouche had noticed that coil of rope the moment he entered the place, and he at once guessed the purpose for which it was there. He lost no time in fastening one end of it to the ring beneath the window and he let the other end drop over the parapet.

The police-officer Gerault was dealing furious blows upon the door with his axe when Cartouche passed out of the window and over the parapet. He had scarcely done so when the door was burst in and Gerault entered.

Of course, the police-officer at once saw how his prey had escaped.

Climbing half out of the window he saw Cartouche a few feet below him, carefully descending by means of the rope.

"Ha, ha! Monsieur Cartouche, you shall each the street sooner than you expect," said he.

Gerault struck a blow with his axe at the rope.

So intensely excited was the man, however, that the first chop was a miss, and did no harm to anything except the edge of the axe. The second cut certainly struck the rope, but did very little injury to it.

The third stroke, however, was more successful; the rope was severed, and Cartouche fell into the street.

Gerault thrust his head out as far as he could

without toppling over himself, and saw his victim lying in the road, not lifeless, but severely injured. He moved his limbs in a spasmodic fashion, but was quite unable to get up or run away. And the policeman laughed loudly.

"Blue death! He is mine now!" Gerault yelled. "I have won the thousand!"

He rushed down the stairs at his top speed, and would have gained the street in a few seconds had he not encountered a stalwart Norman peasant coming up with a load of fire-wood on his back.

This obstacle delayed him, perhaps, fifty seconds, which Gerault occupied in cursing everything he could think of in so short a space of time.

At length he reached the street, where he found the rope only. Cartouche had vanished.

"Holy blue!" the policeman exclaimed. Then he made some remarks about *ventre blue*, which means "blue belly." The French are apt to curse till all is blue.

He looked round this way, that way, and the other, but could see nothing of Cartouche. He asked in a little wine-shop, at a little place where they sold pig's feet, sausages, and things of that kind; he also made inquiry at the store of a dealer in wood and charcoal, but the proprietors of those places could give him no information.

Then Gerault swore a lot more blue oaths and rus ed first to one end of the street, then to the other, but no one had seen Monsieur Cartouche pass.

A couple of police-officers, well known to Gerault, came up, and inquired what was the matter. Being told, it was decided that one of them should be stationed at each end of the street to see that no one passed, while Gerault visited the houses one after another and found out what had become of this audacious ruffian.

Gerault searched, questioned and threatened, but he did not find Cartouche.

What had become of this desperate outlaw?

The reason why the police-officer Gerault did not find him was because he did not search his own house as well as others in the street.

Cartouche was there, although it must seem very unlikely that a prescribed outlaw should take shelter in the house of a police-officer.

Yet, when the outlaw fell there was a man watching from the second-floor window who saw the affair, and at once rushed to his aid.

This was none other than Tomasso the Corsican, who had found it expedient to change his abode, and had engaged a second-floor room in the very house where Gerault occupied the room nearest the street-door.

Tomasso was a mountaineer, quick of thought and quick of foot. There were no loads of wood on his staircase, and he was out in the street in an instant.

Strong as Hercules, he lifted Cartouche in his arms, and ran up the stairs as nimbly as he would have climbed his native mountain side; and he had his captain snug and safe inside that second-floor apartment before Gerault, the street, or the neighbours had looked out to see what it was that fell.

"It is precious risky," the old Corsican muttered, "but I will save him if I can, for he is the only man fit to keep the band together."

Tomasso laid Cartouche on his bed, and felt him over, but could not discover that any bones were broken.

"A dose of cognac is the best medicine I can prescribe," said he, and he at once administered it.

Very soon Cartouche, who had been severely shaken by the fall, opened his eyes and looked round.

"Where am I?" he asked.

Tomasso briefly explained where, and how he came there.

"Louise must know," said the captain.

"I know where to find the Wolf—he can let her know."

"And Gribichon? He is a true heart—but not Red Judas."

"He shall know the point of my dagger when I meet the traitor," old Tomasso growled, as he departed, carefully locking the door.

    *   *   *   *   *

The scene is a garret, and a poorly-furnished one at that, for Marie Dupont, nicknamed Cancan by her associates, lived alone, and did not believe in spending much of her hard-earned money over lodgings.

She was, nevertheless, and indeed in consequence, high up in the world.

Marie spent a little in dress, but that little was very well spent, and on Sundays and holidays she could turn out as neatly and nattily attired as ladies of much higher rank. Let alone a careful and tasty Frenchwoman on that subject.

CHAPTER XVIII.

A LITTLE SUPPER PARTY.

CAN-CAN was sitting at a little table counting over her money now that the day's work was over, and the result hardly seemed to satisfy her.

"Three francs and seventy-five centimes fo. twelve hours' work, and only half of it profit. Oh, dear! I'm afraid I shan't get rich at that rate! Never mind—*vogue la galere!* I'll have my supper, anyhow."

Can-can knew something of the band with which Cartouche was connected, but as yet she had not become a member of it.

Spreading a neat little cloth on the table she produced from a cupboard in the wall a Strasburg sausage, a roll, and a small piece of cheese. The bottle of sour and very small claret—variously named *vinaigre*, *petit blue*, and *piquette* in derision by the poor of Paris—was absent, for the earnings of the last day or two would not admit of it.

Marie commenced slowly enjoying herself on these homely viands, and as she proceeded she thought to herself—

"I wonder what has become of Adolphe Adrien Eugéne Victor and all the rest of him? I wonder whether he'll ever return and pay those three francs?"

At this moment the window opened from outside, and Gribichon, looking very hot, dusty, and tired, jumped in.

Poor Can-can screamed.

"Adolphe Adrien!"

For it was that scamp Gribichon who had given her the card on which was imprinted that fine long string of names, had called her angel, Venus, and all the rest of his stock of endearing terms, and had borrowed her hardly-earned money.

"Flora, my angelic goddess, at last, Flora, my goddess of scents and perfumed flowers, I am with you."

By this time Can-can had recovered herself a little, and so she answered with a pout—

"There, that will do; you called me a goddess when you got those three francs out of me."

"Flora, forget the past."

"Adolphe, you forgot to pay me. But how did you get in?"

"I climbed on the roof of the pigsty and scrambled up the waterspout"

"Why didn't you come in by the door?"

"Because the door was watched and the police were at my heels."

"The police?"

"They were after me, no doubt, by mistake. They took me for somebody else. But, my dear girl, can't you give me something to eat? I am famished."

"Famished? I thought you were rich."

"I mean my run has given me a magnificent appetite. And is that a sausage—a Strasburg sausage?"

"It is—it's my supper."

"Adorable Can-can, for the love of Heaven, give me a bit."

"Well, sit down then."

Gribichon did not wait for any better invitation, but sat down and commenced eating hungrily.

"One would suppose," said Can-can, "that you hadn't eaten for a month."

"I breakfasted early, and have not dined yet."

"What time do you dine?"

"Ahem! Usually at ten o'clock in the evening."

"That is rather late."

"Always—that is usually, generally, sometimes—at ten. All the delicacies of the season —you shall go with me and help me to eat it."

"Where is your hotel?"

"In the Rue de Bastille, the large stone building, you know."

"I thought that was a prison!"

"Vulgar people often think it is, because it's built so strongly. A most fascinating place— once you get inside it's quite difficult to leave it."

"Is it so very handsome?"

"Well, its beauty consists in its grand solidity. No one has ever been able to break into it!"

"Or out of it, I suppose?"

"No," said Gribichon, with a bit of a grimace, "I suppose not. But its inmates are treated like the Royal Family—are always attended by a guard of honour."

"Are you really very rich, then?"

"My riches are unknown. My steward informs me that I am worth millions."

"Then you can pay me my three francs?"

"Three francs! You shall have a hundred!"

A knock was just at that moment heard at the door.

"What's that? Who's there?"

Whoever it might be seemed to hesitate to enter, and at last Can-can opened the door herself.

It was the Wolf, and he evidently wanted to say something privately to Gribichon.

Can-can, with the tact of a better-bred lady, saw this, and retreated to the other side of the room, while Gribichon listened intently to the Wolf, whose whispers in his ear were accompanied by a considerable amount of gesticulation.

The Wolf at last left the room, and went down the stairs as stealthily and noiselessly as he had ascended them.

"Who is that strange-looking individual, and what did he want?" asked Can-can.

"That was my land steward," readily responded Gribichon, determined to keep up his little joke; "he came to tell me that all my tenants had raised their rents of their own accord! But I must leave you, my angel; duty calls me away, the Minister of Finance awaits me. He wants me to advance the Government a million of francs! Good-night."

"Is that the way you run off after eating my supper? I thought you were going to take me to your hotel."

"Not to-night, my love. Call on me to-morrow—ask for the marquis. Good-bye!"

And he hastened down the stairs.

"Well, he's a nice kind of fellow! Ah! here he comes back again," said Marie, to herself.

"By-the-bye," said Gribichon, as he popped his head in at the door hurriedly, "have you got three francs about you? I left my purse on the——"

"Oh, yes, I know; but never mind. Well, here they are. But when will you pay me?"

"I'll give you an order on my bankers for a hundred francs—two hundred—anything you like, to-morrow. Once more, good-night, my angel!"

"Oh, dear," thought poor Can-can, "I expect I've been very silly. I've lost my supper and three francs twice over. I do wonder what kind of a fellow this man of millions will turn out to be!"

CHAPTER XIX.

EUGENE AND HER FATHER.

THE scene is once more changed to a fine old château in the neighbourhood of Paris.

The apartment in which it takes place is handsomely furnished with all the art and luxurious accessories of the period.

The Marquis de Grandlieu, the owner of the place, is seated in a comfortable attitude on a richly-upholstered *fauteuil*.

But the expression on his face is not that of a man at ease.

He has an unpleasant duty to perform—or something which he believes to be his duty.

He is about to separate two loving hearts—that of his daughter and her sweetheart—and, to do him justice, he doesn't much like the job.

In France more particularly, though by no means exclusively there, rank and high birth, wealth and power look for alliances suitable for their standing.

And his daughter's choice is not to his liking; it must be forbidden.

He loved his daughter well, but not well enough to let her have all her own way.

At this moment his daughter, Eugenie, little expecting the thunder-clap about to burst, entered the room.

"Eugenie, my dear, come and sit by my side; I have something to say to you that must be said, though I would fain avoid the task."

"Father, what is the matter—what have I done?" asked the young girl anxiously, noting the sternness depicted on her father's countenance.

"Nothing at present, my darling; it is of the future I have been thinking, and must speak."

"Father dear, for many a long year I hope to be with you; what, then, can happen?"

"Eugenie, I have in view for you a grand alliance, one that will consolidate the wealth and power of two noble families; prepare yourself to receive and accept the addresses of a rich man—one who——"

"But what of François, father?"

"François! a penniless adventurer. Do not mention such a connection again in my hearing."

"But François once saved my life," said poor Eugenie, almost on the verge of tears.

"For which," answered her parent, haughtily, "I evinced my gratitude at the time, and promised to push him on in the world."

"But early companionship, father! François was my early playmate and always my devoted friend."

"You must forget the past," said the old man, gravely, "in the contemplation of the splendid destiny which may so easily be yours."

"Never!" answered Eugenie, bursting into tears—"never!"

There is no telling what might have been the result of this disagreement between father and daughter had not a servant just then knocked at the door and entered.

"Monsieur François Cariol," announced the domestic.

"I will not see him," broke out the marquis, angrily.

"Oh, father, do not drive him so rudely from your door. It would indeed be inhospitable—it would be——"

"Let him then be served with refreshments in the dining-room. But I will not see him."

"Father, father, you'll break my heart," sobbed poor Eugenie.

"My child, I wish for nothing but your happiness."

"I am certain of that, my father. Well then, suffer me at least to see him, and break your determination to him, if indeed——"

"My mind is made up on the subject. Nevertheless, that you shall not deem me too harsh——"

"Dear father!"

"It shall be as you wish; you shall break my intentions to him; I will retire. But remember, Eugenie, this must be your last interview; I shall be near at hand."

And with this the Marquis bowed stiffly to his daughter, repulsing, though not unkindly, her wish to embrace him, and left the apartment.

The old servant, who understood the situation, desired M. Cariol to enter.

François, nothing loth, rushed into the room, upsetting a chair in his haste, and ran to the side of his beloved, whose waist one arm soon encircled, while the other took her hand and raised it to his lips.

"Eugenie—dear Eugenie!"

"Dear François! But no, you must not. I had forgot——"

"What have you forgotten, my darling?" asked François, anxiously, seeing that something had evidently occurred since their last interview.

"I must not betray myself," thought poor Eugenie! "I must try and treat him with coldness and indifference."

So, suiting the action to the thought, she pointed to a chair, and said, in a constrained and frigid manner—

"Will you not please to be seated, sir?"

"Sir! How formal you have grown, dear Eugenie. What *is* the matter?"

Nevertheless, he took the chair and sat down beside her.

"A little further off, if you please, sir!"

"Ah! honestly I don't quite understand. But perhaps these are some of the new city manners to which I am unused. Dear Eugenie, how happy I am to see you once more."

But he really hardly looked it.

"How charming—how delightful is this meeting," continued he, with an assumption of gaiety he certainly did not feel.

"Delightful, François—I mean, sir. A little further off, if you please."

"Have you quite forgotten the old scenes of our childhood, Eugenie?" asked her lover, with some little emotion in his voice.

"Oh, no—I remember the many pleasant hours we have spent together, François—I mean sir."

"I am rejoiced to see you again—and your ather——"

WHILE SPEAKING HE RECEIVED A DEADLY BLOW IN THE BACK.

"My father !" answered the young girl, trembling as she thought, "I must break his heart with the news of our future engagement." But she only went on, "A little further off, if you please, sir ; remember that——"

"Don't you remember the old mulberry tree under which we have so often sat together ?" broke in François, trying to make conversation, while he could see there was something wrong.

"Oh, yes, François."

She had forgotten the "sir" this time !

"Well," answered her sweetheart, noting gladly the omission—"well, they have cut it down."

"Oh, what a shame ! And the old hall ?"

"Has been turned into a workhouse. And they've built a new prison and pulled down the parsonage ; and all the old maids have got husbands because the conscription for the army claimed all the unmarried men, and to save themselves why, of course, all the bachelors got married."

"And how are all my favourites, François ?— the pony, my dogs, the birds——"

"Oh, famous ! And your pretty flower-garden is in full bloom. You should only see the violets and the sunflowers !"

"And the pinks ?"

"And the roses ! But they do not compare to those on thy face, my darling !"

And with this he lost all his previous constraint, and implanted a hearty kiss on her blushing countenance.

"Ah, François !"

"Oh, Eugenie !"

While all this was going on it may well be believed that their senses, being bathed in bliss, so to speak, were not so wide-awake as usual in regard to ordinary mundane affairs.

As a matter of fact, the marquis had entered the room without either of them being aware of the fact, and he now confronted the unlucky pair locked in one another's arms !

"What is this I see ?" thundered out the old gentleman. "Is this how you keep a promise, Eugenie ?"

"Oh, father !"

"To your room at once—say not one word. And you, sir," growled the marquis, as he turned to François, "this is how you repay my hospitality ! Begone, sir ! Quit my roof, and never darken my doors with your presence again !"

"Marquis, I obey you ; you have befriended me, and I can forgive you, for it must seem as though I had committed a breach of faith. Nevertheless, you will live to regret the injustice of this moment."

And the young man left the room with a profound and respectful bow, which the marquis returned, but in his haughtiest manner.

The old noble paced up and down for some minutes greatly agitated.

"My daughter," said he to himself, "must never see that scoundrel again. And yet—well —he is no scoundrel I must admit, for he saved my darling's life. Nevertheless, I have higher views for my girl than such a man, however respectable. I must speak to the servants."

He rang the bell and a footman entered.

"Send Jules, the butler, to me."

Jules was an old and trusted member of the household, who had grown grey in the service of the marquis.

"Jules," said the old man in a tremulous voice, as the butler entered, "remember well that that young man, François Cariol, must never enter these doors again. I must protect my daughter from adventurers as I would myself. Let the whole household understand this."

And Jules, who had rather a secret liking and admiration of young Cariol, nevertheless knew that he must not oppose the will of the marquis, and so bowed assent as he left the room.

Could the marquis protect himself ? Time— and a very short time at that—will show.

For at this moment the wheels of a carriage were heard on the gravel outside as it drew up at the door of the chateau.

A servant entered and announced—

"The Count d'Aubarne would speak with the marquis."

The particular Count d'Aubarne of the moment was no other than Cartouche !

It will be remembered that Cartouche had taken, with other things, from the count an order for a hundred thousand francs. The money had been won by the latter at gambling, and Cartouche, when he stole it, had supposed at the moment that he had simply to present it at the Bank of France for payment.

But on investigating the note he found that while the document was doubtless good enough, it required the endorsement of the marquis, from whose son and heir it had been won.

Cartouche at first did not like the look of this, as it might lead to investigation, but not being easily daunted, came finally to the conclusion that he would call on the marquis, and so, behold him here on the spot, dressed to perfection as a nobleman of the period.

On the other hand, the marquis, a very wealthy nobleman, who, while quite willing to pay the card or other debts of his rather scampish heir, did not care that they should be noised abroad, had himself determined to get the note back, and pay the money himself at the chateau. This was all the easier as his land steward had been collecting rents for some two months past, which had not been paid to his account at the Bank of France.

So when he thus learnt of the arrival of the count he was delighted, and ordered him to be shown in at once.

"The Count D'Aubarne," was announced by the footman.

"My dear count," said the Marquis to Cartouche, "I am delighted to make the acquaintance of a man of whom I have heard so much. I have never yet had the pleasure of meeting you, but report speaks highly in your favour."

"My dear marquis, you flatter me. Whether report speaks justly you shall judge for yourself."

"Rumour, count, has a thousand tongues, and makes free with reputations, I know. But——"

"Oh, yes ; for instance, Cartouche is a good case in point."

"Ah, you have heard of that scoundrel ?"

"My dear marquis, who has not ?" The audacity of that fellow is really remarkable. He assumes the garb of a gentleman, and enters your house under an assumed name, with the most perfect nonchalance. He will even converse with you on various topics, hold you by the buttonhole, and pick your pocket with your eyes open."

And Cartouche suited the action to the word by abstracting the marquis's purse.

"Is it possible ?" said the marquis.

"It is true, I assure you !"

"And without being discovered ?"

"The fellow has acquired such a thoroughbred air that no one would detect him. Even you, my dear marquis, might be deceived in him."

"Oh, no, no," answered the old nobleman, "that's really not likely."

"You might, really. And, between ourselves, I've heard a report that Cartouche has laid a wager to rob you, marquis, of your purse and watch before one o'clock to-day."

"He must be quick, for it only wants a quarter to one now."

"Is your watch going ?"

The polite old gentleman took it out and showed it to Cartouche.

"Look for yourself."

"Rather slow, but it's going."

"Oh, yes, it's going," and, our readers need hardly be told, in a few moments after it had *gone*—into Cartouche's pocket, though the marquis remained unaware of the fact."

"Rob me, will he ? Ha, ha ! An impudent, presuming rascal, I should like to catch him at it," chuckled the old boy.

"By the way, marquis, you will pardon me, I know, making any allusion to such trifles. I have an order on you——"

"Don't apologise, dear count ; I shall have to pay that young scamp's debts of honour, of course. In fact, give me the document, and without further fuss I can at once pay you the money."

Cartouche handed him the paper.

And as he said this he walked to his desk and took out a bundle of bank notes.

"This is all quite satisfactory then, my dear count," said the marquis ; "but, just for form's sake, you know, you may as well give me the pass-word."

"The pass-word ?"

"Yes ; the pass-word that was arranged upon."

"Confusion !"

Cartouche, in *his* confusion, had actually hit on part of it.

"Yes, that's right—that's half of it."

"Half of it," thought Cartouche, quickly, "here goes for a bold venture. Confusion to Cartouche !"

"Yes, that's it ; here's the money. You will deposit it in the bank !"

"Assuredly, in my bank."

"For the benefit of the widows and orphans of Paris."

"Eh ? What did you say ?"

"The winner, you are aware, was to invest it for the benefit of the poor. My young scamp of an heir, bad boy as he is," and here the old man drew himself up proudly, "is not mercenary, and plays only for excitement, not money."

Cartouche was a strange being, and with all his villainy had some noble qualities. He handed the bank-notes back again.

"Marquis," said he, "I would rather not take the money now—it will be safer in your possession."

"Oh, for fear Cartouche may get hold of it ?"

"I think it very likely, if it remained in my hands."

"By the way, count, I have an appointment in your regiment ; I can now comply with the request you named in your letter. Here is a commission with a blank left for the name, which you can fill up at discretion."

At this moment the footman again entered, and announced—

"Another gentleman below, sir, who gives his name as the Count d'Aubarne."

"The devil !" thought Cartouche. "My young colonel of Musqueteers has managed to escape, then ?"

"The Count d'Aubarne !" exclaimed the marquis, in astonishment. "Why, this is the count ?"

"Marquis," said Cartouche, "rely on it this fellow is none other than that scoundrel Cartouche."

"Do you really think so ?"

The real count entered.

"Marquis, I come to—— *You* here ?" said he, the last ejaculation coming forth spontaneously as he caught sight of Cartouche.

"Ah, you didn't expect to see me, I suppose ? Marquis, I was right. See how confused the rascal looks ? It *is* Cartouche !"

"Ho, Jacques, Phillipe, Jean ! Seize that impostor, and hand him over to the police !" almost shrieked out the old marquis, as he pointed him out to the servants, who rushed in at the genuine Count d'Aubarne.

"I assure you I am——"

"Don't let him speak—gag and bind him—away with him !"

The poor count was hurried out of the room by the brave trio of servants, who, having only one man to deal with, pummelled him to their hearts' content.

"The scoundrel !" gasped the poor marquis. "It is fortunate that you were present, count, to recognise the fellow, or the chances are he would have robbed me."

"Are you sure that he has not done so ?"

The Marquis felt in his pockets.

"My watch, my purse, both are gone !"

"Ah, no doubt Cartouche has got them."

At this moment the clock struck one.

"One o'clock—ha, ha! You see, my lord," said Cartouche, shaking with laughter, "that scoundrel has kept his word!"

A glimmer of light broke in on the bewildered brain of the poor marquis. But it flickered out again.

"Here, Jacques, bring back that man!" said he to one of the men-servants.

The real count was again brought in.

"Marquis, you are deceived, imposed upon," said the latter.

"Yes, by you, you scoundrel!"

"No," answered the count, pointing to Cartouche, "by that fellow, who has assumed my name. There stands Cartouche!"

"Then you are really——"

"The Count d'Aubarne."

"Gentlemen, enough," said Cartouche, in an exasperatingly cool and ironical manner; "I am, and there's no mistake, the real original of that name. The only mistakes made have been on your side. Adieu, my lord marquis, my dear count, till next time!"

And, amid a scene of confusion, cries of "Secure him!" "Stop thief!" and the popping of two or three pistols, Cartouche ran down the stairs and drove off in the hired carriage which had brought him.

With the exception of the Count d'Aubarne, who was only just being unbound, and the marquis, who was too old for action, there was a good deal more talk than valour about, and Cartouche had hardly need to hurry himself in the slightest.

And, to do him justice, he didn't.

CHAPTER XX.

A STAB IN THE BACK.

CARTOUCHE remained quietly with the old Corsican, Tomasso, for a couple of days, while all Paris was talking of his last exploit.

The police were simply furious.

That an outlaw, whose form and features were well-known to them, should be able to defy them in this manner, to make them the laughing-stock of France and treat them with contempt, was rather more than they could stand, and they swore——

Well, the rank and file of the force swore a lot of foul oaths which had no particular bearing on the case.

Monsieur Peuchet and two or three other superiors swore they would capture Cartouche, and when once caught he should never have the least chance of escaping from their clutches.

But how to get him was the question.

The police believed to a great extent in the cleverness of Madame Lafarge, and she trusted that she would be able to worm the whole secret from her daughter, La Belle Louise.

We know not how she contrived to get the information, but Madame Lafarge did contrive in some way to learn that her daughter and Cartouche loved each other.

She knew that Louise would be certain to see her lover before long, and therefore Louise should be watched instead of sending men out to search, blind fashion, for a man who did not wish to be seen.

Louise did wish to be seen, and for that purpose presented herself on all the most public Parisian thoroughfares during the twelve or fourteen hours she devoted to business. Louise thought, and with good reason, that the more she remained about the streets the less chance would there be of her being watched by the police.

So Louise kept herself before the public as much as possible.

Of course, she soon heard of the attack made upon their lodging by Gerault, the policeman, and she learned that Cartouche had contrived to get away, but how he did it, and whither he had gone, she could not guess.

So La Belle Louise strolled about the streets of Paris, and when she saw a crowd in the street she pushed forward to hear, if she could, what they were saying about Cartouche.

Nothing, except that he was the most daring outlaw France had ever produced. No one, though, had the slightest idea what had become of him, though the troubles of Peuchet and the disappointment of Gerault were freely discussed.

But Louise did not know that during all this time she was being watched by her own mother.

Such was the fact, however.

A certain young officer of the Archer Guard has already been mentioned in this story as making a bet with Louise that Cartouche would be captured within a certain time; and he was in communication with Madame Lafarge.

The officer, Monsieur Ogilvy, was the descendant of a Scotch gentleman who years before had settled in France, to live, like scores of his brave countrymen, by the profession of arms, or, in other words, to serve as a soldier.

The original Ogilvy had done pretty well in that line and his progeny still better. Some had been killed, of course, and now the sole representative of the house was the Seigneur Capitaine Ogilvy, who was madly in love with La Belle Louise, the flower-girl, and furiously jealous of Cartouche.

Since the interview with Louise in which he made her the bet, young Ogilvy had somehow heard that there was an intimacy between the flower-girl and the outlaw. Also, he had heard from one of the superior officers of police that Louisa was the daughter of Madame Lafarge, who was as anxious as himself to get Cartouche hanged.

So young Ogilvy had an interview with Madame Lafarge, and the result was a bargain by which the Captain of the Archer Guard undertook to pay Madame double the reward advertised if either of them could entrap Cartouche within a week. In return Madame undertook to do all she could to persuade Louise to listen favourably to the advances of Monsieur Ogilvy.

Ogilvy had already made the acquaintance of

Louise, and it will be remembered that Cartouche had overheard a conversation in which it was prophesied that his own liberty would speedily be exchanged for captivity.

Cartouche was none the worse for his fall as may be guessed from his pranks with the marquis. But he was jealous of young Ogilvy, and resolved to keep a watch on him.

The young captain was seen going along the street to the place where Louise was vending her flowers. Cartouche followed.

He could not hear the first words that passed between her and the young swell, but it seemed as though Louise had repulsed him in a way that made him very angry.

The first words Cartouche heard Ogilvy say were—

"Then you refuse me? Very well. I believe you are in league with this villainous Cartouche, and I give you my word that unless you aid me to bring him to justice you will find yourself in the Bastille before long. You can avoid that fate by doing what I have asked—give him up, and then be mine. Louise, you do not know how I love you."

He passed his hand around her waist, and touched her chin with his right hand.

But Cartouche's blood was boiling, and even whilst speaking the young Archer received a deadly blow in the back from the same blade with which the Parisian outlaw had already done fatal work.

Down dropped Ogilvy—dead!

"Away, Louise!" he whispered. "You must not be seen near him."

Louise darted off. Cartouche hastily rifled the pockets of his victim, and then disappeared in the opposite direction. A minute later the dead body was seen, and a few hours later all Paris was talking of the murder.

Cartouche hastened away, and lost no time in putting the breadth of the city between himself and the scene of his latest crime. Arriving at one of the gates he saw a countryman offering a fine horse for sale, but the offers the man received did not suit.

Cartouche whispered to the man—

"Lead him out of the gate for about a mile. I will follow, and give you eight hundred francs for the horse, but say nothing."

The man nodded and went away with his animal. Cartouche followed and soon overtook him.

"Now, where is the money?" the man asked.

"You will get no money from me."

"Then you will get no horse."

"I shall have this horse as sure as my name is Cartouche," said our hero, seizing the bridle.

The countryman gave one gasp and then fled as fast as his wooden shoes could carry him.

Cartouche mounted and galloped off, but without any clear idea as to the course he should pursue.

Presently he heard the sound of wheels, and retired behind some bushes to see what was coming.

A huge lumbering coach, almost as big as a modern furniture van, drawn by four great Flemish horses. Inside was a gorgeously-attired man, who, looking out of the window, espied a rather good-looking peasant girl walking along the road.

Calling to his postilions to stop, this worthy called the girl and told her that if she was going towards Paris she might ride with him, for which offer she thanked him, and entered the coach, which then moved on again.

But in less than a minute Cartouche heard screams, which convinced him that the owner of the vehicle was paying some very pressing attentions to the girl.

"I've done enough crime for one day," he muttered, "but I'll save that poor girl from the clutches of a rascal even if I have to shoot him."

And putting on his mask, he rode up to the coach, calling upon the postilions to stop if they valued their lives. And it seems they did value them—for they stopped.

Then Cartouche, pistol in hand, appeared at the door of the coach.

"Instantly hand over your money," said he.

The owner of the coach trembled with fear.

"Be quick about it!"

The fellow contrived to extract a well-filled purse from his pocket, and handed it to Cartouche, who then said—

"You, young woman, may alight if you please. I think you will be safer walking than in that coach."

The girl, not knowing what was to happen, got out, and Cartouche then bade the postilions to drive on as fast as they could, an order they readily obeyed.

"Why are you going to Paris?" Cartouche asked the girl.

"To take a situation for a couple of years and save money, that I may not be without a portion when Alphonse is ready to marry me," she replied.

"Does Alphonse live in your village?"

"Yes, monsieur."

"Then put this purse in your pocket; go back to him and get married as soon as possible. There is more than two years' wages in it; and when you hear people talking about Cartouche try and think well of him."

And, without waiting to be thanked, he galloped away.

CHAPTER XXI.

CAPTURED.

THE scene again changes; we are in the humble lodgings of Louise, the flower-girl.

François, her foster-brother, has just entered, and Louise has greeted him kindly, for she has a kindly heart, and is grieved to see him so downcast and melancholy.

Nothing she can say, however, seems to warm or animate him, for he cannot forget his last interview with Eugenie, and especially the peremptory hardships exhibited by her father, the Marquis de Crandlieu.

Everything seems hopeless to him, and,

indeed, he can hardly blame the marquis, aristocrat as he is, for rejecting the suit of one unknown to fame and empty of purse.

He knows that Eugenie loves him; nevertheless, for the moment this seems to make matters worse, for is it likely that he will be able to win her?

He sees no way—nothing but blackness and despair all around him. The future opens up no vista of happiness.

"François," said Louise, "you know we were brought up as children together. You were my earliest and kindest playmate, and have helped me out of many a scrape. Is there no way, then, in which I can help you?"

"I know your good heart, Louise, but there is no possibility of what I know you would gladly do for my sake. You cannot give me rank and riches!"

"They are to be won, François—both may be yours, though the way may be long and weary."

"I do not deny the possibility, but, alas! where is the probability? No, dear Louey, Eugenie is lost to me for ever! Her purse-proud father drove me from his door."

"Poor François!"

"I have resolved to remain in Paris no longer. Without friends——"

"Fie, François!"

"I do not forget you nor your well-meant kindness; nevertheless, I am right. Without fortune or hope, but one course remains to me. Paris is no place for a poor man; and yet life outside it will seem sad enough to me, who has tasted deep of its pleasures!"

"Life has some duties also," said Louise, gently.

"Perhaps so," answered the young man, irritably—"perhaps so; I am hardly in a condition yet to take moral lessons with equanimity and patience. Nay, more, I have thought seriously of ending my career once and for all——"

"For shame, François!"

"It would be the easiest way of getting out of my difficulties; it would end them for ever."

"And you consider yourself a man thus to fly from trouble—I might say almost your first trouble?"

"It looks weak; nevertheless, it requires bravery."

"Of what kind?" asked Louise, contemptuously. "Well, I can tell you; the bravery of a braggart or of a madman, but less excusable than the latter, which flashes up momentarily and then expires, leaving crime to be expiated for ever and for ever!"

"Louisa, you are a good girl, but you have not known trouble such as mine."

"Have I not known trouble?" quietly asked the girl, a flush passing over her face, which was succeeded by a deathly pallor. "Maybe I have trouble of a kind which enables me the better to understand yours."

"Poor Louey; are you, too, then, deeply in love?"

The girl did not seem inclined to answer so blunt a question.

"Tell me, Louey, for you interest me once more in life, and if I can help you, you know I will."

"I doubt it not, François; but for the present, at least, there is no way."

"Then are we both in the same fix? Who is the happy man, or the man you would make happy? Surely not this mysterious stranger you have so often named to me?"

The poor girl hung her head, but did not deny the soft impeachment.

"Am I then right? But no, hardly; for you are ignorant of his very name and position, I believe?"

Louise felt herself obliged to answer this last query, inasmuch as it cast some little slur on her prudence.

"His name," said she, colouring up—"at least, the name I know him by—is André; but that he tells me is not his real name."

François shook his head, and the girl continued, still more earnestly—

"He has promised that I shall soon be made acquainted with his rank and family; but of this I am certain, that his intentions are honourable—noble!"

"Be warned, Louise," answered François, seriously; "an honest man need never make a secret of his name and circumstances."

"He promised to visit me this evening. When he arrives I will introduce you to him, and you shall judge for yourself, François, whether I am not right."

"I will wait, then, though I fear you have made a mistake."

"No, no, I will not believe it," answered Louise, smiling through her tears. "François, I have a few little purchases to make; remain here till I return; I shall not be long."

And the girl rapidly put on her hat and shawl, and taking up a basket, quitted the room.

François, left to himself in the gathering gloom of the evening, soon relapsed into the state of melancholy which had characterised him when he arrived.

"It is all very well for Louise," said he to himself, "good, kind girl that she is, to talk hopefully; she has not really known trouble yet; I pray she never may."

This, by the way, is a common idea with many, though most common, of course, among the young, that no one has ever had any trouble worth mentioning excepting themselves.

"No," continued he, muttering to himself; "it will not do. The case is hopeless. And yet without Eugenie I cannot, I will not live! Existence would be a burden to me; life would not be worth the having."

François went to the door; it was latched and there was no sound of footsteps on the stairs.

He took from his pocket a handsomely-mounted pistol, small and compact in comparison

CARTOUCHE,
THE FRENCH JACK SHEPPARD.

"INSTANTLY HAND OVER YOUR MONEY," SAID CARTOUCHE.

with the great clumsy affairs of the day, and regarded it with an earnest seriousness.

"Here I have," thought he, "the means of self-annihilation—no more trouble, no more worry. I am weary of existence—I am alone!"

The bells of a neighbouring church just then rang out solemnly the hour; they reminded him of something he had forgotten.

He fell on his knees and bowed his head in his hands.

He muttered a prayer earnestly but incoherently, and then, with a wild frenzy which showed him to be at least momentarily mad, placed the pistol to his temples, when——

It was dashed aside by a powerful hand, Cartouche having at that moment entered the room by the window, his own clothes showing some signs of disorder.

"My young friend," said he, in a sarcastic tone of voice, which, nevertheless, had a ring of merriment in it, "whose brains are you going to blow out—yours or mine?"

"A stranger," muttered François, gloomily, as he turned his head towards Cartouche; "who on earth are you?"

"No enemy of yours," answered Cartouche, cheerily, "since I have prevented you from accomplishing a very foolish, as well as a very wicked act."

"Do you come here to moralise?"

"No; moralising is not much in my way, or if it was people would very much doubt my sincerity. Why do you wish to terminate your existence?"

"Because I have lost all hope."

"Is your mistress false to you?"

"No, but her father will not suffer me to address her."

"Why so?"

"Because I am poor."

"Ah, a very good reason, and one which most fathers—at all events, those who love their daughters—consider first of all."

"Do you mock me?"

"Not a bit of it; I will aid you. How would you prefer to get rich?"

"By the exercise of my talents," answered François, grandiloquently.

You see he was very young, and therefore could not help being something of a donkey.

"Talents are all very well," laughed Cartouche, "but have a hard time of it usually at first without something else; you want a little influence thrown in."

"Where am I to look for it?" asked François, with all the starch gone out of him once more.

"Why, here; haven't I just promised to help you? And what profession would suit you for the exercise of those talents of which you seemed so sure a few moments ago?"

"Either the bar or the army——"

"The bar! Ha, ha! I've had too much of the bar myself—don't like lawyers," said Cartouche, laughingly, and herein he doubtless spoke the truth; "but the army, that's the very thing. I'll give you a commission."

"You?"

"Yes; here it is,' and he handed him the commission which the marquis had given him when he impersonated the Count d'Aubarne. "I filled it up with your name, you see, for the fact is I expected to see you."

"You know me, then?"

"Yes. Louise has often named you to me—the young man from the country—her foster-brother."

"Louise! then you are——"

"Her devoted admirer!"

There is no telling how the conversation would have continued, for at this moment a commotion was heard outside in the street.

François went to the window and looked out. There was a seething, fighting mass of humanity below, who had followed the gendarmes of the Civic Guard, the latter with M. Bobilet at their head.

All the rabble were shouting and crying out, and looking up at the house.

"Monsieur," said François, "I have no words sufficient to thank you for your kindness. But what does this crowd mean below? What or whom do they want?"

"I suspect shrewdly that they must want me!"

"You?"

"Yes; that's why I sought shelter here."

"Who, then, are you?"

"Why, Cartouche, of course!"

"You—you that desperate villain? If that is so there is nothing else for it. Sorry though I am I must give the alarm!"

"Is this the return for my kindness?"

"I despise your gift as I despise you," and suiting the action to the word François threw down the paper which would have given him rank and standing in the army.

"Don't be a fool," coolly answered Cartouche, "or you'll compel me to act very unlike a gentleman."

"I defy you!"

"Do you? Then I must teach you submission!"

And without more ado Cartouche roughly hustled François into the large corner closet and locked the door.

The noise increased outside, the mob yelling and shouting at the top of their lungs.

The tramp of the guard up the stairs was getting obviously nearer.

Cartouche concealed himself momentarily behind a curtain.

The door was burst open, and M. Bobilet peered cautiously into the gloom, looking as though he did not half like his job.

But observing no one his courage returned, and he shouted out to his followers boldly—

"I don't see him—let's enter. Perhaps he's in the cupboard?"

Cartouche, with the quickness that always distinguished him, darted across the fireplace before he was seen by those on the dark staircase, who were only then just on the point of entering, and was inside and up the chimney in a jiffy.

"Men, search the house !" called out Bobilet, bold as brass in an apparently empty room. "Ha ! I have a keen nose for scenting a thief. I have a shrewd suspicion that he has climbed up the chimney !"

M. Bobilet went to the fireplace, and, screwing his head inside, looked up the chimney.

At this moment a brick, dislodged by Cartouche as he scrambled up inside, fell, bringing down a lot of soot with it.

The brick landed on M. Bobilet's upturned face with a sounding whack, which bunged up one of his eyes, bruised his face, and brought the blood in a stream from his nose.

It is quite unnecessary to remark that poor Bobilet speedily retired from that scene of action, looking a very crestfallen and disreputable-looking person indeed.

The soot and blood together made him look more like a chimney-sweep who had gone in for prize-fighting than an officer of the Civic Guard.

He fell, limp and nerveless, "all of a heap," to speak vulgarly, on the floor, feebly shouting—

"Help ! Murder ! Murder !"

Meantime the gendarmes and the Guard were searching for an opening to the roof, and when they did finally discover it, found that it was also necessary to obtain a ladder.

All this took time, of which Cartouche was not slow to avail himself.

He reached the top of the large, old-fashioned chimney and soon scrambled out on the roof, where he sat for a few moments to pull himself together.

In those days sweeps always climbed inside the chimneys to clean them, as they did in this country till the practice was prevented by Act of Parliament, and at that moment the head of one appeared above a neighbouring chimney-pot, belonging to a different house.

"Here, my friend, come out of that," exclaimed Cartouche, as, none too gently, he hauled him out by the hair of his head ; "we'll change chimneys, if you please. But, here, just give me your blouse, and drop down that one over there "—pointing to the one from which he had just before emerged.

The sweep, who was utterly bewildered by this strange meeting, and to whom a chimney or two, more or less, made no difference, handed Cartouche his blouse, and immediately obeyed, dropping himself down the one indicated, rather glad than not to get off so easily from the clutches of one who appeared more like a madman than anything else.

Cartouche, on his part, prepared to descend the chimney from which the sweep had emerged.

If he could but get into another house he might have a good enough chance of escape.

But he did not, on inspection, at all like the look of the chimney. It was a tall, thin one, and the sweep, who had come up it and had now disappeared by the other, he remembered, was, though, doubtless, lithe and active enough, something of the same build.

There was a good deal more of Cartouche, and, though the active life he had led had kept down superfluous fat, his shoulders were broad and muscular.

He was, in fact, about two sizes larger than the chimney.

Here was a dilemma, not improved by the fact that he could tell from the noises below that the guard had found their way to the trap-door on the roof and were unbolting the latter.

A shout was heard in the street, and Cartouche, cautiously peering over, saw that a long ladder was also being brought towards the house.

"Well," said he to himself, "here goes ; I must make a try."

And he swung himself into the chimney ; but a few moments struggling showed him that was hopeless—it would be a useless attempt.

So he scrambled out again as well as he could, and with a speed born of dire necessity.

"Confound it," said he, "this a nice fix, but it would have been much worse to have got stuck there ; I should have been smothered. There is nothing else for it ; I must stand at bay and defy them."

At that instant several of the Civic Guards appeared on the roof, while the top of the ladder showed above the parapet.

The men, scrambling over the uneven roof, did not seem anxious to begin the fray.

One, bolder than the rest, approached Cartouche, who, quick as lightning, hurled him over the parapet in sight of the surging mob below.

He would give no further trouble.

A second raised his carbine, fired, and missed.

"A bad shot, my friend," calmly remarked Cartouche, as he sent him flying through a skylight on the roof ; "that's a better one !"

Had the Guard and the others arrived one by one, or, for that matter, two by two, it is probable that Cartouche would have held his own.

But now they swarmed on the roof, on the parapet, up the ladder, most of them still giving the distinguished robber a wide berth.

He was unarmed ; he had come on a very different errand—to see Louise.

Now there was a shout in the street ; it announced the arrival of the Musqueteers.

Cartouche began, for once, to see that he had better bow to destiny. He folded his arms with a grim smile, and one by one the men, who had been so cowardly before, regained their courage and sidled up towards him.

At this juncture the Count d'Aubarne, the Colonel of Musqueteers, with a detachment of his men, sprang on to the roof, and the affair was for the time ended.

There was a short struggle, and then Cartouche found himself pinioned.

The count, in spite of having been tricked and robbed and then impersonated, had a secret admiration for the bold and daring robber.

He stepped forward and said, with something approaching a smile—

"At last, Cartouche, I suppose even you'll admit that we've got you? You are our prisoner."

"Well," answered Cartouche, with the most perfect assumption of indifference, "I suppose I must. But who and where is the scoundrel who betrayed me?"

A shambling, sneaking figure, who had just before run up the stairs and emerged on the roof, came forward. It was Red Judas.

"It was I, most unworthy captain. I told you, Monsieur Cartouche, that you had made an enemy of Red Judas. This is how I return your many compliments!"

"Faugh!" said Cartouche, "take that reptile away. I defy him and the lot of you! The prison is not yet built that can hold me!"

CHAPTER XXII.

STRANGE DISAPPEARANCES.

ABOUT this time terror spread itself through Paris in consequence of the extraordinary disappearance of several persons. In the course of four months twenty-six young men, the youngest seventeen and the oldest twenty-five years of age, had been spirited away from their inconsolable families. The most extravagant and contradictory rumours were in circulation upon the subject.

Amongst other gossiping stories whispered about upon this subject it was pretended that a princess, who was suffering from a dangerous liver complaint, had been advised by some foreign charlatan, or quack doctor, to make use, from time to time, as a means of cure, of a bath of human blood, and that the unfortunate missing persons had been immolated for the purpose.

Another equally horrible surmise was that they had been made away with by the Jews, who, out of hatred and derision for our crucified Messiah, were accustomed to put Christians to death upon a cross. Fortunately for the poor Jews this latter opinion took no hold of the public mind.

Whatever the secret cause of these disappearances might have been, terror and desolation reigned in Paris. The Duke de Gevres having mentioned the fact to the king, his majesty sent for the lieutenant-general of police, and reproached him with suffering the existence of kidnapping, which, in all likelihood, he added, must have been followed by violent deaths, as none of those missing had ever been heard of afterwards. Monsieur Peuchet, in despair at the displeasure of his majesty, returned in a very bad humour to Paris, and sent immediately for one of his most experienced agents, named Lecoq, a man whose services on many difficult occasions he had good reason to value.

To him he made known the embarrassment in which he found himself, told him of the king's anger, and held out to him the prospect of so great a reward, that Lecoq, carried away by his cupidity, exclaimed—

"Ah, monsieur! I see that, in order to take you out of trouble, I must renew the sacrifice of Abraham. I ask you to allow me eight days, in which time I hope to give you a good account of the affair."

Lecoq said no more; and Monsieur Peuchet, who looked upon him as his best agent, dismissed him with a sign which gave him to understand that he had at his disposal all the resources of the police. At that time it was a custom in the police department to make use of mute signs on extraordinary occasions of this kind, the meaning of which was known only to the principal and most confidential agents.

Lecoq, who was not married, had a natural son, to whom he was greatly attached, and over whose conduct and education he carefully watched. This lad, called by his companions L'Eveillé, from the precociousness and sprightliness of his disposition, was gifted with no common intelligence. Though little more than sixteen years of age, Nature had not only given him reason beyond his years, but had also been prodigal to him of external gifts. Besides possessing a handsome face, he was tall, and so well and strongly formed that he looked more like a man of five-and-twenty than a youth of sixteen.

L'Eveillé obtained from his father all that could flatter the vanity of a young man, for his handsome person was always set off by costly and modish clothes. He, however, quitted the house but seldom, for the elder Lecoq knew but too well the danger to which handsome young men like his son were exposed in the streets of Paris.

Lecoq, on returning from his interview with Monsieur Peuchet, shut himself up with his son, and had a long conversation with him. In the afternoon of that day L'Eveillé was seen quitting the house alone, and splendidly dressed. Around his hat and suspended from his neck were gold chains; he wore two watches, and, from the chinking of his purse as he walked it was evident that it was filled with good broad pieces of gold coin. But what still more surprised the neighbours (for the profession of the elder Lecoq was unknown to them) was to see the handsome and finely-dressed L'Eveillé go and return home several times four consecutive days, without being accompanied, as had always been the case before, by his uncle (in reality his father) or some friend.

It has been already stated that L'Eveillé, besides the remarkable comeliness of his face and person, was endowed with a lively intellect, courage, prudence, and *savoir-faire*. The confidential conversation he had had with his father had awakened his ambition; and he easily understood that he might acquire both honour and profit should he succeed in discovering, for the lieutenant-general of police, the cause of the extraordinary disappearance of so many young persons.

Accordingly, in the rich dress befitting a young man of family, he walked about the streets, on the quays, in the gardens of the Tuileries and Luxembourg, and in the Salle des

Pas Perdus at the Palais de Justice, and in the galleries of that vast edifice, then a favourite haunt of the gay and idle amongst the Parisians.

Lecoq the elder had conjectured that the young men who had disappeared had been ensared to their ruin by the seductive charms of some frail beauty; and he foresaw that, by putting his son in the way to meet such a creature he exposed him likewise to a similar fate; but, reckoning upon his being forewarned, he hoped he might escape the snare that had proved fatal to so many others.

The fifth day, towards three o'clock in the afternoon, young Lecoq, in all the *eclat* of his fine clothes, was sauntering on the terrace of the garden of the Tuileries next the river, when a remarkably beautiful young woman passed close by him.

She was walking alone, but was followed at some distance by a kind of humble friend, or *gouvernante*.

She appeared to be about twenty-five years of age, was elegantly dressed, and had not only much of beauty in her face and shape, but a certain foreign grace or piquancy in her air and manner.

L'Eveillé gazed, or pretended to gaze, with great interest upon the fine form and striking features of the unknown fair one.

His glances were not thrown away, but were answered by timid and half-downcast looks.

He drew himself up, arranged the frill of his shirt, disposed in better order his lace ruffles—in a word, gave himself the airs of a man who had the presentiment of an adventure, hoping all the time that it was that for which he had his instructions already.

To make sure of this, he passed and repassed several times before the lady, and at length took a seat upon one of the benches of the labyrinth which then existed in front of the Champs Elyseés.

He had not been there many minutes, when he saw the friend, or *suivante*, of his beauty approach the spot where he was, and, after a few turns, seat herself on the same bench. He took off his hat, as was the custom, and soon after entered into conversation; and thinking the game already in his hands, he asked the *suivante* who the young lady was in whose service she appeared to be.

"Oh, sir," replied she, "the history of my mistress is almost a romance."

"A romance!" exclaimed L'Eveillé, "you interest me deeply—probably your mistress is——"

"Yes," replied the *suivante*, in a confidential tone, "you have guessed right; she is that interesting young person of whom all Paris is still talking; and, since you have so readily chanced upon her name, I will no longer conceal from you her history. You must know, my dear sir, that the father of my mistress was a rich Polish prince, who came to Paris *incognito*, and whilst there formed a connection with the daughter of a tradesman in the Rue St.

Denis; a child (my mistress) was the result of this connection. The prince quitted Paris, and never returned. It was said that he had been set upon by brigands and murdered. The King of Poland, however, having been made acquainted with the unworthy conduct of the prince, wished to repair, as far as in him lay, the evil he had done; and for that purpose sent a confidential agent to Paris. But, alas! before his arrival the mother of my mistress had died of a broken heart, and he found her infant orphan alone in the world. The King of Poland, on being informed of the circumstances, caused the child to be declared heiress of the vast wealth of the prince. Happy the man who shall call her his own!"

"Happy, indeed!" exclaimed L'Eveillé, "the man who could entertain even a hope of pleasing her," at the same time heaving a deep sigh.

"Ah, young man, to please you must sometimes dare——"

"To do what?" asked L'Eveillé.

"How should I know?—to be amiable."

"And how is that to be done?"

"Oh, you question me too closely; and, for an intelligent youth, as you appear to be, you ask singular questions. Adieu, monsieur!"

"One word more," cried L'Eveillé; "one word more, I conjure you."

The *suivante*, who had risen, sat down again. It was now L'Eveillé's turn to speak; and he told the old woman, with as much apparent ingenuousness as he could muster up, that he was the son of a wealthy physician of Mans, and that he had been sent to Paris to attend the courses of lectures at the university; and added—

"Here I have been for the last ten days, and, as you see, not ill provided, for my father is generous, having no other child but me; and, besides watches, chains, and rings, I have two hundred pistoles in my purse, and leisure and disposition to devote myself to the task of pleasing so charming a person as your mistress."

The old sorceress chuckled and smiled, with a mingled expression of pleasure and contemptuous pity.

She then took L'Eveillé by the hand, and said—

"You have entirely won my heart, and I feel a kind of motherly affection for you, of which I will give you a proof. Listen to me. You have not escaped my mistress's notice. She was struck with your person and manners, and desired me to find out who you were. I am charmed that her choice should have fallen on one so worthy of her. Station yourself this evening, a little before nightfall, in front of the principal door of the church of St. Germain l'Auxerrois. I will meet you there, and bring you, I have no doubt, good tidings. Take care to come well dressed, and with all your finery; for it might spoil all were you to appear before my mistress in the guise of a threadbare-coated, penniless student."

This being settled, they separated, L'Eveillé,

in his joy, scarcely touched the ground along which he hurried home, as he felt convinced that he had discovered the decoy that had lured so many young men to their ruin and untimely deaths.

On acquainting his father with what had taken place, Lecoq shared in the suspicions and hopes of his son ; but as the hour of trial drew nigh paternal tenderness filled his heart with fear, and he trembled at the danger the young man was about to encounter. However, in order to diminish that danger as much as possible, he summoned a number of his most trusty police agents, to whom he briefly explained the nature of the service, and recommended them to keep close to his son, without, however, compromising by their too near approach the *coup de main* he was about to attempt. He himself was to walk at a short distance before them, resolved that, as far as in him lay, the expedition should not fail.

A little before nightfall L'Eveillé, still more richly dressed than in the morning, proceeded to the place appointed. The church-doors were about being closed, when an old woman, meanly clad, and with her face nearly concealed under a hood, emerged from the church ; and, after throwing a furtive glance about her, recognised L'Eveillé, and made him a sign to approach her.

"I should never have known you," cried L'Eveillé. "What a strange figure you have made of yourself !"

"Oh, it is a necessary precaution, my son, in order to escape the eyes of the numerous adorers of my mistress, who, hoping to gain me to their interests, beset me whenever they see me in the streets. Let us hurry on ; but first put this bandage on your eyes. This is a delicate attention shown by our Parisian gallants to their mistresses, and with which I know Mademoiselle Jaborouski (for so my mistress is called) will be not a little pleased, and will reward you for it."

"No, by my faith !" replied L'Eveillé, "I shall not bandage my eyes. My father expressly forbid me ever to do so."

"Well, then, let us proceed," said the old woman, "without it, since your papa has forbidden you. I shall explain that to mademoiselle."

They walked forward, the old woman a few paces in advance of L'Eveillé, and the police agents following at a cautious distance. They traversed the Rue de l'Arbresec, de la Monnaie, and after various windings, at length stopped in the Rue des Orfèvres, not the least hideous street of that infected and black, mud-covered quarter of Paris. There, near the chapel of St. Éloi, and opposite a tolerably good-looking house, the old woman halted, and said—

"My dear sir, my mistress does not reside in this poor place, but the house belongs to her, and it was her wish to receive you here first. I shall go up and let her know that you are here."

The old demoness entered the house, leaving L'Eveillé at the door.

His father, to encourage him, though he trembled himself, crossed the street and squeezed his hand. He had scarcely moved away when the old woman reappeared, and after again endeavouring, but in vain, to persuade L'Eveillé to let his eyes be bandaged, conducted him into the fatal house.

L'Eveillé, though armed, felt no little misgivings and fears of being attacked as he followed his faithless guide in utter darkness, through a long passage, and up some flights of stairs. However, he met with no obstacle of the kind, and was, after some time, ushered into a room lighted with wax tapers, and richly furnished.

At one end of the room, upon a crimson-coloured sofa, fringed with gold lace, reclined, in a most seductive deshabille, the daughter of the Polish prince, Mademoiselle Jaborouski.

At the sight of the stranger her hand, sparkling with brilliants, readjusted over her half-disclosed bosom the two open folds of her robe, and after saluting her visitor with a welcome smile she made a signal to her duenna to retire.

The young man, forgetful for the moment of the object of his mission, felt as if under the spell of enchantment, and, fascinated by the beautiful person before him, he had scarcely power to speak or move. She, seeing his embarrassment, arose from the sofa and held out her hand, which he eagerly kissed.

This served to put more completely to flight his presence of mind ; and, though conscious of the infamous and dangerous nature of the place where he was, he could not resist taking a seat on the sofa near so charming an object.

The elder Lecoq, who, with the police agents, were impatiently waiting in the street, not hearing the signal agreed upon with his son, put a whistle to his mouth and blew it loudly.

The shrill sound reached the ears of young Lecoq, and put his illusions instantly to flight. He started from the sofa, and the siren, under whose fascination he had been, under pretence of giving directions to her old *suivante*, went into an adjoining chamber.

L'Eveillé, profiting by her absence, made an inspection of the room, in one corner of which stood what appeared to be a kind of Indian screen.

Wishing to see what was behind this he endeavoured to close up its folds, but finding them immovable, he shook them with some violence, when he heard a click, like that of a spring giving way, and one of the folds descended into the floor, and left unmasked a deep and ample recess or cupboard, upon the shelves of which were ranged twenty-six silver dishes, and in each a human head, the flesh of which had been preserved by some embalming process.

A stifled cry of horror burst from the youth's lips, which but a moment before had been breathing accents of admiration and passion. But his agony of terror was still further increased when, looking towards one of the windows of the room, he thought he saw several other cadaverous faces fixing upon him through the panes their glazed but fiery glance.

"I TOLD YOU I WOULD KILL YOU, AND I HAVE KEPT MY WORD," SAID CARTOUCHE.

He grasped at the back of a chair to keep him from falling, his hair stood on end, drops of cold perspiration covered his forehead, his cheeks became paler and more livid than the faces of the dead that confronted him, and his nerves at length giving way, he sunk upon his knees and clasped his hands in a delirium of terror and despair.

At this moment the window was burst in, and his father, followed by the police agents, jumped into the apartment, for the elder Lecoq, alarmed by the silence of his son, and dreading that he might be assassinated, had bravely mounted to the assault of the house, which he was enabled to do by means of ladders, which the agents procured from a neighbouring house-builder's yard.

This fortunate and daring act of Lecoq's did, in fact, save his son's life, for immediately after the noise made by Lecoq and the police agents breaking into the apartment, Mademoiselle Jaborouski, followed by four armed ruffians, rushed from the adjoining chamber; but the police agents being superior in number, and equally well armed, resistance was in vain, and the fair murderess and her four accomplices were secured, and after being manacled were carried off to prison.

A close examination of the house led to no other discovery worth noticing, and inquiry proved the lady to be a most profligate Englishwoman—a modern Messalina. She lent herself to serve as a decoy, by means of which young men who had the appearance of wealth were lured to the den where young Lecoq had had so miraculous an escape. There they were murdered, and their heads separated from their bodies.

The latter were disposed of to the surgical students for anatomical purposes; and the heads, after being dried and embalmed, were kept until a safe opportunity offered of sending them to Germany, where a high price was given for them by the secret amateurs of science—then in its infancy, but which has since made some noise in the world under the name of phrenology.

The Government, dreading the effect on the minds of the people likely to be produced by a public exposure of these numerous and atrocious murders, took measures for the prompt but secret punishment of the culprits. The four robbers were hanged and their female accomplice was also sentenced to death; but destiny ordained otherwise.

The Chevalier de Lorraine, the Marquis de Louvois, and the Chancellor of France happened to be present in the Marchioness de Montespan's apartment whilst the king was relating to her and the Duke of Orleans, his brother, the adventure of young Lecoq, who had been rewarded with a considerable sum of money and a lucrative place.

The marchioness expressed great horror at the profligacy and cruelty of Lady Guilfort (which title, like that of Jaborouski, was one of the many names assumed by the Englishwoman,

her real name having never been discovered), and asked the king if the execution of so base and fiendish a creature should soon take place? Louis replied that the law would take its course, and then changed the conversation.

Soon after the Duke of Orleans and the Chevalier de Lorraine took their leave. After quitting the apartment the chevalier said to his royal highness—

"This Englishwoman must be a rare piece of womanhood; suppose we have her to sup with us?"

The prince cried out, "Shame! shame!" but the very extravagance of the proposal pleased him; and on the favourite renewing his entreaties, he consented.

The Englishwoman being confined in the Bastille, a blank *lettre de cachet* was procured and filled up with an order to the governor to deliver to the care of the bearer Lady Guilfort for the purpose of her *being transferred to the prison of Pignerol*. The governor of the Bastile, deceived by this false warrant, delivered up the prisoner.

Lady Guilfort, who supposed that her removal from the Bastille was only for the purpose of being taken to the Conciergerie, preparatory to her execution, soon perceived, however, that the carriage took the direction of one of the barriers of Paris, after quitting which, and at the end of a two-hours' drive, it stopped.

A kind of equerry came and opened the door, offered her his hand to descend, and, after passing through a long corridor and up some flights of stairs, ushered her into a brilliant and well-lighted apartment. A well-heaped fire of logs was blazing in the chimney, and nothing about the room wore the appearance of a prison.

After the interval of a few minutes three gentlemen entered the room. Though plainly dressed it was evident, from their air and manner, that they were persons of high rank. One of them, immediately on entering, put an opera-glass to his eye, and examined with haughty curiosity Lady Guilfort; the two others threw themselves into arm-chairs. Lady Guilfort, after the first surprise was over, had no difficulty in recognising in the persons before her the king's brother, the Duke of Orleans, the Chevalier de Lorraine, and the Marquis d'Effiat. She quickly conceived the motives which led to her being brought into their presence, and though, under other circumstances, she would have willingly joined in the wildest orgies with the persons in whose company she then found herself, yet the recollection of her dungeon in the Bastille, and the terrible death impending over her, left her no thought but that of making her escape.

Seeming to enter into the spirit of the adventure, she exerted all her powers of fascination, and soon made captive to her seductive influence the Chevalier de Lorraine and the Marquis d'Effiat.

But the Duke of Orleans, never a great admirer of the fair sex, and who could not vanquish his horror of the Englishwoman, tired before long of the scene; and bethinking himself that the gratification of his curiosity might be too dearly purchased by the risk of the king's displeasure should the circumstance meet his Majesty's ears, and having refused to stay for supper, was conducted by the Chevalier de Lorraine and the Marquis d'Effiat to his apartment; for this scene took place in the palace of Versailles and in the lodgings of the Marquis de Lafare, the use of which he had given to the Chevalier de Lorraine for twenty-four hours.

The two gentlemen, after returning to the room where Lady Guilfort was, sat down with her to a *petit souper*.

The most exuberant gaiety, and not the most refined gallantry, was the order of the night. At the close of a supper which had been prolonged into the small hours of the morning Lady Guilfort on a sudden rose up, and, taking up a taper, made her lowest courtesy, and wished the gentlemen good-night. She then quitted the room.

Soon after the two gentlemen moved off to their respective chambers, when Lady Guilfort silently locked the doors of their apartments, and hurried back to the supper-room, where, tying together the table-cloths and napkins, she fastened one end of this *impromptu* rope to the balcony, and, by means of it, let herself down into the park, where she lay concealed until the gates were opened in the morning.

She then slipped out, and, hurrying into the town of Versailles, took the first vehicle that offered, and arrived in Paris before the two imprisoned admirers were released from durance, as they dared not during the night make a noise in the palace by calling or ringing for the servants, to have the doors of the rooms in which they were locked up forced open, lest it might lead to the discovery of their participation in the criminal trick played off upon the governor of the Bastille, and the consequent escape of Lady Guilfort.

CHAPTER XXIII.

HOW CARTOUCHE ESCAPED.

THE police of Paris were almost mad with joy. They had captured the notorious Cartouche and secured also the mysterious Polish princess, or English lady, who had caused the death of so many young and wealthy members of the best society.

The police did not sing "*Te Deum laudamus*" in the cathedral of Notre Dame because they preferred to praise themselves; but they held a big drink at a café situated in a street at the back of Monsieur Peuchet's headquarters. Young Lecoq was there spending his money freely, and those who captured Cartouche had obtained something on account of the reward, so there was plenty of wine and brandy.

Madame Lafarge was drinking by herself in her lodgings to drown her disappointment at not getting the reward, and Louise was taking something a little stronger than water to console her

for the loss of her beloved Louis Dominique. And Can-can, who sat with Louise that night, drank just to set her friend a good example. Tomasso, Gribichon, and the Wolf drank—their toast being—

"Death and confusion to the police, who have taken our captain!"

In fact, all Paris was taking its liquor freely that evening.

At the café behind Monsieur Peuchet's office the president of the evening was Lecoq senior, who, having seen that all present had their glasses filled, said—

"Gentlemen, we will drink to the speedy execution of Monsieur Louis Dominique Cartouche and the Lady Guilfort. They both baffled us for a long time, but now they are caught, safely caged, and they cannot possibly escape. So here is to their speedy elevation on a lofty gallows!"

Hanging, or breaking on the wheel was then the mode of capital punishment in France. Beheading did not come in vogue till after the reat Revolution.

The police drank the toast.

"They can't escape!" said all those who were most intimate with Parisian prison interiors; but—they were both free at that moment.

Just about the time they drank that toast one of the criminal judges entered the cell where Cartouche was heavily ironed.

With the judge came the Count d'Aubarne, Bobilet, and Red Judas, whose treachery had been rewarded by his instant appointment to the position of second gaoler in that prison. And an infamous scoundrel he looked, with his bunch of big keys dangling at his girdle. Half a dozen soldiers with muskets and fixed bayonets blocked the doorway.

Cartouche was seated on his little table, holding up his heavy fetters so that they should inconvenience him as little as possible, when the judge entered.

"What now? Can you not let me rest?" the prisoner asked.

"Listen, Louis Dominique Cartouche; "you, having been found guilty of divers crimes against the law of the realm and acts of violence and murder upon the persons of several of his Majesty's subjects, have been condemned to death by the judges of the Civil Court whose names are here set forth——

"Never mind the details, don't trouble yourself about the solemn old owls who slept comfortably through the evidence, and only woke in time to sign that death warrant. It a joke! I shall see some of them before long."

"You will die in the morning."

"Nothing of the kind. I shall be walking off with some of their plate and jewellery in a few hours."

"I have done my duty in giving you warning, and now I leave you to prepare for death. Will you have a minister of religion to attend you?"

"No—send me a good dinner and a bottle of wine."

The judge gave a shrug of his shoulders and walked out, scandalised at the flippant conduct of the prisoner.

Bobilet, who had been looking on quietly while the judge was speaking, turned to the Count d'Aubarne, and said—

"Well, he is a cool fellow. When he is to be hanged in six hours he talks as quietly of a bottle of wine and a dinner as if he was going to be married!"

"A good idea, friend Bobilet," said Cartouche. "I will go through that ceremony to-morrow."

"Take my advice and don't. I am a married man myself, and I should think hanging is rather less painful."

The Count d'Aubarne came forward.

"Well, Cartouche, you see I have got back my ring! When do you think you will get it again?"

"Why, count, as I am to be married to-morrow, Wednesday, I cannot possibly attend to you before Thursday; but I can promise that you will miss that ring by Friday evening."

"You are a fool! Well, I leave you to prepare for your death. You are to be executed an hour after sunrise."

"You speak wildly, count. The hemp is not sown, grown, or twisted that can hang Cartouche."

"It is, though, noble captain!" exclaimed Red Judas. "I swore I would see you hanged, and I shall be present to-morrow when you dance upon nothing."

"Judas, you have often perjured yourself, and you have once again taken a false oath—you will never live to see me hanged."

"Why should I not live to see you dangle in the air? I am in good health."

"Because I have sworn that I will kill you—and I never broke such a vow as that—nor shall I begin perjuring myself to let you live."

"It will be bad for you if he escapes," Monsieur Bobilet whispered to Red Judas.

"How can he escape? These walls are of solid masonry five feet thick. Look at the bars before the window—see that door cased with iron; and then remember that there are five others equally strong, and outside all a wall thirty feet high, and then tell me how he can escape."

"I will escape, though!" Cartouche exclaimed.

"If you succeed I will give you my life."

"That is a bargain, Judas. Either I am hanged an hour after sunrise or you die within twenty-four hours of the time appointed for my execution."

"Bah! you can't frighten me, Cartouche. Just look at your irons and consider how you will get out of them in the first place."

"They are very pretty ornaments, certainly; but I will outwit you yet, Judas, you creeping, venomous worm, and when you die, which will be soon, the fiends of hell will hesitate to associate with such a wretch."

"Get out of this gaol if you can," said Judas.

Then the rascal carefully examined the irons that had been fitted to Cartouche's wrists and legs.

"All right, eh?" said the prisoner. "Then give me some paper and a pen and ink, that I may make my will."

"It's against the governor's orders. You are not to be allowed the use of pen, ink, or paper."

"I call that very cruel. However, if I am debarred from those luxuries you must let me have some brandy."

"I'll get you some brandy from my place, Cartouche. I have some capital stuff in my cellar," said Bobilet.

"That is against orders too. The prisoner is to have bread and water only."

And Judas brought forward a very stale loaf and a jug of not very pure water, both of which Cartouche threw at his gaoler, the loaf hitting him on the eye, while the jug narrowly escaped fracturing his skull.

"Now, Monsieur Bobilet, how about that brandy?" said Cartouche.

"An excellent idea; a little drop would be a good thing for you, Judas. Won't you go and buy some?"

"Yes," replied Judas.

Bobilet drew a purse out of his breeches pocket, but, suddenly changing his mind, he said—

"On second thoughts I had better go and get some of my own. I am certain there is none better in Paris."

Dropping the purse into the side pocket of his coat he turned towards the door, when Judas, unable to put off his old habits, adroitly filched the pouch, without the jingle of a coin being heard.

But Cartouche saw the action, and resolved to have that purse.

He had been deprived of everything by the police, and knew how necessary it was to have some money to spend as soon as he should find himself outside the prison walls. He did not at the moment know how he was to get out, but he thought it could and would be managed in some way.

Cartouche accordingly, while Judas was watching the retreating figure of Bobilet, gave his chains a good rattling shake, and the new gaoler turned round hastily, thinking the prisoner had perhaps contrived to slip out of his irons in some extraordinary manner.

Judas knelt down by the side of his former chief and again carefully examined every link. While so engaged Cartouche, without difficulty, relieved him of the purse he had just stolen from Bobilet.

"Are the irons right, Judas?" the prisoner asked.

"Yes, and I shall see you hanged in less than twelve hours. The people are already gathering in the Place de Greve to see the fun."

"They will be disappointed. But you,

Judas, had better buy yourself a coffin at once. You will need it before forty-eight hours have passed; but you may as well send for some wine—I'll pay for it."

And he produced the purse.

"Why, that is mine!" exclaimed Bobilet, who suddenly reappeared at the door. "I came back to look for it."

"Mine! Judas stole it from you and I took it from him—the thief!"

"What a den of villainy!" exclaimed Bobilet. "They will steal my teeth out of my head if I stay here!"

And he bolted from the cell just as the Count d'Aubarne reappeared in the doorway.

"All right and safe?" the count asked.

"Safe enough, your excellency. The spectators are already beginning to take up their places, and they will not be disappointed this time."

"They will be disappointed though," said Cartouche, "for I certainly don't mean to be hanged. Where shall we meet to-morrow evening, count? I have sworn to have that ring again, and Judas knows I always keep my oaths!"

"Bah!" exclaimed Judas, going out into the corridor along with the count, as they both heard some noise outside the cell.

A few minutes later Judas returned with a loaf of bread, which he handed to Cartouche, saying—

"Here's something to eat which the governor has allowed to pass in to you, and a bottle of wine which that ass, Bobilet, has been fool enough to pay for."

"Thanks, Judas. But I must keep my oath, and kill you."

"Your brain is certainly turned. Good-night."

When the door of the cell was closed Cartouche tore open the loaf, and took from the inside a note from Gribichon, which ran—

"DEAR CAPTAIN,—We are outside waiting for you, so just write a note with your instructions as to what we are to do. Put your note in the Count d'Aubarne's hat; he has sworn to visit the prison every hour during the night and report to one of his ladies, who thinks she is going to see you hanged, that you are safe. Put the note in his hat and we will soon have it."

Cartouche ate some of the bread and drank some of the wine. In the loaf he also found some paper, a pencil, and a small bottle, which, from the smell, he knew contained laudanum.

"Good Gribichon; but why not have put in a file or two?"

He sat quietly enough till he heard footsteps in the gallery outside, which, he had no doubt, were those of the Count d'Aubarne, coming in fulfilment of his threat to pay a visit every hour till the time of execution.

He was correct in his guess. It was the count, this time without Judas, who had entrusted him with the key of the cell.

"Writing a letter, Cartouche? What folly."

"I am writing to my friends outside to tell them when to expect me," the prisoner replied.

"You are certainly mad. How can you send out a letter?"

"I may persuade you to take it."

"Mad as can be," said the count.

In the meantime Cartouche, having finished his writing, folded it and rose to his feet.

He had sufficient length of chain to let him move a yard or more, but not to touch the wall.

"Having finished my writing, and since you are determined to hang me, I suppose I ought to rehearse my last dying speech and confession. I come on the scaffold and bow thus—— Stay, that will not do! Count, will you honour me with the loan of your chapeau for a minute? I must have a hat in my hand when I make my last bow to the public."

The count, anxious to see how far Cartouche could go in eccentricity, handed him his hat.

"And I bow thus—once to those in front, once to those behind, once to those on the right, and once to those on the left."

During this piece of stage business the prisoner contrived to place the note inside the lining of the count's hat, which he then returned.

"A thousand thanks! And now I address the people. 'Kind Christian friends who have come hither to see me die——'"

"I am afraid you are but ill-prepared for death."

"Then, count, will you do me the favour to send in a priest? Father Lorraine, who lives on the other side of the street, is a splendid hand at sending sinners to heaven."

"If his administrations will be of any use I certainly will."

"They will be of the greatest service. Thanks!"

The count departed, and Cartouche chuckled.

Anxious to save a poor sinner's soul, the count left the cell and walked out of the prison, where many people were assembled; but he was scarcely a yard from the door when his hat was snatched from his head by the Wolf, who handed it to Tomasso, who passed it to the Ferret, who ran with it to Gribichon, who was not many yards off.

Gribichon's nimble fingers soon found the paper inside the lining, and, beckoning the Wolf to follow him, he walked away.

The count, however, procured a new hat and followed up his threat of visiting the prisoner every hour.

It wanted but three hours of the time fixed for the prisoner's execution when he entered the cell to say that he was unable to find the Father Lorraine Cartouche had spoken of. And he had scarcely disgorged himself of that message when Judas entered, saying—

"Visitors for the prisoner. A lady of title and her black servant; but they can only remain one hour."

And there entered to the prisoner Gribichon, very nicely got up in brocaded petticoats, and the Wolf, who had blacked his face, and in the guise of a negro page-boy was holding his companion's train.

The Count d'Aubarne had some sense of delicacy left, and retired to the remotest corner of the cell.

Then Gribichon said—

"My poor boy, why did you not take my advice—the advice of your poor aunt—and avoid these evil courses which have brought you to the gallows."

"I am not on the scaffold yet, aunt."

"But you will be soon," said the count. "Hark! there is the bell tolling for the funeral service."

"And they won't bury me," said Cartouche, in low tones.

"Oh! oh! oh!" sobbed the pretended lady. "Why did you leave your aunt and your affectionate parents to begin a career of crime, which has landed you in this damnable—detestable, I mean—predicament. It is enough to break the heart of a parish pump. Hold my tails up, Pompey."

Pompey obeyed literally, and exhibited so much of Gribichon's calves that the count at once cried out—

"There is something wrong here! This is no woman!"

"Nonsense! What, do you doubt my sex?"

"Most certainly I do!"

"Count, you have made a good guess," said Cartouche, in low tones. "This is one of my most devoted friends, who has come at the risk of his own life to bid me adieu before they send me to the next world. You will not betray him?"

"Certainly not," responded the count.

"And you won't refuse to drink to 'my escape from a life of crime,' whether it's to another world or remain in this?"

"I will drink that toast with pleasure. I wish you well in this world or well out of it. And here is to your speedy reformation!"

The count seized a goblet, quite unaware that Leopold Dominique Cartouche had just put about half an ounce of laudanum into the flask.

And the result was that when the young nobleman drank the wine he was suddenly seized with a great inclination to go to sleep, and promptly availed himself of a quiet corner in the cell, where he coiled himself up for a jolly good nap.

"Now, then, Gribichon, what have you for me?"

"A couple of the sharpest files in Paris, so that you may cut through the irons, and two pair of your old pistols. Also fifty feet of rope, with a hook at the end."

"Hand them over."

Gribichon at once delivered up the articles to his chief, who had scarcely secreted them about his person when Judas entered, shouting—

"Now, then, all visitors except the most noble Count d'Aubarne must leave. It is the governor's order that the prisoner shall remain undisturbed for two hours previous to his execution in order that he may have leisure to repent."

"Go, my dear aunt—leave me!" said Cartouche.

"Nephew, I trust we shall meet in another and a better world," responded Gribichon, as he walked out of the condemned cell, with the Wolf acting as train-bearer.

"We shall meet on the scaffold, Cartouche," said Judas.

"You lie, scoundrel! I shall not be there."

"I shall, perhaps, have to carry you, but that does not matter. I shall have the pleasure of seeing you dangle at the end of a rope. Make the most of your two hours, for I shall be very punctual in fetching you out to the place of execution."

Cartouche made no reply, and Judas went out, locking the door, quite oblivious of the fact that the Count d'Aubarne was fast asleep in one corner of the cell.

"Now for it!" said Cartouche, as soon as he was alone. His hands were as thin as a woman's, and he at once slipped them through the bracelets. Then a few strokes of the file cut the manacles from his legs, and he stood erect and unfettered.

"Now for the window!" said he. "These tattling fools have told me which way to go, and thus I take my leave of this prison, which was not built to hold me."

Gribichon had put a crowbar in two parts, along with the file and the cord. One wrench took away one of the iron guards from the window, a second pull made sufficient space for him to pass through. The ground was only twenty-five feet beneath, so instead of hooking the rope on to the remaining bar, he simply passed one end round and went down the doubled cord.

Thus he was able, after crossing a courtyard, to throw the hook of the rope up on the top of the outer wall, where it caught, and he swarmed up hand over hand.

Judas told a lie when he said there were three walls to be crossed by any person trying to escape; he found only one, and having easily scaled that he was at liberty. And when Judas opened the door to lead out the prisoner to execution he could only find the count.

Cartouche ought to have been executed at seven o'clock in the morning; at eight p.m. the sightseers in the Place de Greve were informed that Cartouche had escaped, and just about the same time Red Judas was kicked out of his situation.

What should Judas do?

It was a delicate question rather, for now that Cartouche had escaped the traitor knew that his own life was in danger. Worst of all, he knew not from what quarter the blow might be struck.

Judas walked into two or three wine-shops to aid his brain with a little stimulant, but he soon found that would not do, for it was necessary to keep his head clear. Presently he went into a restaurant to get some food, when the waiter said—

"There are two gentlemen upstairs, mon-

CARTOUCHE,
THE FRENCH JACK SHEPPARD.

"I LOVE YOU, AND YOU ONLY," SAID CARTOUCHE.

sieur, who would be glad if you would honour them with your company. They want to know all about this villain Cartouche."

Judas was always glad to eat and drink at other people's expense, and snapped at the bait.

He walked upstairs into a room, and he had no sooner entered than he heard a sound as though someone was locking the door upon him. He looked round and saw Tomasso in the act of putting the key into his pocket, while Cartouche stood by with a couple of rapiers under his arm.

"I told you I should kill you within forty-eight hours, but I did not think I should have that pleasure within so short a space. I could have stabbed you as you entered the room had I chosen; but, reptile as you are, I will give you a chance. Take one of these swords and defend yourself."

"But there are no seconds! This is not a fair duel," Judas moaned.

"It is fair enough for you."

"And with permission, messieurs, I will act as second for both parties," said Tomasso, drawing his sword and resting the point of it on the ground. "Off with your coats, gentleman and scoundrel; one of you answers to the latter name and keeps his coat on, but Cartouche, who in this affair has acted as a man of honour, is already in his shirt-sleeves. Off with your coat, Judas; we want to sell it when you are killed, so Cartouche doesn't like to spoil the price by making holes in it and soiling it by your muddy blood."

Judas saw that he was in the hands of his foes.

"If I should win in this passage of arms shall I be allowed to pass out of the house?"

"Yes. Let him go if he can vanquish me, Tomasso."

"I will," said the Corsican.

Judas pulled off his coat and took his choice of the two rapiers.

"*En garde!*" shouted Tomasso. And the blades clashed together.

Red Judas in the course of his lawless career had picked up a pretty good notion of fencing; but he was no match for Cartouche, who said—

"I shall only lunge three times at you. One!"

A thrust *in quarte*, which Judas parried.

"Two!"

That was rather more difficult—but still Judas put it aside, and began to hope that after all he might stand a little chance, although the odds were fearfully against him.

In avoiding Cartouche's attack the rascal had retreated till he now found himself close to a door between that room and the next, and he had not space enough to defend himself, when Cartouche shouted out—

"Three!"

Judas felt something, and dropped his sword to the ground. Cartouche's rapier had passed right through the scoundrel's body, and he was pinned against the door.

"*Mort bleu!*" groaned Judas.

"A blue death for you, but a more respectable one than you deserved. I told you I should kill you, and I think I have kept my word. Are you dead yet?"

Judas was too far gone to answer the question, but Tomasso said—

"I think so, captain, and now we had better go."

Cartouche, with some difficulty, withdrew his rapier from the door and the body of Judas, who fell dead.

"Now then, away," said Tomasso.

The Corsican had been loitering about the prison when Cartouche effected his escape, and had brought him to that restaurant where neither of them were known. But now that a fatal duel had taken place on the premises it was necessary to run away at once. So they went.

CHAPTER XXIV.

LADY GUILFORT'S PLOT TO MURDER LECOQ.

ON arriving at Paris Lady Guilfort hastened to the Rue Plat d'Etain, where, in an obscure and miserable-looking house, but admirably contrived inside for the purpose of concealment, lived one of the chief agents of the band of malefactors with whom she was connected. There, after explaining to her accomplice the means by which she had recovered her liberty, she found a secure asylum.

In a little time, aided by this villain, Lady Guilfort organised a new troop of bandits upon whom she could reckon.

She, as chief of the association, planned the expeditions, appointed to each the part he was to play, partitioned the booty, and, at times, took a personal part in the expedition. The individual in whose house she had taken refuge was named lieutenant of the troop.

As it was no longer possible to allure victims to the den by means of Lady Guilfort's personal attractions, the efforts of the band were principally confined to house robberies; but murders were avoided, unless where they became necessary to the safety of the robbers.

Besides, the feeling of hatred arising from the loss of four of the troop, including the captain, and the diminution of their gains effected by young Lecoq's interference, Lady Guilfort nourished a deep desire of personal vengeance against him for having been duped by him, and resorted to the following stratagem to gratify that feeling.

Young Lecoq, enriched by the bounty of the king, and possessed of a lucrative place, led a regular life, undisturbed by any fears of Lady Guilfort's vengeance, he supposing her to be dead; when, one day, a grave-looking and respectably-dressed man called upon him, and after requiring a promise of secrecy with regard to what he should tell him, asked if he should like to be put in the way of detecting a set of smugglers, who carried on an extensive trade between Belgium and Paris, in Brussels lace and other prohibited goods.

Lecoq, whose ruling passion was avarice, eagerly accepted the offer, and agreed to the terms proposed. His informant was to point out Lecoq as a sure agent, to whose house the smugglers might consign their bales and cases of contraband merchandise.

Ten or twelve days after the conclusion of this bargain a cart stopped at Lecoq's door, and from it were taken two large wooden cases, which, according to Lecoq's orders, were placed in a store-room on the ground-floor of his house. The carter, after in vain searching his pockets for the keys, said that he must have left them at the stage where he had stopped the night before; but that he would return thither, and bring them to Lecoq the next morning.

From some over-acting on this man's part, and from observing that these cases were perforated in seven or eight places with small holes, Lecoq had his suspicions awakened. He communicated his doubts to a friend of his, a courageous and resolute young fellow; and in the evening, when everything was quiet in the house, they both, armed with pistols, took their posts near the door of the store-room, which had been left purposely unclosed.

They had been for a considerable time on the watch; and Lecoq's friend, getting impatient, was about abandoning his post, when an indistinct noise from that part of the store-room where the cases were placed struck their ears.

They redoubled their attention—the noise increased; and they were soon able to ascertain that it came from the cases.

Lecoq squeezed his friend's hand—the signal was understood—they both cocked their pistols.

" John," said a voice in the lowest possible whisper, " are you there ?"

" Yes."

" We appear to be alone in the house. Let us breathe a little air ; for I am stifled in this cursed box. We can lie down again when the people of the house come back."

" Do you think they have any suspicion ?"

" Not the least ; with all his cunning Lecoq is blinded by his avarice ; the Englishwoman judged him rightly, and to-night, at twelve, she may satisfy her vengeance in the heart's blood of the infamous *mouchard* (police spy)."

" Fire !" cried Lecoq, at the same time discharging his pistol in the direction of the cases.

His friend did the same, and the explosion was followed by a double cry of agony—the balls had taken effect.

Lecoq ran into an adjoining room, where he had placed a lighted lamp in a cupboard, and bringing it with him into the store-room, he and his friend saw the robbers stretched at the bottom of the cases, one dead, and the other having his thigh broken.

The noise of the firearms brought several of the neighbours and the patrol to the house.

This circumstance greatly annoyed Lecoq, as the public rumour of the discovery of the two robbers would, if it reached the ears of any of the band, prevent them from keeping their engagement for midnight.

Lecoq now endeavoured to repair as much as possible the evil he had wrought in using fire-arms, by enjoining silence on those who entered the house.

He also informed the lieutenant-general of the police, who sent him a company of soldiers disguised, and who came to the house only one by one, where they were conveniently posted for the reception of the robbers.

It had scarcely struck midnight when the noise of several feet was heard approaching, and soon after they stopped opposite the door of the house, whilst at the same time five knocks were given upon one of the panes of the window of the store-room.

The door, after a moments' delay, was cautiously half opened, and four men successively entered, followed by another figure in female attire.

The door was then slammed-to violently, a slight whistle was blown, and instantly numerous torches and tapers were brought from the adjoining rooms, which lighted up the hall, and exhibited to the stupefied banditti the muskets of thirty soldiers levelled at them.

In despair they dropped their arms, and were seized, bound, and carried off to prison. Before their departure Lecoq went up to the female figure, and, putting a lamp to her face, beheld features totally unknown to him. The woman was not Lady Guilfort. Lecoq's disappointment and astonishment were extreme.

The next day, however, he received a note, which in some measure cleared up the mystery. This note, which exists in the archives of the police, was brought to him by a porter, who said it had been given to him by a lady in a thick veil.

The contents were as follows :—

" Tremble ! One of us must perish. Yesterday I was near your house, when the impatience of my two agents rendered my plan abortive ; but wishing to revenge myself on the new captain of our troop, and the unworthy rival he has preferred to me, I did not warn him of the fate of our advanced guard, but allowed him to proceed on the expedition, knowing that he would thereby become your and the police's prey. I have succeeded, and they will now expiate the scorn they treated me with. You may judge from this that my vengeance knows how to reach those that incur it. It is your turn next, young fanfaron, who imagine that you are secure from my blows by having made yourself a *mouchard*, when at best you are good for nothing else than to be . . ."

After reading this letter, the conclusion of which is expressed in too energetic terms to be repeated to ears polite, the police-officer Lecoq swore quite enough to put himself on a level with the writer of the billet.

Old Peuchet, too—his book in which this affair is described is still in existence—was at his wits' end. To be baffled by Cartouche and this Englishwoman was too much.

" Send that Madame Lafarge to me !" he

said; and the mother of Louise was invited to visit Monsieur Peuchet without delay.

CHAPTER XXV.

HOW GRIBICHON ESCAPED—AND WAS CAUGHT.

GRIBICHON and the Wolf knew well enough that their share in the escape of Cartouche would bring the police upon their trail, so they resolved to separate for a time.

They remained in Paris long enough to hear the whole city in an uproar at the news of Cartouche's escape, and then went off into the country, each choosing a different route.

Louise was informed of their proceedings, and they promised to let her know, as well as they could, where they might be found, promising, moreover, to return to Paris the moment they heard that Cartouche had any need of their presence in the city.

Gribichon resolved to go to the west—the Wolf, therefore, had to go either north, south, or east.

Gribichon could not leave Paris without an interview with Can-can, the enchanting seller of sweet scents, whom he found in the act of preparing her simple breakfast.

Can-can seldom had more than two meals a day. Sometimes when trade was good she would treat herself to a glass of wine and a cake at mid-day; but, as a rule, it was a breakfast of coffee with bread and butter before starting in the morning, and such a supper as we have already seen her sharing with Gribichon.

"You here?" she exclaimed, as Gribichon entered.

"Yes, my charmer."

"You must not come so early any more. Why, I was in bed only an hour ago."

"Well, if I had only known that I would have——"

"Hush!" said Can-can, holding up her finger.

"What is the matter?" Gribichon asked.

"You must not talk nonsense. Now tell me what brings you here so early."

"The king wants me——"

"He always is wanting you it seems."

"I wish to heaven he didn't," said Gribichon. And Can-can went on to inquire—

"What does he want you for now?"

"I am to go to Cherbourg to construct a dockyard and arsenal from which he can send out fleets and armies to conquer those confounded English with whom our country has always been at war."

"Bravo! but you don't know how to make a dockyard. I saw them doing it at Toulon, and it took two thousand men nearly a couple of years to make it. If the king thinks you can make a dockyard while you live, why the king is a donkey!"

"Can-can, I know what you can do."

"What is that?"

"Make lovely coffee. It has a delicious scent."

"I does smell nice," said Can-can.

"You know things are very deceptive. I should really like to know if that coffee tastes as nice as it smells."

"You shall have a cup," was Can-can's cheerful reply.

Gribichon sipped the fragrant drink, then set down his cup and frowned horribly.

"What is the matter?"

"I have no doubt it is very good coffee, but unless I have some bread-and-butter to put my tasting powers in proper order I shall not be able to do justice to it."

"Help yourself," said Can-can, pushing a loaf about two feet long towards him.

Gribichon cut the loaf in halves and adroitly slipped one half into his coat pocket. Then he began to cut thick slices from the remaining half and crammed it into his mouth as fast as he could.

"Why, where is all the bread gone?" Can-can asked, she having had her back turned from the table for a few seconds.

"I have eaten it, my dear. This Parisian bread is nothing but wind in a fit, and I could eat forty of these French loaves with the greatest of ease."

"Well, don't eat it all, please. I want two slices."

And Can-can was eating with a good appetite, when there was a noise heard below, and she looked out of her window.

"The police!" she exclaimed.

"Then I must be off and make that dock-yard. I suppose the king is angry because I have not commenced yet, so I must make a beginning."

"Don't offend the king, so run away."

Gribichon ran away. On the stairs he encountered half a dozen police, but his charge was so impetuous that he burst through the party and was away in the street before they could stretch out a hand to arrest him.

But in a few seconds they recovered, and were after him in full cry.

Gribichon made for the nearest gate, but as he approached it he perceived that the warder was in the act of closing it in response to a signal given by a whistle which one of the police carried with him. The man was stooping down to do something with the socket into which the lower bolt should shoot, when Gribichon came flying along and took a leap over his shoulders, and in a moment was outside the city of Paris.

The police followed. Gribichon was perhaps more terrified than the occasion required; he kept on the main road for a league or more, still occasionally hearing the pursuers behind. Presently it occurred to him that if he kept on the causeway he would certainly be taken, so he resolved to go across country.

Crossing I don't know how many fields and heaths, and leaping a number of ditches which he found in his way, Gribichon arrived at the side of a wood, and was just going into it to conceal himself, when all of a sudden two men on horseback appeared before him, and called out—

"Who goes there?"

Gribichon's surprise prevented his making a very prompt response, so one of the horsemen rode up and shoved the muzzle of a pistol against Gribichon's head, and asked in low, but very distinct accents—

"Who are you?"

Gribichon told his name.

"Whence come you? What is your business in the forest?" the man asked.

"I don't know. I am running away from Paris," replied Can-can's sweetheart.

"Why run away from Paris? A smart young fellow like you ought to be able to get a living there."

"The king wants me to do too much work," replied Gribichon, who had an idea that his questioner was, like himself, beyond the pale of the law.

"What?"

"The young man means that he would be sent to the galleys if he was caught," said the second horseman.

"I am in no more danger of being chained to the oar than you are yourself."

Both the men laughed loudly, and the elder bared his chest, exhibiting the brand with which all felons were marked in those days.

"I have worked for the king, you see," he said.

"And I don't want to work for him."

"You will be safe enough with us, so come along to our den."

The other robber whispered to his confederate for a few seconds, and then the man who had done the greater part of the talking said—

"What have you done that you are wanted by the police? We must know something about you before we take you to our place."

"I have stolen snuff-boxes, watches, rings, and so forth."

"Bah! that is nothing."

"But I helped Cartouche to escape from prison."

"Bravo! then you are the Wolf?"

"Certainly not, monsieur."

"Then you must be Gribichon?"

"I have the honour to bear that name."

"You are wanted by the police, there is no doubt. There is a reward of fifty crowns for you—but we will not give you up, so you need not fear. But where is Cartouche?"

"I don't know," replied Gribichon.

"Well, come along. You need food and rest —you will be safe enough in our place."

The two men led the way into a part of the forest where the underwood was very thick. Presently they were obliged to dismount, and one of them whistled in a peculiar manner.

In response to this signal another man appeared, who took the horses and led them away.

"Follow us, and keep close, for you might easily get lost in this thicket," said the elder of the two men.

Gribichon thought that was very likely indeed, so he held on to the coat-tails of his guide, who at length paused before a tangled mass of brambles, into the midst of which he thrust his hand and drew up a rusty iron chain.

"Pull!" said he.

The three men pulled with all their might, and the bramble bush, which grew on a very steep slope, rolled aside, disclosing the narrow mouth of a cave.

"Do as I do," said the first robber.

Seating himself on the ground he slid down into the bowels of the earth out of Gribichon's sight.

"Now down you go," exclaimed the other man.

Gribichon seated himself as the first man had done, and launched himself into the depths of the cavern, wondering where he should find himself. After sliding down some fifteen feet in a way that threatened serious damage to the hinder part of his breeches he came to a stop, and his arm was grasped by the man who preceded him.

"Wait a moment till Jerome comes, and then we will shut the street-door."

Down came Jerome, the second robber; then another chain was put into Gribichon's hand, and they all gave a long steady pull which caused the mass of brambles to resume their original position over the mouth of the cave.

"Now we are safe, and will have a light," said Jerome.

The man produced from some recess a flint and steel, and soon was sending a shower of sparks upon a piece of tinder, at which he kindled a brimstone match, and then lighted a large wax candle, which looked uncommonly as though it had once decorated the altar of some church.

"Come along—sharp to the right—two steps forward—now sharp to the left. Here we are."

Gribichon, obeying the instructions of his guide, found himself in an underground apartment about thirty feet long and half as broad. It was so low that a tall man would be able to touch the roof in many places.

There was a rude table in the middle of this cave, half a dozen roughly made stools were scattered about, and at the far end of the place was a hearth with some sticks of wood smouldering upon it. Half a dozen piles of dry fern round the wall seemed to be used as beds.

"Snug enough," said Gribichon.

"Too snug for an old she-bear and her cubs, so we killed them, and took possession of her retreat," said Gribichon.

On the table were a couple of goblets, which, like the candle, had an ecclesiastical appearance.

Jerome went to a sort of recess near the fire-place, and drew forth a large black jack or leather bottle, from which he filled the goblets. The other man found in the same recess a huge joint of venison, some loaves of bread, and wooden platters.

"Fall-to," said he.

The bread was very coarse and dark-coloured, so Gribichon took from his pocket the half of poor Can-can's loaf, and invited his companions to take part of it, an act of courtesy which pleased them greatly.

"Ah!" said Jerome. "It is not very often we get such bread as this."

"Why not? It is cheap enough when you don't pay for it."

"That is all very fine. You, in Paris, of course, can steal your bread, but we who live in the forest must be on our best behaviour with the villagers of whom we get our provisions, or they would soon be up against us."

"Do they sell venison?" Gribichon asked.

"No, we find that in the forest, and help ourselves when we want any. The foresters are friendly enough; that was one of the king's foresters who took the horses, which he will keep at his hut and feed them with corn and hay which he procures from the royal hunting-lodge."

"Ah, this is rich! You gentlemen doubtless live by plunder, and the king finds provender for you and your horses. This wine, perhaps, comes from the royal cellars."

"No, from the Abbey of Beaulieu. The sacristan there is a friend of ours, and helps us from the abbot's store. The candles, which are far better than we could buy in the village, are also from the abbey."

"And the goblets?"

"No, we found them in a little church out the other side of the forest. But come, eat and drink."

Gribichon was doing both in first-class style. The meat was tender and the wine of excellent quality. The dinner service was a little rough, it is true, but then Gribichon had not been brought up in the lap of luxury.

At length he declared himself satisfied, and then Jerome's friend, whose name was Charles, said—

"Now, then, tell us all about this wonderful devil of a fellow, Cartouche."

"He is a wonder! You have never seen him?"

"No, or I would have joined his band."

"So would I," said Jerome. "We have contrived to pick up a living here in the forest, though it has been a hard pinch at times, but if we had been working with him we could have been rolling in wealth by this time."

"Not a bad idea. If he knew of you and your cave it would be very useful at times when Paris grows too warm to be pleasant."

"He is a born leader of men, and we will put ourselves at his disposal. Now tell us all about him."

Gribichon told all he knew about Cartouche, and the two men reiterated their desire to enlist under the banner of so redoubtable a chief.

"When will you see him again?" Jerome asked.

"I don't know. I don't even know where he is, but as soon as it is safe for me to go back to Paris I will find him."

"We can disguise you—we have plenty of wigs and things of that sort, and can fit you up so that your own mother won't know you."

"Then I'll go to-morrow," said Gribichon.

"And by way of preparation for your journey you had best lie down and have a good sleep. It is sunset now, and we'll let you be till sunrise."

Gribichon drank another cup of wine and threw himself on one of the fern couches. He slept soundly for some time, and found himself alone when he awoke. But he knew where to find the "black jack," so he filled himself another cup of wine and composed himself for another snooze.

"It will be time to get up when they return and find me that wig they spoke of," Gribichon remarked to himself, as he turned over and began his second sleep.

CHAPTER XXVI.

HOW CARTOUCHE MET THE LADY GUILFORT.

AFTER killing Red Judas, Cartouche and Tomasso thought it advisable to separate.

The Corsican had two well-filled purses in his pocket, one of which he slipped into his captain's hand, so that the movements of Cartouche were not to be hampered by poverty.

Tomasso went back to his lodgings, and Cartouche stood for a moment to think what he should do.

He dared not go to any of the lodgings he had occupied with Louise, as he knew that now the police would watch every known haunt of his. Nor could he speak to her in the street, as every movement of hers would be watched by some *mouchard* or police spy.

"A change of clothes first of all," said he. "These things are too well known to the police to be worn with safety."

There were plenty of second-hand clothes dealers in Paris, and Cartouche went into one of them.

"I am to play in a private theatre to-night," said he, "and I require a shabby black suit. I am to be an old advocate or notary."

"I have just the thing, monsieur. The dress will fit as though made for you."

"Produce it then, my friend."

The man hunted among his stock, and then displayed a pair of faded black velvet breeches and a threadbare black cloth coat and waistcoat.

"I shall want black stockings as well."

"And you shall have them. What think you, monsieur; will the dress suit you?"

"I doubt if it fits me. Can I not try it on?"

"Certainly—step this way, monsieur."

The dealer led the way into a room behind the shop and assisted Cartouche to array himself in the seedy black clothes.

"They fit, certainly—but I don't look much like an old lawyer, do I?"

"Pardon, monsieur, I have had much experience in these things; a few touches of powder on the face, a few wrinkles drawn upon the forehead and about the corners of the mouth will make the disguise perfect."

"Let me see how you can do it."

QUICK AS LIGHTNING LOUISE DREW ONE OF HER WEAPONS AND FIRED.

The man rapidly "made up" Cartouche, who gave himself an approving glance in the glass.

"I will keep this suit on," said he. "I will go among my friends, and I shall be very surprised indeed if any of them recognise me."

"And these clothes of yours, monsieur?"

"Pack them; I will send a servant for the parcel in the evening," Cartouche replied.

The dealer bowed, and Cartouche, having removed his valuables to the pockets of his new suit, quitted the house.

A couple of hundred yards along the road he met Louise, who accosted him with—

"Buy my flowers, learned sir."

"Louise! well, if you don't know me my disguise is perfect."

"Great Heaven! is it you, Louis?"

"Yes, but don't get excited, for, no doubt, you are watched."

"That is certain. But where are you going—what will you do, my brave lover?"

"I know not. What is the last news about me; are the police on my trail—have they any idea what has become of me?"

"No; they are at fault. They tried to capture Gribichon, but he managed to escape; and the Wolf, he is still at liberty."

"Tell the Wolf to be at the quai, by the side of the Pont Neuf, at ten o'clock to-night, and let him bring me all the money you can spare me, Louise."

"I will. Have you any?"

"Only two or three francs. I want more than that."

Louise slipped a piece of gold into the hand of her lying sweetheart, who pocketed it, saying—

"I would like to kiss you, but that would be dangerous, as, no doubt, some mouchard has his eye upon us. Don't forget to send more by the Wolf, and, by the way, let him bring me my small pistols."

"I won't forget, never fear," said Louise.

"Won't you buy a flower, sir?" she added, as a man she suspected of being in the pay of the police sauntered up.

"Not I; go away, you bold bad girl," Cartouche replied.

"You are a nasty old man, and if I knew where to find your wife I would tell her how you have been going on with me, you wicked old wretch."

Cartouche walked on, and had much difficulty in keeping from laughing at the way in which he and Louise had played their little comedy. He thought of the coin she had given him, and for a moment it occurred to him that he had acted rather meanly in taking it and demanding more, when all the time he had Tomasso's purse in his pocket; but he soon dismissed that thought from his mind.

All that day he haunted the law courts, and looked so very grave and learned that twice he had offers of legal business, which he refused on the plea that he already had as much in hand as he could manage.

When the courts were closed he repaired to a little tavern, where he dined, and there sat till it was time to go out and keep his appointment with the Wolf on the quai at the end of the Pont Neuf.

The Wolf was punctual to the moment. He felt considerable pride in being once more the confidential medium of communication between his chief and the pretty flower girl.

Louise had described to the Wolf how Cartouche was dressed, so they recognised each other at once.

"What have you for me?" Cartouche asked.

"This purse to begin with, captain," the Wolf replied, as he handed over a far more weighty pouch than Tomasso had given him.

Louise had been prudent lately, and saved up the money Cartouche had lavishly supplied her with.

"How much did you take for yourself, Wolf?"

"Not a franc, not a sou, captain."

"I believe you. Here, put these twenty francs in your pocket."

Cartouche did not believe the youth, but he knew it would not do to quarrel with him, as he was to be the means of keeping up communication between himself, Louise, and the other members of the band.

"Have you anything else for me?"

"A brace of pistols, captain, and they are beauties, too!"

Wolf heaved a sigh as he handed over the weapons, as though loth to part with such pretty toys.

"Here is the powder-flask, captain, fifty bullets, and the mould, so that you can amuse yourself by casting more when you have nothing else to do."

Cartouche loaded the pistols and placed them in his pocket.

"Any news of Gribichon?" he asked.

"No, captain. I can't think where he is hiding."

"Nor I. Well, tell Madame Louise that I shall keep out of sight for some days, so she, perhaps, will not see or hear anything of me. You will come here every night at this time and wait for an hour; then, if I don't show up, you can go away home."

"All right, captain; any more orders?"

"If you see or hear anything of Gribichon let me know. Bring him with you if you can manage it."

The Wolf promised strict obedience and caution.

"Off you go!" said Cartouche; and the street-boy disappeared.

Cartouche slept that night and several more nights at the tavern near the law courts where he dined.

He still kept up the appearance of an elderly lawyer, and it gradually began to be believed that he was a wealthy old advocate from Orleans who had come to Paris to watch the progress of a suit.

Cartouche, however, found this very slow work. He missed the frolics he had been used to, he missed the blandishments of La Belle Louise, and he pined for something more exciting than this hide-and-seek life he was leading.

One day, as he was walking round near the courts, he saw a lovely woman in front of him. It appeared as though she was desirous of being observed, and Cartouche had a good look at her.

The female was elegantly dressed. She had a figure of medium height and well-developed proportions; her curly hair was of a bright, golden tint, and her complexion was clear, white, and pink.

Poor Louise was forgotten in a moment, and Cartouche resolved to achieve the conquest of this fair stranger clad in silken attire.

"But she won't look at me in this dress," was his first reflection. "I must be something more like my old self before I speak to her. I will follow this girl, though, and see where she goes."

He followed, and presently saw her enter a dingy-looking house in the Rue Plat d'Etain, the door of which she opened with a key.

"Then it is pretty certain she lives here," said Cartouche to himself.

He thought over the matter as he paced up and down. Then he went to a tailor's shop and ordered a fashionable suit, thereby making the tradesman think the old lawyer a lunatic to dream of dressing like one of the young swells about the court.

Next he hired a small room in a house near the tavern he resided at, still keeping his apartment there.

The tailor worked in a leisurely fashion, and it was five days before the fashionable suit was made.

But every one of those days Cartouche wandered out towards the Rue Plat d'Etain and saw that lovely young female stroll out through the principal streets of Paris and return again alone, although her object evidently was to draw attention.

The young men of Paris, however, had not forgotten the fate of those decoyed by Lady Guilfort, and would not be tempted by any new siren.

Little did they or anyone else imagine that this was the real Lady Guilfort or Princess Jaborouski—yet so it was.

The adventuress was as clever as Cartouche himself in the matter of disguises, and by the aid of hair dye and cosmetiques was able to set the police at defiance.

Her hair, originally dark brown, was now yellow as gold, and her skin, formerly tinged with brown, was now transparently white—and so she boldly flaunted to and fro in the metropolis of France. But she kept as much as possible from places where it was likely she would encounter the police lieutenant Lecoq or his son.

At length the fashionable suit was finished, and Cartouche had it deposited in the new apartment he had engaged.

Walking out of the tavern as an old lawyer he entered the other place, from which he emerged half an hour later attired as a wealthy young nobleman might be—coat of dark blue velvet trimmed with gold lace, long waistcoat of fawn-coloured silk with embroidered lappels over the pockets, white buckskin breeches, and boots of the pattern worn by our lifeguards—a three-cornered cocked hat covered his head, and an elegant rapier hung by his side.

"Now for this fair one!" said he.

He had not far to go before he met her.

The lady was walking in front of him eating some grapes she had purchased, when some rude fellow, who must have been drunk, snatched the fruit from her hand.

She screamed. Cartouche at once ran up and gave the fellow a blow in the face, which floored him.

"Mademoiselle, pray pardon my rudeness, but I could not help chastising the fellow when I saw him offer such an insult to you."

"No apology, monsieur, but pray accept my thanks for your timely interference."

Cartouche bowed.

"The streets positively are not safe at times," said he; "permit me, therefore, to escort you to your destination, wherever it may be."

"I cannot think of putting you to such inconvenience."

"Nay, it will be a pleasure, I assure you. Your society in itself is a thing that many men would give half their lives to enjoy. Now, which way do we go?"

"To the Rue Plat d'Etain."

"Then we must pass by the police-office, unless we go round by the Rue Martin," said Cartouche.

"Yes, that is the nearest way."

It may well be imagined that neither was very anxious to go near the police quarter, but neither made any demur, lest the other should suspect there was something wrong.

So behold Cartouche and Lady Guilfort, the two greatest criminals Paris had known for many a long year, promenading arm-in-arm in front of the office of Monsieur Peuchet, who, looking from his window, saw them, but little guessed they were the people he most of all wanted to lay hands upon.

The Rue Plat d'Etain was soon reached, and the lady, whose name she told Cartouche was the Countess Tubalhoff, paused before the door of her dwelling. Cartouche paused also.

"I would ask you to enter," said she, "but I fear my humble dwelling would scarcely be to the taste of such a gentleman as you evidently are."

"Mademoiselle, the dwelling which is honoured by you residing in it is a palace fit for a prince."

The Countess Tubalhoff made a low curtsy, and opened the door.

"Enter, monsieur," said she.

Cartouche followed her into the hall, the door was closed, and the countess beckoned him to follow her up the staircase—an invitation which the amorous Cartouche readily obeyed.

On the first floor was a tolerably well-furnished room, into which the murderess ushered her guest.

"You will pardon my leaving you for a few seconds," said she. "I will just get rid of my hat and wraps, and then come back to you."

We have already stated that the lady had for the present given up the advancement of science by collecting heads for phrenological examination. Murder was a trifle too dangerous now, for the Parisians were so thoroughly alarmed that if she had been recaptured they would have hanged her to the nearest pillar or balcony rather than let her escape a second time. So she had no intention of killing Cartouche, or causing him to be killed, although she certainly had made up her mind to have his purse and the diamond brooch he wore in his neck-cloth. She did not know that it was as great a sham as her own titles whether English, Polish, or German.

Cartouche looked round the room during the fair one's absence, to see if there was any small but valuable piece of portable furniture which might be conveyed into his pocket.

Plenty of trifles all very elegant in their way, but not of the least value to the people who usually relieved Cartouche and his friends of the articles they found in their travels.

Having satisfied himself that the place contained nothing worth his trouble, he began to consider how he should begin his love making, and had not quite settled that question when the Countess Tubalhoff reappeared, looking more lovely than ever.

"Be seated, baron," said she, placing herself on a chair. Cartouche had told her that he was a baron of the Roman Empire.

"Nay, I cannot be so rude as to seat myself in the presence of a goddess. I will stand—unless you permit me to kneel at your feet."

"No, no! you must not kneel, for that signifies worship——"

"And I worship you, I adore you!" cried Cartouche, flopping down on his marrow-bones and seizing her hand, which he covered with kisses. "I love you, and you only," he said, unaware of the fact that the barrel of a pistol was within a yard of his head.

Yet such was the case. Whilst making his extravagant protestation of love the door opened noiselessly, and a very ill-looking ruffian appeared, holding his weapon close to Cartouche's body.

"I adore you, I love you!" said Cartouche, passionately; and then he fell to work kissing her hand again.

Presently pausing in this refreshing sport and looking up for some sign of encouragement, he perceived that the lady was shaking her head at some one, and that one certainly was not himself.

Like a flash of lightning Cartouche sprang full four feet back, and, standing erect on his feet, flashed out two pistols, one of which threatened the countess, whilst the other covered her associate.

"What! would you kill me?" he shouted.

"No, no, you are mistaken, my dear baron," said she; "it was only a jest."

"A fine jest truly, for it might have cost two lives—yours and that fellow's."

"We are pretty well used to that sort of thing," the fellow growled—but at a signal from the countess he lowered his weapon.

That remark enlightened Cartouche, and he at once guessed who the lady was. Of course, like all the rest of Paris, he had heard of her achievements in the way of making murder a pleasure.

"Ah, then I am in the presence of the celebrated Lady Guilfort!" he exclaimed. "I wonder I did not think of it sooner. My dear countess, you may dismiss your attendant, I am quite equal to the task of taking care of myself and you."

"What devil are you?"

"I have been called a devil so often that I take the word as a compliment when it comes from your lips."

"I confess I am the Lady Guilfort, but who are you?"

"I am Cartouche."

The ruffian in the doorway dropped his pistol.

"Pardon, monsieur," he said. "Had I known it was you I would rather have pointed the muzzle against myself."

"Right, friend, you would have found it almost as profitable, for I am a very quick shot, and should probably have sent a bullet through your skull long before you had half finished pulling your trigger."

Then Cartouche turned to the lady.

"Well, countess, shall we come to terms."

"What terms can we make?"

"We can agree to work together for our mutual benefit."

"Go on—explain."

"You have associates and accomplices, so have I. If the two parties worked together it would be easy enough for them to enrich themselves at the expense of the fat citizens of Paris, and laugh all the time at the clumsy police.

"I agree," said the Lady Guilfort.

"Then I will undertake to direct the operations of the two parties," said Cartouche.

And thus two of the most dangerous criminals the French metropolis had ever known became leagued together.

Cartouche spoke the truth when he sent word to Louise that it might be some time before she heard anything more of him; he found the society of Lady Guilfort so pleasant that it was some days before he quitted the house in the Rue Plat d'Etain.

The Wolf promenaded the *quai* by the Pont Neuf night after night, all to no purpose, and Louise mourned for her lost lover, without dreaming that the unfaithful rascal had transferred his affections to another.

Louise looked in every direction for Cartouche as she plied her business as flower-seller. She met Tomasso and two or three other members of the band, but they could give no information.

"He must have left Paris," she thought.

CHAPTER XXVII.

THE FURTHER ADVENTURES OF GRIBICHON.

At length the two robbers returned to the underground cavern to which they had conveyed Can-can's sweetheart.

"Now, my friends," said Gribichon, "I want to return to Paris and find out what Cartouche is doing, so if you have those wigs and other things just let me have a few of them, and I will start."

"Right!" exclaimed Jerome; "and when you see Cartouche don't forget to tell him that we are ready to put ourselves under his command. Ah! there were a dozen of us in this cave once—all regular devils—now only two."

"Three! I am here, and am I no one?"

"Only a visitor, Monsieur Gribichon; but come, let me dress you for your part in the play."

Jerome then lifted a flat stone, from under which he dragged a good-sized box full of all sorts of theatrical properties, such as wigs, false moustaches, dresses, and so forth.

Gribichon's hair was black naturally, so Jerome chose a light-coloured wig and clapped it on the young man's head. Next he shaved off Gribby's eyebrows and stuck on a false pair which agreed in colour with the new head of hair. Then with tincture of iron he splashed some artful freckles on Gribby's face.

"Now you will do; your own mother would not know you. Off you go to Paris, and find out all about our brave captain, Cartouche."

"A little money, if you please, brother Jerome, to help me on the road. I am penniless, but Cartouche will repay you anything advanced to me. And you may charge him for my night's lodging too."

The robbers were not very wealthy; trade had been bad, travellers had avoided that road, or had travelled together in such numbers that it was not safe to attack them. They had plenty of bread and meat and wine—but very little silver.

However, they managed to find five francs for Gribichon and after giving him directions how to find his way to the mouth of the cave, they set him on the road with his face towards Paris.

But it was a long walk, and after a time Gribichon thought he needed refreshment.

A little roadside inn presented itself to his view, and he entered with the intention of having a glass of wine and a crust of bread.

Jerome had disguised Gribichon as a peasant, with wooden shoes and a blue blouse, &c.

Gribichon well knew the part he had to play, but unfortunately he forgot the difference between the speech of a countryman and a Parisian. And when he entered the house and called for his refreshments the landlord of the place stared.

"Eh? you are the first peasant I ever heard speak in that fashion,' said he. "How long have you followed the plough, my young friend?"

"Ever since I was born."

"Come over to this window, young man."

Gribichon obeyed, and the landlord pointed to a plough which had been left on the other side of the road, just by a field gate.

"You see that plough?"

"Yes, of course I do," responded Gribichon, who, when he first set eyes upon the implement, did not know what it was.

"Then to which end of it do you harness your horse?"

"Why, you old idiot, that is plain enough!"

"Of course, then you will tell me."

"I should naturally put my horse between the shafts," said Gribichon, pointing to the handles or stilts by which the plowman directs the implement, so that it shall turn up a straight furrow.

The landlord laughed loudly.

"Ha, ha, ha! you are a fine ploughman. My boy, you are a thorough Parisian rascal, and you are masquerading for some purpose; let me see——"

The old man stared hard into Gribichon's face for some few seconds; then he said—

"You are not Cartouche, but I think you must be one of his gang. So I will keep you."

"I'll be hanged if you will!" shouted Gribichon.

Dashing at the landlord of the inn, Gribichon hurled the old man to the floor and rushed out of the place. A man dressed in the garb of a forester was coming along the road leading half a dozen big, fierce-looking dogs in leashes.

"What is the matter?" this man asked.

Gribichon made no answer, but sped away as hard as he could down the road.

"Stop him!" yelled the innkeeper, coming out to the door.

Gribichon was too nimble to be stopped by any forester in the pay of the French king; but the man at once slipped his dogs.

"Hi, dogs! after him!" he cried.

Gribichon leaped the ditch and plunged into the forest with half a dozen savage hounds on his trail.

"Good heaven! to think I should be hunted in this style!" sighed Gribichon. "This is making game of me with a vengeance."

Gribichon was sharp witted, and he remembered to have heard or read that water would not hold scent and that any animal might baffle hounds by crossing a stream. He also remembered that about a quarter of a mile from the inn there was a riverlet which came from the forest, so he doubled back to get to it.

The hounds were in full cry.

Man-hunting was their usual occupation, for the forester kept them to hunt up the poachers and deer-stealers who infested the neighbourhood. Jerome and his companion had more than once been obliged to run before those dogs.

"If I can only reach the stream!" said Gribichon.

On he sped. He fairly distanced the forester, but the great question was, Could he keep away from the hounds? Luckily for him the animals had not been bred for speed—they were not intended to run down an animal in the open, but to follow slowly, though surely, and keep the game afoot till it gave up from exhaustion.

"What would Can-can say if she saw me?" he thought. "I would give something to be in her room now, with a nice sausage and a bottle of wine, and the door closed between me and these savage devils of hounds."

Presently he saw the brook.

At that part of the forest it was broad but shallow, so Gribichon dashed in and waded up the watercourse for a couple of hundred yards.

"Here's a chance!" he exclaimed, suddenly.

A huge tree growing by the edge of the stream dropped one of its branches almost down to the water. Gribichon caught hold of this branch and scrambled up into the thick, leafy covert at the top of the tree.

"Look, Carlo! Seek him, Wolf!" he heard the forester say, as his hounds came to a stand at the edge of the water.

The man and the dogs thoroughly examined both banks of the stream for at least half a mile in each direction—up and down—but, although they knew where Gribichon entered the water, they could not discover how or where he left it.

For an hour or more the forester kept up the search, and more than once he passed under the tree where Gribichon was seated.

"If those dogs smell me it will be all over with me," Gribichon sighed. "That forester with his gun would shoot me down out of this tree as he would an old crow."

Luckily the hounds did not scent him in his airy retreat, and after a time the forester took them up in leash again and led them away, saying, loud enough for Gribichon to hear him—

"Well, I'll make that old Pierre the inn-keeper pay for sending me on this useless hunt. I am the king's forester, and these are the king's hounds, and any person who employs us on any business not connected with the king's forest will have to pay a pretty stiff price for the luxury."

"I wish he would hunt the innkeeper," Gribichon thought.

"I will have a bottle of that old burgundy wine now, and he shall send a dozen bottles up to my house," said the forester.

"What a greedy villain!" Gribichon said to himself.

The forester with his dogs strolled slowly away in the direction of the roadside inn, and Gribichon descended from the tree.

The artful young Parisian intended to keep him in sight till he and his hounds were safe inside the public and in full enjoyment of the bottle of wine; then he would creep round the back of the house and come out on the main road some half-mile or so beyond it.

Which programme he carried out exactly, though he was a long time before he could be quite certain that he did not hear the forester's hounds baying behind him.

It was quite ten miles from the house where the hunt began to the next place where refresh-ment could be procured, and Gribichon felt almost exhausted when he reached it. But a trifle of good liquor, with some food and a short rest, reinvigorated him, and he resumed his walk, reaching Paris only a few minutes before the time appointed for closing the gates in the evening.

"Now what shall I do?" he questioned.

A brief thought convinced him that he must find out the Wolf or Louise. He could get no news of Cartouche except through those indi-viduals.

So Gribichon looked about for the Wolf.

That young worthy had, however, thought proper to take up fresh lodgings. Louise was not to be seen at her usual haunts, so Gribichon had to go to bed at a very cheap inn without having heard anything of his chief, except the gossip of the tavern and the street. And Paris was still talking of the wonderful escape of the young outlaw.

Most people seemed, in Gribichon's opinion, to think that Cartouche would never venture to show himself in Paris again.

"Very much mistaken, my friends," Gribi-chon thought. "He is in Paris now—and Louise knows where. I wish I could see her."

But Louise kept for some days away from her usual haunts—so Gribichon did not see her.

The sham countryman managed two or three clever bits of pocket-picking, and so kept him-self supplied with money.

He had been back in Paris quite a week when one evening, just as it was growing dusk, he saw the Wolf pacing along the street in front of him.

Gribichon made a spurt, got some distance ahead of his friend, then turned and waited.

The Wolf, with his hands in his breeches-pockets, sauntered along, whistling softly.

Evidently he did not recognise Gribichon.

"How are you, Wolf?" asked the sham countryman.

"Eh? Who are you?"

"Don't you know me, Wolf?"

"No—no; yet you are not unlike a friend of mine, only his hair was much darker than yours."

"Well, I am Gribichon."

"Nonsense! Go away!"

"It is a fact, old Wolf. I am Gribichon, and it is a wig I am wearing over my own hair."

"You are done up well! I thought you were some young fellow from the country."

"Where is the captain, Wolf?"

"That is what I want to know—so does Madame Louise."

"You mean to say she has not a notion where to find him?"

"No; and when I saw her this morning she was crying because she had not heard anything of him."

"Have you seen Can-can?"

"Yes, she is a jolly one, she is!" exclaimed Wolf.

"Look here, she is my girl—so don't you go on in that way, or we shall quarrel, Master

CARTOUCHE,

THE FRENCH JACK SHEPPARD.

IN THE NICK OF TIME HE TOOK A FLYING LEAP INTO OLD GREGOIRE'S BOAT.

Wolf !" said Gribichon   "Go and find a sweet heart for yourself if you want one "

"All right, my boy   But tell me, where have you been ?"

Gribichon narrated his adventures—except the hunting

"That must be a jolly place, that cave," said Wolf

"It is   Our captain could not wish to have a better hiding place   I wonder where he is ?"

The two young rascals were at that moment passing along the Rue Plat d'Etain, little guessing that their captain was there in the company of the handsome adventuress known to the Parisian public as Lady Gulfort.

"I have to go down to the Pont Neuf every night," the Wolf said   "That is the captain's order, so I suppose he will show up one of these evenings "

"I'll go with you this evening—what is the hour ?"

"I am to go every night at ten, and wait for an hour , if he does not show up then I am to consider that he doesn't want me "

"All right, where are you going now ?"

"To see Madame Louise   She writes a letter every day which I am to give him if I see him—but I always have to take it back to her "

"I should like to see her "

"Come along then," said the Wolf

Wolf was well known to many of the light fingered gentry of Paris, who thought he was in luck—that he had captured some silly country youth with more francs than brains   "We must meet Wolf when he has done the trick," said they to each other, "then we shall have plenty of wine "

None of them recognised Gribichon, so good was his disguise

Presently they saw Louise at the place she had appointed to meet the Wolf

"It will not do for both of us to go up to her together, so let me have a few words first, and I will tell her that you are waiting to speak to her," said the Wolf

"You are right," Gribichon answered

The Wolf darted forward, exchanged a few words with Louise, to whom he returned the loving letter she wrote to her faithless lover the previous day, receiving from her an equally affectionate billet to be delivered that night if the Wolf saw Cartouche

It was little that Louise had to tell her lover except that she loved him, and the infatuated flower girl was never tired of reiterating that statement

The Wolf left Louise, and then the sham countryman slouched up to her

"Is that you, Gribichon ?" she asked   "I would not have known you if the Wolf had not told me who it was "

"Yes, Madame Louise, it is Gribichon   I wanted to see the captain to tell him that there is a famous hiding place in the forest near Beau lieu, and a couple of stout devils of fellows who have heard of him and are anxious to join his band."

"I wish I knew where to find him !" Louise sighed

"What shall I do, then, madame ?"

"You had better wait in Paris till to morrow morning   Perhaps Wolf will see the captain to night "

"I am going with him to the Pont Neuf "

"And if you don't see the captain you had best return to your friends in the cave and tell them that Cartouche is not visible to anyone for a few days because the police are so active   Say anything you like so that you keep them in the mood to become sworn members of the band "

"I will , farewell, Madame Louise "

And Gribichon darted after the Wolf

The sham countryman arranged with his friend as to time and place where they should meet at night, and then lounged about the streets looking for Can can   He did not care to go to her lodging because he had no doubt that she was closely watched, and any visitors would be scrutinised by the police

At length he met the pretty scent smeller

"Buy a bottle of essence of roses, monsieur ?" said she   "It smells as sweet as the flowers that grow at your own cottage door, and lasts longer "

"But how about its looks ?" said Gribichon

"Don't you think that's a very pretty flask ?—only half a franc "

"Pretty flask !   Pretty girl, you mean !"

"Who is a pretty girl ?"

"You are , and well you know it "

"Good gracious, monsieur from the country ; you had better not let my sweetheart hear you talk like that !"

"Where is your sweetheart ?" Gribichon asked

"I don't know," said Can can, and her eyes assumed a very watery appearance

"What is he ? Does he sell scents ?"

"No—are you going to buy any ? "

Gribichon took the bottle she held out to him, and put it in his pocket

"Half a franc, if you please, young man "

"I never pay for anything "

"If my sweetheart was here he would beat you to a mummy for cheating me   I wish I knew where to find him "

"I am Gribichon," said the owner of the name

"You ! yes you are ! why I must have been blind that I did not know you before   My dear Gribby !"

The affectionate girl threw her arms round Gribichon's neck and kissed him

"Eh ! what is this, Can can ?" said an old police officer, who happened to be passing at the time

"My long lost brother from the country, if you please, sir," replied Can can, demurely "We haven't seen each other for so many years that we did not know each other at first "

"Are you certain it is your brother ? How do you recognise him ?"

"I know him by the freckles on his face, sir "

The police-officer looked closely at Gribichon.

who felt very much disposed to sink into his wooden shoes to avoid that keen gaze, which seemed to penetrate to his very soul.

"Well, Can-can, I hope it is your brother. Don't make a scene with him in the streets."

"Very well, sir," the girl replied, very demurely indeed.

And the police-officer walked on, to the great delight of Can-can and Gribichon.

"Is it true that you are one of Cartouche's band?" Can-can asked when they were once more alone. "I have heard it said lately that you are one of them, and that it was you who aided Cartouche in his escape from prison."

"You heard the truth, Can-can."

"Then I am in love with a——"

"Exactly so—I am a——"

"You are a thief, Gribichon. That is true, is it not?"

"Yes—I suppose I must tell the truth."

Can-can dropped a few tears and then said—

"Gribichon, if I love you as much as ever, or more than ever, will you give up stealing and earn an honest living?"

"I will," responded the unblushing rascal.

"Then I will love you more than ever I did in my life," she replied, giving him another of those kisses which had already sent two young fellows almost mad with jealousy and envy.

"Well, Can-can, I must go away now. Do you live still in the same place?"

"The very same place where you ate my supper, and afterwards came without invitation to breakfast when the police wanted to get hold of you. Ah, I had a bad time of it for two days through those police—who told me who and what you are."

"The police do not seem to know me, so I suppose I may pay you another visit."

"Come as often as you like, my Gribichon."

"I must go away now, but I shall be at your place before midnight."

"Do you want any money, Gribichon?"

"Yes, my dear Can-can, I'm awfully poor—and you say I must not prig any more."

"I haven't much, but take this—only two francs, but I have bread at home and the rent is paid."

Gribichon, without compunction, pocketed the coins, and then went away muttering to himself—

"Eh! I am to earn an honest living, am I, Can-can? I don't know how to do it, my girl."

CHAPTER XXVIII.

HOW GRIBICHON AND THE WOLF MET CARTOUCHE.

AT nine o'clock that evening the Wolf and Gribichon might have been seen in a little wine-shop which was swept away years ago to make room for the North of France Railway terminus.

They were playing dominoes and drinking wine till the clock struck, then, admonished as to the hour, they rose and went out into the street.

"I have an idea that the captain will turn up to-night," the Wolf said, as they walked in the direction of the Pont Neuf.

"I hope so. But is not that Tomasso in front?"

"By Heaven, it is! I wonder if he is going to our rendezvous?"

"Best go on and ask him."

The two young fellows hurried after the Corsican.

"Are you looking for the captain?" the Wolf asked.

"What captain?" demanded the Corsican, scowling at Gribichon.

"Our captain—Cartouche."

"Be careful how you talk in the presence of strangers," the old Corsican growled.

"This is a joke—he doesn't know me. Never heard of Gribichon before, did you, Tomasso?"

The Corsican whistled shrilly.

"You Gribichon? Of course you are, though."

"Isn't it a good disguise, Tomasso?"

"First-rate. But where are you going?"

"To take my usual evening walk at the foot of the Pont Neuf," the Wolf replied; "and Gribichon goes with me."

"If you see the captain tell him I am all right and ready to do anything he bids me. You know where to find me, Le Loup?"

"Perfectly, Signor Tomasso. I thought, perhaps, you would like to go with us."

"Best not go in too great force. One or two might pass without notice, but the police would be certain to look at three or four of us if we walked along together."

"Quite right, signor. If we see the captain and he has any commands for you I shall not fail to let you know."

Tomasso lifted his hat to the two young fellows, who walked on and arrived at the quay by the Pont Neuf full five minutes before the clock of the neighbouring church chimed the hour of ten.

"We keep good time, at all events," said Gribichon.

"And the captain is not here. Well, let us walk up and down for a time; he is so much looked after that we must not be surprised if he is a little bit late. I should like, though, to know how he has been getting on this week past—playing some devil's pranks, I'll warrant."

To which speech Gribichon made no response. The two young men walked up and down till nearly eleven o'clock, when as they turned about they found themselves face to face with Cartouche, who, fiercely seizing the Wolf by the throat, hissed in his ear—

"You shall die, you dog! But first tell me who is this you have brought down with you."

The Wolf was unable to reply, so tightly did Cartouche compress his throat. But Gribichon caught hold of the arm of the enraged captain, and said—

"What, don't you know me—don't you know Gribichon?"

"Why so it is! What a splendid get-up, Gribby."

"First-class. I can stand and talk to a policeman for half an hour without his guessing who I am."

"Well, we must not stand here long. What news, Wolf?"

"This note from Madame Louise," the Wolf replied, handing the letter to Cartouche, who read it.

And then, as conscience was not altogether dead within him, he began to reproach himself for having neglected the beautiful flower-girl.

"I love her!" thought he, "and she has gone through great risks for my sake, so I must not neglect her. Poor Louise! She is a darling girl, but then——"

The image of the Lady Guilfort floated before his mind's eye, and like his English contemporary, Captain Macheath, he felt inclined to say, "How happy could I be with either were t'other dear charmer away." But he did not see his way to getting rid of either of the dear charmers; so after thinking for a minute he said to the Wolf—

"When will you see Madame Louise again?"

"Early in the morning."

"Tell her to meet me at eight o'clock to-morrow night."

"Good, captain. And shall I come at ten as usual?"

"No. I shall see her, and can tell her what is to be done. Did she send any money?"

"No, captain."

"Ask her to bring some to-morrow. Now, Gribichon, what have you to say for yourself?"

Gribichon related his adventures—how he had fallen in with Jerome and Charles, who were anxious to place themselves and their cave at the service of so celebrated an outlaw as Captain Cartouche.

"Very good business, Gribby. I will have those two fellows, they will make famous additions to the band, which has been very sadly thinned out by the police during the last week or two. Have you seen Black George?"

"No, captain," replied both Gribichon and the Wolf.

Black George was a member of the gang in whom the captain, Cartouche, had very little faith. In fact, he suspected that Black George had gone over to the police, but he had no proof of it.

"Well, Gribby, you had best go back to your cave. Jerome and Charles must come here with you at midnight, two nights hence, and they shall be sworn as brothers of the band. And they shall see a sight, too, which will convince them that they had better keep the oath. Now then, be off with you—right-about! March!"

Gribichon and the Wolf walked a few paces, then they both looked back over their shoulders —but Cartouche had vanished.

The Wolf went on to his lodging, and Gribichon once more took supper with Can-can, though on this occasion he purchased the sausage, the cheese of Camembert, and the wine.

Cartouche walked up and down the street leading to the quay, then he resolved to walk along by the office of the Chief of Police, and see if any new placards had been issued relating to himself.

Just as he approached the place he saw a female leave it.

"Surely I know that figure," he mused.

It was, in truth, Madame Lafarge.

Monsieur Peuchet had sent for her again and again. The amorous old Chief of Police still believed that by the agency of "that magnificent woman," as he called Madame Lafarge, he would recapture Cartouche. Besides, he had his own little designs and desires to gratify.

And he had just been treating Madame Lafarge to a sweet mixture of flattery and bullying, something to the effect that if she helped him to capture the French Jack Sheppard she should live in his favour for ever, with a good stipend, but if he was not captured very soon she would be likely enough to find herself in the apartments lately occupied by Lady Guilfort at the Bastille.

So Madame Lafarge was going away with rather slow step and downcast looks.

Cartouche recognised her, and resolved to follow, and so ascertain whither she went.

Madame Lafarge passed along three or four narrow streets, then she paused, and looked about as though rather expecting to see someone. And presently that someone appeared.

"Black George, by Jove!" said Cartouche.

Our hero had procured another false beard and whiskers, and these he slipped on. Fearless in his disguise, he followed and listened to their talk.

"What news, George?" asked Madame Lafarge.

"It is pretty certain Cartouche is in Paris. I saw Gribichon and the Wolf together just now, and I heard the Wolf say that Cartouche and Louise were to meet at eight to-morrow evening."

"Where?"

"I could not catch that."

"Well, George, you have done well, and if I do succeed in capturing this Cartouche I will take the reward and marry you."

George bowed as politely as he could, and went on to say—

"I gathered that the Wolf and Cartouche met on the quay by the Pont Neuf, so I think it very likely Louise will go there to see him."

"Just so—but no, I think not—he is too artful."

Madame Lafarge did not want anyone to share in the killing or capture of Cartouche. She wanted the reward entirely to herself, and had not the slightest intention of allowing Black George or anyone else to participate in the glory or profit of ending the career of Cartouche.

"Dead or alive!"

Such were the terms of the proclamation, and Madame Lafarge resolved that it should be— dead!

She would kill him, and that would save a vast deal of trouble.

Black George, quite unaware that he had the Chief of Police as a rival for the possession of Madame Lafarge's charms, walked on, making love in a clumsy fashion, and Cartouche walked along noiselessly behind (he had on his felt-soled boots), and listened.

Presently the black one and Madame Lafarge parted, and Madame Lafarge exclaimed aloud—

"It will do. I will go to the Pont Neuf and kill him while he is with Louise."

At which Cartouche chuckled. And, having thus learned the plans of the enemy, he strolled away.

"Black George shall suffer for this," he said to himself. "He shall be made an example of when Gribichon's friends are sworn in. It will be well to let them see what they are liable to if they break the oath they must take."

Very thoughtfully he returned to the Rue Plat d'Etain, and entered the dwelling of the Countess Tubalhoff, alias Lady Guilfort.

CHAPTER XXIX.

HOW LOUISE AND HER MOTHER MET.

THE Wolf duly conveyed his message to La Belle Louise, who was delighted at the idea of seeing Cartouche once more.

"Of course he wants money, and he shall have it," said she.

And next morning she sold or pawned every article she had that was saleable or pawnable; and at the appointed time she was on the quay by the Pont Neuf.

Louise walked up and down several times, wondering from which direction Cartouche would come, when as she was turning she found herself face to face with him.

Of course Louise kissed him—most lovingly—and Cartouche, as he held her for a moment in his arms, wondered why he had become so infatuated over Lady Guilfort.

"Have you seen anyone loitering about, Louise?" he asked.

"No, dear. I kept a good look-out so that the police should not track me, and I am quite certain I dodged them. You know the inn of the White Horse?"

"Yes, of course I do. The entrance is in the Rue St. Stephen."

"Right. I went in there, but I passed out at the back into the Avenue Saint Pierre."

"Good girl! I did not know there was a back way."

"I looked round when I got out, but there was not a soul in sight, so I suppose if any of the police shadowed me they are still waiting. And now, Louis dear, tell me what you are going to do."

"I cannot tell you, Louise; I have no plans fixed as yet."

"Tomasso, the Wolf, Gribichon, and other members of your troup are still about, and will work for you. They are all good fellows to do

what they are told to do, but they need a leader—one who can plan for them, as you can."

"Come this way, Louise. We shall be noticed walking about here on the quay, so let us go up this street."

They turned up a narrow thoroughfare leading from the riverside, and then Cartouche thought that he had made a mistake in having anything to do with the Lady Guilfort.

True, she had two or three ruffian associates who would not hesitate to murder or steal at her command, but she was, he felt bound to admit to himself, a false, treacherous devil, who would sell him to the police if she thought the bargain could be made with safety to herself."

But Louise had been tried, and proved faithful.

"How can I get rid of the Englishwoman?" Cartouche thought.

Finally he resolved to tell Louise all.

"There will be the deuce of a rumpus for five minutes, and then she will say I am forgiven."

So he told her that for a week past he had been with this celebrated murderess.

He was quite right. There was a rumpus for a few minutes—Louise pulled his hair, slapped his face, and called him a variety of bad names; then she sobbed for a minute or two.

Cartouche waited patiently; he was tired of Lady Guilfort—she would be little use to him because she was not able to be about much, for fear of the police, and he, Cartouche, had already made sure of her male associates.

"Now listen, Louise," he said.

"I wish I never had listened to you!"

"That is not quite true."

"It is! it is! I hate you, Louis Cartouche!"

"Then why don't you go away and give me up to the police?"

"I can't, Louis dear—you know I can't."

"Then listen. I did wrong to you when I went after this English siren, and I will not do so again. But she will kill me."

"No! she dare not lift her hand against you."

"She does indeed, so I have not long to live."

Louise sobbed. They were still in the narrow street, one end of which opened down to the quay; they stood facing each other, and had no fear of being overheard, as all the houses were fast closed.

Suddenly in the midst of her sobbing Louise saw what filled her soul with dread.

Behind Cartouche, standing in the shadow of a doorway, was a woman who held uplifted a dagger which she was about to plunge into the back of Cartouche.

"It must be the Englishwoman!" thought Louise.

Her thoughts and actions alike were prompt. She had taken to carrying pistols of late, and quick as lightning she drew one of the weapons from her dress, and fired at the person who was about to stab Cartouche.

"She is dead!" Louise exclaimed.

"Who? What is it?" asked Cartouche.

"That Englishwoman was about to stab you,

Louis, but I know how to shoot, and she will never injure either of us again. I have saved you, Louis!"

"You have, dear Louise."

Cartouche had a dark lantern with him. He turned the light on to the prostrate figure.

Louise had not bragged without cause when she said she knew how to shoot—the bullet had struck plumb centre on the forehead of her mother, Madame Lafarge.

That misguided woman, in pursuance of her threat, had tracked Cartouche, and fully intended killing him to earn the reward offered by the police, when her earthly career was cut short by her daughter's pistol.

"Come away!" said Cartouche.

And he hurried Louise from the spot without allowing her to have a fair sight of the face of the woman she had shot.

"Was it the Englishwoman?" Louise asked, when they paused a little in their hasty flight.

"No, you were mistaken."

"It was some enemy of yours, Louis, so I do not regret what I have done. I would shoot any man or woman who dared lift a hand against you, my lover!"

"Come away, Louise, come away!"

Cartouche was about as callous a scoundrel as lived, but he had not courage enough to tell the girl he loved—after his fashion—that she had shot her own mother.

Louise's lodgings were a considerable distance from the Pont Neuf. Cartouche accompanied her thither, and the Lady Guilfort saw no more of him for some time.

The good people of Paris wondered what had become of Louise, but she was happy enough with Cartouche, who would not let her go out till he judged that people had done talking about the woman who was found shot near the Pont Neuf.

CHAPTER XXX.

HOW JEROME AND CHARLES WERE SWORN INTO THE BAND.

CARTOUCHE, although he compelled Louise to remain in her lodging, went out a good deal himself.

He was bent on reorganising his band of outlaws. Tomasso, Gribichon, the Wolf, and two or three others were safe for anything, and Lady Guilfort's male friends would prove valuable recruits he doubted not. Jerome and Charles, the men who entertained Gribichon in the forest by Beaulieu, would also be good-working members of a fraternity whose aim was to prey on society.

Cartouche first of all fixed upon a place where he and his men could meet without fear of interference.

The police, of course, were watching all his old haunts, so he hired a house in a part of Paris which he had never before frequented.

"We will all meet in our new home to-morrow night at ten," said he to Tomasso; "so pass the word to everyone—except Black George."

"Why will you leave him out, captain?"

"I shall not leave him out, but I want to get him there before he has a chance of telling the police where we meet."

"But after the meeting——"

"He will be dumb."

"I see."

"He will not see."

The old Corsican laughed, for he knew that Cartouche intended to inflict some terrible punishment on the man who was justly suspected of being a traitor.

Gribichon was then sent off to the forest to bring Jerome and Charles to Paris, so that they might swear fealty to Cartouche.

"I will manage Black George myself," said the captain.

It was rather late the next afternoon when Black George, strolling along one of the streets of Paris, found himself confronted by his captain.

"Well, George, how are you getting on?" Cartouche asked.

Black George felt very much inclined to call a police-officer who was on the other side of the street; but he thought twice, and resolved that he would do nothing of the kind till he was able to betray *all* his old associates—the whole lot of them—into the hands of Monsieur Peuchet.

"I am doing very little, captain," said Black George. "Our old band seems broken up, and I cannot work alone. I must have someone to help me."

"The band is not broken up; we are going to admit two new recruits in an hour's time, and I have provided a place where we can meet at all times. Come along."

He took Black George by the arm and marched him away down the street.

"What a fool this Cartouche is to put himself in my power in this fashion," thought George.

"I have you fast enough now," was Cartouche's speech to himself as he led his victim along. "And when I have done with you I defy you to give information to the police."

After walking a mile or so they halted in a quiet street.

"That is the house, with the green door. We won't go in together, so you go first."

"What is the word, captain?"

"Word and signal just the same as at the old place. Tomasso keeps the door at present, and he knows you."

"You are a wonder, captain," said the traitor.

And, without further remark, he walked up to the door, knocked, and was admitted by Tomasso, who greeted him with a very grim smile.

Cartouche remained pacing up and down the street till he saw Gribichon coming, with the two forest robbers who were anxious to join his band.

He went in first, and himself admitted the new-comers who were not to know the password till they had taken the oath binding them to the fraternity.

Cartouche led the way into a large room. At one end of the apartment was a table and chair slightly raised above the floor ; down both sides of the room were chairs, most of them occupied by members of the band, about a dozen being present.

Cartouche seated himself on the raised chair and spoke—

"Gentlemen, we have met for the first time in our new home, and the pleasing business we have first to transact is to enrol the two new members, who are desirous of joining us. Gribichon will tell you who they are and how he met them."

Which Gribichon did.

Jerome and Charles were then brought up to the table, the oath was administered to them, and they signed the roll of membership.

"Now, gentlemen, we have another duty to perform, that is to drink success to the new members of the band. Wolf, produce the champagne."

"Certainly, captain."

A basket containing half a dozen bottles was set upon the table with glasses, and in an instant the corks were flying in every direction. The health of the new members was proposed by the captain, and each man swallowed a bumper.

Who so happy as Black George?

But after a few minutes spent in laughing and joking Cartouche called his audience to attention.

"Gentlemen, we have yet another duty to perform."

"What! more business to-night, captain?" said Gribichon.

"Yes ; and it had better be done at once. Guard the door, Tomasso; let no one go out or come in till I give the word."

The Corsican said nothing, but he rose from his seat, placed his back against the door, and drew a long dagger from the inside of his vest.

"Listen, you two gentlemen who have just been admitted to our fraternity. You have heard the oath of brotherhood, and you have sworn it. Now you shall see how we punish traitors. Seize Black George!"

Gribichon and another at once collared the rascal and dragged him into the body of the hall.

Black George was too much astonished to make any resistance.

"Gentlemen," said Cartouche, "you see before you one who, having sworn the oath and signed the roll, conspired with a woman who was shot—to hand me over to the law dead or alive, as the bills say. Whether he had any evil against the rest of you I cannot say, but I overheard his conversation with that woman. Search him!"

Gribichon's nimble fingers never picked pockets so very willingly and thoroughly as they went over Black George's clothes.

A pistol, a purse, a knife, and one or two other trifles were handed up to Cartouche at the table,

but still Gribichon seemed to think there was something wanting yet.

Presently he found a secret pocket in Black George's vest, and in that a packet of letters.

"Now we shall know something !" said Cartouche.

"Captain—comrades," said Black George——

"Don't call me comrade !" exclaimed Gribichon, hitting him a heavy blow on the mouth.

"Wait, Gribby, don't disown him yet. Let us see with whom the fellow is in correspondence," said Cartouche.

The first letter settled the business, for it was from Lecoq senior, well known to all the band as the lieutenant of Monsieur Peuchet, the Chief of Police.

Cartouche was about to open some more of the letters when old Tomasso interfered—

"Don't waste time, captain. You have read quite enough to show that he is a thorough traitor."

CHAPTER XXXI.

THE PUNISHMENT OF BLACK GEORGE.

"What say you, gentlemen, is Black George guilty or not guilty ?" demanded Cartouche.

"Guilty !" was the unanimous reply of all.

"Then, captain, you had better pronounce sentence at once ; and if no one else cares for the job my dagger is at your service," said Tomasso.

"I shall call upon the new members to execute the decree that will be pronounced upon the wretch."

Jerome and Charles rose and bowed, to express their readiness to execute Cartouche's orders.

"Bring the prisoner up to the table."

Black George struggled, but feebly. He was in the hands of four strong men and had to go.

"George St. Claire—for that is the name by which you enrolled yourself a member of this band—you swore true brotherhood and fidelity when you signed the roll, and you wished the hand that held the pen might perish if ever you proved false. Your falsehood has been sufficiently proved—Jerome, lop off the traitor's right hand."

Black George yelled and struggled, but it was no use, Gribichon and the others held him. Charles caught hold of his fingers and forced the offending hand down on the table. Jerome drew a heavy cutlass, or hunting-sword, which he wore, and in two blows severed the offending member.

"Now cut off the other, to prevent his writing any more lies," said Cartouche.

Jerome and the others cheerfully obeyed the command.

"Now, lest he bleed too much to undergo the remaining part of his sentence, you, Charles, sear his wounds with this red-hot poker," said Cartouche, taking the implement in question from the fire behind him.

"With pleasure, captain !"

Black George had yelled and moaned pretty loudly whilst his hands were being amputated, but his screams were positively awful when the red hot iron was applied to the raw flesh. However, it had the effect of stopping the flow of blood.

"We will soon quiet that noise," said Cartouche, and he smiled one of his worst-looking smiles as he spoke. "The prisoner is a little faint, give him a glass of wine."

Black George, who was on the point of fainting, greedily swallowed the liquor that was held to his lips, and felt a little better after it.

Black George was not very wise, or he would not have opened his mouth; but thinking his punishment was over he very foolishly said—

"You have prevented my writing to the police, but, you fool! you forget that I can speak to them."

Cartouche smiled worse than before.

"I forgive your anger, Black George, but I cannot overlook your folly. Do you feel better?"

"Yes."

"Then we will proceed to the next part of the punishment. I have not half finished with you yet."

Black George was perfectly white with terror when he heard those words.

"Gentlemen," Cartouche continued, "that handless fellow who sits there once swore the oath we have all taken; he swore falsely, and having broken his oath he now has the imprudence to tell us that he possesses the power of giving information to the police. He shall no longer possess that power, for I decree that his lying tongue shall be cut from his mouth. Who will volunteer to do it?"

The new members of the band, anxious to prove their zeal in the common cause, at once offered to execute the order, in spite of its brutality.

But old Tomasso stepped forward.

"Captain," said he, "I believe I am the oldest surviving member of this band, and I think I am entitled to have a hand in the game. Besides, cutting out a man's tongue is a delicate operation, requiring a sharp weapon and a firm hand. It is an operation I have performed twice, and I think with my experience I could make a good job of the present case."

"Then do it, Signor Tomasso."

Black George did not yell, and he was too weak to make much resistance. He was forced back into a chair, and there he sat with his teeth clenched.

Tomasso was as cruel as any cat playing with a mouse. He approached his victim with what he intended to be a pleasant smile.

"Open your mouth," said he.

Black George shook his head and sat with his mouth firmly closed. He would not open his teeth to say a word.

"Well, if you are obstinate I must use my instruments," said Tomasso.

The Corsican had been occupying himself the early part of the day in fitting up the place, getting in furniture, and so forth. He had a few carpenters' tools with him. Catching up a pair of pincers he struck Black George on the mouth with the implement and broke off two of the unfortunate rascal's teeth; a chisel was then inserted in the gap, the obstinate mouth was forced open, and a piece of wood being inserted between his jaws, Black George was unable to close it again.

Tomasso then deliberately drew out the poor devil's tongue with his pincers and cut it off as near the root as possible.

Finally Black George's eyes were rendered sightless, and then Cartouche exclaimed—

"So may all suffer who prove faithless to their captain and comrades."

"Amen!" said all the members of the band.

But some of them felt very sick—such deliberate and diabolical cruelty was rather more than their stomachs could stand.

As for the victim, he was senseless, and only a slight pulsation told the others that he was alive.

Cartouche wished him to live as an example to all the band, for Black George would have to beg for a living, and his late comrades would not fail to see him as he wandered about while they were on their predatory expeditions.

So some restoratives were administered to the poor maimed rascal, and when he was able to walk they led him out into the street.

More merciful than Cartouche, Gribichon, who conducted Black George to the door, set him with his face in such a direction that if he walked straight on for about three hundred yards he would certainly tumble into the Seine, and so end his wretched life.

But fate ordained that Black George should live.

CHAPTER XXXII.

MORE OF LADY GUILFORT.

LADY GUILFORT, alias the countess, alias the princess, &c., &c., was rather surprised that Cartouche did not return to her.

He was not taken or all Paris would have known it; so the lady could only suppose that the too pressing attentions of Peuchet, Lecoq, and the police generally, had compelled him either to quit Paris or keep entirely within doors. She knew nothing of his connection with Louise.

Cartouche, too, had not revealed to Lady Guilfort the meeting place of his band, so that she knew not in which quarter of Paris it was most likely that she would meet with him.

She went out every day it is true, and she wore a different wig and different complexion each time she went out.

Lady Guilfort's male servants or associates had been told that they were to join the band of Cartouche, and they also wondered when they were to be introduced to their comrades in villainy.

But Cartouche himself, knowing her to be a cold-blooded murderess, thought he had best be off with the new love and keep on with the old. If Lady Guilfort should happen to discover that his absence was due to Louise, he fancied that his head and the flower-girl's as well might go to decorate the study of some old-spectacled German professor.

So Cartouche remained with Louise.

The day after the punishment of Black George, however, the flower-girl was permitted to go out and resume her occupation in the streets.

Cartouche wanted to know what the Parisians had to say about the eyeless, handless, dumb man, who had appeared in the streets, but he did not wish to ask any questions.

So he sent out Louise with strict instructions to find out anything extraordinary that had happened lately.

"For instance, you may say you have been away in the country, and inquire, in a joking way, how many murders and duels a day have been committed during your absence."

"Not many, I suppose, or you would have told me of them. I should like to know who that woman was whom I shot the other night."

"I have not been able to find out yet."

The police had, as a matter of fact, identified the body, which was buried at the expense of Monsieur Peuchet, but that gentleman, for reasons of his own, commanded all his subordinates to keep the name of the deceased a secret, and in his official report of the matter stated that the murdered woman was unknown. And that report was issued to the public.

"Also, you may ask if anything is known of that rascal, Cartouche," continued the owner of that name.

"Well, you know——"

"I want to know the latest rumours."

"I understand," Louise responded.

So kissing Cartouche, Louise caught up her basket and hied away to the market, where she bought a good stock, the dealers being glad to see her again, as she was a profitable customer.

"Eh, Louise! why, where have you been?" was the question asked on all hands.

"To visit my aunt in the country. Why should not I take a holiday sometimes?" she replied.

Having made her purchases Louise went to a neighbouring archway and sat down to tie them up in small bouquets.

While so engaged Lady Guilfort came along.

"What pretty flowers!" she said. "What is the price of this bunch?"

"A franc, mademoiselle."

"I will take it—here is the money."

The wind blew the Lady Guilfort's mantle aside slightly as she took the coin from her pocket, and the flower-girl distinctly saw the butt of a pistol and the handle of a dagger in the folds of her dress.

"A queer sort of lady," thought Louise.

But the Lady Guilfort always went armed, and was fully resolved to make a desperate fight if any police-officer should make another attempt to arrest her.

Louise handed her the bouquet and pocketed the coin.

"Are you the girl they call La Belle Louise?" the lady asked.

"I am," was the response.

Louise had a sort of half suspicion that she was speaking to the notorious murderer whose escape from justice was still common talk in Paris in spite of later novelties in crime.

"I don't wonder that all the young swells of the town are in love with you, Louise."

The flower girl smiled as she answered—

"It is lucky for me that you are not likely to go into the flower business, or I should have a dangerous rival."

"Of course I am not such a fool as not to be aware that I am good-looking, but I am not going to start in the business against you."

Louise made no reply; she had resolved to say as little and hear as much as possible. Her suspicions were on the increase.

"Of course, having such a vast number of admirers, you have selected one upon whom to bestow your heart?" the lady asked.

"Certainly, what would life be without a sweetheart?"

"A handsome fellow, doubtless!"

"And a brave one," said Louise.

"Is he rich?"

"Now what does this woman want to ask all these questions for?" thought Louise, and she warily answered—

"Sometimes he makes a good deal of money, but he is very generous to me and extremely extravagant."

"How does he earn his money?"

"What a question! However, if you must know, he gambles—and frequently wins. How do you get money—have you large estates?"

Lady Guilfort gave an affirmative nod.

"Yes, I have in Normandy. But I hate living there because it is so dull."

"That accounts then for your not talking like a Parisian. I thought from your speech that you were a foreigner—an Englishwoman or a German," said Louise.

While uttering these words the flower-girl pretended to be busy with her stock-in-trade, but all the time she was keeping a very close watch upon the countenance of her lady questioner, across whose face there flashed a sudden look of intense fury, which, by a mighty effort, she changed to a smile, but rather a severe one.

Her ladyship, on this occasion, was wearing black hair and eyebrows, and had her skin browned a little to match.

"You are a silly child! you cannot find Englishwomen or Germans so dark-complexioned as I am. My parents were Spanish, and I was born in Spain, though they took me to Normandy when I was very young indeed. But what is the name of this lover of yours?"

"Philip Damas," replied the unblushing Louise.

"Of course, you hear all the news of the town?"

"I have not much to-day, and I only returned from the country late last night."

"Then you have not heard of that poor wretch who was found last night with his hands cut off, his eyes blinded, and his tongue torn out ?"

"No ! was there a man found in that state—who could do such a cruel thing ?"

"People say it was Cartouche, but I don't believe it."

"It is impossible !" said Louise, impetuously, and her cheek flushed so that Lady Guilfort began to suspect that she had a rival.

"Do you know Cartouche ?"

"I knew him some years ago, before he was so famous," was the guarded reply of Louise. "He was very generous and gentle then, and I will not believe he can have changed into a monster."

"I think with you that it cannot be Cartouche," said Lady Guilfort. "Well, Belle Louise, shall I find you here other morning with your flower-basket ?"

"Not always ; I go in different directions as fancy prompts me. Now I must go and meet my lover."

"Then I must hasten away."

Lady Guilfort hastened away, but after going a few yards she looked back, intending to watch the flower-girl.

Louise had risen, but instead of going to meet her lover she was watching Lady Guilfort's movements.

For some few minutes there was some artful dodging between these two ; at last Lady Guilfort contrived to escape into a labyrinth of narrow passages and alleys, and Louise was quite convinced that it was no use to follow. But she felt quite certain now that she had been talking to the Lady Guilfort.

Louise then went off to the place where she expected to find Cartouche.

CHAPTER XXXIII.

AN AFFAIR WITH THE MILITARY.

TOMASSO and Cartouche met by appointment in a little street at the back of the Cathedral of Notre Dame.

They were both to some extent disguised, but each recognised the other by a peculiar signal given with the fingers.

Their object was to plan another expedition, for the exchequer was getting rather low, none of the band being noted for thrift while money lasted.

Cartouche's men were not, as a rule, drinkers to any great extent, but each of them, from the captain down to the Wolf, had a lady-love—some two or three.

Cartouche had just proposed a raid upon the Jesuits' college at which he was educated, and was proceeding to discuss the details when Louise was seen approaching.

"Good girl !" said Cartouche, pretending to examine her basket of flowers. "What news ?"

Louise did not know much of her husband's companion, and therefore rather hesitated to open her mouth.

"Don't be afraid of Tomasso, he is a good old friend and a trusty one. Speak out, my Louise."

"Well, Louis, there has been found in the streets a poor wretch whose hands and tongue had been cut off and his eyes destroyed—and they say you did it."

"That man intended to betray us all—the whole of the band—into the hands of the police," said Tomasso, seeing that his chief hesitated to reply. "Every one of us would have been in the Bastille to-night if his treachery had not been detected."

"Why did you not kill him ? that would have been far more merciful."

"There are two others of whose truth we are doubtful, and it was necessary to read them a fearful warning."

"You see, Louise," said Cartouche, "it was necessary that there should be a living example of the vengeance that overtakes traitors."

Louise heaved a deep sigh.

"What do they say of this fellow—where is he ?"

"They say that you did it, but the people cannot think why, as he was by his dress a poor man."

"You know why, but you must not give that piece of information to anyone. What has become of him ?"

"The police found him wandering about, and sent him to the hospital till his wounds are perfectly healed."

"And then ?"

"I don't know what will happen to him then. But now I know why it was done I have less pity for him."

"Who told you about him ?" Cartouche asked.

"A lady who bought flowers of me. And, Louis, I verily believe it was that Lady Guilfort of whom you told me about some little time ago."

"Well, Louise, why do you think it was the lady in question ?" Cartouche asked.

Louise detailed her reasons for suspecting the woman, and repeated, almost verbatim, the conversation they had, giving at the finish a minute personal description.

Cartouche frowned and said—

"It must be that cursed woman."

"I wonder why she should question me ?"

"I know not, my love. If you ever see her again be very careful in your answers, and, if you can do so, track her to her home, and let me know where it is. Now run away and sell your flowers, girl. I would like to kiss you, but we don't want to attract too much attention."

Louise nodded and tripped away.

Cartouche and Tomasso strolled away to a little wineshop not far distant, where they arranged their plans for the attempt upon the Jesuit seminary.

"But," said Tomasso, when the details were nearly settled, "is the game worth the candle ?"

"How ?—what do you mean, Signor Tomasso ?"

"Are we likely to get a booty worth the trouble we must take and the risks we run. It is vacation time, you tell me, and the pupils, both rich and poor, are away. Have the few fathers who remain there anything worth our trouble?"

"Plenty. I know exactly the spot where stands the chest in which the funds of the college are kept, and this is just the time when they receive their rents."

"Good. I hope those Picardy farmers have been punctual with their payments."

"If a few of them are behind with their rents there is still the chapel to exploit; you have never been there, Signor Tomasso?"

"No, monsieur the captain."

"It would make your mouth water and your eyes twinkle to see the solid silver candlesticks almost as tall as myself, and the solid gold cups and plates upon the altar, and the gold ornaments all over the place."

"How shall we get them away?"

"Why, we must take a file or two and cut them up into small pieces, and put them in a sack."

"It will make our shoulders ache to carry that sack away," observed Tomasso.

"Never mind, we can rest afterwards. So if you are in the humour we will astonish Paris by plundering the college to-morrow night."

"Right, Captain Cartouche," said the Corsican. "How many men shall we take with us?"

"Only one—old Gregoire as boatman. He knows how to handle the oars."

"How many men are there in the college?"

"Only three old priests, and the gardener and cook."

"We can manage the men. How many women are there, my brave captain?"

"Signor Tomasso, you speak scandalously. Do you imagine the holy fathers would allow anything feminine inside their walls? No, signor, not even a female cat—all the mousers in that establishment are of the male sex."

"Ha, ha, ha! you are jesting, captain."

"No, I assure you."

"Well then, captain, proceed with your plan of campaign. How shall we get there?"

"We had best not go together; so, good friend Tomasso, I will go in the boat with Gregoire, who will provide the necessary implements, and you walk or ride as best suits you to the scene of action."

"Where and at what hour shall we meet?"

"There is a little tavern about a hundred yards before you reach the school by road—the Silver Star it is named."

"I know it—bad wine there."

"There is better inside the school walls. We will meet at the Silver Star at half-past nine of the clock. It will be best not to go together, for everybody is watched now by those confounded police."

"True; and as if there were not enough of them about the town they must needs put a number of soldiers on police duty, men who have been doing duty at Toulon and Marseilles, the galley-slave depôts—men who know the face of every discharged convict who ever tugged at the oar."

"They are not likely to know mine. Is yours familiar to them, Signor Tomasso?"

"No; but I should not like to show it at Corsica or even in Genoa."

"Then stick to Paris, my good friend. Well, we have agreed how to get to Clermont and how to meet outside. I know how to enter the place, and will show you when we get there."

"Good, and till half-past nine to-morrow night we had best not be seen much together."

"You are right, Tomasso. You will bring your pistols, of course, in case force should be necessary."

"I shall bring pistols and my dagger."

The two worthies then separated.

Cartouche went to one or two places where he expected to see Louise, but not seeing her he decided on returning at once to his—or rather her lodging.

Walking fast and by the most direct route, he overtook the flower-girl, who, having sold out her stock, and not finding anything that suited her in the market, was returning home with some dainty articles of food in her basket to form a savoury dinner for herself and Cartouche.

"I am very tired, Louis, and cannot keep up with you at this pace," said Louise, when they had gone a few yards together.

"Then we will walk less rapidly, my pet."

And they strolled on together, quite oblivious of the fact that they were being watched by no less a person than the Lady Guilfort.

That worthy adventuress had, after much thought, come to the conclusion that Louise knew much more about Cartouche than came out in their conversation, and so resolved to keep a watch upon the movements of the flower-girl as the best way of finding out the hiding-place of her truant lover.

It was just after Louise parted from Cartouche near the cathedral that the wily adventuress caught sight of the flower-girl, and since that time Louise had been closely watched.

Now she saw the meeting between Cartouche and his pet, and the demon of jealousy at once filled the soul of the fashionable murderess, who at once condemned Louise to a violent death or such disfigurement as had been inflicted upon Black George.

Determined to find out whither they were going she called a sedan-chair—a kind of conveyance very popular in Paris just then, a thing something like the hinder part of a cab, but only wide enough for one person inside. It was carried by two porters, who fixed poles to the sides of the machine, and so bore it along. There were public ones for hire, just as now we have cabs.

"Keep those two persons in view," said the Lady Guilfort to the chairmen, who promised obedience, as it meant extra pay.

But as the men moved off with their burden the cry was heard—

"Make way for his highness the Dauphin !"

And a dozen or more mounted servants rode up the street—which had no sidewalks—driving the people into doorways, courts, and side streets to enable the lumbering coach containing the king's son to pass up the street.

Cartouche and Louise were unceremoniously thrust up a narrow entry on one side, and the chairmen were pushed down a street on the other side.

"Let us go through to the next street," said Cartouche ; "it is quite as near a way."

Louise assented, and so Lady Guilfort missed her prey, a circumstance which added considerably to her anger.

Cartouche then quietly made his arrangements with old Gregoire, a boatman who had often assisted the gang to plunder the barges on the river ; he was to row Cartouche to the point nearest the Jesuits' college, and there wait till the plunder was brought down to the waterside in the vehicle which Tomasso had agreed to have in waiting at the Silver Star.

Gregoire was to be waiting at one of the quays at seven in the evening, an hour which would give Cartouche ample time to keep his appointment with Tomasso at the little inn near the Jesuit college.

He was strolling down to the water in a leisurely manner, smoking a cigar—a fashion just recently adopted from the Spaniards, when Lady Guilfort caught sight of him.

For a minute anger predominated over love, and seeing two of the soldiers who had just been sent to aid the police, she ran up to them and exclaimed—

"See ! that man with the cigar—it is Cartouche !"

Without even waiting to thank her for the information the soldiers started in pursuit, fixing their bayonets to the muzzles of their clumsy old muskets as they ran.

The clattering of their heavy shoes on the ill-paved road attracted the attention of Cartouche, who looked back over his shoulder to see what was the matter.

"Hullo ! halt, Monsieur Cartouche !" shouted one of them.

"Stop, my good fellow," cried the other, "or we shall be compelled to shoot you !"

Cartouche replied by drawing a pistol from his belt and firing as he ran. The bullet missed, and he fired again with no better success.

"The reward is the same—'dead or alive,' says the proclamation," one of the soldiers remarked as Cartouche bounded away down the street ; "so halt, comrade, take a good aim, and—fire !"

"Bang !" went the two muskets, and the bullets whistled very near Cartouche's head without touching it.

"Follow on, comrade ! if we can only overtake him we shall do the business."

They were hardy athletic men, and they pressed Cartouche so much that he was glad when he saw the quay at the end of the street, and old Gregoire, with a patch over one eye, in his boat about a couple of yards from land.

Of course the soldiers could not stop to load their muskets or their quarry would escape. The bayonet was just the thing, though, i they could only get near enough to administe a thrust.

And they drew so near Cartouche as h approached the edge of the quay that it seemed very likely he would feel the points of thei weapons. But just in the nick of time he took a flying leap into old Gregoire's boat.

"Pull like the very devil !" exclaimed Cartouche.

Gregoire needed no exhortation, but with on sweep of his sculls sent the heavy craft far out into the river.

Then, like a prudent man, observing that on of the soldiers was reloading his piece, the boat man sent his craft behind a long string o barges anchored in mid-stream, and soon wa beyond range.

The other soldier, by-the-bye, unable to hal soon enough, had gone head-foremost into th water, therefore shooting was out of the questio so far as he was concerned.

In a very disconsolate condition the bol soldiers returned to their station to report wha had happened and to be laughed at by thei comrades, while Gregoire and Cartouche spec merrily over the surface of the river, indulgin in quiet chuckles at the discomfiture of thei foes.

Everything was quiet upon the river, and th boat touched land again without observation.

"Will you go back with me, captain ?' Gregoire asked.

"Can't say ; all depends upon how we ge along, but you may expect to have either Tomasso or myself for passengers on the retur voyage ; and, of course, we are not going to b such fools as to land where we started from."

"Nor yet where my boat is usually moored They would not know me with the patch ove my eye, but they might recognise my old skiff.'

"Well, be ready to shove off the moment yo hear us coming down the road."

Gregoire promised to be wide awake.

Cartouche then walked away in the directio of the Jesuit school.

CHAPTER XXXIV.

A GOOD BAG !

IT was ten minutes earlier than the ti appointed when Cartouche entered the little i called the Silver Star.

Tomasso was there, however, and no ot guest. The vehicle, with its driver, stood the roadside about half way between the and the place to be exploited.

"One glass of cognac, Signor Tomasso, then we will proceed to business," said C touche.

"We tried the wine and it is filthy, so le have a taste of brandy to purify the palate.

"Is 'The Driver' all right ?"

CARTOUCHE,
THE FRENCH JACK SHEPPARD.

CARTOUCHE TOOK GOOD AIM AND SENT A BULLET INTO THE FELLOW'S BRAIN.

"Perfectly," replied Tomasso.

The man who brought Tomasso to the Silver Star was one of Cartouche's band. He drove a public carriage for hire in the streets of Paris, and few of the band knew him by any other name than "The Driver."

As Cartouche and Tomasso passed up the road to the school they saw that The Driver was seated on the box of his vehicle, whip and reins in hand, and the horse turned in the direction he would have to go when a start was made.

Then they came to the building.

It looked a difficult place to get into without permission—at least, so Tomasso thought as he surveyed the high wall, crowned with spikes, and the lofty iron gates.

"How are we going to get in, my captain?" Tomasso asked.

"Like gentlemen. We shall ring the bell and enter by the front gate—those you see before you."

"But see the notice, my captain—'No person admitted under any pretext after eight o'clock in summer and in winter six?' And now it is nearly ten."

"My good friend, Tomasso, I intend to ring that bell. The gardener, who acts as porter during the vacation, will come. I shall hold him in conversation and you will seize him by the throat. Then we shall bind and gag him."

"But, Signor Capitano, ringing the bell will arouse the good fathers, who, doubtless, are just sinking to sleep on their wooden couches."

"Those wooden couches have good thick woollen mattresses between them and the bodies of the reverend fathers; no hard boards there, Tomasso, except for refractory pupils, such as I was. Besides, having once secured the gates and the porter's keys, we need not hurry, but can give the holy gentlemen an hour or so to fall asleep again ere we begin our work."

"You are a great general, so begin as soon as you like, Signor Cartouche."

The captain of the Parisian banditti gave a good tug at the bell-handle and whispered Tomasso to stand aside so that he should not be seen.

In a few minutes the gardener-porter came up the path, swinging his lantern in his hand.

"Who is here at this time of the night?" he growled. "You cannot come in if you are the king himself."

"Friend, open the gate, and do not speak any more treasonable speeches, or you will find yourself in the Bastille before sunrise. I come from the king."

"How am I to know that?" demanded the gardener, who had been asleep for an hour.

"You will have to take my word for it," said Cartouche, sternly; "so just open the gate, and then I will trouble you to show me to the presence of Father Renard, the principal."

The gardener was cowed by the threat of being sent to the Bastille, whither so many went and whence so few returned, and he at once opened the gate.

Cartouche walked in, and, pretending to stumble over something, fell upon his hands and knees. The gardener turned to see what made his visitor swear so, and Tomasso seized the unhappy menial by the throat with such an iron grip that he could scarce breathe, much less cry out. Cartouche was quickly up, and bound his arms and legs, and a gag was placed in the poor fellow's mouth. Then they carried him outside and laid him against the wall, some twenty yards from the gate.

That done, and having secured the gardener's lantern, Cartouche and Tomasso went inside the grounds, and the leader of the expedition coolly locked the gates, having taken the keys from the poor fellow outside.

"Now cover up the lantern, and we will hide in this clump of evergreens," said Cartouche.

"You are as artful as Satan, Captain."

"Thank you for the compliment, Tomasso!"

"I believe you could steal the devil's pitchfork if you wanted it, but hang me if I see the use of hiding in these laurels when there is work to be done!"

"Don't argue, friend Tomasso, but come along and keep particularly quiet, too."

The Corsican obeyed, and followed his leader into the clump of evergreens, and they had not been there many minutes before another lantern was seen coming up the path towards the gates.

Very soon the two robbers could see that it was borne by the Father Renard, the superior of the college.

"The old rascal!" whispered Cartouche, "I can feel the sting of the whip now. I shall never forget that stroke he gave me as I climbed over the wall."

"What shall we do with him, captain?"

"Same as the gardener—only don't handle him quite so roughly, for he is an old man and I don't want to kill him."

"That would be a very easy job. However, as you want him to live I won't stop his breath."

On came the reverend father.

Father Renard was fairly active considering he was sixty-five years of age. He had heard the bell, and, in fact, sent the sleepy gardener to inquire who was ringing at such an unusual hour. Now he came to find out why that gardener had not returned.

"It is very strange," said the father, holding up his light and examining the gate. "All safely locked—but where is the gardener and where are the keys?"

"I have them—I, Louis Dominique Cartouche."

"Villain!" exclaimed the father; but before he could utter another word Tomasso had him by the throat, and the reverend superior of the college was speedily bound and gagged.

"Well done, Tomasso!" said Cartouche.

"Ah! but what will my father confessor say when I next tell him my little budget of sins?"

"What did he say when you confessed last?"

"Told me to walk two miles every day to hear mass with peas in my shoes."

"And did you, Signor Tomasso?"

"I did, religiously, Captain Cartouche."

"They must have hurt your feet."

"On the contrary, signor Capitano. I always boiled the peas till they were quite soft—the father said nothing about that part of the business."

"Bravo, Tomasso? If I can rob the devil of his pitchfork I believe you can cheat him out of his horns. But now, having laid our reverend gentleman aside under these laurels, where the winds will not blow upon him too harshly, let us perform the remainder of our business."

"How many men do you say are there?"

"The cook and two or three fathers. The cook is fat, and could not walk twenty yards in five minutes, the fathers are very feeble old chaps, but awfully learned. The Greek, Latin, Hebrew, and Egyptian languages come as naturally to them as swearing does to a wood-carter bringing faggots from Fontainebleau."

"What is to be done with them?"

"Get them all into one room and lock them in. But have you searched the Reverend Father Renard? What did you find on him?"

"A horsehair shirt next his skin—and that is no use to us, Signor Cartouche. Here is a breviary, a crucifix, and a bunch of keys. No money, no jewellery."

"We will keep the keys and let the reverend gentleman keep the rest of his property. Be quiet," he added, turning to Father Bernard, "and no harm will happen to you, and we shall soon set you at liberty."

Then he and Tomasso walked towards the house, putting on their crape masks as they went.

The front door was open, as the gardener and Father Renard had left it, so they walked in without any trouble.

As they crossed the entrance-hall they ran against the fat man—cook of the establishment—who should have been in his bed two hours before.

"Where are you going?" demanded Cartouche.

"To the wood-cellar for fuel, holy father," the fat fellow managed to stammer.

"I am not a holy father, but a robber; and you know well enough that fires are not allowed at this hour. What key is that you have in your hand?"

"Key of—wood-cellar—holy robber," the poor fellow said.

Cartouche snatched it, and compared it with one of those he had taken from Father Renard.

"A very neatly executed duplicate of the wine-cellar key." However, you shall go to the wood-cellar.

"Shall I show you the way, holy gentleman?"

"I know the way as well as you, so go on as fast as your fat legs will carry you."

The cook trotted off at a pace which broke the record of his last ten years' pedestrianism, for Tomasso, though silent, had been extremely eloquent in his looks and gestures.

"This is the wood-cellar, holy sir," said the cook, as he paused before an underground door.

"Go on, this won't do," said Cartouche.

The unhappy cook trotted on till they came to another door, when Cartouche cried—

"Halt—what door is this?"

"Wine cellar, holy sir."

"In you go, then," said Cartouche, turning a key in the lock, and thrusting the lying cook into a vault where a quantity of fuel was stored. Locking the door and bolting it on the outside he said to Tomasso—

"We will have all the fathers down here. They may shout themselves hoarse without being heard, and we can go quietly over the place."

Cartouche then led Tomasso up into that part of the building where the Jesuit fathers attached to the college had their quarters.

"Father Joseph lives here," said Cartouche, pausing before a door in a long corridor.

"What is he?" asked Tomasso, who was not quite certain that he was not committing deadly sin in thus invading the lodgings of men who were supposed to dwell in the odour of sanctity. And if Messrs. Rimmel could only bottle up some of that odour wouldn't we all be very nice?

"Father Joseph is a very clever mathematician," replied Cartouche. "He will prove that two and two don't make five, and demonstrate to the satisfaction of everybody that the two halves of a thing are much greater than the whole."

"That's all my eye!"

"No matter, let us have the reverend genius out of his cot. Ho! Father Joseph! come out!"

There was a sound as of two persons conversing in low tones, then in a louder voice—

"Who disturbs my nightly prayer?"

"I want to confess, father."

"Go to—Father Peter," said the voice.

"He is no use. I must tell you all the sins I have ever committed, or mean to commit, and they are such a lot that it will take at least half an hour to catalogue them."

"Away, you rascal; this is no time for confession!"

"It is for committing crime, though, so come out, father."

Father Joseph made no response, so Cartouche gave a very vigorous kick, which burst the lock of the holy gentleman's door, and, followed by Tomasso, he walked in.

"Great heaven! what do I see?"

What he saw was the reverend father Joseph just struggling into the breeches he usually wore. But Cartouche noticed something else; there was apparently a pile of blankets on the couch fitter for a winter at the North Pole than the mild atmosphere of Paris.

"What have we here?" said he.

Jerking back the blankets there was disclosed to view the stout form of a middle-aged female, who had taken up Madame Lafarge's trade of supplying the scholars with fruit cakes and other things beloved by schoolboys.

"Ha, ha, ha!" laughed Tomasso, heartily. "I thought, Signor Cartouche, women were not admitted?"

"Smuggled goods—no duty paid at the gates. Don't interfere with the lady, Tomasso—but, Father Joseph, you must come down to the wood cellar and make confession, or——"

"I shall give you absolution with this," said the Corsican, showing the long, keen dagger with which he had frightened the cook into a proper frame of mind.

"I don't know why I should move," Father Joseph stammered.

"You are professor of mathematics, and don't know that when an irresistible force meets an immovable object there is bound to be a smash? Come out!"

Father Joseph, in his breeches and shirt, came out very promptly into the corridor, and stood like a lamb waiting to be slaughtered by the side of Tomasso, who looked quite capable of killing him and hanging him by the hind legs at the gateway of the college.

"You old scoundrel, if you move or speak without permission I'll let you have the full length of this! It is only eight inches, but that is enough for you, I guess."

And the Corsican flourished his long dagger before the eyes of the mathematical father, who cried—

"Mercy—mercy!"

"Keep quiet and you won't be hurt," said the Corsican. "What are you going to do with the girl, captain?"

"It must have been ages since she was a girl, but—look here woman, if you venture to move from that bed till Father Joseph returns, I will kill you as sure as my name is Cartouche."

"Cartouche!" she screamed.

"Silence!" cried the owner of that magic name.

"Cartouche," moaned Father Joseph. "Then I am——"

"You are not damned yet, father, but you soon will be if you don't hold your tongue," said Tomasso. "Now come along with us down to the wine cellar, where we have your friend the fat cook safely locked up. You may drink as much as you like, you know."

"It is rather dry hospitality you are offering the reverend gentleman," Cartouche observed.

"The cook said that was the wine-cellar, so it ought to be moist enough."

"The cook is a liar. However, come along Father Joseph."

And the unhappy mathematician was led away, and thrust into the wood cellar along with his friend the fat cook.

"Now, captain, I suggest that we get to work upon the portable property as soon as we can," said Tomasso.

"We may as well lock up the other chaps, so that we shall have no interference."

"As you like, captain. Only say the word and I will tie them together, neck and heels, and pitch them into their own fish pond. The carp and tench would have some rare picking from their bones."

"No, we won't drown them, Tomasso, we will lock them up in the wood cellar with the others."

So the remaining inhabitants of the Jesuit College were thrust into the prison with their confrères, Father Joseph and the fat cook. But, to the credit of the establishment, be it said, Cartouche found no more ladies.

Having locked up the father of the seminary the two robbers proceeded in the first place to the steward's office, where they expected to find the money which should have been paid as rent by a score or more of farmers who held land of the college. Father Joseph, as a great arithmetician, had for some time held the post of steward and treasurer; but his office was bare; the rents were not due till a couple of days later, and, of course, were not paid.

After bursting open two or three iron-banded chests, which proved to be empty, Tomasso said—

"Well, captain, this is not a very profitable game, so I vote that we have a look into the chapel."

"Right, Tomasso—we will."

One of the fathers locked up in the wood-cellar acted as sacristan and custodian of the chapel. Cartouche had the key of the sacred building, but he declined to make use of it.

"I want the good people of Paris to see my handiwork," he said; "so lend me your crowbar, Signor Tomasso."

The Corsican with a polite bow handed the "jemmy" to his captain.

"Locks, bolts, and bars fly asunder!" exclaimed Cartouche, as with a powerful wrench he forced the chapel door from its hinges and laid it on the pavement with the disused key upon it.

"By Jove, captain, this is a sight!" exclaimed Tomasso, as his eye ran along the chapel.

The Jesuit College was a very wealthy one. The original founders had bestowed wealth enough for all purposes, but some of the great ones of France educated there had greatly increased the revenues of the establishment. Gifts of plate also had rolled in; the great Cardinal Mazarine had given such a set of plate as few altars in France could show. Richelieu had supplemented that gift with a dozen tall candlesticks of solid silver, one or two of the kings of France had testified their devotion to the church by donations of great value, and altogether the church of the Jesuits College was the most richly furnished in Paris.

The candles at the altar were kept burning day and night as a rule, and they were alight when Cartouche and his companion entered the place.

"Leave them for a time—the cups and plates first, friend Tomasso."

"Right, my captain. I leave the direction of the business to you—so give your orders and they shall be obeyed to the best of my ability."

"Then first put those gold plates and cups into the bag—don't spoil them by doubling them up for they are works of art, and will fetch more than their value as metal."

"But where will you sell them, my captain?"

"In England. I have an agent there, and the beef-eating race will pay through the nose for such things as these?"

Tomasso ripped the cloth covering from the principal seat, and wrapped each article carefully so that it should not be damaged, after which he transferred them to his bag.

"Now for the candles, Signor Cartouche."

"You see now why I wanted a couple of good files," said the captain of the banditti. "These candlesticks are of solid silver, and we shall have to cut them in three or four parts before we can put them away comfortably in that bag you are carrying, Signor Tomasso."

"Then give me one of the files and I will begin my apprenticeship as a silversmith."

Cartouche handed him one of the tools and they both set to work.

The cardinal's candlesticks were heavy and solid; there was no hollow workmanship about them. But Cartouche and his friend contrived to break them up, and then they fitted into the sack to a nicety.

"Now, off we go, Tomasso. We have been long enough about this job," said Cartouche.

Tomasso tried to shoulder the bag, but it was so weighty that Cartouche had to give him a hand with it.

"That is it. Now, captain, let The Driver get us back to old Gregoire's boat as soon as possible."

"That shall be done, but, Signor Tomasso, you forget that we have left a reverend gentleman lying——"

"He can't lie very well this evening, Signor Capitano. I gagged him so that he cannot say a word, truth or lie."

"I don't mean that, Tomasso; but he is taking his rest under the laurel bushes."

"Why should we disturb him? If anyone wants him in the morning they can look round and find him."

"Good, my Tomasso; but I want to give him a treat in payment for the stroke he gave me with his whip when I went out over the wall. So let me give you a hand with the bag down to The Driver's waiting-place, then we will return and pick up the Padre."

"I should like to leave him there for a month."

"I want to have a game with him, so I shall not leave him. Come along with the bag, old man. It is a jolly heavy one this time, and no mistake."

CHAPTER XXXV.

WHAT BECAME OF FATHER RENARD.

CARTOUCHE and his friend Tomasso lugged the bag of church plate along to the place where The Driver was waiting and placed their plunder under the seat of his vehicle.

"You will have to take three of us back to old Gregoire's boat," said the captain.

"Eh! three, captain?"

"I have said it."

"Well, I would take thirty with pleasure—

but, my captain, consider the stability of the vehicle and the power of the horse."

"It is not far down to old Gregoire's boat."

"True—and if your passenger is not too heavy he shall go along with us."

"He is only one of the fathers of the college."

"Eh! I see! you are going to put him in the boat and then drop him overboard for fear of accidents."

"Nothing of the kind, Driver. Do you think I would drown a poor Jesuit with his arms tied to his sides?"

"Don't know, captain."

"Well, I don't intend to drown him; so if you hear of a man being found at the Quai de Nemours to-morrow you may know that Father Renard is safe."

Cartouche and Tomasso then went back to the college grounds and brought out the reverend principal, whom they placed in the vehicle, still bound and gagged.

Next they paid a visit to the gardener—left in the ditch outside the college—and tucked in his girdle the key of the wood-cellar in which they attached a label, with the words—

"This is the key of the fathers' wine-cellar—and very dry wine you will find it. Look also in Father Joseph's dormitory."

"That will be enough for this side of the town. Our dear old Father Renard who whipped me as I climbed over the wall will go back to Paris with us."

The Driver took them swiftly down to the riverside, where Gregoire and his boat were waiting.

"Put the sack on board," said Cartouche. "That is more valuable than either or all of us."

As soon as the bag of church plate was placed on board the skiff Father Renard was tumbled into the craft in a rather rough, unceremonious manner.

"Be at the rendezvous to-morrow—or rather to-day, at noon, Driver," said Cartouche, as the boatman with a good strong pull at his oars sent the boat out into the stream.

"Right, captain," responded The Driver, who then went away to employ his time as best he could till the gates of Paris should open in the morning when he could re-enter the city.

The boat with Gregoire, Tomasso, Cartouche, and Father Renard on board swept along the shining bosom of the bright river Seine.

In due time they arrived at the Quai Pont Neuf, where, in spite of Gregoire's protestations, Cartouche insisted on landing.

"You are playing the very devil with me, captain," said the boatman.

"And I shall play something else with the father. Bring the old customer ashore."

Father Renard accordingly was landed just as though he had been a bale of goods to be delivered this side up.

It was about four o'clock in the morning, and Paris was about as quiet as one could expect that city to be in the early part of the eighteenth century.

"What shall we do with him, captain?" said

Gregoire, as he made fast his boat to a pile driven into the bed of the river.

"First of all we must dress him," was the reply of Cartouche.

The chief of the Parisian outlaws had, with a laudable consideration for the health of his victims, brought away the holy father in the dress he mostly preferred, namely, a shirt of woven horse-hair and black breeches which had been worn for many years by some other person before they came into the possession of the college.

In the bottom of Gregoire's boat was an old blanket.

Why it was there would be difficult to tell, but the gay captain of the Parisian banditti caught it up, and in the twinkling of an eye threw it round the body of the holy father Renard.

"Now you are one of us," said Cartouche. "You must have the rest, though."

And an hour later a member of the police force, wandering up the Quai Pont Neuf, espied a very curious-looking object—that is to say a man who apparently had nothing on him but a blanket; outside the blanket, however, was a ticket upon which he had written—

"THIEF!

"This man robbed Cartouche, and there's the revenge of L. D. Cartouche!"

With this ticket upon his back they sent the venerable preceptor of the Jesuits College on shore at the Quai Pont Neuf, where, in the course of half an half, he was surrounded by about a thousand young imps of the gutter, who hooted and yelled till someone was good enough to give the reverend father into the care of the police.

Cartouche and Tomasso got their bag ashore without any difficulty, and took the swag up to the place where Cartouche and his lovely Louise were residing.

CHAPTER XXXVI.

LOUISE HAS A BAD TIME.

LADY GUILFORT, having once ascertained to her own satisfaction that the flower-girl was Cartouche's favourite, and, therefore, her rival, was determined to do her best to consign Louise to prison or death, or any kind of fate that would keep her out of the way.

The Lady Guilfort wanted Cartouche herself, and was determined that no one should share his affections with her. "A low-bred flower-seller!" she muttered, as she walked back to her lodging, after Cartouche made his flying jump into Gregoire's boat.

Lady Guilfort was about as artful as they made folks in those days, and Monsieur Peuchet was no fool. But in dealing with Cartouche the Chief of Police was matching himself against a rogue of no ordinary cabibre—and the Lady Guilfort considered herself a match for all the police of Paris; so that between the two, Monsieur Peuchet, to whose memoirs we are greatly indebted, found himself in a very considerable fix.

Monsieur Peuchet was seated in his office conversing with Lecoq the elder, when a lady was announced.

"Name?" demanded Peuchet.

"She refuses to say, monsieur."

"Age and personal appearance?"

"Can't tell, monsieur."

"Why not, fool?"

"She keeps her veil down."

"Ass! how long have you been in the police force?"

"Fourteen years, monsieur."

"And you don't know yet how to make a woman expose her face? I shall put a mark against your name and you may wait fourteen years more for promotion."

The man gave a military salute and was silent.

Peuchet ran over in his own mind the list of female correspondents with whom he had to do since the death of Madame Lafarge, and at last told the man to show her up.

So Lady Guilfort was ushered into the place where she was most wanted, and the chief of police said to her in his most polite manner—

"Pray be seated, madame, and let me know what I can have the pleasure of doing for you."

"Monsieur Peuchet," said the lady. "I believe you are desirous of capturing Cartouche."

"Certainly, madame."

"I can assist you, I think."

"I should advise you to do so."

"Shall I share the reward if we succeed in bringing him to justice?"

"You may share the reward if you act fairly with me, but if you play me false you shall have a taste of his punishment."

Lady Guilfort had disguised and painted herself to such an extent that she could neither blush, nor frown, nor look angry. Her countenance was fixed behind a thick coating of paste and varnish.

"You say I shall have a taste of his punishment—pray what will that be?"

"Death! madame. When he is caught he will be hanged."

Lady Guilfort laughed as she said—

"You promised me a taste of his punishment—pray how much will you hang me?"

"A devilish nice-looking girl," thought old Peuchet, "and one with a temper too. Well, I like them with just a touch of the fiend in their composition."

And after a few seconds' thought he said—

"Madame, I have no wish to hang you—unless it should please you to clasp your arms round my neck, and then you may hang there till doomsday."

"You are facetious, monsieur."

"Very serious, madame."

"We were speaking of Cartouche. He robbed me, and I wish to know whether, if I assist in bringing him to the gallows, I shall have any part of the reward offered."

"Half, madame, if through your agency we capture this rascal who is at once the curse and the pride of France."

"I do not follow you quite."

"Madame, Cartouche is the curse of France on account of the many robberies he commits; but he is also the pride of the country because he does his business in such a bold, audacious manner. Cartouche is no common thief; he is a man of genius, and, although one of these days I must catch him and bring him to the gallows, I shall always have a respect for the daring fellow who gagged me in my own office."

"I can put you in the way of taking him."

"Do so, madame; you did not honour me with your name——"

"Signora Romano. I am Italian."

"I should have guessed that from your hair and complexion. You are married, of course, signora?"

"I have been, but alas! he is dead."

"You may yet find one to fill his place."

"Never!"

"Signora Romano, I, the Chief of Police, though far advanced in years, have still a heart that beats warmly. It is only a few minutes since my men brought you to my room, but during that time I have learned to love you. Signora, I adore you!"

"You don't know to whom you are speaking, my dear Monsieur Peuchet," replied the lady, satirically.

He certainly did not, or he would have clapped the handcuffs on to her wrists at once.

"Do not be angry, my charmer," said he.

"I am amused," quoth she. "But touching Cartouche."

"I wish I could touch him."

"Now I will tell you how it may be done——"

"And when it is done, my charmer, may I hope——"

"You may."

"Then tell me how we are to circumvent this artful rascal who defies the police."

"Listen, you know La Belle Louise?"

"Who in Paris does not?"

"She knows more of Cartouche than anyone else. She is his wife, though whether any ceremony of marriage was performed beyond jumping over a broomstick I cannot say."

"How do you know anything of this, madame?"

"Louise herself told me that Cartouche was her lover."

"And where do they live?"

"Heaven only knows! According to the statement of Louise they change their lodging every night."

"Humph! then how am I to catch Cartouche unless you can tell me where he and Louise are living?"

"Capture Louise. Cartouche is wildly in love with her—curse her!—and when he finds she is locked up he will soon come out and look around for the best means of rescuing her from your clutches."

"That is not a bad notion," said Peuchet. "Of course Louise is always about the city selling flowers; it will be easy enough to have her arrested."

And then as he reflected on the matter the Chief of Police said to himself—

"This woman is certainly in love with that rascal Cartouche, and therefore she is jealous of Louise. I wonder who she really is?"

The Lady Guilfort did not feel inclined to give her correct name—or rather that by which she was known to the French police—so Monsieur Peuchet remained in ignorance of the fact that he was conversing with one of the two most notorious criminals France possessed.

"It shall be done as you suggest, madame," said the Chief of Police, "and if the affair results in the capture of Cartouche you shall share the reward with me."

"Then, monsieur, I will take my departure."

"Permit me, madame, to conduct you to the door. Your carriage is waiting for you, I presume."

"A chair only."

"Bid the lady's chairmen be in readiness," Peuchet shouted down the staircase to his satellites below.

Then with a great deal of old-fashioned politeness he led her to the door, and saw her safely shut up in the chair.

"To what part of the city shall they convey you, madame?" he asked, standing, hat in hand, by the side of the conveyance.

"Home," was her brief reply.

And the chairmen trotted off with their load.

"Ahem! she might have been a trifle more civil. However, I have to catch Cartouche, so I will act on her suggestion and get hold of Louise first."

Monsieur Peuchet re-entered his office, and in less than five minutes despatched two of his men with orders to arrest La Belle Louise.

"You know her usual haunts," said he. "There should be no difficulty in finding her within a couple of hours."

"And where shall we take her, monsieur?" one of them asked.

"Bring her here and place her in one of the cells."

The two men gave a military salute to their chief and departed on their errand.

But instead of being only two hours over the business it was more than twice that time before they caught sight of the fair flower-seller.

Peuchet was waiting with some impatience for their return, when he heard a knock at the door.

"Enter! Have you caught her?"

The man who entered simply said—

"A letter for monsieur."

"Eh? Who brought this?"

"One of the city porters, monsieur. He said it was given him by a lady who got out of a sedan chair in the gardens of the Louvre."

"Send those men to me as soon as they bring in Louise, the flower-girl."

The man saluted and made his exit. Peuchet opened the letter, the contents of which caused him some surprise, not to say annoyance.

"I must be an ass!" he ejaculated.

The letter was worded as follows:—

"Monsieur Peuchet, you are an old donkey! You plaster the walls of Paris with bills offering a reward for my apprehension, and yet you politely escort me out of your office when I have told you the best way to capture my faithless lover, Cartouche. I hope you may catch him, though, and don't forget to punish Louise, who is the hated rival of your friend—The LADY GUILFORT."

"Ten thousand devils!" exclaimed Peuchet.

Meanwhile the two men were hunting for Louise, and at last they found her.

Frequent change of residence was, as already explained, one of the reasons why Cartouche was so very successful in evading the merry men of the police force, of whom thehead was Monsieur Peuchet.

Cartouche and Louise had gone to reside in a little low street where they had not previously resided. He had been at home all the day, and Louise had just gone out to purchase some dainties for their supper, when she was tapped upon the shoulder by one of the two officers.

"Ha, Louise, we have been looking for you," said he.

The flower-girl gave him a good slap on the face by way of answer.

"Gently, girl! don't you know that we are police officers?" said the man.

"I only know that you are a blackguard to insult me thus."

"Keep calm. I tell you I and my friend are police officers."

"Then go away. I am not a thief."

"Perhaps not, but you are the reputed wife of the most daring and successful thief in France. So you must come along with us, Madame Cartouche."

"That is not my name."

"Perhaps not. It should have been, though, if that rascal had taken you to church when he married you."

"Insolent!"

"We are used to hard names, so spit out as many of them as you please."

The other man thought he must have something to do in the matter, so he caught Louise by the arm, and said—

"We are wasting too much time over this girl, Henri Let us take her along without delay."

"You are right," responded the other.

The two police officers little guessed that their conversation had taken place just under the window of the room in which Cartouche was secreted.

He had overheard everything, and was rather puzzled how to act till they rudely laid hold of Louise; then anger overcame all other considerations. He had his pistols with him, and he resolved to use one of them at least.

So Cartouche took careful aim, and sent a bullet crashing into the brain of the fellow who had so rudely assaulted Louise.

The police-officer lived just long enough to clap his hand to his forehead, then he tumbled down dead. But his companion dragged off Louise, and had her safely up a neighbouring alley before Cartouche could get his second pistol ready for firing.

And then, when the chief of the Parisian banditti saw the dead man upon the roadway, he realised that he must at once take measures for his own safety. A policeman could not be killed in the street whilst performing his duty without some notice being taken of the fact.

"Captain!" whispered a voice.

Cartouche turned with the second pistol in his hand, and he beheld Gribichon.

"You don't want to shoot me, captain?"

"No, Grib. But how did you get here?"

"You don't know what trouble I have had to find you, captain," said Can-can's lover.

"And now that you have found me I must be off again."

"Don't go out at the front door, captain—follow me; I happen to know this place much better than you."

"Lead on, then, Gribichon."

"I can get you out of this house in a twinkling. Come along."

Gribichon led the way to the top of the house and out on to the roof.

"Captain, I have seen you jump a greater distance than from here to that house, so just fly across."

The house in question was at the back of Cartouche's late residence and had its front in another street.

"Set me a go, Gribichon. Show me the way."

"Then follow me, captain," exclaimed Gribichon.

And he took a leap across the intervening space; the tiles of the other house rattled a little as he alighted on them, but he was ready in a couple of seconds to extend a hand to Cartouche, who came flying after him.

"Where are we now, Gribby?"

"Rue St. Just—that is just about where we are."

"Whose house is it?"

"An old gentleman who owns a long and rather curved nose and sometimes purchases snuff-boxes, watches, and other trifles I find."

"A very nice person to know; what is his name?"

"I call him Moses, Red Judas used to call him Isaacs, but his real name may be anything else in the world."

"Well, Gribby, let us get out of this as soon as we can. Which is the way down?"

"Come along, captain."

"After you, Gribichon."

On the roof of this house there was a trapdoor, very similar to that from which they had emerged from Cartouche's lodging.

"Come along, captain, we will cheat Peuchet and his men yet. There are only two policemen in Paris that I care a rap for."

"Who are they?"

"The Lecoqs—father and son."

"They are dangerous customers, and no mistake."

"Hold your head down, captain, while I bolt the trap; if anyone feels inclined to follow us he will have some trouble to lift up this door now that the iron is properly in the socket."

Gribichon securely fastened the trapdoor on the inside, and then led his chief down a dark and rather narrow staircase. Half way between the roof and the street door they encountered a middle-aged man of a slightly oriental cast of countenance.

"I am honoured by this visit from the great Captain Cartouche," said this individual, pulling off his cap and making a low bow.

"You know me, then?"

"Well, monsieur?"

"Then be silent as to my visit."

"Not a word, monsieur. At any time when you have diamonds or jewellery of any kind to sell will you think of me? I'll give as good a price as any man in the trade—cash down."

"You are the man for me."

"Gribichon will tell you how to get here, Monsieur Cartouche. But then, I shall know you if I see you again. When you come on business, Monsieur Cartouche, ring the bell three times."

"And in the meantime be good enough to go before us and see that the street is clear. I am in no mood for an encounter with Peuchet's people just now."

"And you have left your pistols, captain," said Gribichon.

"The devil! so I have," growled Cartouche.

"I have some excellent pistols for sale, captain," said the owner of the house. "Fifty francs for a pair of them, and I will load them for you if you like."

"Let me have them."

"Loaded, captain?"

"Of course. Empty barrels are useless."

Isaacs, or whatever his name was, trotted off down to his shop to get the weapons, and Cartouche whispered to his friend Gribichon—

"Go and find out what they have done with Louise."

"I will; but I am afraid that hasty shot of yours will make things uncomfortable for her."

Off bolted Gribichon, and a minute later the man of the house came up with a pair of very handsome pistols.

"These never missed fire since they were forged," said he.

"Certainly they are handsome weapons."

"Not only handsome, but none in France can throw a bullet nearly so truly, Monsieur Cartouche. And they are cheap, too."

"What did you give for them?"

"Nothing."

"Then how did you get them?"

"Found them in the street, Monsieur Cartouche. It is not unusual to find things in the street. I believe you have sometimes picked up a trifle or two."

"Right you are—we won't discuss that matter, though; but here is the money for the pistols. And tell Gribichon to meet me at the old place at ten to-night—I forgot to make an appointment with him."

"Where is the old place, captain?"

"He knows well enough."

"But I don't."

"Nor is it necessary that you should."

"Bravo, Captain Cartouche; you are just as close and secretive as a captain ought to be."

"Is the street clear?"

"Not a soul stirring, and if you go into that little café opposite you can walk through into the next street without the least trouble. If you see a red-headed waiter there give him a few sous and he will swear against all the police in Paris that you have never been within a mile of the place."

"My friend, I foresee we shall have a good deal of business together," said Cartouche. "May I ask your name?"

"Monsieur, I am from the land of Perfidious Albion, and my name is Jones—Sir Jones."

"Good indeed! Then, Sir Jones, for the present adieu."

And Cartouche hurried out into the street.

The fact is he heard certain sounds that convinced him his enemies were on his track and had followed him from his own house to the dwelling of "Sir Jones." They were trying to raise the trap-door.

Luckily the street was empty, so he dashed across the road into the restaurant.

"A glass of wine, quickly!" said he.

"It is here, monsieur," said the red-headed waiter.

Cartouche took the liquor and demanded the price.

"A franc, monsieur."

"Take two, and don't say that I have been here. There is a way out here at the back?"

"Certainly, Monsieur Cartouche."

"What, you know me?"

The man bowed.

"Then be silent as to my visit or you may come to grief."

"I can be as dumb as that door-post, monsieur."

"Be as dumb as ten francs can make you, and remember that although I can be liberal I am also very vindictive when anyone injures me."

"I will not forget it, monsieur, and I trust to enjoy your liberality for many years to come. This way, monsieur."

The man led the way through a back yard into another house, and then into a street.

"You are safe, now, monsieur."

"These people will be silent, think you?"

"Yes, monsieur—I will guarantee they shall say nothing."

Cartouche darted out into the roadway, wondering very much what was to be his next move.

"I will not leave Louise; I must make some effort to find out what they intend doing with the girl, for she has been good and true to me."

He walked along for some distance when he saw in front of him a female form which seemed familiar.

A second look showed him that he was not mistaken.

"The Lady Guilfort, by all that is holy!" he ejaculated.

Cartouche paused for a moment to reflect.

"She must have found out about Louise and put the police on that business," was the decision he came to. "So as she has declared war, why, I'll let her know that I'm not to be trifled with. Here, boy!"

"What is it, monsieur?" said the street arab Cartouche had spoken to—a regular young imp.

"You see that lady walking on in front?"

"Certainly ; she is in evidence, monsieur."

"You have heard of the Lady Guilfort who cuts off the heads of her lovers?"

"All Paris has heard."

"There she is ; give her into the hands of the police and the reward is yours."

"Monsieur, are you certain?"

"Positive. She wanted to cut off my head, but I was just a little too clever for her. I don't want the reward, but it will be a fortune for you."

"You are generosity itself, monsieur," cried the boy, as he darted off intending to keep the lady in sight till a police-officer was visible.

Cartouche did not wait to see what would be the result of his ruse, his only notion for the present was to put himself in safety. And he did so, as he thought, by turning in the opposite direction to that taken by the Lady Guilfort.

But as he turned the corner of the street he stumbled against the man he most wished to avoid—Lecoq senior.

"Pardon, monsieur," said the police-officer.

"A thousand pardons, monsieur! I trust I have not injured your foot by treading on it?"

"On the contrary, monsieur."

Both gentlemen raised their chapeaus in the genuine Parisian style, and Cartouche at once saw that he was not recognised by Monsieur Peuchet's lieutenant.

"So I can have a game with him," thought the bold brigand. "Here goes!"

And with a sublime smile upon his face, he said—

"Monsieur, I have caused you some inconvenience, I know. Pray allow me to invite you to take a glass of wine while you recover from the pain I must have caused you."

Lecoq senior was very fond of wine, and there happened to be close by the place where Cartouche ran into his arms a dirty little cabaret, noted throughout Paris for selling the finest wines of Burgundy and Bordeaux. It was rumoured that sometimes the king's ministers went there for a good bottle, and it was no secret that Monsieur Peuchet often imbibed at The Blue Pig, as the little place was called.

"You are kind, monsieur," said Lecoq.

"Don't mention it," replied Cartouche.

Arm-in-arm the thief and the police-lieutenant walked into the dingy back room of the house.

CHAPTER XXXVII.

CARTOUCHE DISCOVERS LOUISE'S PRISON.

"WHICH vintage do you prefer, monsieur?" Cartouche asked the police-lieutenant.

"I like St. Emillion, if that suits your palate," replied Lecoq.

"Excellently. And now what is the latest news in Paris?"

"You are a stranger in the city?" said Lecoq.

"Not exactly—but I have been at Lyons for two months, and so don't know what has been going on."

"Well, then I can tell you. That villain Cartouche has been keeping us alive."

"Ah! what is the last thing about him?"

The unsuspecting police-officer related how Black George had been found mutilated—supposed by Cartouche—how the college was plundered and the father insulted—by Cartouche—and a variety of other misdeeds which made Cartouche think himself insulted by having them fathered upon him.

"Ah, and they can't catch this fellow?"

"I think we shall have him soon."

"Yes ; I hope you will."

The police-lieutenant drank a second glass of wine and said—

"I don't mind telling you, as you seem a honest, decent man, that I am a police-officer— pretty well up in the service too."

"Ah! then, of course, you know everything."

"I know that our men collared Cartouche's mistress, Louise, the flower-girl, this afternoon——"

"And what have they done with her?" Cartouche asked.

"She is in one of the cells under the office. But that devil shot one of our men while they were taking her."

"He is a devil!"

"I wish I could lay my hand on him," said Lecoq, putting his fist upon Cartouche's arm.

"Ah! he would have a poor chance then."

"But do you think it safe to imprison her in the police-office—I mean the flower-girl?"

"Certainly."

"Would not the Bastille or the Prison of St. Pelagie be a more secure place?"

"No, my friend. As sure as fate that devil of a Cartouche would get her out of the Bastille, but he won't dare venture within a hundred yards of the police-office."

"You think he won't?"

"Not he! Why, there are a score of police-officers waiting in the office at all times."

"Ah!" said Cartouche, "then Louise will have a bad time of it. What crime is she charged with?"

"None at all. We are going to keep her till we find Cartouche."

"Rather hard on the girl, isn't it?"

"Not at all. She will get plenty to eat and drink; her apartment is on the ground floor, looking out on the Rue Martin—nice and airy. If Cartouche only dared venture down the street he could shake hands with her through the window bars."

"Of course he won't venture there; you have men watching for him at each end of the street?"

"Not a man! we know that he won't venture into the neighbourhood, so why should we worry our men by telling them to watch for a man who won't come? We feel perfectly secure on that point, monsieur, and Louise is as safe as she would be if we put her in the centre of the Bastille."

"Ah! and you expect to hear something of Cartouche soon?"

"Yes. The poor devil is awfully fond of this girl, and when he finds that she is locked up he will go mad, and commit some act of folly that will bring him within our reach."

"Just so. And then, of course, he will be hanged."

"Undoubtedly! Unless the judge orders him to be broken on the wheel, which will be better fun."

"Yes. I shall be there when Cartouche is broken on the wheel."

"And when we have settled him I mean to make Louise my own particular little friend."

"Indeed! Do you think she will have anything to say to you if you are the cause of her lover's death?"

"Yes. I believe I am not an ill-looking fellow, monsieur."

"By no means! Decidedly handsome."

"And you know what our herald says when the king dies?"

Cartouche began to think that his companion was either mad or drunk to ask such questions.

"I do not exactly comprehend, monsieur," he said.

"When the king dies the herald proclaims, 'The king is dead—long live the king!'—that is to say, the new king. So it will be with Louise; one lover dead she will take on another at once—and I shall be that favoured individual. Well, monsieur, I must go; but, believe me, we shall all soon hear something more about Cartouche."

So saying the police-officer marched out of the room.

"What an ass!" exclaimed Cartouche. "How on earth came he to reach such a position in the police force?"

Not being able to solve the enigma he gave it up, muttering—

"Yes, they shall soon hear something of Cartouche! They shall hear something that will rather surprise them."

He finished the bottle and sauntered out in the direction of the police headquarters, and walked down the street where he was informed he could shake hands with Louise through the bars of the window.

There were at least a dozen grated apertures about six feet above the roadway.

"Which of these places is it, I wonder?" thought Cartouche. "I would look into all the windows if I thought I could do so without being observed by the folks on the other side."

Cartouche then remembered something he had read when a boy at the school of Clermont —how a certain English king being missing was eventually discovered by a minstrel, who visited half the castles and gaols in Europe, and sang outside of them a song the missing monarch was very fond of. Sometimes the minstrel got coin, sometimes kicks; but one day his trouble was rewarded, for when he had got through the first verse of his song the missing monarch sang the second from his dungeon. Then the minstrel walked boldly into the castle instead of standing at the gate, had breakfast at the expense of the proprietor, sang two more songs, and departed with a bottle of wine and a few shillings in his pocket just to keep him going. And he knew that he had left his sovereign in the castle.

"I will do that little dodge, and see if it is as successful now as it was five hundred years ago," said Cartouche, and as he sauntered down the street he whistled the air of a song Louise was very fond of.

Cartouche sauntered very slowly and whistled very loudly, but by the time he reached the end of the street there was no response.

"I will wet my whistle and whistle my way back again. Louise is there, but perhaps she did not think of answering. But she is a quick-witted girl, and when she hears it a second time she will know that it is a signal from me."

So, having refreshed himself with a glass of wine, he retraced his steps, whistling the same tune as he went along slowly.

Presently he heard the girl's clear voice trilling out the melody, and he said to himself—

"History repeats itself! I am the modern Blondel, and my king, or queen rather, is imprisoned here, and to prevent any mistakes I will take the liberty of making a little chalk mark on the wall, so that there shall be no mistake when I return. Yes, Monsieur Lecoq, I think you will most certainly hear something more of Cartouche before long."

At that moment a hand was thrust out between the bars of the window above, and a scrap of paper fluttered down to the ground at the feet of Cartouche, who, of course, at once picked it up and read what was written thereon.

"Louise—cell No. 12."

Such was the very simple inscription on the two square inches of paper that Cartouche lifted from the mud.

"Louise, I will see you this evening," said he.

"I hear you," responded the voice from within, "and I have no fear now that you know where I am."

Cartouche did not reply, but walked away still whistling the air of the song which Louise was warbling in her prison cell.

Feeling perfectly confident since his interview with the police-lieutenant, Lecoq, that he was not recognised by the force, Cartouche thought himself at liberty to visit any part of Paris except the lodgings he had recently occupied.

So, having purchased a few things which he considered necessary for the liberation of Louise, he strolled down to a café opposite the Cathedral of Notre Dame, resolved to have one more good dinner if he never had another.

But, besides the dinner, Cartouche had a second object in view when he directed his steps to that café.

It was one of the most notorious gossip-shops in Paris. Anyone who wanted to hear the latest rumours, true or false, about anything, had only to repair to that café, and if they had not a sufficiently sensational lie on hand one would very soon be invented.

Cartouche had no doubt that he would hear something very new to him about himself and Louise, and he was not disappointed.

"You have heard the news, monsieur?" said the waiter who brought him his soup.

"No—anything great?"

"They have—the police, of course—have captured Louise the flower-girl, the mistress of Cartouche."

"All Paris knows that."

"But, monsieur, all Paris does not know the decision the authorities have come to."

"Perhaps not. What have they decided upon?"

"That if Cartouche does not surrender himself within a week she shall be flogged through the streets of Paris, and then be hanged in the Place Gréve."

"What for?" asked Cartouche.

The waiter shrugged his shoulders and was quite unable to say why Louise should be tortured or hanged.

"Doesn't it seem hard to think that a girl against whom no crime is alleged should be murdered because her lover happens to be a thief?" said Cartouche.

"Well really, monsieur——"

"Look here, comrade, we are too much governed. Why should they even imprison this girl?"

"They want to get hold of Cartouche."

"So they imprison a girl to catch her lover! Is that justice?"

"It is not, monsieur. But then who dares interfere?"

"The time is rapidly approaching when all France will interfere to prevent such a sin against justice."

The waiter shook his head and did not seem to see it.

Cartouche died years before the great French Revolution commenced, but the waiter lived to see it when he was a very old man, and he used to totter about his house saying—

"Cartouche was right; he said we should turn things upside down."

But Cartouche had not the least idea that he

was prognosticating the upheaval of the whole system of life in France.

Our bold robber was anxious to know all the rumours about Louise, and now that he had ascertained she was to suffer unless he surrendered within a week his mind was quickly made up.

Neither event should happen. Louise should receive no injury and he would still set the police at defiance.

"I wonder what Gribichon has heard," thought the outlaw, as he finished his dinner. "I did not tell him where to meet me, but I suppose instinct will lead him down to the Pont Neuf."

They had met there so often that Cartouche looked upon the embankment by the bridge as the natural rendezvous of the band of which he was the acknowledged chief.

And when he arrived there he found his good friend Gribichon.

"Have you heard anything?" he asked.

"Not a word," answered Gribichon.

"I have heard a good lot. They are going to torture Louise unless you show up in time to prevent it."

"I shall not show up, and Louise will not put the tormentor to the expense of stretching his ropes," replied Cartouche.

"But how will you manage it, captain?"

"I shall do very well, my Gribichon."

"It is a great risk."

"If I wish to be chief I must be prepared to risk my neck against everything."

"Then you intend to have Madame Louise out of that place?"

"I do. So now all you have to do is to be ready when I do the trick, so as to give me all the help you can, Gribichon."

"I will, captain, for by the great and immortal shade of Rabelais you are the only person fit to lead us to death or glory."

"I want to lead you to safety, my Gribichon."

"And where shall we meet again?"

"Here, Gribichon. This is a very convenient place, and I shall look for you here twice or thrice in the day. I may have nothing of importance to say, or there may be great business, but I shall expect to see you here every noon, and every evening at eight, unless I give you warning that I shall be in some other part of the country."

Gribichon saluted his captain and went away. The chief of the Parisian banditti proceeded to measure his strength against Monsieur Paul Lecoq and Monsieur Peuchet, the Chief of Police.

"I will have Louise out in spite of all their locks, bolts, and bars!" said he, and he meant what he said.

––––––––

CHAPTER XXXVIII.

HOW CARTOUCHE BROKE INTO PRISON.

HAVING ascertained exactly the number and position of the cell in which Louise was confined Cartouche lost no time in liberating her.

CARTOUCHE,
THE FRENCH JACK SHEPPARD.

THERE WAS A HAND HOLDING OUT TO HER A FILE AND A LETTER.

Waiting until it was quite dark he wandered down the street by the side of the police-office and whistled the same old tune.

It was answered as before.

Louise was sitting in the cell to which the kindness of the Parisian police had consigned her, and was wondering who it was who whistled that tune which she heard a few hours ago. Was it Cartouche himself, or Gribichon, or some other friend?

While still thinking over this she heard the same old tune.

"If it is not Cartouche it is someone he has sent to find out where I am, so here goes for a reply."

And she sang, as she sung in the morning, the answering verse of the song.

The furniture of the cell to which the police of Paris had consigned La Belle Louise was not so very sumptuous. There was a tiny bed, a very small table, and a three-legged stool. That she might not starve the gaolers gave her a small loaf of coarse bread and a large jug of not very clean water, at which Louise smiled.

"I will have something better than this for supper when Louis comes to take me away," she said.

But would Louis come?

She heard his whistle in the morning, and she was quite certain he knew where she was incarcerated when darkness came on.

"Now is the time—his time!" she ejaculated.

Her gaolers had left her a candle, the rays of which sent a cheerful glimmer through the otherwise cheerless street at the side of the police-office.

Cartouche whistled the air and Louise replied.

Next moment she almost jumped from her seat with joy, for she saw between the bars of the window a hand, which held, as though offering it to her, a file, a letter, and a small bottle.

Louise jumped up and clutched them at once. She kissed the hand, not knowing whether it belonged to Cartouche, Gribichon, or Tomasso; and having concealed the file and the bottle in the bosom of her dress, she kissed it again.

"I know you are there, Louis!" she said.

"Be quiet and read the letter," said the owner of the hand, which at that moment was withdrawn from the window of the cell.

Louise sat down and read the scrap of paper, on which she found the words—

"File through the bars four-fifths of their thickness and then use the acid. Don't try to come out to-night, but at midnight to-morrow you will find waiting outside your own lover— LOUIS DOMINIQUE CARTOUCHE.

"P.S. The acid in the bottle will bite through the bars very much quicker than a file—but don't use it unless you are driven to desperation. If things come to the very worst drink it, and die like the splendid girl you are."

Louise tore the letter to fragments, which she burnt, and said—

"I will prove myself worthy of the love of the greatest thief and prison-breaker in France."

She set to work with the file, and soon found that she had gone through three-parts of the thickness of the iron bars which lay between herself and freedom.

"The acid will do the rest when the time comes," she said to herself; and then she slept very tranquilly for some hours, and presented a most refreshing look to the female gaoler who brought her breakfast.

"You look gay, Belle Louise," said the official.

"Of course! why not?"

"You have little to be jolly over."

"Much! My lover is coming to take me away from this den."

The female gaoler laughed.

"I should like to see Cartouche within half a mile of this place," she said.

"You won't see him, but he will come."

"You are dreaming, Belle Louise!"

"Not at all; he has written to say he is coming to set me at liberty next Sunday, and he always does keep his word."

"Next Sunday, eh?"

"Yes," replied the artful little liar, Louise.

"Then you won't get away."

"I have no doubt my lover, Cartouche, could take me away at any time; but, as I have said, he appoints next Sunday, so I shall remain here very quietly till he calls for me. So don't worry yourself."

The woman gave a quick glance round the cell.

Everything seemed right. Louise had cut through the bars with the exception of a small bit, but she had very artfully concealed her work by filling the gap made by the file with moistened bread crumbs. So nothing was suspected, and the female gaoler *took her hook*—to use a modern slang expression.

Louise remained very quiet all that day and till the next night came on. Then she began to get a little excited.

As soon as it was quite dark she finished cutting through the bars with the exception of a thin film of metal just enough to keep the things in their places till Cartouche should put in an appearance.

That done the brave girl lay down, ready dressed, upon her prison bed, but with no intention of sleeping. She was simply resting till her lover should call and take her away.

It was nearly midnight when she heard someone whistling the air which she now recognised as the means of communication between her lover and herself. Very softly, but distinctly, she sang the following verse, and the next moment she saw the countenance of Louis Dominique Cartouche at the window.

"Have you cut through the bars, Louise?" he asked.

"Yes, except just as much as will hold them together," she replied.

"Then here we go!"

With which words Cartouche wrenched away three of the iron bars which crossed the window of the cell Lecoq had imprisoned Louise in.

Then he thrust himself through the aperture and jumped into the cell.

"My darling!" said he, as he clasped her in his arms and kissed her very fondly. Louise said nothing, but she submitted very patiently to her lover's caresses.

After a few minutes, however, they began to think of their future proceedings.

"Louis, how can I go out through that window?" said Louise.

"I don't intend you to go that way."

"How then, my boy?"

"We will always do things boldly. We will depart by the front door, and leave a card for Monsieur Peuchet. One also for my friend, Lecoq."

"Is he a friend of yours?"

"He told me where to find you."

"What an ass! But you are so artful, Louis, I believe you would deceive the devil."

"If the devil is not more clever than the Paris police it would not be a difficult task. But come away."

"My door is bolted outside."

"They are very careful of you, Louise. However, you must take a little outdoor exercise for the benefit of your health, my girl—so we will soon spoil that bolt."

He set to work with a very fine saw, and soon had cut away sufficient of the woodwork to enable him to use the file and the acid in an effective manner.

"Come along, my darling," said he, as he threw open the door.

"But, Louis, this leads up to Monsieur Peuchet's apartments," said Louise.

"We are his guests for the time—so come along."

Louise had perfect confidence in her lover, so she permitted him to have his own way.

They walked along the passage from the cells and got into the passage leading to the front door.

And then a big policeman confronted them.

"Halt, monsieur!—I do not remember admitting you," said this functionary.

"Pray what has that to do with me?" said Cartouche.

"Why," replied the police-officer, "unless I am quite certain as to admitting you I can't let you go."

"Monsieur Peuchet admitted me."

"I did not have the pleasure of seeing you, monsieur."

"He allowed me to enter by the back way so that I should not be seen."

"Pardon, monsieur. I trust I have not given such offence that you will think it necessary to report me to the chief?"

"Certainly not, my man; you have done your duty, and as soon as you are relieved spend these five francs with your comrade and drink my health."

"You are a prince, monsieur."

"Not at all. You will drink to my health."

"Certainly, monsieur; but by what name shall I drink to you?"

"Well, just for the fun of the thing, and as Monsieur Peuchet does not want my real name to be known, suppose you call me Cartouche. Ha, ha, ha! he is a lively fellow, isn't he? Drink to the health of Cartouche!"

"This is an excellent jest, monsieur. I will certainly drink to the health of Monsieur Cartouche. Permit me."

And with a most profound bow the official opened the street-door to usher Louise and her lover into the public street, where they laughed long and loudly at the folly of the men Monsieur Peuchet had placed in the chief posts in the police force.

"And what shall we do now, dear?" said Louise.

"We must find a home."

"I know a place where we can be safe, so come along, my Louis Dominique."

"You are a grand girl, Louise. But how do you find all these safe places to live in? We have had a dozen different lodgings during the last six months."

"I am always making inquiries, and if we should be disturbed at the place I am taking you to, why I have three or four other lodgings in reserve."

CHAPTER XXXIX.

GRIBICHON'S HOLIDAY.

GRIBICHON was having a good time of it. Can-can had been made thoroughly acquainted with the character of her lover and his associates, but she loved him none the less for that knowledge. Perhaps she envied Louise a little; but then, most girls prefer the captain to the ensign.

But Gribichon and Can-can had both of them sufficient sense to know that they must not be seen too much together. They were suspected of belonging to Cartouche's gang, or some other predatory association; so it would not do to be seen walking about the streets of Paris.

"Can-can, I owe you three francs," said Gribichon.

"Six, you rascal, and a sausage."

"I had forgotten. But listen, my charmer."

"I am listening, my love."

"Let us have a holiday to-morrow. Let Paris go without scent-bottles for a day, and we will go up the river to the sign of the Golden Perch at Beaumont and have a jolly time."

"I agree—— Now don't do that again, young man."

Gribichon had kissed the scent-seller, and she was making a mild protest.

"I won't—I give you my word I won't do it till I have another opportunity."

"You are a bad boy, and had better go away—but where shall I meet you in the morning?"

"Let me see. Why, at the Pont Neuf. We must cross the bridge to get out of the city."

"I am not going to walk to the Golden Perch."

"A carriage shall convey you."

"And if I condescend to ride with you,

Gribby dear, you will promise not to hug me too much ?''

"Not more than you wish, Can-can."

They parted then, for they noticed that one of the police was looking on rather attentively.

Next morning found Can-can at the Pont Neuf as soon as the sun had fairly risen.

The girl had her stock of goods with her, and sold at least five francs' worth before Gribichon appeared.

"You lazy rascal !" she said, smiting him on the cheek with her open hand.

"Look here, that hurts !" said Gribichon.

"I mean it to hurt.'

"You are a savage, Can-can."

"I am nothing of the kind.   But I believe I am a fool for having ever taken any notice of you !"

"Can-can ! withdraw those words, or I won't take you to the Golden Perch."

"Well, and what then ?"

"You won't have a chance of riding in a carriage with me and being hugged on the road."

"Well, I won't hit you again, Gribichon."

"Come along, then, Can-can, there is our carriage waiting, and I have sent on word that we want breakfast the moment we get there—an omelet with fine herbs, a cutlet, and a bottle of wine."

"That will be glorious !"

Without any more fuss Can-can and Gribichon got into the carriage, and, after a proper time, they were deposited at the door of the Golden Perch, a riverside hostelry a few miles beyond Paris—a place much frequented by anglers and holiday-makers.

The breakfast was ready a few minutes after their arrival, and they both enjoyed it thoroughly.

"But," said Can-can, as she looked from the window which commanded a good view of the road from Paris, "who is this standing in front of the house ?"

"By Jove ! it is Bobilet—attached to the police-department of the Civic Guard. You have heard of him."

"I have heard of him, of course. The old rascal used to pretend to love me," said Can-can.

"Well, if he does any love-making this morning there will be a row in the house, that is certain."

"I don't want to see him."

Gribichon wanted, though, to know what errand had brought Monsieur Bobilet out to the Golden Perch.

So, observing that the Civic Guardsman was wandering about the bank of the river in a rather shiftless way, it occurred to Cartouche's lieutenant that he might as well go out and have a little talk with the gentleman.

Monsieur Bobilet was indulging in a little talk with himself.

"I am getting sick of this business," soliloquised Bobilet, "and I shall resign my position in the Civic Guard——"

"Why ?' asked Gribichon, appearing suddenly at Bobilet's elbow.

"Eh ?—who the devil are you ?" asked Bobilet.

"I am not one of the Civic Guard, and therefore am not able to understand why you dislike it.   I thought it a very pleasant service."

"Indeed !   Well, I get knocked about here and kicked about there, and then my wife goes and gets jealous of that perfume-girl, Can-can."

"Not without good cause, I expect, monsieur."

"Well, she certainly is a jolly girl, and I should like to be a trifle more intimate with her than I am.   But, lor' ! she will have nothing to do with me except to smack my face.   And she can give a smack, too."

"She can, and no mistake !'

"So, now, I ask you if it is not absurd of Madame Bobilet to be jealous of a girl who only hits me when I want to kiss her ?''

"Very, indeed," said Gribichon.

"And then, again, in my official capacity I am lost entirely.   They have sent me out here to catch Cartouche !"

"The devil !"

"You are right, monsieur, he is a devil. They might as well tell me to catch a sunbeam ! I hope he won't catch me !"

"But it is expected that the great Cartouche will be in the neighbourhood to-day."

"It is known, for a certainty, that he will come here to lunch.   And I am here to catch him.   Why did they not send a whole regiment of soldiers.   And, to make things worse, here is my wife.   I wonder who the devil told her I was here."

Madame Bobilet was there certainly, and she began at once.

"So, you villain, you are at your old tricks again."

"Madame Bobilet, be calm.   What tricks ?"

"Looking after the girls, you old rascal."

"Surely, Madame Bobilet, you don't call this young gentleman a girl, eh, my dear ?"

"Don't *dear* me !   You were not looking at him.   I have heard, on very good authority, that the perfume-seller, Can-can, came here with you.   Can you deny it ?"

"I can, and do."''

"Well, I am going to search the house till I find her."

Gribichon thought this was a favourable opportunity to step forward and remark—

"Pardon me, madame, can I save you the trouble by making the search for you, whilst you keep Monsieur Bobilet in conversation so that he cannot communicate with her ?"

"A fine plan.   I shall be much obliged, indeed, if you will go and hunt up the bold hussy while I once more ask Monsieur Bobilet what he is doing here."

"I really cannot explain, my dear.   My duty——"

"Your duty is to go home—so off you start at once."

Monsieur Bobilet started, and Madame followed close behind to quicken his pace when he felt inclined to halt.

CHAPTER XL.

THE FATE OF YOUNG LECOQ.

THE place Louise had selected for the joint residence of herself and Cartouche was near the bank of the river.

It was essentially the home of the poor people —men and women who worked hard at the markets or in the factories had their homes there for the simple reason that it was a cheap neighbourhood, and therefore it can be well imagined that it was not so nice as some of the more expensive parts of Paris.

But fate had ordained that they were not to reach that place without an adventure.

Lecoq the younger—he who had that perilous adventure with the Lady Guilfort—was, like most of the young men of Paris, an admirer of Louise.

He had heard from his father and other of the police officials that Cartouche was the favoured lover of the flower-girl.

Young Lecoq was sauntering home at an early hour in the morning, with considerably more than one glass of wine muddling his brain, when he met Louise and Cartouche.

Louise he knew, of course, but he was not so certain about Cartouche's identity.

"But Louise is locked up!" he muttered to himself. "I must be dreaming—or drunk! Yet I am certain it is her."

He walked up to the girl as steadily as he could, and said—

"Hillo, Louise, what are you doing out at this hour?"

"That is not my name."

"Nonsense! everybody in Paris knows La Belle Louise, the flower-girl. But old Peuchet had you locked up, and you have no right to be out of your cell at this time."

Neither Louise nor her lover said anything, but Cartouche thrust his hand into his breast-pocket so as to get hold of his trusty dagger.

"No right to be out, Louise, so I must do my duty and take you into custody. Don't want to knock up any of old Peuchet's people though, so I'll take you to my place till daylight—just for safety."

The young man caught Louise by the arm, and was about to drag her away, when Cartouche stepped forward, and, with a single blow, struck the young man dead.

"What have you done, Louis?" said the flower-girl.

"Saved you from prison and from flogging, which was the fate in store for you, and which you certainly would have suffered had I permitted that fellow to take you away. But come along; we must get out of sight at once."

Louise and her lover hurried away, and soon were safe in the lodging the flower-girl had thought of while in the prison of the police-office.

It was a place she had resided in before she finally decided to link her destiny with that of Cartouche, and it was easy to gain admission at any hour of the day or night.

A peculiar knock was given, the door was opened, and, as soon as they had entered, it was closed again.

Cartouche found himself in total darkness, but Louise held his hand.

"Who are you?" said a rough, masculine voice.

"La Belle Louise," responded the flower-girl.

"You here, Louise? I heard the police had you?"

"They could not keep me when my husband determined to have me out of prison."

"Husband! Are you married, Louise?"

"I am the wife of Cartouche, and he is here with me. We need shelter for a day or two."

"You shall have it; come along, Captain Cartouche."

The great outlaw felt his other hand grasped, and he was then led along a narrow passage.

"Down three steps, captain, now turn to the right, and now twenty steps up," said the man.

Having safely accomplished this journey they came to a halt, and Cartouche's unseen guide said—

"Show a light here—quick!"

A door was opened and a hand thrust out a lighted candle set in a bottle.

"Don't tell anyone in the house who I am, ' Cartouche whispered to the man, who was a burly, elderly, rough-looking fellow, with huge brawny arms, unconcealed by the shirt-sleeves, which were rolled up to his shoulders.

"Not a word shall pass my lips, captain. Madame Louise knows of old that this is a safe place."

"I should not have brought you here if I had not felt certain of that, Louis."

"I have not been visited by the police for a couple of years or more. The last meddlesome fool who wanted to search my place was carried out, and they found him dead in the Seine next day. Which room will you occupy?"

"I should like the one I had when I lived here before, if it is not occupied," said Louise.

"It is at your disposal, madame."

The man led the way up another steep staircase and along a winding passage into a room which was plainly but comfortably furnished. The door of the apartment was a very solid-looking affair and had bolts inside fit for a castle-gate.

"You will be safe enough here, captain," said the man. "Can I get you any refreshment?"

"A bottle of wine and some bread will suffice for the present. In the morning, doubtless, you can furnish a better meal," said Cartouche.

"Anything you desire."

He walked away and returned in a few minutes with a loaf, a bottle, and two glasses.

"Make your minds at ease," said he. "You are as safe here as if you were five thousand miles away. Madame and monsieur, I wish you good-night."

He departed, and Louise carefully bolted the door.

Meanwhile the body of young Lecoq lay

unnoticed in the street where Cartouche's hand struck him down.

A peasant, with a heavy waggon full of vegetables for the market, passed along that street in the early morn, and he stumbled over something which, on examination, he discovered to be the body of a man.

Before he could check his horses the wheel of the ponderous vehicle passed over the head of the prostrate body, crushing the handsome features into an almost unrecognisable mass.

Frightened out of his wits almost, the man hastened on, and left the body where he found it.

Day was breaking when a police-patrol, sauntering along, discovered the corpse, and, after emptying the pockets of everything valuable, he sounded an alarm.

The corpse was recognised chiefly by the clothes; the stab in the heart showed that a murder had been committed—but, strange to say, no one attributed it to Cartouche.

The elder Lecoq did not doubt that his son had fallen a victim to the vengeance of Lady Guilfort or her associates.

CHAPTER XLI.
THE FLIGHT FROM PARIS—LADY GUILFORT AGAIN.

For three days neither Cartouche nor Louise dared leave the house in which they had found shelter.

The old man who kept the house was staunch and true, and informed them of the extraordinary efforts that were being made to discover their retreat.

As those days wore along it became evident that the police, instead of giving up the search, were hunting more vigorously than ever for three persons—Cartouche, Louise, and Lady Guilfort, who was suspected of having contrived the murder of young Lecoq.

It was even said that a house-to-house visitation would be instituted, and great was the consternation and dread of the criminal classes of Paris at the idea of having their secret dens and hiding-places overhauled by the prying underlings of Monsieur Peuchet.

Yet every hour brought confirmation of the rumour. Some gossiping soldiers let out the news that no less than two regiments were to be under arms at midnight to assist the police, who would begin their search two hours later.

Parties of the military were to be posted at the ends of streets, and patrols were to be on the move in every direction, with orders to secure anyone who might be found out of doors.

On the other hand, the police would enter the houses one after another and search them thoroughly from cellar to garret.

"And then they will not capture me," said Cartouche.

"What will you do, then?" Louise asked.

"Leave Paris three hours before midnight."

"The gates will be watched, Louis."

"What care I when I do not intend to leave by any gate?"

"I know you are very daring; but what will become of me? I am not so strong and active as you."

"I shall not leave you behind."

Louise looked earnestly at him and could see that he really meant what he was saying, so she plucked up courage and resolved to venture upon anything that Cartouche might tell her to do.

"How much money have you, Louise?" Cartouche asked.

Louise exhibited her purse, which was well-stocked with gold pieces. Her gaolers had not searched carefully, and she kept the treasure.

"You had better let me have half," said the always-selfish Louis Dominique.

"Have all, if you like," replied the flower-girl.

"No; only in case we get separated by accident we ought both to have coin."

"I hope we shall not be separated."

"I don't suppose we shall; but it is always well to be prepared for anything that may happen."

He counted out the golden coins—fifty-eight in number—and putting thirty of them into his own pockets, which were already well lined, allowed her to have the purse with the rest.

"It is nearly nine now, Louise, so we must be off while there are plenty of people in the street. We shall not attract attention as we should if all the roads were nearly empty."

"You are right, Louis."

They had come to the house without luggage, and they now left it in the same way.

But Cartouche took care to pay his host liberally, for it might be necessary to take shelter there again when Paris was once more safe.

"Now listen, Louise. If any accident should compel us to separate, go as speedily as you possibly can to Rouen."

"Why to Rouen, Louis?"

"I think we shall be safer there than in many parts of France; and there are boats at Rouen by which we can sail to England or Spain."

"But how will you find me?"

"There is a tavern near the waterside called the Great Dog. Go there, and you will be treated with civility; but don't mention my name or your own—call yourself Nanette Bigorne."

"Well, Louis, I will remember; but I hope we shall not have occasion to part."

This conversation took place outside the house. It was a tolerably fine night, plenty of people about, and no signs of any intention on the part of the police to make a big raid on the thieves' quarters of Paris.

"Walk on quietly, Louise, to the quay at the Pont Neuf; I want to warn old Tomasso and the others, if I can. I will soon overtake you."

Louise walked on.

Cartouche could not find Tomasso or Gribichon, but he met The Wolf, whom he desired to

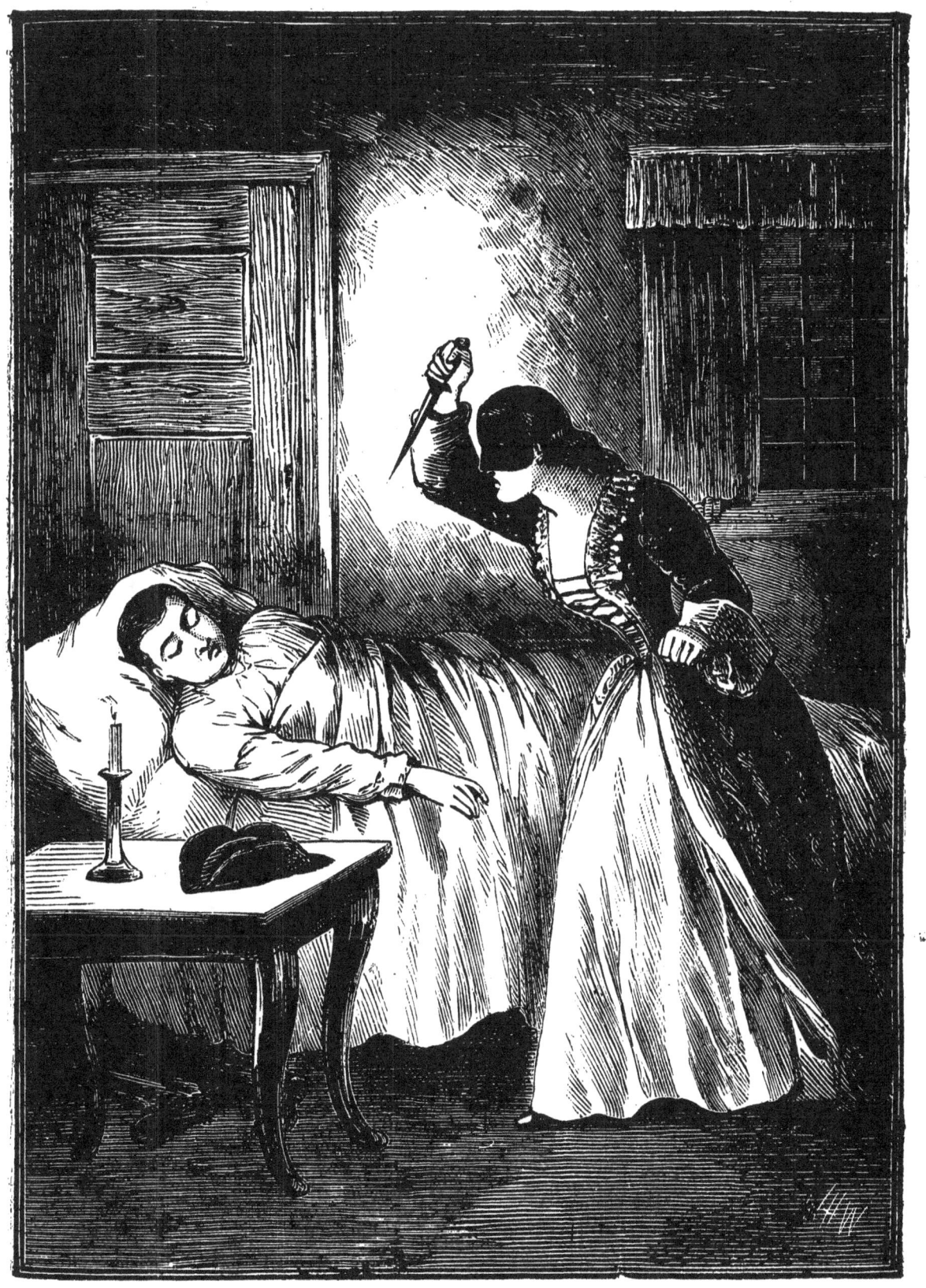

"THE TRAITOR MUST DIE!" SAID SHE, UPLIFTING A DAGGER.

go and warn the others that the police would be uncommonly active that night, and The Wolf at once undertook to put them all on their guard—at least, as many as he could find.

Meanwhile, Louise walked on and reached the quay.

She was pacing up and down near the water's edge, wondering in what way Cartouche would contrive their joint escape from Paris, when her foot slipped and she fell over into the stream.

There had been much rain the two days before, and the river was much swollen and running with great rapidity.

Louise gave one despairing scream as she felt the cold waters close around her; then as she rose to the surface she fought wildly with the eddies, the result being that she was swept out from the shore.

That, however, proved her safety, for she was carried within reach of a huge pile or beam which had been driven into the bed of the river to moor boats and barges in the stream. It was four or five yards from the edge of the quay.

Louise desperately clutched this, and then again she cried at the top of her voice for help.

Cartouche, who was just coming on to the quay, heard her voice, and guessed what had happened.

He ran forward, pulling off coat and waistcoat as he ran, and paused only at the edge of the quay to divest himself of his huge boots, in which it would scarcely be possible to swim.

"I am coming, Louise," he cried, as he jumped into the water and struck out vigorously for the mooring-post.

Cartouche was a strong swimmer, but both his strength and skill were tested before he could cross that swift eddy and reach the mooring-post to which Louise was clinging.

"Cheer up, my love. I will save you or perish with you," said Cartouche.

He then gave her a few whispered instructions as to the way she should lay hold of him whilst he was conveying her to the shore, and as she implicitly obeyed him the quay-side was soon safely reached, though some yards lower down stream.

Having safely got her ashore, Cartouche fetched his hat, clothes, and boots, which he left in her charge whilst he once more swam out to a tier of boats anchored in mid-stream.

He loosened one, and having found a pair of oars in another, he rowed back and took Louise on board.

Having got the craft back into the middle of river, he gave a few powerful strokes, and then directing Louise to crouch down as he did himself, he allowed the boat to drift with the current, steering it with an oar just so as to avoid obstacles.

Soon the city was behind them, and on either side of the stream nothing but sombre woods and meadows just visible by the light of the stars.

Louise shivered with cold, and Cartouche took up his coat, which was dry, with the intention of wrapping it round her shoulders. As he lifted the garment he remembered that he had, by way of preparation for the journey, put a good-sized flask of brandy in one of his pockets.

"Drink," said he; "take a good long pull."

Louise did so, and the powerful spirit seemed to put new life into her body.

"Now off with your gown and put on my coat. It will keep your shoulders and chest warm."

Louise promptly obeyed him.

Cartouche then took a good pull at the brandy himself, and, sitting down in the boat, began to work the oars with a will.

For hours he pulled, till a faint gleam in the east reminded him that day was at hand.

By that time his clothes were dry, or if there was any moisture in them it was more perspiration than the waters of the River Seine. Cartouche was fatigued, and he began to look about for a landing-place.

Some distance down the stream, which was now much broader than at Paris, the dim outline of a large village could be seen.

Cartouche resolved to make for this point, for it was quite necessary that Louise should be able to dry her clothing thoroughly. She had dried her gown to some extent by wringing it and then holding it up to the night winds, so that when Cartouche ran the boat ashore a mile or so above this village she was able to resume it.

And Cartouche, having put on his coat and boots, left the boat in a reed-bed a little way up a muddy creek of the main river, marched boldly on to the village, which he recognised as one he had visited in the course of his gipsy wanderings. In fact having a pretty good knowledge of the whole country between there and Paris, he felt certain he could tell some very pretty lies as to the route by which he came to St. Jean, as the place was named.

"Remember, Louise, we were misdirected, and found ourselves in the meadows, where you had the misfortune to tumble into a rivulet, from which I rescued you with difficulty. Do not pretend to know anything except that we are going to Rouen, walking because we are too poor to ride."

"I understand, Louis," she responded.

One or two of the very early ones were just appearing at their cottage-doors before commencing the day's drudgery, and they looked curiously at the travellers.

"Good-morning, father," said Cartouche to one of the elders of the village. "Can you inform me where I and my wife, who have been walking all night, can find a bed on which to rest ourselves for a few hours?"

"Why walk all night, my son? You could have rested at St. Pol, which you must have passed long before midnight."

"Some rascal of a forester of whom we inquired the road misdirected us, and we have been wandering about all night. My wife fell into a brook in the darkness, and I thought was lost. Her clothing is very damp, and I am anxious that it should be thoroughly dried before we go on our journey."

"The inn will not be open for two hours, but if Madame does not object to share the bed of my daughter, who is crippled with rheumatism, she is welcome, and my wife will dry her clothes at our fire."

"And I can wait till the inn opens, when, no doubt, I can be accommodated. Nan, you may trust yourself in the house of this honest man, and I will see you at noon."

Louise did not like the idea of being parted from Cartouche, but she was shivering with cold, and knew that only speedy rest and warmth would save her from serious illness.

So she kissed Cartouche and speedily was snug between a pair of coarse blankets along with the invalid, and sleeping soundly.

Cartouche shared his brandy-flask with the old peasant, and made a few inquiries which led to his learning that the police only came along that way every third day, and had been there the previous evening. The common belief concerning himself was that he, Louis Dominique, was hanged some months ago.

Nor did Cartouche think it necessary to undeceive the simple villagers.

When the inn was opened he entered and ate heartily, commanding a good meal to be ready for himself and Louise. Then he retired to bed.

But when noon came Louise was so ill from excitement, cold, and exposure, that she was unable to rise, so it was agreed that she should remain where she was till next morning and Cartouche pass the night at the inn.

Like a prudent general, Cartouche surveyed the village.

"That is the only house in the place worth my trouble," said he, looking at a dwelling which belonged to the bailiff of the lord of the district.

But it would not do to break into the place now, for that would call attention to the presence of strangers.

So after a good look, and deciding how an entrance *could* be effected, he retired, being closely watched by an inmate of the house, whose eyes followed him till he entered the inn.

Cartouche went to bed early that night.

His room was rather humbly furnished, but still, he had been in much worse lodgings. There were two windows, on opposite sides of the room, and a large chimney.

Having bolted the door, Cartouche quickly undressed, and fell asleep with his pistols under the pillow and his candle burning on the table.

Although he slept it was a restless sleep, troubled with vague dreams, which seemed to threaten evil.

And it seemed as though calamity would overtake him, for suddenly one of the windows was opened, and a lady wearing a mask stepped into the room noiselessly.

She approached the bed and looked upon the sleeper.

"I was not mistaken. The traitor shall die!" said she, uplifting a dagger which she plucked from the bosom of her dress.

But before striking she paused.

"Yet I loved him once, and if that hated flower-girl could be slain I would save him."

During that brief pause, and while the lady was thinking rather than speaking the above words, Cartouche's good angel, or the fiend, rather, who had him in keeping, interfered, and the sleeper at once opened his eyes.

He comprehended the situation at a glance, and sprang up and seized her wrist.

"So, Lady Guilfort, we meet again," said Louis Dominique.

"It appears so, Monsieur Cartouche," she answered, faintly.

"And you would kill me, eh? Why, when once you pretended to love me?"

"We might have been happy but for that jade, Louise."

"Oh!" thought Cartouche, "that is the business, is it? Sit down, my lady, and tell me how you came to be here."

"Paris was not safe, so I left it, intending to journey to Rouen, and thence—well, I know not whither. Just by this village the carriage I hired broke down, and I, being slightly injured, was taken to the bailiff's house, where I have lived ever since. I saw you looking at the house."

"So as I did not pay you a visit you thought you would come to me?" said the outlaw.

The woman began to weep. She, after a fashion, had conceived a passion for Cartouche.

"Leave Louise and fly with me. I can love you better and I am richer," she sobbed.

A desperate resolution entered into Cartouche's head.

"I will go with you—I will leave Louise," he said, as he began to dress. "I will fly with you to Rouen, and then we will decide where our home shall be."

"Hasten, then—but how shall we get away from this house?"

"I have a boat concealed about a mile from the village; we will go in that, for water leaves no trace."

Trembling with impatience, the woman stood by till he had completed a hasty toilet. Then she led him out through the window on to the roof of an outhouse, and so by a ladder to the narrow passage at the side of the inn.

The village street was deserted, not even a dog barked as they glided noiselessly along.

Cartouche speedily reached the boat, and they were soon floating down the broad river towards the sea.

"I will do it!" said Cartouche.

Little was said for some time by either Cartouche or the Lady Guilfort as the boat drifted down the Seine.

Cartouche scarcely used his oars till he had passed the village where Louise was sleeping; the noise of the oars might attract the attention or some wakeful villager—at least, that was the explanation he gave his fair companion when she inquired the reason of his inactivity.

And she was satisfied.

"I will do it," were the words she had heard him say, and the expression sufficed to put her mind at ease.

Having got past the village without being observed, Cartouche began to use the oars, and sent the boat down stream at a slightly accelerated pace, keeping well in the middle of the river. Then he rowed hard for an hour.

"Now we shall be happy," said the Lady Guilfort, getting nearer to the oarsman. "Embrace me, Louis."

Louis Dominique Cartouche did embrace her. Clasping the lady closely in both his arms he lifted her from the place where she had been sitting.

"Now I shall be happy," she said.

"I hope you will," replied Cartouche.

As he spoke he thrust her from him by a violent effort, and hurled her into the broad, deep, and rapid river.

The unfortunate woman would have screamed, but the waters, as they closed over her head, drowned her voice.

She rose at once, and Cartouche could see her struggling for life ; but she was far from either shore, and what chance had she against that powerful tide ?

"That is better than dagger or pistol," Cartouche muttered to himself. "There will be no signs of violence more than any corpse might receive in floating about the river, and those who find the body will certainly think it an accident."

He turned his boat round, and, having to row six or eight miles against a strong current, set to work with a will, being anxious to get back to his quarters at the village inn before any of the early-rising inhabitants of the place were stirring.

But it was destined that the chief of the Parisian banditti should not have everything his own way.

He was pulling away as hard as he could, when his boat experienced a violent shock, and, starting up to see what was the matter, he perceived that the craft had struck against the trunk of a tree which had been uprooted by some gale, and was floating down to the sea.

"Here's a pretty state of affairs !" Cartouche exclaimed. "There's a hole in the bow of the boat which will swamp her in less than five minutes."

Cartouche extricated his craft from the obstacle with which it had come in collision, gave a quick glance to the right and the left, to see which shore of the river was nearest, and then pulled with all his might.

The land he was making for was many yards nearer than the other bank, but by the time the nose of the boat grated on the shingly shore there was a foot of water in it, and the much-damaged craft could not have kept afloat another minute.

As Cartouche stepped out the water nearly reached the tops of his boots.

He paused a moment to think. Then he took up one of the oars, and with it thrust the boat out as far as he could into the stream, where it soon sank.

"And now how am I to get back to Louise ?" was the question he asked himself.

Cartouche had his dagger carefully hidden away in a sheath, which was fastened inside his waistcoat ; he had his pistols, which were loaded, and he had a pretty good sum of money. So that personally he was not in any difficulty, and could easily support himself.

But he was determined not to forsake Louise.

The flower-girl had risked life and liberty for him, more than once she had saved him by bringing intelligence of the plans and schemes of his enemies, and gratitude, the only virtue he had remaining in his composition, would not allow him to desert her.

When Cartouche handed the Lady Guilfort into his boat and uttered the words, "I will do it," he did not mean that he would elope with the murderess, but that he would free Louise from all risk of falling into the power of a cruel, jealous, and bloodthirsty rival. That was why he hurled the Lady Guilfort into the stream.

How to get back to Louise was the question which now had to be solved, and Cartouche at once set his active mind to work out the solution.

He was on the opposite side of the river to the village where Louise was, he doubted not, slumbering peacefully, and he could only cross by means of a boat or a bridge. It was many miles to a bridge, and he did not remember any village on that side for leagues where he could obtain the services of a ferryman.

There was nothing for it but to walk on and trust to chance—or luck, as he called it.

"I can't get back till long after daylight, that is very certain," he murmured, as he struck across a marsh with the idea of finding the nearest road.

It was some time before he reached a thoroughfare, and then it was broad daylight.

"No getting back into the village without being noticed, and what will Louise be doing in the meantime ? She will think one of two things—either that I have been captured or have deserted her. I must push on."

He did so as well as he could.

The road, however, followed pretty accurately the windings of the river, and as there seemed to be no other path Cartouche was obliged to follow it.

Presently he reached a little hamlet consisting of about half a dozen mean cottages ; on the front of one was a board stating that there one might obtain the best of food and wine.

Cartouche doubted the quality of the entertainment, but as he felt in need of something he entered the place, and ordered breakfast to be got ready as quickly as possible.

The hostess lost no time, and speedily he was attacking a good-sized sausage highly flavoured with garlic, a loaf of bread a yard in length, and a flask of rough wine. An omelette followed the sausage, and having fed sufficiently Cartouche began to ask questions about the locality, and what was the best way of crossing to the other side.

"It is a league and a half down the river to the nearest ferry, monsieur," said the woman.

"But I want to go up stream."

"Then monsieur will find it two leagues."

"And the bridge—how far, madame?"

"Three leagues at the least, monsieur."

Cartouche considered for a minute. If he crossed the river in a ferry-boat he would be one of, at the most, half a dozen passengers, and could not escape notice, perhaps recognition.

On the other hand, several scores of persons would be crossing the bridge, and therefore less notice would be taken of a stranger going over the water in that manner. So, turning to the landlady, he said—

"Madame, will you add to the kindness you have already shown me by pointing out the nearest way to this bridge you speak of?"

"Certainly. You see the wood yonder?—there is a road just behind the church, and if you follow that road you will reach the Bishop's-bridge, by which you can cross the river."

"It is a long road. Are there any houses of entertainment this side of the bridge?"

"Not one, monsieur."

"Then I will take with me a bottle of your wine and some slices of sausage and bread. And is there any place where one can purchase gunpowder and bullets, for I must load my pistols ere I venture into that wood. Who knows what robbers may be lurking there?"

"Ah, indeed, monsieur! And they say that Cartouche has escaped from Paris. However, I sell powder and bullets to suit many kinds of pistols."

"Then supply me quickly, madame, if you please. Cartouche may be hiding in that very wood."

"I pray Heaven not!" exclaimed the woman, as she hastened away to get the things required by Cartouche.

Having provided himself with powder, a score of bullets, and a stock of provisions, Cartouche bade the hostess good-morning, and set out on his journey. He was rather anxious about Louise, but he knew she would go on to Rouen if he did not quickly rejoin her, or send some message.

The road through the wood was rough. It was bad enough for a pedestrian, and must have been awful for the vehicles which sometimes traversed it. But Cartouche, being strong and active, pushed along till he had accomplished half the distance, as he guessed, when he withdrew behind some thick bushes to rest, and refresh himself with some of the provisions he had brought.

While thus engaged he thought he heard voices.

Peeping out cautiously from his leafy shelter he beheld a lady and gentleman carefully picking their steps along the broken road, which the male party cursed vigorously.

A little way up the hill was a carriage which had lost a wheel, and was in other ways too much damaged to continue the journey.

"By Heaven!" exclaimed Cartouche, when the couple were a little nearer; "the man is Monsieur Peuchet!"

He looked again, hardly believing his sight, but the second stare satisfied him that he was right.

The lady was quite unknown to Cartouche; she was richly dressed, tolerably good looking, though rather stout, and probably a little over forty years of age. When they came quite opposite Cartouche's hiding-place this lady protested she was so fatigued that a rest was absolutely necessary.

There happened to be the trunk of a tree lying close by the road, and Monsieur Peuchet led the lady to it and seated her thereon.

"This is a judgment on me for leaving my husband!" sighed the lady.

"But then you know, my dear, Monsieur Bobilet is such an ass that it was impossible for you to live with him."

"True, Bobilet is an ass, and I believe he is not the only one in the Civic Guard."

"You are right, my charmer."

"But still it was wrong of me to leave him. I shall be excommunicated by the clergy, and I don't know what will become of me."

"Pooh! his infidelities with that young scent-seller Can-can quite justify you in leaving him and getting a divorce."

"Ah! that is all very well. However, I have done it, and now Bobilet will have to work for a living; for while he was away on that house-to-house search for Cartouche I sold all the stock of the shop and brought away every franc I could find in the place."

"That is good! Now, my charmer, when we reach the place I am taking you to you must wait there quietly while I return to Paris, and, first of all, get you divorced from him."

"Don't have him executed," said Madame.

"Certainly not, my charmer—unless you wish it. But I think he must see the inside of the Bastile."

"A pretty state of affairs this!" muttered Cartouche. "Here is the Chief of Police eloping with the wife of a prominent member of the Civic Guard, and the poor husband to be incarcerated. But I'll have that money, though."

He was thinking how to proceed, when both Peuchet and Madame Bobilet spoke—

"I wonder what has become of Cartouche?" said the lady.

"I would give anything for a bottle of wine," observed Peuchet.

"Here is Cartouche, and he has a bottle of wine to sell for cash," said the outlaw, suddenly appearing before them with a pistol in each hand.

The chief and his lady-love leaped to their feet.

"Gently, Monsieur Peuchet—madame, do not be alarmed," said Cartouche. "But I think we will move a little way into the wood while we talk about the wine—this place is rather too public."

Peuchet and the lady both looked hard at the speaker, but they saw that the outlaw was in no mood for trifling.

"Right-about-face—forward!" said Louis Cartouche.

They obeyed, and went on as well as they could till they reached a little open space perhaps a couple of hundred yards from the main road.

"Now halt, turn about, and drop down on your knees. Be quick, or Paris will need a new Chief of Police and Monsieur Bobilet will certainly be a widower."

Down they went on their marrow-bones, Peuchet cursing the ill-luck which made him forget to bring his pistols from the broken-down carriage. But then he was so enamoured of Madame Bobilet that forgetfulness was excusable.

"Now," continued Cartouche, "before I part with one drop of wine I must have payment, so down with your purse, your ring, and your watch, Monsieur Peuchet, and you, madame, produce at once the money you brought from your husband's house, and take off those bracelets and earrings; keep your wedding-ring for poor Bobilet's sake."

They began to sob, but Cartouche kept his pistols levelled at them, and sorrowfully they dropped all their valuables on the grass.

"Now retire into the wood a short distance, and if you value your lives don't attempt to follow me."

The crest-fallen couple, crying like children, obeyed the mandate, and Cartouche speedily gathered up the plunder.

Having done so he walked back till he came to the road, when he espied the driver of the vehicle hastening along to procure assistance at the village Cartouche had come from.

"What a fool to leave his horses!" exclaimed the outlaw. "I shall ride now instead of walking."

The man had actually tethered his horses by the roadside with no one to look after them.

Walking up to the spot he selected the best of the pair, which he mounted, having first shot the other to render pursuit more difficult, and ransacked the vehicle.

"Why on earth did Peuchet hire a carriage? but I suppose that woman never rode on horseback," he muttered, as he rode gaily along.

Presently the wood began to clear, a few cultivated fields were seen, and Cartouche began to imagine that he must be near the Bishop's-bridge. So he dismounted when he had ridden into a clump of bushes, and killed the second horse with his dagger, after which he walked boldly down into the village, which stood near the end of the bridge.

CHAPTER XLII.
CARTOUCHE IS OUTWITTED.

At the first inn Cartouche came to he inquired if there was a horse in the place that could be hired or bought.

There was one; and the landlord took him to the stable, where Cartouche saw three horses, but two of them so worn with travel that at least a day must pass before they would be fit to move a leg.

"A lady and gentleman in a carriage changed here three hours ago," said the landlord.

Cartouche nodded, purchased the third horse, and rode away.

But when night came on he was still a distance from the place where he left Louise sleeping, and not being quite certain as to the road he resolved to put up at the first inn he came to.

The place, when he did reach it, was not of an appearance that would recommend it to the travelling public generally; it had an air about it as though any wealthy person going there to stay for the night might lose his valuables, if not his life, before morning.

The landlord was a black-browed, sullen fellow, his wife was a hungry, fierce-looking woman, whose features, if there be any truth in physiognomy, showed that she would rather give her guests poison than wine; the ostler looked like a man who stole more horses than he groomed—and the servants generally were just the sort of people to suit such a place.

"Can one sleep here, madame?" he inquired as he dismounted.

"Certainly—if you do not object to a room in which there are two beds?"

"No objection whatever—the second bed is occupied?"

"By a traveller who arrived half an hour ago."

"And where is he now?"

"Eating his supper."

"Then I will join him as soon as I have seen my horse properly stabled and fed."

The landlady nodded and retired.

Cartouche led his horse to the stable and handed it over to the ostler; but he stayed to see every morsel of corn devoured and the rack above the manger filled with hay before he thought of attending to his own supper. Not that he had any affection for the animal, but food was necessary in order that its strength and vigour might be maintained for the next day's journey.

"Now, madame, supper, if you please," said Cartouche, as he entered the house. "And where is my fellow-traveller?"

"This way, monsieur."

Cartouche was not sorry that his apartment was to be shared by some other person.

He did not know the people of the inn, and therefore was not disposed to make himself known to them. The innkeeper might be a very honest fellow, but the place and people were to be doubted, and if he—Cartouche—was attacked during the night, no doubt the traveller who shared the room would assist.

"He must be a tolerably plucky fellow, or he would not risk his life in a den of this sort," Cartouche thought to himself.

The landlady of the Black Dog, as the inn was called, led the way into a room near the kitchen, and there, hard at work on a tough old fowl, was Gribichon.

CARTOUCHE,
THE FRENCH JACK SHEPPARD.

CARTOUCHE KEPT HIS PISTOLS LEVELLED AT THEM.

"Ah, my old and trusty friend," said Cartouche; "let all the world desert me you will stick to me still."

"Yes, captain—"

"Louis is my name," said Cartouche, in a low whisper.

"Yes, Captain Louis, I always will stick to you like sealing-wax or a creditor."

"I don't know why you should feel all this affection, Gribby."

"Why, Captain Louis, didn't you take pity upon me when I was a poor miserable fellow, and reclaim me from the streets, where I was good-for-nothing but sneaking children's bread-and-butter and prigging old gentlemen's handkerchiefs? You did, and you made me one of the best thieves in Paris."

"Hush! don't talk too loud."

"Quite right. I'll stick to you, captain. Are you the gentleman who has the other bed in my room?"

"Yes."

And then raising his voice a little Cartouche said—

"You have come from Paris, monsieur?"

"By the most direct route. The plague is abroad, so I thought it best to retire into the country for a time."

"What plague?" asked Cartouche, adding the word "fool" under his breath.

"An epidemic of police-officers," Gribichon replied, in low tones.

"Well, if you have just come from Paris you can tell me the latest news about that rascal?"

Cartouche spoke those words loudly, for he saw that the landlady was listening.

"What rascal do you mean?" Gribichon asked.

"Why, Cartouche, of course," said the owner of that name.

"Oh! ah! yes, of course, everybody is rather suprised that he so easily gave the police the slip."

"Gave them the slip, eh? Then he is at liberty?"

"Unless he has been captured since I left Paris, which I should think unlikely, as he left some hours before me."

"What do the Parisians say about him?"

"Why, his name is in everybody's mouth and his portrait in every picture-shop. In fact, his name is to be seen in nearly every shop-window in Paris."

"How?—what do you mean?"

"Why, if you look in a tailor's shop you see nothing but Cartouche coats, warranted to resist any amount of rain-fall, forty-five francs each; Cartouche shirts, Cartouche hats, and Cartouche boots are to be found in every street in Paris."

"The villain is popular, then?"

"So popular that yesterday when I left there were six-and-twenty babies christened by the name of Cartouche."

"Wonderful!" ejaculated the landlady, who came in at that moment to inquire if her guests wanted anything more.

"He is a wonderful man, madame," replied Gribichon. "It was only the day before yesterday in the Palais Royal I met a swell musketeer officer, and asked him why he wore his moustache twisted in such a peculiar way. 'Oh! aw! it's the Cartouche fashion,' says he. All the world of Paris is Cartouche mad."

"And Cartouche laughs at them," said the landlady.

"He does—ha, ha, ha! But bring us another bottle, my good hostess. I and my companion here have known each other in Paris, and we must celebrate our meeting here."

The bottle was brought, and the two confederates were left to discuss it.

"What brings you here?" Cartouche asked, in a whisper.

"I expected to find Tomasso here. We had an idea that you had gone to Rouen, and we wanted to know what we are to do, so we came away, but judged it best to travel separately. Is there another inn?"

"I don't know. But let us be getting to bed, Gribby. I, for one, want to be off early in the morning on the road to Rouen, where I expect to find Louise."

The two friends then retired to their bedroom, but before they lay down a compact was arranged that one of the two should be always awake, the watch to be changed every two hours.

Morning came—Cartouche and Gribichon were both of opinion that the rats at the Black Dog were numerous and very lively. Cartouche protested that some of the vermin wore wooden shoes, but Gribichon doubted it.

The pair breakfasted together, and then Gribichon departed.

It had been agreed that they should not travel together.

Gribichon wanted to find Tomasso, and Cartouche was quite as anxious to see Louise and assure her that he was safe. The French Jack Sheppard was not quite certain whether he would tell Louise how he had disposed of the Lady Guilfort or leave that to chance disclosure.

About an hour after Gribichon's departure Cartouche went to the stable to see his horse properly fed and groomed before starting.

"What do you want, sir?" asked the ostler, who met him at the stable-door.

"Why, my horse, of course."

"Haven't seen any horse of yours, monsieur. When did you bring the animal here?"

"Why, last night, you vagabond!"

"The game is not worth the candle," said the ostler, shaking his head. "That's a very old dodge—a man comes here at night on foot, and in the morning calls for some horse he has dreamt about. It won't do, monsieur."

"Why, you villain—"

"Madame!" cried the ostler, to the landlady, who chanced to be passing across the yard, "did this traveller come on foot or on horseback?"

"I saw him on foot only," said the landlady.

who well knew the horse-stealing propensities of her ostler, and shared the profits with him.

"Then monsieur had better pay his bill and depart as he came—on foot."

There was no appeal. Cartouche could not appeal to the local police, who were provided with accurate descriptions of his personal appearance, so he put on the best face he could, and said farewell to the mistress of the establishment—who said—

"Farewell, Monsieur Cartouche ; had I known you last evening I would have given you a better supper."

"So I am known," thought Cartouche as he strode down the street. " I must be careful."

He walked on for some hours, wondering whether he would overtake Gribichon and Tomasso. But when he came to the village where he had left Louise he had not found them, and on inquiry he was told that Louise had departed.

"Rouen—I gave her an address there, so like the true girl she is she will go there."

So argued Cartouche as he pegged away down the road leading to the capital of Normandy.

But presently Cartouche felt fatigued, so he jumped over a fence into a plantation, and sat down to have a rest.

Now our hero was under the impression that he was going along without attracting particular notice, but he was under a very great mistake. He was being shadowed by one of the cleverest police-officers in Paris.

For Cartouche had not been in the place more than ten minutes, and had hardly closed his eyes for a gentle forty winks, when Monsieur Peuchet appeared at the roadside with a couple of the local police.

"That is the man," said he, pointing to the snoring outlaw. "Bind him, and bring him along."

"Right, colonel. But had we not better shoot him first ?"

"By no means ! If you bind him while he is asleep he can do no harm. Have you any cords ?"

"Enough to bind a haystack," responded the man.

"Then bind him. I don't want to be seen in the business, but secure him."

The two men were fully armed—that is to say, they had muskets and bayonets.

They crept carefully into the thicket where Cartouche was snoozing, and in the twinkling of an eye had the outlaw's hands bound.

"What the deuce is the matter ?" demanded Cartouche, whose slumbers were thus roughly interrupted.

"Captured, Captain Cartouche, so you may as ll come along quietly," said the first of the officers, Peuchet having disappeared.

"And you may bet that I will be as fairly rescued," said Cartouche.

That was a bit of bounce on the part of the Parisian bandit, for he did not know but that he would be led right away to the gallows.

(N.B.—The guillotine had not been invented in the days of Cartouche, when criminals sentenced to capital punishment were hanged.)

Cartouche and the two men of the rural police went for a couple of miles or so through the forest towards the place which Peuchet had indicated as the spot to which they were to take their prisoner.

But suddenly there was a halt.

"Release your prisoner !" exclaimed a voice.

Cartouche halted, so did the two soldier-policemen who formed his escort. Gribichon and Tomasso appeared.

"Release your prisoner !" said they.

"I'll blow his brains out if you don't lower those pistols," said one of the escort, as he put the muzzle of his musket to the back of Cartouche's head.

Tomasso and Gribichon at once lowered the muzzles of their weapons, and it seemed as though Cartouche would once more see the inside of a prison.

But Tomasso whispered to Gribichon—

"Your pistols are loaded ?"

"Of course !" replied Gribichon.

"Then aim at the feet of the villains. You will find everything come right in the end."

"But those fellows will shoot the captain."

"Not they ! the moment a bullet goes through their feet they will drop their guns and run."

"Then give the word, and we will all fire at once," said Gribichon. "One—two—"

"Three !" exclaimed Tomasso ; and at that word four pistols exploded, and four human feet had holes neatly drilled in them. The two policemen dropped their two muskets, and Cartouche said—

"Cut this infernal rope and let us be off."

"In a moment, captain," replied Tomasso.

"What in the name of the foul fiend are you waiting for ?"

"The spoils of war, captain."

"As how ?"

"I mean to have muskets, cartridges, purses —if they have any—coats and hats. We will spoil the Egyptians, and I am sorry I did not spoil their faces as well as their feet."

So Tomasso and Gribichon rifled the pockets of the wounded gens d'armes and then appropriated their weapons, which they cast into the next brook, leaving the officers bound with the same cord which a few minutes before had confined the limbs of Louis Dominique Cartouche.

They arrived within half a dozen miles of Rouen and then parted company.

Tomasso and Gribichon thought it best to go by themselves, and Cartouche was only anxious to find Louise.

But he also remembered that he had relatives in the town, the uncle who saw him after his first journey with the gipsies, and a young man who was to be his brother-in-law.

First of all Cartouche went to the place where he had appointed Louise to meet him.

She was not there ! Had anyone been at the house making inquiries ? was the question Cartouche asked.

The reply was that a young woman had been there, and had gone away feeling much disappointed at not finding a young gentleman there. She stayed one night and then returned to Paris.

"To Paris—to the devil!" exclaimed Cartouche. "Have I come all this way to go back again?"

"Mademoiselle said she would return."

Cartouche twisted the moustache which, though it did not grow upon his lip, was so popular in Paris. Then he moved off towards the city gate.

"What is the matter?" he asked, seeing a big crowd at the principal gateway.

"Monsieur Peuchet is coming."

"And who is he?" Cartouche demanded.

"Why the chief of police in Paris. Haven't you heard how Cartouche robbed him?"

"No; that is scarcely possible."

"Cartouche robbed him twice—once in his own office and once in a wood not many leagues hence."

"Then, why does he not go back to Paris and capture this daring ruffian? He should return at once."

"He thinks Cartouche is in Rouen, or will be here very soon," replied the man.

"Then I will bet you a louis d'or that Cartouche, if he is here, will rob Monsieur Peuchet again before he gets back to Paris."

"He did it once, monsieur, but he will never have the chance of repeating his daring trick."

"No doubt, then, this Monsieur Peuchet will be accompanied by a number of his men from Paris?"

"Not so; he comes alone—or, at least, he has only madame, his wife, with him, so I hear. He has sworn that if he finds Cartouche he will take him single-handed."

"That would be a great thing to do. But is it true that this Cartouche is in Rouen?"

"One can hardly say, monsieur, but I don't think he is."

"And I don't think Cartouche would venture to remain here," said the owner of that name. "He may be a daring fellow, but he would hardly stay when, as everybody seems to know, the great chief of the police is expected."

"That is the general opinion."

"But come, monsieur," Cartouche added, "I have occupied much of your time; what say you to a bottle of wine in this café?"

"I wish to see this great Peuchet."

"There is a window from which one may have a good view."

"True! Then I accept your offer with pleasure."

Cartouche and his companion entered the house, a bottle of the best vintage was produced, and they were clinking their glasses together merrily when there was an extra noise outside.

"Ah!" said the gentleman of Rouen, "a body of our own local police coming up to receive the Parisian chief with the honours due to his exalted rank."

He and Cartouche rose from their table and placed themselves at the window. There were some other customers, too, who wanted to see the great Peuchet, so there was a little crowding, during which Cartouche contrived to secure three watches and four purses. Then he thought it time to go.

Hastily rushing to the gate he passed through the archway and was in the open country some quarter of an hour before it occurred to Peuchet to issue orders to close all the portals.

And about the same time the Rouen man with whom he had been drinking thought it time to return to his business, and felt for his watch to see the hour.

But the watch was gone!

The other customers who had been crowding at the window found that they were in a similar plight, and then came the question—Who was that very affable stranger?

"What was he like?" demanded one of the Rouen policemen who entered at that moment; and a description was given.

"By heavens, that was Cartouche!" the man exclaimed.

*   *   *   *   *   *

The visit of Louise, the flower-seller, to Rouen was, as we have seen, a short one.

Louise heard that Monsieur Peuchet was coming—that he was, in fact, at a village a few miles off, and was only waiting for the arrival of half a dozen of the Parisian police to enter Rouen and capture Cartouche—if he could be found.

While laughing at the absurdity of the police chief in thus making known his object and intention in visiting the Norman city, Louise had wit enough to be well aware that Rouen would no longer be a safe residence for her.

No doubt a house-to-house search would be made, and there was not one of Peuchet's men who was not acquainted with her features, from her having been so many years selling flowers in every part of Paris, so that she would have no chance of escape unless she got away at once.

So she left word with the people of the house where she lodged for that one night that if the young man she expected to find there made his appearance he was to be told that she had returned to Paris.

"He will hear of Peuchet's visit to Rouen, and will know that is why I do not remain here," she thought.

The journey by the nearest road was about eighty miles—no inconsiderable walk for a girl of twenty; but Louise started on the journey without hesitation.

She had made some changes in her dress, which now somewhat resembled that common to the peasant girls of the country, and her feet were clad in *sabots*, or wooden shoes, which were necessary to withstand the rough roads she would have to travel by.

Louise did not look like one worth plundering, so she had little fear of being robbed; besides, Cartouche had provided her with a pair of pocket pistols, which she well knew how to use if necessity arose.

It was the noon of the day before Cartouche entered Rouen that Louise left it.

She walked on merrily till she guessed it was within an hour of sunset, when she looked around for some place where she might rest for the night, and, seeing a cottage at some little distance, she went up to the door and demanded shelter, saying to the woman—

"I am poor, and can only pay a few sous for the accommodation, but I am tired, and do not care to be abroad in the dark."

"Come in; my husband is dead, my two daughters are working in the fields, but they will be here soon, and then we will shut the door to keep out the wolves."

"Are there wolves here?" Louise asked.

"Aye. At this time of the year you can hear them howling in the woods and fields all night long. Sometimes they come and try to tear down the door."

"Are you not afraid to live here?"

"No. See here, where their teeth and claws have almost made a hole in the bottom of the door. But they won't hurt me."

"Then why close the door if you are not afraid?"

The old woman—she was ugly as well as old—gave a peculiar look at Louise, and hesitated to speak.

But at length she said, in an undertone, which perhaps was not intended for Louise's ears—

"We are good friends."

"Then why do you fear them?"

"Did I speak, my dear? Why, I was thinking that the wolves would not hurt me because they could not get a meal off my old bones. It is for my daughters I fear—they were born before my husband became—"

"Became what?" Louise asked, as the old woman had come to a full stop.

But the hostess affected not to hear her, and continued her few household preparations for the return of her daughters.

There was a pot simmering on the scanty fire, containing very little meat, more vegetables, and plenty of water; on the table was a loaf of coarse bread, some salt, a few spoons, and a brown stone jug of cider.

"It is the best fare I can offer you," said the old woman.

"Good enough for a poor traveller like me," Louise replied.

Then she fell thinking about the strange words and manner of the old woman.

"The daughters were born before her husband became—what did he become?" Louise thought.

And suddenly she remembered wild legends she had heard that in France and other countries there were men who had the power of transforming themselves into wolves, and after committing a night's havoc amongst their neighbours' flocks and herds could resume their human shapes again.

"Great heavens!" thought Louise, "can this woman be the widow of a wehr-wolf, as the Germans call them?"

It seemed so, and Louise argued that the woman's fearlessness on her own account was from the knowledge that the wolves would not injure the widow of one who had been a wolf himself, while the same clemency would not be extended to her daughters, who were born before their father made that fearful compact with the evil one.

Louise was still thinking of this when the daughters entered. They were tall, gaunt women, clad in the scantiest and coarsest clothing, with hands and faces tanned dark brown by exposure to the weather. They earned a few sous and a portion of meal weekly for working in the fields of a neighbouring farmer, who was wealthy enough to be able to hire a little labour beyond what his own family could supply.

Supper was soon put on the table, and Louise found that the soup, though weak, was well flavoured. One of the daughters, in the course of conversation, informed Louise that during the day she had been harnessed to a plough, along with a donkey, and compelled to drag the clumsy implement up and down the field whilst the proprietor held the two handles so as to turn a straight furrow.

As soon as supper was over preparations were made for retiring. Louise and the two daughters were to sleep on some straw on a sort of half loft or platform raised seven feet above the floor of the cottage, and to which access was attained by means of a ladder. The old woman, not being afraid of wolves, had her truss of straw in a corner below.

Louise's bed-fellows removed very little of their clothing except their wooden shoes, and the flower-girl thought fit to follow their example, as she wished to be prepared for any emergency that might occur, and she took care to have her pistols in readiness.

In a few minutes loud snores announced that the two agricultural labourers were asleep, and about the same time some dreary howls outside proclaimed that the wolves had come out of the forest.

The old woman kept quiet, although in the course of half an hour the house was, judging from the sounds, regularly besieged by the howling pack.

Once or twice amidst the din Louise thought she could distinguish human voices, but she could not be certain about it, and the two women slept on.

As day began to dawn the din slackened a little, and Louise, peeping from the little hole crossed with iron lattice work, which did duty for a window, saw the last of the pack trotting into the forest half a mile off.

An hour later all the inmates of the cottage were astir—the old woman being busily engaged warming some milk and bread for her daughters before they departed to their labours.

"Did the wolves disturb you, my dear?" the old woman inquired as Louise descended from the loft.

"Not much. I heard them, of course, but as

you were not afraid to stay down here I was not afraid to be up there."

"Mother, what were those two men called who came in while we were having our noontide meal yesterday?" one of the daughters asked.

"From their conversation I learned that one of them—he with the black beard—is called Tomasso, and the younger one is known as Gribichon."

"They are Parisians—what do they here?"

"I believe they were going to Rouen, but they heard that Monsieur Peuchet was coming down to arrest Cartouche, so they decided to return to Paris."

"Then they must be members of his band?"

"Have no doubt of that!" exclaimed the mother.

Louise, having taken some bread and milk, produced twelve sous (halfpence) from her pocket, and proffered eight of them to the old woman, explaining that she must keep the other four to get to Paris with. Of course she had plenty, but she did not choose to let the widow of a wehr-wolf know that she carried gold.

The old woman expressed satisfaction, and set off, hoping to overtake Tomasso and Gribichon, so as to travel in their company to Paris.

CHAPTER XLIII.

AN EXECUTION—AND A SCENE AT THE GALLOWS.

IT was just as the old woman had said.

We have already described how Tomasso and Gribichon parted from Cartouche, thinking that it would be better to enter Rouen separately.

But the cheerful Corsican and his young friend turned aside, out of the straight road, and finding in a bye-lane a house that appeared to be occupied by a prosperous person, they resolved to ransack that house before making their appearance in the city of Rouen.

It proved a very unlucky venture for both of them, for Tomasso was captured and Gribichon had to run for his life without being able to make any effort to rescue his friend.

It was about daybreak in the morning after Louise passed a night that they made the attempt; but the owner of the house happened to have three stalwart sons, who, having served in the army, were home on furlough.

They made quick work with the burglars—Tomasso was captured, and Gribichon had to run for his life with a pistol bullet in his shoulder.

It was unlucky for Tomasso that he and Gribichon had selected that particular house, for the owner happened to be a baron and lord of the soil for many miles round, and by a grant from one of the early kings of France he had power to execute any refractory vassals or any criminals who were taken red-handed within his demesne.

As a consequence of this right Tomasso was condemned to be hanged at sunset.

"It is the first time I have made use of my right," said the baron, "so let the gallows be erected at once."

The village carpenter had not had a job for a month, and at once started building a gallows on a heath, across which the main road passed.

Louise went along there in the morning after the night described in the last chapter. She asked what was going on, and they told her, although they were not able to give the name of the unfortunate who was to die.

Louise did not want to see an execution, so she hurried on, and walked till night once more compelled her to seek a frugal lodging.

In the meantime the carpenter was short of wood, or his tools were blunt—at all even's he had not finished his job till the sun disappeared.

And then Tomasso was brought out on a cart, bound, to die.

The hangman was an amateur, but he adjusted the rope round the neck of Tomasso; then the cart was removed, and the Corsican was left hanging.

"But I'm d——d if I shall die, except of starvation," thought Tomasso, as the spectators hurried away, being afraid of the witches who were supposed to haunt that part of the heath.

The fact is the amateur hangman was an ass, who did not know his business.

Tomasso was not choked by the noose, nor was his spine dislocated by the fall; he was simply suspended by the neck, and, as he said, likely to die of starvation.

But there was another chance for him.

Cartouche was hurrying along the road. He had heard that Louise was not far in front of him, and was anxious to overtake her when he came to the place where Tomasso had been executed.

He beheld a gallows from which hung a man's body, whilst beneath stood a strange, wild-looking woman, who pointed at it.

"Look, Cartouche!" she exclaimed. "See what you must come to."

"Away, you hag!" cried Cartouche, "or I will send a bullet through you."

"Away yourself—or I will call the wolves!"

"They will come without your calling—so will the ravens and crows. But let me see who this is."

"He is called Tomasso," the woman replied.

"My friend!" cried Cartouche.

A deep groan was heard from the gallows.

"He lives—and down he shall come though all the witches and wolves on earth said no!"

"Blasphemer, away!"

"Cut and run, old woman, or I shall end your comedy in a tragic manner."

The old woman—the same in whose cottage Louise had slumbered the previous night—gave a loud cry and fled at full speed.

Cartouche nimbly climbed the gallows, and, unfastening the rope, gently lowered the body, from which, after a few minutes, came the words—

"Captain, this has been a close shave!"

"Take a suck at my flask, Tomasso."

And Tomasso did suck, till the flask was empty.

"LOWER YOUR PISTOLS OR I'LL BLOW HIS BRAINS OUT!" CRIED ONE OF THE ESCORT.

"Now, then, captain," said he, as he scrambled to his feet, "we will walk all night, for I feel my legs are much rested since I have not been using them. That hangman fellow will never be worth a pinch of salt; why, the noose didn't slip, so I was not suffocated."

"Let us get out of this neighbourhood," was the response of Cartouche.

"Right, captain. It is not a healthy district for either of us," Tomasso remarked.

And t ey walked on briskly, though the Corsican certainly felt a little weak from the adventure he had gone through.

At the early morn they rested at a little wayside inn for a couple of hours, but nothing could they hear of Louise or Gribichon.

So they went on, Tomasso greatly rejoicing at his very lucky escape from the hangman's rope.

"But how shall we get into Paris?" said Cartouche.

Tomasso shook his head, and replied that he could not venture a suggestion. Cartouche said—

"You will have to disguise yourself and go in first. I will wait at St. Denis for you."

"Disguise myself! How can I do that, my captain, when my black beard is known to every police spy in Paris?"

"Then cut off your beard."

"Holy blue! I had not thought of that."

"You must do so, Tomasso"—who replied—

"Anything for the good of trade! So the next barber's shop will see the last of my beard."

A village was soon reached, and there Tomasso parted with the ebony-hued beard, which had previously been the pride of his face. Then they went on till the environs of Paris were reached, and Tomasso prepared to go in and inquire the news.

By way of preparation for his work of espial the Corsican changed his dress—or rather made some alterations in it, so that with his shaven face he would scarcely be recognised even by his friends.

Then off he started, leaving Cartouche in a little roadside inn a couple of leagues from the city.

It was well that Tomasso changed his appearance, for on entering the city he found that the guards were doubled, and a member of the detective police was there on duty to watch all who passed in or out.

Tomasso recognised the man, who was one of the ablest of old Lecoq's assistants; but the detective did not recognise the Corsican, who passed along as swiftly as he could, without exciting suspicion.

"Now what shall I do?" thought he.

A wine-shop was close at hand, and as Tomasso was both warm and thirsty after his hanging and walking, he resolved to rest and drink while considering over matters. For to tell the truth, from the time he left Cartouche his mind was mostly occupied with the question whether he would be able to get into Paris without being captured.

But that part of the business had been accomplished, and Tomasso had now to find out whether Louise and her esquire Gribichon were within the city.

"If I could only run up against The Wolf I would soon know what is going on. I wonder if that young rascal contrived to get himself arrested by Peuchet's men?"

It seemed pretty clear that he could only work with the assistance of The Wolf; so having finished his wine the Corsican resolved to visit some of the places most frequented by that youth.

Tomasso felt pretty certain that even if he did not see The Wolf he would hear something of him on the quay by the Pont Neuf, where the young ragamuffin was in the habit of running errands for the boatmen and performing other services, which he varied by diving for coppers when the water was not too cold or he was in want of a meal.

So to the Pont Neuf went Tomasso.

There were a lot of young rascals playing about, but The Wolf was not of the number.

Tomasso shouted out his name, and the others looked up.

"Where is The Wolf?" the Corsican asked.

"Not here, monsieur," said one. "I can run errands and dive just as well as The Wolf, who has not long gone away."

"You will not do. I want The Wolf. I sent him on an errand this morning and he has not returned. Do you know where to find him?"

"I think I do, monsieur."

"Then five sous for you if you bring him."

The boy held out his hand for the money.

"When you bring him," said Tomasso, with a grim smile.

The lad looked irresolute for a few seconds, but presently scampered off, crying out—

"I will bring him, monsieur."

Tomasso lighted his pipe and walked up and down the quay.

The Wolf was easily found in a very small and disreputable café playing dominoes with a youth about his own age, and cheating him in a most barefaced manner.

"Wolf, you are wanted," said Tomasso's messenger.

"Who wants me?"

"Don't know—the gentleman did not tell me his name."

"What dressed like?"

"Much like a peasant, except that he does not wear wooden shoes."

"Dark complexion or fair?" The Wolf demanded, coolly altering the arrangement of the dominoes on the table while his adversary was staring at the messenger.

"Very dark. He said you sent him on some business this morning and had not been back."

"He tells lies! Now, then, Charles, I have won the game, so just pay up twenty sous, and then I'll be off to see this mysterious person. Lead on; I should like to see the individual who can truthfully say I ever cheated him."

"Of course, you don't cheat," said Charles, handing over the coin.

"Nobody ever caught me at it," responded The Wolf, which was true to the letter.

Then he hurried off, wondering who it could be who wanted him at the quay.

"I have not been sent on any errand this morning," said he, "so if I find any young rascal has been using my name I will half kill him."

The messenger protested that he was innocent, so The Wolf went on muttering all kinds of vengeful threats till they came to the well-remembered quay.

"Where is the monsieur?"

The messenger was at first unable to point out Tomasso, and The Wolf was just preparing to administer a severe beating when the Corsican appeared on the scene. Finding his messenger longer gone than he expected, Tomasso had been taking another glass of wine.

"Here are your sous—now away with you. Wolf, you come along with me; I want to have a chat with you."

"But may I not have the pleasure of knowing your name, monsieur?" demanded The Wolf, who did not recognise the Corsican without his beard.

"The devil! If you don't know me I am safe," said Tomasso.

The Wolf stared, but, the messenger being by this time many yards off, the Corsican went on—

"I am Tomasso. Do you know me now?"

"Why, yes, signor; but what a change!'

"Yes; it won't do to be seen looking too much like one used to resemble in the old times."

"Quite right, signor; but have you seen the chief lately?'

"Yes; I left him only a few hours ago. Have you seen La Belle Louise, the flower-girl?"

"No, not for many days. I fancy she must have left Paris, Signor Tomasso."

"She has been to Rouen, but left that city to return to Paris when she heard that Peuchet and some of the Parisian police were expected."

"I have not seen her, signor. If I should meet her how can I communicate with you or the captain?"

"I have thought of that; but before I make any arrangements I must see the captain. Where do you live, Wolf?"

"In the catacombs—such a jolly place!"

"Bah! nothing but ghosts and dry bones."

"The bones don't hurt anyone, and they make good fires with a little wood. And the ghosts don't trouble me."

"See here, Wolf. Look about the city as much as you can and inquire as much as you dare about Madame Louise. Don't spare time or trouble. Have you any money?"

"A little—not much, though."

"Take this," said Tomasso, thrusting a handful of silver into the youth's hand. "Get about as much as you can to-night, and meet me here to-morrow morning at nine."

"Right, signor; trust me—I will do all I can."

Tomasso then turned about and sauntered out of the city gate.

It was dark by the time Tomasso got back to the little roadside inn where he had left Cartouche.

There was a light inside the building though, shedding a cheerful glow through the red window-curtain that screened the common-room of the pla   and the night air outside was pregnant   a savoury smell of cooking.

"Ah! I shall not go to bed supperless," Tomasso muttered, as he   ened the door and passed into the house.

"Just in time for supper, Signor Tomasso," said a female voice, as the Corsican entered the room.

Tomasso stared and rubbed his eyes, not being quite certain that he could believe the evidence they presented him.

A second rub, however, convinced him that he was wide awake and his optics unimpaired.

"Heavens! is it you, Madame Louise?" ejaculated Tomasso.

"It is," replied the young lady the Corsican had just been inquiring about in Paris.

"Then I have had my walk for nothing. However, I don't mind that, since it has given me a great appetite, and I can smell something very nice."

"First take something to wash the dust out of your mouth and throat, that you may enjoy your supper the better," said Cartouche, handing his lieutenant a glass of wine.

Tomasso swallowed it, and was about to question Louise as to her adventures since parting from Cartouche, but the chief interposed—

"No tale-telling till we have had our supper, for I am as hungry as you, Signor Tomasso, and so is Louise."

"And here comes the supper," said the flower-girl.

A smoking dish was set upon the table, and for some time nothing was heard but the clatter of plates, spoons, forks, &c. But when hunger was appeased their tongues were loosened.

Louise, it seemed, had not met with any particular adventure after leaving the hut where she passed the night surrounded by wolves. She took a slightly different road from that travelled by Gribichon and also by Cartouche and Tomasso after the cutting down of the former from the gallows; but at the village where they were then sitting those roads joined.

Poor Louise was weary and footsore from walking in the clumsy wooden shoes when she reached the little inn intending to remain there for the night.

Judge her astonishment when, before she could open her mouth, she found herself clasped in the arms of Cartouche, who claimed her as his wife.

Tomasso did not want to hear any more—there they were in evidence; there was only one thing remaining to be explained, and the Corsican put the question to his two companions.

"What, then, has become of Gribichon?"

"He must be in P ris," said Louise. "I have heard more than once of a man much resembling him, who passed along the road some hours in advance of me."

"I think if he had reached Paris The Wolf would have told me," said the Corsican.

"Did you ask Wolf?" said Cartouche.

"No; I was only with him a few minutes, and that time I spent in finding out if I could what had become of Madam G. But I have appointed to meet him early in the morning, and then we shall know if he has seen Gribichon."

"Has Wolf any place for us to live in? It will not do to go to any of our old lodgings."

"Can't say. He lives in the catacombs."

Louise gave a shudder at the idea of going to those dreary vaults which she had heard so much of, though she had never in her life visited them.

"I don't know but it might prove a good hiding-place. But see Wolf to-morrow—inquire about Gribichon, and, if you have time, take a look at this place in the catacombs."

"I will do so. And you, of course, will remain here till I return, Captain Cartouche?"

"Of course, I shall not be fool enough to do anything of the kind, Signor Tomasso."

"Then how shall I find you—or where, rather?"

"I must think that out during the night, and in the morning we will arrange. And as our good landlord is now yawning much I think we had better retire."

Of course, it can easily be guessed that there was no one in the room while this talk was going on.

A few minutes later the three travellers were shown to their rooms, and long before midnight peace and perfect quietness prevailed in the little village, and the weary travellers slept soundly till the first rays of morning light roused them from their slumbers.

CHAPTER XLIV.

GRIBICHON'S ADVENTURES.

How fared it all this time with Gribichon, whom we left running for his life with a pistol bullet in his shoulder?

He looked upon Tomasso as utterly beyond human help, and thought the best thing he could do was to hurry back and reach Paris as quickly as possible.

"But I must avoid all my old haunts and old friends, too, except, of course, the captain, Tomasso, and Can-can," Gribichon thought to himself as he hastened along.

Gribichon did not keep to the highway, but hurried across fields, through woods, and over heaths, in what he thought was the right direction.

Cottages were few and far between, but the peasants, though poor, were hospitable, and never refused him a share of their food or a drink of their cider.

At length it was evident that night was coming on, and Gribichon looked round for some place where he could sleep. His arm, too, where the bullet was lodged, gave him much pain and evidently needed attention, which could only be given by some fellow-creature.

Not a house of any kind could he see.

"Well, I must make myself as comfortable as I can under some bush or other in the wood yonder," the young man muttered to himself. "I would give something, though, to be safe inside the walls of Paris."

Gribichon walked on, and had reached within a couple of hundred yards of the wood in which he proposed to pass the night, when a loud and dismal howl was heard near the point to which he was making.

The sound was answered by a similar howl at a little distance, and then two great gaunt wolves came out of the wood, and, sitting down on their haunches like dogs, surveyed the scene.

Gribichon halted instantly.

"What a mercy I didn't go into the wood," he muttered.

At that moment other howls were heard deeper in the forest, which were answered by those two advanced sentinels.

Gribichon forgot his fatigue and his pain; he turned about and ran with all the speed he was capable of across the open field.

He had nearly reached the low boundary-wall of an enclosure when he stumbled, and in recovering himself looked back towards the forest.

The two wolves had viewed him, and were standing with their faces towards him, yelling like fiends to their comrades in the wood to come and join in the chase.

Gribichon leaped over the wall.

The enclosure was only a few hundred yards in extent and afforded no safety, so the young man sped on, and quickly bounded over the wall at the other side.

But whither should he go—which way bend his steps? Before him was a wide open heath, with here and there a solitary tree; not a house to be seen.

"I must take to one of the trees," thought Gribichon. "I shall be torn to pieces in five minutes if I don't contrive to get out of their reach."

He sped with the swiftness of a hunted deer towards the nearest oak that looked capable of affording shelter, and saw with satisfaction that its trunk was quite as thick as his body, and the principal branches were at least twelve feet from the ground.

There were two smaller shoots growing out from the trunk, one about six feet from the ground, the other two or three feet higher.

Gribichon caught hold of the lowest of these two minor branches and scrambled up the trunk with the agility of a cat; he reached a place of safety, and then paused to recover breath.

The wolves were more than a minute behind him, a score in number, at least, yelling like demons.

For a few minutes they made frantic efforts to jump up to where Gribichon was seated, and howled fearfully at finding that they were unable to reach him.

"It is lucky for me they can't climb," thought Gribby. "But I must stay here all night, that is certain."

Having come to that conclusion he resolved to make himself as secure as possible, and, drawing a piece of thin but extremely strong cord from his pocket, he lashed his body to a stout, upright branch which grew from that he was sitting on.

The wolves had left off jumping, and were watching Gribichon's proceedings earnestly.

"No fear of falling down amongst you, my beauties, so you may yell yourselves hoarse. Here's confusion to you," he added, sucking at a flask of brandy he purchased at the last village.

The wolves ceased their loud howls, but kept up a sort of snarling noise.

"Having a debate as to what is to be done, are you, messieurs?" said Gribichon. "You had best go away, for I don't intend to descend."

But the brutes seemed to have no such intention. On the contrary, three of the biggest began to gnaw at the trunk of the tree as though they intended to tear it down.

Gribichon let them continue at this for some time, then it suddenly flashed across his mind that he had a pistol and a good supply of powder and ball in his pocket.

"Now, my beauties, I'll have some fun with you," said the tree'd one.

He loaded the pistol, took steady aim at the back of one wolf, and then pulled the trigger.

When the smoke cleared off Gribichon saw that his aim had been true—the monster's back was broken, and the others had retired to a more respectful distance.

"But they don't mean to go away, that is the worst of it," Gribichon moralised, as he reloaded.

He was besieged.

The sun went down, but the sky was beautifully clear, and soon became thickly studded with stars, which, with the young moon, gave Gribichon sufficient light to see the movements of the enemy.

Posting themselves round the tree at intervals they resolved to tire Gribichon out, but he felt no inclination to surrender.

Presently he heard a distant church clock strike the hour of eight, and then he perceived that his adversaries were gradually drawing in towards the tree.

"Let them come a little closer," said Gribichon.

Very slow and stealthy were the movements of the animals, but presently Gribichon got a good aim at one of the pack and stretched him on the turf.

But guess his surprise when the others, instead of going away fastened on their wounded companion and began to eat him, snarling and growling over their feast in a horrible manner.

"What nasty cannibals!" Gribichon exclaimed, loading his pistol as rapidly as possible, and firing again at haphazard into the throng, from whence came a fearful yell which told him his shot had taken effect.

"Three of them done for! Hurrah! Come closer, my beauties, and I will settle the lot of you!"

Gribichon took another slight sup at his flask, and then made ready to fire a fourth time, which he did with the same success.

But the wolves, finding that those flashes of light from the tree meant death to one of them, withdrew to some distance, though they did not give up the siege. On every side of the tree they could be heard howling most dismally.

Long, chill, and weary were the hours of night, and Gribichon could only drive away the cold which attacked him by repeated applications to his brandy-flask.

At length a faint streak of light appeared in the eastern sky, and evidently the day was at hand.

The wolves began to draw in towards the tree as if they intended to try once more to make a meal off the bodies of their relatives.

An idea flashed through Gribby's head. He would make some money out of those wolves; so he drew the bullet he had already placed in his pistol and substituted for it one he had cut in halves.

On they came, hungry and disappointed, but warned by the growing light that it was time to retire to their dens in the thick forest.

Gribichon allowed them to collect round the body of one of the slain, and then he fired.

Two death screeches were heard, and then one was seen writhing upon the ground, while another was scarcely able to limp after his companions, who were hastening away towards the wood at full speed, evidently not intending to show themselves any more that day.

Gribichon loaded his pistol and then descended from the tree.

"Five heads to take to the next village and get paid for. Why, I am really earning a honest living—for the first time in my life," Gribichon muttered.

Then he began to sever the heads of the slain from their bodies and tied the five of them together with his cord.

Having heard the clock several times during the night he had no difficulty in deciding in which direction he ought to go, and set out at a brisk walk to warm his thoroughly cold body and limbs.

He soon saw the church whose clock he had heard.

It seemed a good big village or small town. Some of the inhabitants were about, and stared to see Gribichon with the wolves' heads.

But Cartouche's friend quietly refreshed himself at the first inn he could find, and then made his way to the house of the magistrate who was to pay the reward for each head.

CHAPTER XLV.

HOW CARTOUCHE GREW JEALOUS.

Tomasso slept very soundly the night after his trip to Paris and back, for he was fatigued.

It was broad daylight when he awoke, and recollecting in an instant that he had appointed to meet The Wolf again, he jumped from his bed and dressed hurriedly.

"What time is it, madame?" said he to the hostess, as he reached the common room.

"Seven in the morning, monsieur."

"And my friends with whom I supped last night, where are they, pray?"

"They have gone. But they desired me to say that they would see you again before reaching Paris."

"A crust of bread and a cup of wine, if you please, and I will hurry after them."

The refreshment was brought, and Tomasso demanded how much he had to pay.

"Nothing, monsieur; all is paid."

Tomasso drank his wine and departed munching his piece of bread, and muttering—

"He is a devil of a fellow! But why did he go away?"

Half way along the road to Paris he passed two persons, a man and a woman, who called after him—

"Why such hurry, Signor Tomasso?"

"I know that voice. Why, it is you, captain—and Madame!"

"We are going into Paris with you."

"I think you may do so safely, so well are you disguised."

Cartouche had not altered his dress much, but his hair was white, and some artful artist had drawn lines on his forehead, about his eyes, and at the corners of his mouth, which, with a touch of red at the tip of his nose, made him look like a convivial old country tradesman. Louise also had put on evident signs of age in the shape of a few grey hairs and (sham) wrinkles upon her countenance.

All this had been accomplished by a barber whom they found just outside the village, a man who had often disguised Cartouche, and who had, in consequence of the fact being suspected by the police, judged it prudent to leave Paris for a time.

This being explained the three confederates marched on together and entered Paris.

First they went to the quay of the Pont Neuf, but The Wolf was not there—it was an hour past the appointed time of meeting. So leaving Louise in a little wine-shop not far from the quay Cartouche and Tomasso started to hunt for their young coadjutor in other parts of the city, but for a long time they sought in vain.

"Hunt elsewhere, friend Tomasso, for another hour, while I go back to the quay and wait in case he comes," said Cartouche—and Tomasso nodded assent.

Returning towards the Pont Neuf Cartouche passed down the street where he had left Louise. He did not intend entering the house, but he glanced through the open window, and to his astonishment saw her sitting opposite to a man whose back was turned towards him.

Jealousy took possession of Cartouche.

He drew a pistol and aimed at Louise, then he lowered the weapon, muttering—

"No, I cannot kill her. But he shall die who has supplanted me in her affections!"

The man evidently was making very amorous advances to her.

Cartouche again raised his pistol and fired. Then conscious of the danger he had incurred, he turned and ran away, but had not gone many yards when a man darted out of a shop exclaiming—

"Assassin! I saw you fire that fatal shot!"

There was no time to draw another pistol, so as the man tried to seize him Cartouche brought the butt of it with terrible force on his head.

The fellow fell like a log, and Cartouche darted up an alley and was speedily a good distance from the scene of his last exploit.

Having stopped running for fear of exciting suspicion, he was just turning a street corner when he met Tomasso and The Wolf.

"What is the matter, captain?" the Corsican asked.

"I have just shot a man," he replied.

"Where, in Heaven's name, and what for?"

"Why, where we left—that woman!"

"What woman are you talking of, my brave captain?"

"Louise! I ought to have shot her!"

And Cartouche related what he had seen.

"It seems to me, captain, that you have been very hasty in this matter. Likely enough she was only trifling with some fellow whom she recognised as a police spy. You should remember that she knows many of them."

"But why should she—"

"To get information—to wheedle out of him the latest moves of the police in regard to yourself."

"Tomasso, I believe I have been an ass!" said Cartouche, after a moment's reflection.

"Likely enough. Mortals cannot be wise at all hours. But go you with The Wolf to some place, and I will make a few inquiries."

"Right, my friend; and if you can bring away Louise, do so."

"This is a place where we can wait, captain," said The Wolf, pointing to a wine-shop over the way; "the place where he had been playing dominoes when inquired for by Tomasso the previous day."

"It will do. Come back here, then, my friend."

Tomasso nodded and departed.

Cartouche was about to enter the house when Wolf plucked him by the sleeve.

"Captain," said he, "there are some queer fellows go there, and you are not dressed one bit like the regular customers; so we had best play a game at cards, and I will make believe that you are some old countryman I have picked up and am going to cheat out of all your money."

"What for?"

"Because I don't want any of the fellows to know that you know more than all the lot of them. If they thought anything of that kind they would begin to wonder who you are, and then you would be talked about."

"All right, Wolf; cheat me as much as you like."

CARTOUCHE,
THE FRENCH JACK SHEPPARD.

"LOOK, CARTOUCHE!" SHE EXCLAIMED. "SEE WHAT YOU MUST COME TO!"

There were about a dozen young fellows, of ages varying from fifteen to eighteen, in the house. They all stared at Cartouche and winked at each other when he accepted Wolf's invitation to play.

It amused Cartouche so much that he could scarcely maintain the character he had assumed; however, he contrived to lose a small handful of silver in a blundering style before Tomasso returned.

When Tomasso returned Cartouche rose and went out, first bestowing a very paternal blessing on the boys.

Wolf followed to get instructions as to his future movements, and, knowing that he was watched by his young companions, contrived to rob Cartouche of a pocket-handkerchief ere he returned to them.

"And what is the news, Tomasso?"

The Corsican seemed highly pleased at something.

"Is the man dead?" Cartouche continued.

"No, nor even injured, although much frightened. You did not see his face, did you?"

"I did not."

"It was our old acquaintance of the Civic Guard, Monsieur Bobilet. Your hand was unsteady, or Madame Bobilet would have been a widow."

"And Peuchet a married man. But where is Louise?"

"Close by. She has been interrogated by the police, and swears the shot was fired by a very tall, dark man, for whom they are now searching."

"The man I knocked down with my pistol will tell them a different tale," said Cartouche.

"He is dead, captain," answered Tomasso.

"Then let us go to Louise—who is waiting close by, you say, Signor Tomasso."

"Waiting anxiously, to explain to you how she happened to be in the company of Monsieur Bobilet."

Cartouche and his friend then went to the place where Louise was anxiously expecting her lover. A few words set every suspicion at rest, and then they retired to refresh themselves and consider the future.

"Wolf, let us see this place in the catacombs which you think would suit us," said Cartouche.

"With pleasure, captain," responded the Wolf.

They were walking together, and had not got more than fifty yards when half a dozen police pounced upon them from a narrow little alley.

"We have you now, Captain Cartouche!" said one.

"I am not certain of that!" he exclaimed, struggling violently to get his hand to the breast-pocket where he always kept his trusty dagger.

It was a hard tussle, and all six of the police seemed to have only Cartouche upon their minds. So Tomasso, The Wolf, and Louise quietly withdrew, seeing that other police were hastening to the spot. They knew well enough that they could help Cartouche best by not sharing his captivity.

So the chief of the Parisian banditti was led off to prison, and all the metropolis rejoiced at the capture of the renowned outlaw who so long had been a terror to the people.

And they laughed rather when they remembered that it was not Monsieur Peuchet who gained this great victory. And Monsieur Bobilet thought to himself—

"If I had half the pluck of this Cartouche I would certainly kill the man who has decoyed my wife from her home."

CHAPTER XLVI.

THE REWARD FOR WOLVES' HEADS.

WHEN Gribichon went to the mayor, or head man of the village, with his five wolves' heads, that worthy gentleman stared.

He stared because, in the first place, he had never known one man present so many trophies at one time; and, in the second place, he was rather doubtful whether the village contained the quantity of coin which he must pay down to the successful wolf-hunter.

For it seldom happened that the most daring and successful forester in the district could claim for more than one head of a full-grown wolf during the year, and that a man should have five of them all freshly killed was something very extraordinary indeed.

"How did you get those heads?" demanded the mayor.

"I cut them from the wolves' bodies," replied Gribichon.

"Who killed the wolves, dolt?"

"I did, of course," responded Gribichon.

"You couldn't kill all those wolves. How do you pretend you did it?"

"I sat up in a tree and shot them."

The mayor continued to grumble that there was no proof of Gribichon having shot the wolves; but the successful hunter, pointing with one hand to the heads upon the floor, called the attention of the mayor to a placard on the wall:—

"Any person bringing the head of a wolf to the mayor of this or any other town or village shall receive a reward of five livres without any delay and without deduction. The said mayor to pay the money at once and to destroy the heads, so that they be not presented a second time."

"So I will trouble you for the money at once, Mr. Mayor," said Gribichon. "There is nothing here about proving that I killed the wolves—and it must occur to you that any man who kills a wolf and does not take its head must be either a very big lord or a very great fool."

The mayor's secretary, whose principal duties were feeding his worship's hogs and looking after the goats, entered, and after whispering to the great man, placed a little bag in his hand.

"Young man," said the mayor, "I can only pay you for four of those heads—"

"You are to pay without delay and without deduction."

"But there isn't enough money in the village!"

A bright idea struck Gribichon. The passport system was then very strictly observed; not only were foreigners entering France obliged to show papers establishing their identity, but the natives passing from one part of the kingdom to another were liable to be called upon to show their passports. Gribichon, of course, had no such document, but he resolved that he would have one without delay.

"Listen, Monsieur the Mayor," said he.

"I am all attention," replied the great man.

"If I report you to the king's huntsman for refusing me the head-money for five wolves you will get into very serious trouble."

"I know I shall,' responded the great man, beginning to shiver and think himself very small indeed.

"Very serious trouble indeed, Monsieur the Mayor."

"I will do anything you can suggest rather than have the king's huntsman finding fault with my administration.'

"Then listen again, monsieur. The wolves devoured my wallet in which I had papers of importance, including a passport enabling me to circulate freely in the north-western provinces of France. Now, if you will write me another passport in place of that torn in pieces by the wolves, I will be satisfied with the money for three heads while signing you a receipt for the reward for five."

"Excellent! You shall have it at once."

The mayor sat down to write.

"Your name, if you please, monsieur."

"Eugene de Gribichon. Remember the 'de,' if you please."

"Certainly. Your place of birth and residence?'

"This village, monsieur, as you are well aware."

Monsieur the Mayor stared, but Gribichon pointed very significantly to the wolves' heads, so it was written down that he was an inhabitant of the village of Louvet, and that he had permission to circulate freely in all parts of France.

When this precious document was stamped and signed by the mayor and his secretary De Gribichon put it in his pocket and in turn signed a document acknowledging that he had received the proper reward for killing five wolves.

"And now, monsieur, when I have tasted the good wine which, doubtless, you keep in store, I will bid you good-morning and resume my travels."

The mayor produced the wine, and Monsieur De Gribichon, having partaken, was about to depart, when a carriage rolled up to the door of the house.

"Monsieur Peuchet!" exclaimed Gribichon, as he looked upon the form of the individual who alighted from the vehicle.

"Eh?" exclaimed the mayor. "It cannot be!"

"It is, though!' said Gribichon; "I know him."

"Then, monsieur, I doubt not you will do me the honour of introducing me to the great Chief of Police."

"With pleasure. Take your seat, with your secretary at your left hand. Now assume your badge of office, and do not move till I bring the Chief of Police to you."

The mayor put on one of the badges he had to wear, but Gribichon had already secured the other, and was wearing it when he descended the two steps of the mayor's house to meet Peuchet.

"You are the mayor?" said the Chief of Police.

"Just so. And I am off to Paris on important business."

"Ah! May I ask what that is?"

"Oh, there can be no doubt that fiend Cartouche has sent some of his gang down here to see the best way in which we can be attacked. So I am going to Paris to request that a garrison of soldiers may be put in the village of Louvet to protect the inhabitants."

"Then ride with me, monsieur. I and my lady are going to Paris, and I merely called to know if you had heard anything of that villain, Cartouche. You can tell me as we go."

Monsieur De Gribichon bowed and entered the carriage, which rapidly rolled away towards Paris.

Gribichon told Peuchet a number of extraordinary lies as they went along, and Madame Bobilet, who was with Peuchet, stared hard at the young man, of whom she had some vague recollection.

CHAPTER XLVII.

IN PRISON.

THE robber and the Chief of Police rode along in the most friendly manner till Paris was reached, which was at rather a late hour in the afternoon.

Peuchet and his carriage being recognised the guard at the gate turned out to receive him with the respect due to his rank, and Monsieur De Gribichon had the honour of being received by a company of infantry, who with their captain at their head presented arms to him and his companions as the carriage passed through into the city.

"See what a fine thing it is to be Chief of the Police," said Peuchet. "Now, only a few days ago my lady and I were robbed of all we possessed by that villain Cartouche, yet I went boldly on, and at the first town I reached I demanded horses and money in the name of the king, and was instantly supplied with everything I required."

"Ah! very much Cartouche's style, only he demands things in his own name and does not make the king an accessory to his acts of robbery."

"No, of course he does not. Well, I shall

have Cartouche soon. He has escaped me many times, but it will not happen again."

Gribichon was not of the same opinion, but he did not think it advisable to air his sentiments on the subject lest suspicion should be directed to himself. So he simply said—

"Monsieur, as we have arrived at the corner of the Rue Francini, will you have the kindness to permit me to alight?"

"With pleasure; and thanks for your company."

The coachman pulled up, and Gribichon stepped from the carriage, to the great astonishment of a number of police, both in uniform and plain clothes, who were loitering about.

Gribichon walked a little way down the Rue Francini, and then, hearing some shouts, and seeing other people run in the direction of the spot where he left Peuchet's carriage, he turned back himself to see what was the cause of the commotion.

There was a troop of dragoons surrounding Cartouche, whose hands were bound behind him.

It was evident that the French Jack Sheppard was caught and they were conveying him to prison.

"My good friend Peuchet had not the honour of making the capture, that is certain," mused Gribichon.

Then, tapping one of the police on the shoulder, he asked whither they were taking the prisoner.

"Why, to prison, of course—St. Pelagie."

"Ah! what has he done?"

"Robbed everybody and murdered a lot of folks."

"And who is this terrible criminal?" demanded Gribichon.

"Why, you must be a fool not to know Cartouche!" the police-officer replied.

Gribichon kept as near as he could to the procession, and he was certain that Cartouche saw him. But the question Gribichon had to consider was—How could he rescue his captain from the gaol to which the soldiers were taking him?

And then came also the question—How did it happen that Cartouche was captured.

To explain which it will be necessary to revert to the previous chapter, in which we left Cartouche, Tomasso, Louise, and The Wolf on their way to the catacombs.

Cartouche had some notion of taking up his abode in the subterranean retreat The Wolf had indicated, and Louise, now that the little fit of jealousy was over, was, of course, prepared to accompany him anywhere.

But as they were passing along the street, Tomasso and The Wolf in front, Cartouche was suddenly pounced upon by a party of police far more watchful than their chief.

Louise and the others were entirely ignored; the police knew Cartouche, and they meant having him, so they surrounded him in such numbers that Tomasso saw how hopeless it was to make any attempt to rescue his friend. So

he and Louise thought it best to seek their own safety, as did Wolf.

Cartouche, being secured after a very severe struggle, was being conveyed to prison when Gribichon saw him.

Nor did Gribichon leave the procession till he saw his chief conveyed inside the prison, the gates of which were immediately closed.

"Now, I would give something to know which of those dismal rooms they have put him in," said Gribichon to himself.

As though in answer to his question a white handkerchief was waved at a window on the second floor of the prison, and Gribichon at once concluded that his chief was there.

"No difficulty now," said he.

Gribichon at once went to a shop and purchased a couple of files and a small jointed crowbar, with a few other articles, which he packed up in as small a parcel as possible.

Returning to the prison just as it grew dusk he found no one on guard outside, and without difficulty pitched his parcel through the window, which had only one bar across it.

So far all seemed well; the parcel of tools actually reached the hand of Cartouche, for whom they were intended, and he had commenced operations upon the iron bar, which was about the only obstacle between himself and liberty, when he heard the noise of approaching footsteps.

He at once desisted from his work and concealed his tools. Having been thoroughly searched when he entered the prison, he had no fear of being examined again.

"Come along, prisoner," said the chief gaoler, as he entered the apartment and glanced round. "You are too near the street here, so we will give you an apartment in the interior of the building where you will not be disturbed by the noises that are going on outside."

"You are too careful, monsieur."

"On the contrary, Monsieur Cartouche. It is not often that I have the happiness of entertaining such an illustrious guest, so I must do all I can to promote your health and security."

Cartouche bowed in his best style.

He judged it prudent not to prolong the conversation for fear of rousing suspicions in the minds of his custodians.

"I am at your disposal, monsieur," said he.

"Then this way," said the gaoler.

Cartouche was conducted to a cell, the window of which commanded a view of a small courtyard surrounded on all sides by windows which were closely barred.

"And when shall I have the pleasure of an interview with my noble friend the judge?" the prisoner asked, as he took possession of his new apartment.

"It seems to me that you are impatient," replied the gaoler. "Most men wish to put off that interview as long as possible."

"That is not the case with me, though."

"Well, Monsieur Cartouche, to-morrow being Sunday you can scarcely expect to be brought to the court, but Monday, or, more probably,

Tuesday, I have no doubt he will tell you when you are to be hanged."

"If he tells me I am to be hanged he will tell a lie! The hemp is neither sown, grown, nor spun to hang Louis Dominique Cartouche."

The gaoler smiled in a pitying manner. He was accustomed to prisoners who thought they were going to evade the last penalty of the law but who never succeeded in doing so.

"Will you eat the prison fare, Monsieur Cartouche, or will your friends send you what you desire?'

"The prison fare, if you please. I have no wealthy friends upon whom I can call for support."

"And yet I'll be sworn La Belle Louise would give her last sou for your comfort."

The gaoler knew that Louise was "wanted" by the police, and he thought there was just a chance of catching her through her affection for Cartouche; but in this case he made a mistake, for the prisoner thoroughly understood the trap set for him, and avoided it.

"Louise will probably hear of my escape before anyone tells her of my imprisonment," said he.

"She must be already aware of your incarceration, since she was with you when we had the felicity and honour of taking you," said the gaoler, who was angry with himself for not having captured Louise as well as her lover.

Cartouche was not inclined to prolong the conversation, so after having a good look round the room to see that everything was secure the gaoler departed. But at least once an hour all that night he visited the cell to see that his prisoner was safe.

CHAPTER XLVIII.

HOW CARTOUCHE GOT OUT OF PRISON.

Louise, Tomasso, and Wolf held a consultation as soon as possible after the capture of Cartouche to consider how he could be released.

They were not aware of Gribichon's return to Paris, and of course knew nothing about his having conveyed a packet of tools to the prisoner.

It seemed to them a hopeless case.

"If we only could have a few words of conversation, or send a letter to him, or receive one from him, something might be done," said Louise.

It was the Sabbath morning, and the three had met on the bridge—the Pont Neuf, instead the quay, their usual place of meeting.

At that moment a youth about the same age as The Wolf appeared on the bridge and gave a peculiar whistle.

Wolf started when he heard the sound, and hurried towards the person from whose lips it proceeded.

"What is the matter, Sucking Fish?"

"Why, you know Captain Cartouche, don't you?"

"I have seen him once," responded The Wolf, who was not certain how far his friend might be trusted.

"Well, my mother goes into the gaol every morning to clean up the cells for the prisoners and so forth. She has just brought out this letter, which I am to give to you, and Cartouche says that you know for whom it is intended."

The Wolf took the document, which had no address upon it, and slipped it into his pocket, remarking—

"I think I know what the captain means. Run back and tell your mother you have given it to me."

The Sucking Fish hastened away, and Wolf lost no time in conveying the missive to Louise. The letter was:—

"Be outside the wall at two hours after midnight. Bring a coat, a sword and pistols, and I will manage the rest. If you can find Tomasso and Gribichon let them be at hand in case I need their assistance."

"I will be there, Madame Louise. And now I think we have nothing to do till the appointed hour arrives; we had best not be seen loitering about near the prison."

"And I must set to work to procure what he requires."

Tomasso undertook to provide the weapons as he understood such things rather better than Louise, and, everything having been arranged, they separated with a promise to meet at midnight.

"I wish I knew how to find Gribichon," Tomasso thought, as he strolled away from the bridge.

* * * * *

Gribichon, having supplied Cartouche with tools to accomplish his escape, knew they would be skilfully used, so he did not wait to see what might happen.

He was in total ignorance of the whereabouts of Louise and Tomasso, and therefore could not concert measures with them.

Inside the prison Cartouche was quiet enough. At the time Tomasso, Louise, and the Wolf were holding their meeting he was listening to a very pious and eloquent sermon delivered by a friar, who attended every week to convert as many sinners as felt inclined to give up their evil courses, and his devout manner so impressed the reverend gentleman that at his own expense he sent a capital dinner and a bottle of excellent wine to the criminal.

Cartouche dined, and then went to work.

He was not well acquainted with the inside of the prison, but he knew that if once he could get out of that cell it would be a strange thing if he could not get into the street.

The door was locked on the outside, so Cartouche thought it best to cut through the window bars, and get out into the courtyard which formed the interior of the prison.

That was easily done, then the difficulty was how to scale the outer wall, which was about twenty feet high and tipped by a row of formidable spikes.

"Sheets and blankets tied together are just

the thing, so I must go back and fetch them," said he.

Cartouche had noticed that his apartment was No. 31, so he very soon found his way to the door, and cut away the padlock which secured it.

"Now they will think I have had some help from outside," was his thought, "and that will puzzle them more than enough."

He wasted no time, however, for he knew not how often the turnkey would visit his cell during the night.

Hastily catching up the bedclothes with which he had been provided, he tore them in strips, and formed a rope which he had no doubt would bear his weight.

"Now to find the way out !" thought he.

The courtyard had an archway leading from the interior of the building to the front gate— but that was locked.

Cartouche gave one look round, and seeing no other chance he threw up one end of his improvised rope with such fortune that it caught on some of the spikes that decorated the wall.

"Ho ! there !" cried a voice. "Help ! a prisoner is escaping."

"I yield—I yield !" said Cartouche.

The wakeful turnkey was anxious to have all the glory of preventing Cartouche's escape, so, instead of waiting for assistance, he ran up to the prisoner and caught him by the collar.

"Die, dog !" exclaimed Cartouche, who held in his hand a sharp-pointed file which he had been using.

Down fell the turnkey, pierced through the throat with that weapon ; and Cartouche lost no time in climbing up to the top of the wall. He had left his coat behind in the cell, and wore only his waistcoat, breeches, and boots, but he saw that Louise and Tomasso were waiting with a fresh equipment for him.

It took hardly five seconds to fix the rope again and to descend.

"You are saved ! you are safe, my life !" Louise ejaculated.

And Tomasso, who had disguised himself as a peasant, looked fiercely round to see if there was anyone who would interfere with the safety of his captain.

"Safe, my love, thanks to you and Tomasso. But which of you was it pitched that packet of files through the window of the cell I was first put in ?"

Neither of them could answer.

"Well, we must hurry off as quickly as possible, so come along, my Louise, and let us visit The Wolf's home in the catacombs."

CHAPTER XLIX.

IN THE CATACOMBS.

GRIBICHON was resting.

He did not know what to do to aid Cartouche's escape after pitching those tools into the prison, so he thought he had best keep out of sight till he heard something.

Gribichon had a notion that The Wolf and one or two of the younger members of Cartouche's band had a snug little dwelling in what was afterwards known as the catacombs.

In the outskirts of Paris a quantity of stone had been excavated for building purposes, and in the quarry were numerous galleries leading Heaven knows where. A few bones had been discovered by the workmen, and that circumstance gave rise to a rumour that in olden times the place had been used as a cemetery, or place of burial. Long after Cartouche's time the Provisional Government of Paris ordered that those vaults should be used as a last resting-place for the bones gathered from the Parisian graveyards.

Gribichon knew whereabouts these catacombs were situated, but he was not quite certain as to the mode of entering the place.

He lounged about, hoping that he might see someone enter ; but other people imitated him, and a couple of hours passed without anyone going in or coming out.

Gribichon was thinking of retiring when he heard the sound of wheels, and looking round he saw a travelling chariot in which a rather stout lady was seated. And the stout lady called out at the top of her voice—

"Stop, young man ! Stop, stop !"

Which, of course, Gribichon did.

"Where is my husband ?" she asked.

"I suppose Monsieur Bobilet is——"

"I don't mean him ! I have divorced myself from him, and I am now Madame Peuchet, wife of the Chief of Police, with whom you rode to Paris."

"Wife !" exclaimed Gribichon. "I expect you were married without benefit of clergy if you are Peuchet's wife."

"Impudent rascal, I will have you sent to the Bastile !"

"Never mind if you send me there—I daresay I can get out."

"Now I know you, villain ! I was looking at you as we came along in the carriage, and I am certain you are the impudent rascal who used to keep company with that wretched girl who sells scents."

"Madame, you know too much."

"What do you mean ?"

"May it please you to alight from your carriage and walk a little way with me, then I will tell you."

Madame Bobilet hesitated only for a few seconds.

Madame could not imagine that the beloved (as she thought herself) of the Chief of the French Police, would be made the victim of a trick.

So in a very affected way she descended from the coach, the driver of which was instructed to return to Monsieur Peuchet's office and there await orders.

"Madame," said Gribichon, "I know you feel a grievance against a young woman named Can-can—you suppose she gained the affections of your husband—I mean Monsieur Bobilet ?"

"That is so," said Madame.

CARTOUCHE AGAIN RAISED HIS PISTOL AND FIRED.

"I can take you to the place where Can-can is to be found, and then you can do as you please."

Gribichon was prompted to make this declaration by the fact that he at that moment saw The Wolf walking towards the place where he supposed the entrance to the catacombs to be.

Gribichon gave a peculiar whistle, which was at once answered by The Wolf, who then, in obedience to a gesture from Gribichon, walked on.

"Are you sure we shall find Can-can here?" said Madame.

"Quite certain," replied Gribichon.

"It looks very nasty and dark."

"Well, that cannot be helped. Can-can will show you to a very much better place, where there is more light."

Madame Bobilet looked rather suspicious, but she very much wanted to exercise her finger-nails on the countenance of the scent-seller; so she was prepared to risk a little.

Gribichon followed The Wolf, who dived down into one of the deepest recesses of the place.

"I don't like this," said Madame Bobilet.

"We all have to put up with unpleasant things sometimes," responded Gribichon, who then whispered to The Wolf—

"Have you got a place here where we can lock her up?"

"Yes. But what is the use of doing it?"

"Why, we will keep her here till Peuchet liberates the captain."

The Wolf shook his head in a doleful style.

"Peuchet is not the man to let Cartouche go."

"Then we will not let the lady go. And if Cartouche hangs, why she shall dangle at the end of a lamp-post."

"And what do you think Peuchet will care?"

"Never mind; let us do something."

So Madame Bobilet was invited to enter one of the galleries, and as soon as she had done so a big door was locked upon her.

"Now, madame," said Gribichon, "you must remain here till Cartouche comes to release you. Come along, Wolf."

"Give the poor woman some bread and water before going."

"Hang it! why, she is not worth so much trouble."

"If we hold her as a hostage we must keep her alive."

"You are right, I believe. So let her have some food and drink."

"And what shall we do with her then?"

"Heaven only knows!".

Wolf pushed a coarse loaf of bread and a mug of water through the doorway, and then wandered off with his friend Gribichon.

Neither of them knew exactly what Cartouche was doing, but by a kind of instinct their steps led them towards the prison of St. Pelagie.

"Hold there!" cried a masculine voice as they sauntered along by the wall. "Stand and declare yourselves!"

"We are only two poor homeless vagrants who have no place to go to," said The Wolf.

"That answer will not do for me."

"Can't give you any better reply," Gribichon retorted.

"Then stand!" shouted the man, who was one of the Civic Guard—one of Bobilet's men, in fact.

Neither Gribichon nor The Wolf felt the least bit inclined to stand and be overhauled by the official. Gribichon, however, turned very unexpectedly, and, finding the point of a sword held by the aforesaid official within an inch of his breast, he determined to make a bold stroke for life and liberty. So he caught the blade of the officer's weapon in his left hand, and with his right clutched the fellow by the throat with such a squeeze that he was unable to cry out for assistance.

"Now, Wolf, quick!" cried Gribichon.

"What shall I do?" The Wolf asked.

"First wrench the sword away from him; be sharp, for he is strong."

The soldier was a muscular man, and struggled violently; but Wolf twisted the sword from his hand, and then united with Gribichon in an endeavour to pull the owner of the weapon to the ground.

Their joint effort succeeded, though all three came down together. But the soldier struck his head against a stone, and lay there senseless.

"I'll stop him from crying out when he comes to his senses," said Gribichon; and by way of doing so he drew the tie of the soldier's cravat as tight as possible, and then, crossing the ends over his mouth, tied them behind his head, so that the soldier was effectually gagged even if he escaped being strangled.

"We had better tie his hands behind him," said The Wolf. "I have plenty of cord in my pockets."

"I know a better plan than that. Give me some cord."

The Wolf handed his companion a long piece of well-spun hemp, quite as thick as a modern lead pencil.

"Now bend up his left leg and slip this noose round his ankle," continued Gribichon, who, for the greater convenience to himself, was seated on the soldier's back.

The Wolf obeyed the command, and then Gribichon, with a few clever turns of the cord, soon united the soldier's right wrist to his left foot. Wolf laughed, but very quietly, for they knew not how near another patrol might be to them, and Gribichon tied up the right foot and the left hand of his unhappy victim.

"Now before we go away let us search his pockets. He is one of the Civic Guard, and may have some cash or valuables," observed The Wolf.

They searched, but did not find much money to reward them for their trouble. Then they left him, and he was found dead—strangled—a very short time after.

"How did you find me at the catacombs?" Wolf asked.

"Saw you and followed. You answered my whistle."

"Yes, I knew it must be one of our lot, but I hardly thought to see you with a lady."

"Hush! keep close in this doorway. Some-one is coming out of the prison," Gribichon whispered.

Our two youths were exactly opposite the main gateway, which was suddenly opened, and a dozen soldiers with torches issued from the prison.

"Outside patrols be on the alert," shouted the officer in command of the party. "Answer to your numbers—Number one."

No response came to this challenge.

"Number one!" the officer bawled at the top of his voice; and then, as there was still no answer, he challenged Number two in the same manner.

Still all was silent.

"A pretty state of affairs!" the officer ejaculated. Here's Cartouche escaped, and the patrols who ought to have stopped him apparently have deserted."

"Perhaps Cartouche has killed them, cap-tain," an old corporal suggested.

"Perhaps you are a fool!" was the answer of the angry officer. "How could an unarmed man kill two armed soldiers?"

"He is a devil, this Cartouche," muttered the corporal.

"I believe those curs I posted here were afraid of him and ran away. Follow me, men, and we will look round the prison."

Away went the officer, and soon he found Number one, just as Gribichon left him, except that he was dead. And further on was Number two—just as Cartouche left him.

As soon as the officer and his men had got a little way from the gateway Gribichon whispered—

"Now we know he has escaped we had best get away from the neighbourhood."

"Right you are—keep close in the shadow of the houses, and cut away as fast as possible."

Gribichon and his companion were Parisians born and bred, and knew almost every crook and turning of the French metropolis, which had not then been renewed and beautified, but was as full of winding streets and narrow courts as our own London before the great fire of 1666. So they hastened on.

But day was breaking, and it was time to think of some definite plan of proceeding; so they slackened speed a little just to get suffi-cient breath to talk, and then The Wolf said—

"Now, what is the game, Gribby."

"Into this cabaret for five minutes' rest and a mouthful of something to eat and drink, and then we can talk."

The house Gribichon pointed to was a very poor-looking place. It was frequented by labouring people whose necessities compelled them to be abroad early to earn a few sous at the markets, or at any place where early and disagreeable work would bring a trifling remuneration. Even these poor devils must have a humble meal.

Gribichon and Wolf had their humble break-fast, and then, walking on more leisurely, Gribichon asked—

"Are the police after you, Wolf?"

"I think not, for I have been about as usual. They might have collared me at any time if they had wanted me."

"But I believe they want me; so if you don't mind having me for a lodger for a week or two at your place in the catacombs I think I will go there. I have money enough to pay the rent."

"That is right, and I will see that you don't starve."

"You, not being wanted by the police, can go about in the usual manner, and pick up any information you are able to get hold of about the captain and Louise—and don't forget to inquire about my sweetheart Can-can."

Wolf smiled at the latter words.

"Now let us go," said Gribichon.

And they went, by many a devious and wind-ing way, to the place where was the descent into the series of vaults which The Wolf had chosen for his abode.

They were still a quarter of a mile from the spot when The Wolf suddenly stopped, and, pointing to three figures some little distance ahead of them, exclaimed—

"Behold! the captain."

CHAPTER L.

A NEW HIDING-PLACE.

CARTOUCHE, Louise, and Tomasso, after the escape of the first-named of the worthy trio, determined to pay a visit to the catacombs and see if Wolf could provide them with that hiding-place of which he had spoken to Tomasso.

The search throughout Paris would be of the strictest kind, and whatever place of conceal-ment they might choose would have to be very artfully contrived.

All three knew the neighbourhood of the catacombs, but neither of them was certain of the entrance.

These catacombs were certain subterranean vaults and galleries from which, in times past, stone had been cut for some of the public buildings of Paris. The disused underground quarries became the refuge of homeless vagrants and criminals, and often corpses were found there; hence the name was given. But it was not till long after Cartouche had ceased to exist that these vaults became, by order of the first revolutionary government, a receptacle for all the bones that could be collected from the churchyards of Paris.

"I don't much like the idea of living down there with ghosts and what not," said Louise.

"I assure you there is no cause for fear, Madame Louise," said Tomasso.

"I will eat any ghost who dares to interfere with you," Cartouche added, "or shoot any human being who is guilty of such rudeness."

"But I wish I knew the way in," Tomasso continued.

At that moment they heard a whistle.

"That is one of my band," said Cartouche,

It came, in fact, from Gribichon, to whom The Wolf had just pointed out the figures of their captain and his companions.

By this time it was broad daylight, but there were not yet many people about. Still, caution was to be observed in all their movements.

"Cut along, Wolf, and show them the way," Gribichon said.

"Won't you come !"

"After them. Hurry on, lad."

Wolf ran ahead, and as he passed the captain he said in low tones—

"Follow me, captain ; I know the way."

Keeping a few yards in advance, Wolf crossed what was then a waste piece of ground, and disappeared in an opening between two disused limekilns.

Cartouche and Louise followed together ; Tomasso strolled a few yards behind them, and Gribichon brought up the rear.

Gribichon, as we know, had been there before, and fancied he knew the way—but—

Cartouche and Louise found The Wolf waiting for them a few yards inside what looked like an entrance to the infernal regions. The descent was very steep, but they felt quite safe with their young guide, who, probably because he had some Irish blood in his veins, declared he could show them over the whole place without a light.

"Is that you, Tomasso ?" Cartouche whispered, as another person joined them.

"You are correct, as usual, Signor Captain."

"Then let us proceed. Gribichon knows the way, you say, Wolf ?"

"Yes, captain."

"On then, and let us reach some place where we may have a little light to cheer us."

The descent as aforesaid was steep for a time, but after progressing some way downwards their path became tolerably level, though by no means smooth, and Louise, who no longer wore her wooden shoes, frequently bruised her feet.

"Halt now, captain, while I get a light," said The Wolf, after they had made several rather abrupt turnings.

"Right, my boy ; let us have one by all means."

From some secret recess in the rocky walls the youth produced a lantern and candle, and Louise was then able to see what sort of a place she was in. It was a roughly-hewn passage not more than about seven feet high or five broad, in which the quarrymen who cut it found the stone unsuitable for building purposes, and therefore continued their way deeper.

"But where is Gribichon ?" Tomasso asked.

"He will see the light, and follow," The Wolf replied. "Do you know I have a prisoner here, captain ?" he added.

"Who is that ?"

"A lady, captain."

"You rascal ! you are much too young to bring your sweetheart down here, and keep her prisoner !" said Louise.

"Sweetheart, madame ! she is not at all to my taste, I can assure you—almost old enough to be my grandmother."

"Who is it then, Wolf ?"

"Madame Bobilet ! She left her husband for the sake of Monsieur Peuchet, so Gribichon decoyed her here, where we intend keeping her as a hostage for your safety."

Cartouche and Louise laughed greatly at this, the captain saying, however—

"Now that I am free you ought to release her."

"You may get captured again, captain, so I think we had better keep her. But, captain, you will laugh when Gribby tells you how he entered Paris in Peuchet's travelling chariot along with Madame Bobilet and the Chief of Police."

"You are a pair of young devils !" said Cartouche.

"We have served under a clever master," replied Wolf ; and he made a very polite bow.

They went on for some distance, and then The Wolf whispered—

"That is where Madame Bobilet is."

He pointed to what seemed a rocky wall, but it was in reality a door of wood on which some skilful mason of past times had fixed thin slabs of stone so artfully that only a very close inspection revealed the truth.

"The door of the place where you shall stop is like this ; there is not much furniture in it though."

"Enough for us, I daresay," Louise replied.

"You must be good enough to share another cell with me and Gribichon, Signor Tomasso."

"As you like, if it is not a police prison-cell."

The Wolf then touched some spring or other contrivance in what appeared the solid wall, and a door opened within which was a cell about twelve feet square. It was, as Wolf had said, poorly furnished, containing only a couple of wooden stools, an iron stove, a few cooking utensils, and a coarse bed in one corner.

"We will try and make it better," said Wolf. "Tomasso and myself are on the opposite side of the passage, and if you please, captain, I will show you how you may call either of us when you desire."

All this was explained, and then, whilst they were drinking a bottle of wine, which Tomasso had prudently purchased, the question was again raised as to the reason of Gribichon's non-appearance. Wolf volunteered to go and look for him, and Louise at the same time gave him some money to purchase provisions.

*   *   *   *   *

The Wolf was not able to find Gribichon, for the simple reason that he was not in the catacombs.

Gribichon had made a little mistake when he thought he knew his way about underground Paris. He turned to the left when he had gone twenty-five paces, which was quite right, but then he turned to the right and found that he had gone wrong entirely.

He wandered for an hour or more along the dark passages, cursing his own folly in not having kept nearer the rest of the party. But cursing was no use, and he began to bless his stars when he saw a glimmer of daylight ahead of him, which looked very much like the entrance.

"If ever I trust myself in these infernal caverns again without a guide I ought to wander around till doomsday," he muttered.

He found his way out, but found when he once more gained the upper earth that it was not the opening by which he entered the caverns. However, that mattered but little.

Gribichon went to a place he knew, made some changes in his dress, and then wrote a letter to the Chief of Police.

"MONSIEUR,—The lady with whom you have been travelling is now in the custody of Cartouche's friends. If any harm happens to Cartouche you will find her hanging from the lamp before your office. I shall expect to find a written answer to this epistle exhibited publicly on the front of your office."

Having despatched this missive, Gribichon wandered away to hear if he could gain any tidings of Can-can. But no one seemed to know what had become of the scent-seller, so her lover found his way down to the quay of the Pont Neuf, where he hoped to find The Wolf.

But The Wolf was not there, nor could Gribichon find him for several days, during which time he heard nothing of Cartouche, except that all the citizens of Paris spoke of him as the most daring law-breaker who had ever infested their city.

CHAPTER LI.

A FIGHT AT THE CITY GATE.

FOR three weeks Cartouche, Louise, and Tomasso lived in the underground hiding-place to which The Wolf had brought them.

Much they wondered at Gribichon's absence, but that young man judged it prudent not to be seen much in the neighbourhood of the entrance to underground Paris, and The Wolf seldom went down to the quay.

Madame Bobilet remained in captivity, but she was treated as well as possible under the circumstances; and little did she guess that the day after the receipt of Gribichon's letter Peuchet caused a large sheet of paper to be inscribed with the words—"Madame B——t may hang for anything I care. I am determined to have C—t——e."

Much the Parisians wondered at this. They guessed that the letters at the end signified Cartouche, but they could not make out who Madame was, and gave their Chief of Police credit for being a very deep, artful fellow indeed.

Three weeks underground was quite as much as Cartouche was capable of enduring. He was anxious for fresh air, and also for news, so he determined to risk all and take a look at the sun once more.

So under the guidance of The Wolf he reached the opening between the two limekilns, leaving Louise and Tomasso below.

"You had better wait about the neighbourhood for me, Wolf. I shall never be able to find my way back alone," said Cartouche.

"Right, captain, I'll be here."

Cartouche first walked down to the Pont Neuf, but there was no Gribichon there. Then, emboldened by finding that he was not recognised, he actually walked past Peuchet's office and read the mysterious notice, the meaning of which he guessed.

Then he tried three or four restaurants in the city, and still no one recognised him as the man whose name was in everybody's mouth.

"I wonder if they will know me at the gate," he thought. "I will try it at any rate."

Cartouche walked away to one of the many gates Paris then possessed, and had a look. There appeared to be only one soldier actually doing duty as a sentinel, so Cartouche sauntered up as though about to pass out.

"Halt!" bawled the sentinel.

"Are you shouting at me?" demanded Cartouche, in an indignant tone of voice.

"No doubt of that, monsieur," replied the soldier, bringing his bayonet down to the charge. "Your passport before you can walk through this gateway."

"Away, scoundrel! If you do not know who I am I shall have to teach you."

The sentinel still kept his bayonet directed at the body of Cartouche, who, being in one of his dare-devil moods, drew his sword, exclaiming—

"Well, if you will have it so, we will see if you are able to stop an officer of the guard of the palace."

"A nice palace guard you would be, monsieur," said the soldier, with a broad grin. "But, still, you don't go out."

"I do!" Cartouche exclaimed, advancing.

The soldier made a thrust, which Cartouche parried.

Then the soldier threw himself into the position which English soldiers know as "shortening arms," so that although Cartouche was closer to his adversary—and it was not his object to close—he had no real advantage.

Two or three men were looking on, but as Cartouche had proclaimed himself an officer of the Palace Guard they did not interfere.

They would almost as soon have ventured to interfere with the King of France as with one of those officers, who generally behaved as though they thought all Paris belonged to them, in right of their office.

Four or five fierce thrusts were made by the soldier, then Cartouche saw an opening which proved fatal to the unfortunate wielder of the bayonet.

"You are a dead man!" cried Cartouche, as he lunged with full force and sent his blade through the body of the soldier, who fell, feebly muttering—

"Well, this is better than hanging or dying in bed. So hurrah for France!"

Cartouche looked with considerable respect

upon the veteran who could meet death so easily. Then he began to think about his own prospects. Should he go out or go back?

On! was the decision he came to. He had called himself an officer of the Palace Guard, and fought the sentinel in that character, so it would not do to turn back.

Cartouche haughtily beckoned one of the men who had been looking on at the duel, and said—

"Here, fellow, run to the main guard, tell the captain what has happened, and ask him to oblige me by posting another sentinel at this gate."

The man doffed his hat and hied away upon his errand, without stopping to ask the name of the brave officer who had slain the sentinel. And Cartouche passed out of Paris.

"What next?" he thought, when he had walked half a mile or thereabouts. "How shall I act now?"

Looking back he saw that soldiers had already arrived from the main guard, that two sentries were placed at the gate instead of one, and that other soldiers were looking after him, as though they had some idea of following.

"It won't do to hurry, and yet I must make haste. I am in the country now, and when I shall get back to Louise is a question I cannot answer. The only thing is to do some deed of daring in the country that shall set them all talking, and then get back into the city while they are looking for me a hundred leagues away. And that is what I will do!"

So he walked on leisurely, occasionally glancing back to see whether he was followed.

But the guards at the gate moved not an inch beyond the portal they were appointed to look after. An officer of the Palace Guard was not to be impertinently followed merely because he had slain a private soldier.

As soon as hedges and trees concealed him Cartouche began to mend his pace.

He thought a good deal of Louise, Tomasso, and The Wolf. They had so often helped him when in dire distress that a feeling of gratitude had been hammered into his otherwise hard heart by the mere force of circumstances. He felt that it was scarcely the right thing to desert them; yet there was nothing else to do.

As usual, Cartouche had contrived to fill his own pockets with the greater part of the money Louise and Tomasso had when they accompanied him to the vaults, so for the present he had not much to fear in the shape of hunger or want of shelter. Moreover, he had his sword, a brace of good pistols, with which he could compel those not given to charity to fill his purse with gold and silver.

So he walked on.

The gate by which Cartouche left Paris on this occasion was one he seldom passed in or out at. The road led to the north-east of France, and that was a part of the country our hero did not often visit, for the people were poor and the climate was cold.

Instinctively Cartouche edged off by some cross-roads towards the south, and presently found himself at a little village which, although it was not a couple of leagues from Paris walls, he did not remember having visited before.

"And so much the better for me," thought the escaped one. "If I don't know the people they are not likely to know me."

It was a small place. The two or three farmers had built the walls of their barns and other buildings towards the open country, so that by breaking up the village and barricading it at both ends of the street it would form a place capable of defence against a regiment, unless the soldiers had artillery.

The street was open, and Cartouche passed into the village.

"Only one little tavern!" ejaculated Cartouche. "And not a customer in at this hour of the day, I will warrant."

Cartouche entered—and found he was mistaken.

There were two customers in the common-room of the place, who appeared very tired, or intoxicated, for they were both asleep.

One was a man of middle age, who, for the sake of ease during his nap, had pulled off his coat and hung it over the back of his chair. The other man was reclining on a settle near the fireplace, and at first Cartouche could not see his face, but as the fellow turned uneasily in his sleep he exclaimed—

"Blue death! it is Gribichon!"

Yes, Gribby in a sound slumber. From the state of his boots and the size of the empty bottle before him it was pretty certain that fatigue, not drink, had overtaken Can-can's lover.

Without disturbing either of the sleepers Cartouche went out to seek the landlady.

"I do not wish to disturb your sleeping customers, madame," said he, "but pray let me have a bottle of wine, some bread, and sausage of Lyons. I will take them into the room myself."

"As you please, monsieur. No doubt they are fatigued."

"Probably friends travelling together, madame."

"Not so, monsieur."

"Inhabitants of your village then, doubtless?"

"Monsieur Barbet has come to gather the rents for our grand landlord who wastes all his money at Paris. The other gentleman I do not know."

"I will be careful not to disturb them. Give me the viands, madame, and I will recommend that you don't let anyone else come in till they have finished their sleep."

"Not a soul shall enter, monsieur. You are very considerate."

Cartouche took his wine, his sausage, and his bread into the room, and set to work—looking from one sleeper to the other.

He soon came to the conclusion that Monsieur Barbet was heavily intoxicated, and formed his plans accordingly.

"A change of dress will not do me any harm," thought the bold robber. "Barbet's coat will fit me, I think."

He tried, and it did fit as though the tailor had measured him for it, so he transferred his

CARTOUCHE,

THE FRENCH JACK SHEPPARD.

"YOU ARE SAVED, MY LOVE!" LOUISE EJACULATED.

stols and a few other matters from his old
at to the new garment he had appropriated,
the pocket of which was a bag, which felt
ery much as if it contained the rents the in-
xicated Monsieur Barbet had collected, and a
air of pistols.

"A brown coat—yes, that is a colour that
asses unnoticed, and as it fits, why I will wear
," Cartouche muttered.

Then he turned towards the slumbering
ribichon, and shook him smartly.

Gribby jumped up at once, but he was too
ell trained to make any noise till he saw what
ere was to halloa about; and, moreover,
artouche's hand was over his mouth, so that
e could not shout.

"You know me?" said Cartouche.

Gribichon nodded, that being the only way
which he could make an affirmative answer.

"Then get up at once, drink the wine you
ill find in the bottle upon the table, and follow
e.   Turn to the left when you get outside the
oor, and don't for Heaven's sake wake that
or gentleman who is sleeping so soundly."

"Not for the world!" Gribichon replied.
Is he one of Peuchet's men?"

"No.   Why do you ask?"

"If he was one of that lot I would not wake
m.   He should sleep on for ever."

And Gribichon made a gesture as if to indicate
at he would produce that endless slumber by
itting the breathing apparatus of the sleeper.

"No violence, no noise!"

With this caution Cartouche stole quietly out
the room.   He paid his bill in an equally
lent manner, and then walked off with the
lf-satisfied air of a citizen of France who had
ne his duty.   And at five minutes' interval
ribichon slouched after him, looking very like
man who did not know whether he ought to
kicked or made first minister of the King of
ance.

"What in the devil's name is he up to now?"
ibby muttered.

They were a full half-league beyond the village
fore Cartouche shortened his martial stride so
to allow Gribichon to come up alongside of
m.   Cartouche spoke—

"Well, young man, and where have you been?"

"Looking for you, captain."

"Of course.   Looking for anyone else?"

"Why, I can't find Can-can, captain,"
ibichon replied, and Cartouche smiled.

"I thought you had been hunting for someone
sides myself.   Now then, what is your
oposal?"

"I have no proposal to make."

"Well, what plan had you? you must have
en travelling on some fixed idea."

"Well, you see, captain, there have been
veral fairs lately within ten or twelve leagues
Paris, and as I could not find Can-can in the
y I thought she might be making a suburban
ur, so I came out for a day or two to look for
r."

"How are you going to get back into Paris?"

Gribby smiled very proudly, as he produced

the document signed and sealed by the Mayor
of Louvet, authorising Monsieur Eugene de
Gribichon to pass through all parts of France.

"Your paper is worth nothing in Paris," said
Cartouche; "because, doubtless, the mayor and
Monsieur Peuchet have met by this time, and all
has been explained.   But keep the document,
Gribby—it may prove useful with the rural
police."

Gribichon laughed very heartily.   He well
remembered the Mayor of Louvet, and the way
he obtained that passport which, as Cartouche
reminded him, might enable them to travel
freely outside the barriers of Paris.

"The rural police, captain! They and the
rural mayors are the most contemptible asses I
ever met with."

"I quite agree with you," said Cartouche,
who, after thinking matters over, continued—

"Now listen, Gribichon.   It would be very
dangerous indeed for either of us to attempt to
get back into the city at present.   The police
believe I am hidden away in some part of Paris,
but I want to convince them that I am not, so
we have to do a big thing, and prove to them
that we are a hundred miles at least outside their
confounded walls and gates."

"I'm game for anything; but I want to find
Can-can."

"The sooner we do what I have suggested
the sooner we can dodge back to Paris; so come
along."

The worthy couple walked on for some hours,
and then once more entered a wayside inn for
rest and refreshment.

"What is going on?" demanded Cartouche,
who noticed that a great deal of excitement was
prevailing in the house.

"The Lyons mail, monsieur—the *diligence* is
expected."

"We wish to go to Lyons.   Can we have
seats?"

"Undoubtedly.   No one has booked from
this place as yet."

"Then I and my friend will set a good example
by taking a seat each.   How much must we pay,
madame, if you please?"

The hostess named a price, which Cartouche
paid.

"Why do you wish to go to Lyons?"
Gribichon asked.

"As well there as any other place.   It will
be a change of scene, at all events, and we shall
do some business on the road."

Gribichon was silenced.

In a short time a lumbering vehicle drew up;
three passengers alighted, three remained;
Cartouche and Gribichon were invited to take
their seats on the Lyons mail.

And if the reader thinks they robbed that
mail coach the reader is much mistaken; they
did nothing of the kind, but travelled very
quietly for about thirty hours till they were
about twelve miles short of their destination,
when they descended from the vehicle, and said
that, being tired of the jolting, they would
finish the journey on foot.

"Now, what are we to do in Lyons?" Gribichon asked

"Wait a time. Something will turn up."

Cartouche took Gribichon to a quiet hotel in Lyons, where they stayed for a couple of days. The rent in Monsieur Barbet's coat—that is to say, the bag of money—was a good one, and they felt there was no fear of immediate want.

Towards the close of the second day Cartouche said—

"We will go on to-morrow, friend Gribichon. Whither as the fates lead us. But, as they say in the new world of America, water leaves no track, so we will travel by a passenger-boat which goes down the river to-morrow."

"As you like, captain. I will go anywhere with you, but I wish I could find Can-can."

"Gribichon, you cannot possibly love Can-can more than I love Louise ; but as I told you before, we must do something to convince the police that we are three or four hundred miles from Paris before we venture to return to that city where we both wish to be, and where we shall, without doubt, find our sweethearts waiting for us."

"Go ahead, Captain Cartouche."

"We cannot go till the boat starts."

Gribichon and Cartouche went back to the hotel.

"Have you heard the news, gentlemen?" said the host as they entered.

"I have heard little since I came to Lyons," Cartouche answered, as he seated himself.

"They have captured him !"

"We will have our dinner at once if you please," said Cartouche, who, after ordering a good meal for two, with wine to correspond, turned to the host and said—

"Now you may tell me who it is they have captured, also who are they that captured him."

"Surely monsieur, you know of whom I speak ?"

"I assuredly do not ! If I knew, why should I take the trouble to ask a question ?"

"Then, monsieur, you, like all other good citizens of France, will rejoice to hear that the vile scoundrel, Cartouche, has been captured once more."

"What need to capture him again ? Why, we all knew long before I left Paris that he was in the prison of St. Pelagie."

"He escaped, monsieur, but the great Peuchet captured him only five days ago in a ruined old abbey about twenty leagues to the west of Paris."

"If your news is true, monsieur, I will wager that Peuchet does not give him another chance of escaping."

"Thank heaven for all mercies !" exclaimed one of the guests. "Now I can travel freely."

"But surely you don't fear Cartouche down here ?" said our hero, with a smile.

"I have much money in my bag, monsieur, and I have been afraid that rascal Cartouche—he can smell gold, I firmly believe—would hear of it and rob me. But now I snap my fingers at the rascal since Peuchet has him again."

"You are right," replied Cartouche. "Do you travel far ?"

"I go to Valence ; there is a big fair there in two days, and I want to turn my money to some account amongst the silk-dealers of the south."

"Quite right, and, I hope, your cash ; how much did you say you had ?"

"Twelve thousand livres, monsieur."

"I hope the merchants who throng the Valence fair will give you good value for your money."

"They will, without doubt, Cartouche being as good as hanged."

"A fate he well deserves."

"Why, then honest merchants being no longer afraid of the great robber—"

"Can go and rob each other. Ha, ha, ha !"

The merchant joined in Cartouche's laugh, and then another guest at the hotel of the White Lion joined in the merriment.

"I also have from twelve to twenty thousand livres," said the second guest ; "but I did not let anyone know till I was certain Cartouche was recaptured. But now I can go as I like ; there is no other robber in France who dares rob Adolphe Sprenger."

"You are not a Frenchman," said Cartouche.

"No."

"Then I would advise that you keep your tongue quiet, for there are many Frenchmen who would enjoy the joke of robbing a foreigner."

Adolphe Sprenger snapped his fingers.

"There is not a man in France now that Cartouche is laid by the heels who can rob me of my thirty thousand livres," said he.

"You have added ten thousand to the sum you first named ; do you know, Monsieur Sprenger, you are inviting all the robbers of France to try for your portmanteau ?"

"I say bah ! to the French robbers. There isn't one who knows how to steal now that Cartouche is captured."

"Well, if any accident happens, don't say you were not cautioned. Some of Cartouche's friends are very clever thieves."

"He means me," thought Gribichon.

"Again I say bah ! to all French robbers."

Cartouche did not say anything more just then, but when he retired from the dinner-table with Gribichon he said—

"We will have those thirty thousand livres, Gribby."

"I thought you meant doing it, captain ; but then, how about the fellow with the twelve thousand ?"

"Why, my good boy, I intend that he shall be worth thirty or forty thousand by the time the fair is over, and then we can ease him. We had better let him have four or five days to earn a little money for us."

"Captain, you are a wonder !"

"No compliments, Gribby, but just attend to me."

"That I will do ; what is the game ?"

"By the time the fair comes to an end the money will be in a very few pockets—half a dozen, perhaps—and you ought to know by this time, Gribichon, that it is much easier to pick six pockets than fifty."

Gribichon promised to attend to every hint his captain could give on the subject of robbing merchants who travelled with a lot of money in their pouches.

In the morning they went down together to the quay, or landing-place, and walked on board the boat which was to float them several leagues down the river to the town of Valence, where the fair was to be held which was the cause of the gathering of all these rich merchants.

Cartouche and Gribichon landed, as did most of the other people who came from Lyons.

"What is the next move, captain?" said Gribichon.

"Go to the mayor of the place, have your passport countersigned by him, and get a new one for me. My name is Adolphe Sprenger, and I am a native of North Germany."

"You are a real devil, captain!"

"You are one of my imps, so you will have to obey my command!" was the response of Cartouche.

Gribichon left his chief and took a good look at the fair at Valence, before he ventured to ask the simple question—

"Which is the office of Monsieur the Mayor?"

And the countryman to whom the question was propounded laughed loudly and vulgarly—

"Don't you want to buy a horse, monsieur?"

"No, nor do I wish to sell an ass."

"Do you consider me an ass?"

"A very bad specimen."

"How—explain yourself, monsieur.'

"Your ears are not long enough and your brain is too small. You are a contemptible donkey."

The countryman judged from the smiling faces about him that he had the worst of the badinage, so he contented himself with the sulky reply—

"Turn to the left, monsieur."

"And then how shall I follow on—"

"Follow your nose, unless you think proper to turn your hind parts to the front."

Gribichon bestowed a mental blessing—of the back-handed kind—upon the countryman, and took the left-hand turning, which brought him to the mayor's office.

"What can I do for you?" the clerk asked.

Gribichon replied that his friend, who was too ill to attend, wanted his pass countersigned, and that he himself required a renewal of the documents with which Eugene de Gribichon used to travel.

"Undoubtedly!" said the Mayor of Valence.

"I have given you a correct description of my friend," said Gribichon, smiling.

"I could draw his portrait from your description," replied the mayor; "so tell your sick friend not to worry himself, but to do the best he can for himself during the time the fair lasts. Here is a passport for him."

"But, monsieur, he had one permitting him to travel freely in all parts of France, and you have given him one which only permits him to travel between the two cities of Lyons and Valence."

The mayor apologised, and in two or three minutes had signed another paper with a good description of Egbert Gribichon upon it. Egbert Gribichon was Cartouche.

And as they were about to retire to bed Gribichon said—

"Look here, captain, there is too much money about this fair. I think we ought to have some of it."

"Did I not tell you we are to have all of it? So, my dear friend Gribichon, just keep your hands from picking and stealing for a couple of days, and leave the rest to me."

CHAPTER LII.

HANDS UP!

GRIBICHON obeyed his captain's behests, and during a week, or thereabouts, that he remained at Valence he took not the least liberty with any person's pockets. But the fair came to an end.

"And what now, captain?" said Gribichon.

"Back again," was the reply.

Gribichon smiled in a grim fashion.

"What is the use of going back again?" he asked.

"To get what we missed when we were coming down the river, friend Gribichon. There will be at least a hundred thousand livres on board the boat when we go back to our old quarters at Lyons.'

"I said before, you are a perfect devil, monsieur.

Cartouche nodded a short acknowledgment of the compliment, and then made his arrangements to take a passage back to Lyons by the next boat that was going up the river. And that was a very different matter from going down the stream, which was easy enough.

"How many of these good gentlemen go with us?" said Cartouche the morning they were to leave Valence and be towed up the stream by the power of eight horses.

"They all go with you, monsieur," said the hostess.

"They are foolish," said Cartouche.

"Why?" asked the hostess.

"They might be robbed."

"Nonsense! Cartouche is in prison, and there is no one else who would venture to rob the boat."

Cartouche smiled, and booked two places on board the clumsy boat, which at that time conveyed people up and down the river Rhone.

When he and Gribichon took their places on board there were only four other passengers—who all kept very much aloof from each other. But Cartouche could see plainly that they had all done well at the fair at Valence, and were taking home their money.

Of course the journey was a slow one, but in

the due course of route the boat reached a point which Cartouche remembered as distant only three leagues from Lyons. It was time to do something.

"You have pistols, Gribichon?" queried Cartouche.

"At your service, captain."

"Are they loaded?"

"With powder and bullets. Enough to drive a hole through Peuchet's head if he interferes."

"How many men are there beside the passengers?"

"Only two; the captain and the man at the helm."

"Have your weapons ready—now!"

In a loud voice Cartouche exclaimed—

"Let every man on board this boat hold up his hands in the air. Anyone who goes fumbling in his pockets for a pistol or any other weapon will be shot."

There was a considerable amount of confusion on board the boat, but the peaceful tactics of Cartouche prevailed, especially as Gribichon backed up the business with a pair of pistols, which all on board might see.

The merchants held up their hands, so did a very stout old lady, who got on board the boat about a league from Valence.

"Now, gentlemen, I will trouble you for the money you have brought with you from Valence," said Cartouche.

"I did not make any," said Sprenger.

"That is not the first lie you have told. I will take sixty thousand livres from you."

"Ach Himmel!" sighed the German, "I never in the life of me had so much money."

"You had thirty thousand livres when you came down the river, so it is pretty plain you must have doubled them at the fair—so down with it!"

The German sighed deeply as he handed over his bag, which contained over seventy thousand livres.

The other passengers followed his good example, and in less than half an hour the two confederates had quite as much money as they were able to carry.

"That is good business!" said Gribichon.

"Believe me!" ejaculated Cartouche.

"You have done those fellows brown!" cried Gribichon.

"I know it; and now we have to get on shore as soon as we can."

There were two landing-places between the point on the river where the robbery took place and the quay at Lyons where the boat was to finish its journey. At the first of these landings Cartouche cried aloud—

"Gentlemen, you who have paid for my passage be good enough to go below."

"This is not gentlemanly," said Sprenger.

"Perhaps not; but go down, or I will shoot you first and throw you overboard afterwards."

So Herr Sprenger went down to the cabin, and as soon as the boat was moored Cartouche and his friend went on shore, neither the captain nor any of his crew daring to say a word.

"Remember, gentlemen!" said Cartouche, as he shot one of the horses to make the others pull up stream, "the name of the person who has borrowed your money is Cartouche—the man the old fool Peuchet thinks is in Paris. But you see I am far outside the bounds."

Gribichon was overweighted with silver and gold. He had all the money that had been taken at Valence fair, and, naturally, he wanted to know what his chief was going to do with it.

"Come along, Gribby. I know a place not far from here where we could all hide for a year or so. I wish I had brought Louise down here."

"And I wish I could find Can-can," said Gribichon.

"Hold your tongue and follow me," said Cartouche.

Many long weeks ago it was told in the course of this story that Cartouche in his travels with the gipsies got to be acquainted with many old places in which lodging could be had, and where human beings did not walk as a rule, lest they should find some ghost there.

It was, in fact, a fine old ruin in which a score of people might hide.

The entrance was underneath a pile of ferns and other things, that were carelessly thrown over a little gap in the wall.

"Come along!" said Cartouche.

"I'll follow you," replied Gribichon.

Cartouche had not been in the ruin for many years, but he knew exactly how to get to the underground part of the building.

A sharp turning to the left brought them to the place where a brass tablet invited all people to pray for a noble knight who never imagined that his tomb would be the doorway of a robber's den.

"This is all right, captain," said Gribichon.

"Hold your tongue, and see that we are not followed."

Gribichon winked in a most artful manner.

Having got within the walls of the ruined abbey Cartouche led the way down a steep staircase.

"Hold hard, captain!" said Gribichon

"What is the matter?"

"Look at this!"

Looking in the direction indicated by Gribichon's finger Cartouche saw upon the wall a shadow, which represented, most exactly, a hand holding a dagger.

"We are betrayed!" exclaimed Cartouche.

And then Gribichon smiled.

"You can look again, captain; it is all right. There is only the shadow of a drunken man's fist, with a very small stick in it."

At that precise moment the shadow on the wall disappeared.

"You are wrong again," said Cartouche.

"How do you mean, captain?"

"That is neither your shadow nor mine, so it must be that of an enemy."

Gribichon did not care for shadows—he only wanted to find the substance—i.e., Can-can. But, of course, he did not expect to find her in the vault of a ruined abbey, half-way between Valence and Lyons.

"I will see what this means!" exclaimed Cartouche.

He took the torch with which Gribichon had illumined the underground passage, and had a good look, thinking that he had, perhaps, in former times left some nook unexplored.

But he could find nothing.

CHAPTER LIII.

TWO GIRLS AT THE FAIR.

LOUISE and Tomasso still dwelt in the catacombs.

Monsieur Peuchet and all his merry men could not get into their heads the simple idea of searching those vaults, which were suspected to be the haunt of more thieves than ever Cartouche could assemble by sounding his whistle. It may be that personal safety had a little to do with the matter.

Cartouche, when he went out from the catacombs, promised Louise that he would be back within twelve hours, or she might know that he was once more captured by his old enemies the police.

Louise, therefore, waited for twelve hours before she ventured to go out in search of her lover.

Tomasso was much against her going out at all.

"What will you do?" he asked.

"Who can say? I may kill Monsieur Peuchet, unless he very much mends his manners."

But Louise had no notion of slaying the Chief of Police; she did not know what had become of Cartouche, so she bethought her that Can-can was Gribichon's very particular sweetheart, and it was possible that the scent-seller might know something about both the missing young men.

It was the fair of St. Germains.

Louise remembered the day well enough, for was not that the very day upon which Cartouche first claimed her as his love?

Cartouche was Heaven only knew where, and his name seemed to have faded out of the minds of the volatile Parisians—at least, they did not talk of him.

Louise had a good deal to think about—how she first went to the fair and how she got home. This time she had also to think of her mother's death.

"But that was not my fault," Louise thought, as she went on the fair-ground at St. Germains.

So, dismissing her dead mother with a brief sigh, Louise looked round the fair.

The first man she saw was Tomasso.

"Why, I thought you were safe at home in the catacombs."

"Not so, Madame Louise."

"Then why are you here?"

"Like yourself, I wish to know what has become of our chief," responded Tomasso.

"We had best not be seen talking together though," said Louise, who did not wish to be paid any particular attentions by the police force.

So Tomasso bowed and walked away.

Louise continued her ramble for a very short space of time, when she stopped short and exclaimed—

"Why, that must be Can-can!"

It was the scent-seller, who said—

"Why, Louise, how is it you are here without your basket of flowers?"

"Can-can, how, or rather where, is your sweetheart?"

"Which of them?"

"You naughty girl, have you more than one?"

"Half a dozen at least."

"Well, you are a very naughty one! I mean the one who—"

"I know! the fellow who used to eat my sausage and then borrow the money to pay for more." •

"I think his name was Gribichon."

"*De* Gribichon, if you please, Madame Louise."

Cartouche's lover made a very grand curtsey.

"I readily admit the *De*; but what are you doing here, Can-can? Where are all your smelling-bottles!"

"I am looking for Gribby; I have two kinds of sausage and a clove of garlic in my pocket, and he may have all if he will only come back to me!"

"He is a lucky fellow. But tell me, have you heard anything of Cartouche?"

"Only that he blew down the walls of the prison and walked out of the place. Why do you ask me, though?"

"Because I believe Gribichon is with him wherever he may be."

Can-can shook her head.

"Look!" said Louise; "here is Peuchet coming."

The Chief of Police was strolling leisurely down the middle avenue of the fair. He was not searching for anyone in particular.

Peuchet had not received any response to his note to the effect that Madame B—— might hang if he secured Cartouche; in fact, he had almost forgotten the existence of the wife of the officer of the Civic Guard.

But when Peuchet saw Louise and Can-can having a talk together his eyes twinkled.

"I did not come to the fair of St. Germains for nothing," said he, to himself. "These two girls are worth five hundred crowns each—at least, that is the reward which ought to be given for their apprehension, and I don't see any reason why I should not honestly earn a thousand crowns by arresting them."

Peuchet thought over the matter for a few minutes.

No Government order had been issued regarding either of the young women, but Peuchet knew—no one better—that the King's minister would sanction anything that might lead to the extirpation of Cartouche's band of robbers.

THE MAN MADE A THRUST WITH HIS BAYONET WHICH CARTOUCHE EASILY PARRIED.

So the Chief of Police beckoned to one of his men, who happened to be standing near.

"At your service, monsieur," said the man, saluting.

"I wish you to go back to Paris."

"I will fly on the wings of the wind, monsieur," said the fellow, proud of being noticed by his chief.

"Then hasten away—this to the printer with all speed. You will wait till they have printed what is here ordered, then you will come back to me."

"And you will be here, monsieur—in this place?"

"I shall be here; so away with you, rascal, and if you breathe but a word of the business I have sent you on to anyone you shall spend the remainder of your life in the Bastile."

The policeman knew as little about the Bastille as the general public did. He had an idea that it was a place where dreadful torments were inflicted—a prison easy enough to get into, but from which no prisoner was ever released except by death.

To avoid the Bastile he resolved to do his errand speedily.

But the best laid plans sometimes fail.

As the policeman entered Paris he met a man, none other than Tomasso, who, being tired of the rather confined atmosphere of the catacombs, had come out for a breath of pure air.

Tomasso, it has already been mentioned, once lodged in the same house as a policeman, and this particular man who was now hastening with Peuchet's letter to the printer was a visitor there; consequently the two men were slightly acquainted.

"How do you do?" said Tomasso.

"In excellent health, I thank you."

"But you look pale. I hope you are not suffering from the plague which has been devastating the south of France."

"Pale, am I?"

"You look very ill indeed."

"I have walked fast. Monsieur Peuchet will have no loitering, so I came from St. Germains at my best pace."

"What! is he at the fair? But you look so ill that I am afraid something will happen."

"I feel well, I assure you."

"Better have a glass of brandy—that cannot do you any harm, and it may save you from death."

The policeman liked brandy and hated the idea of death, so he very willingly acceded to Tomasso's proposition.

They entered a little cabaret, and Tomasso promptly paid for the liquor which was set before them.

"I can't stay long—I must be off soon," said the officer.

"What hurry is there?" Tomasso asked, and the officer, under the influence of the brandy, divulged the important business on which he had been sent by Peuchet.

"Now, I say it is a shame," cried Tomasso—"a shame that Peuchet should work his men to death in this fashion!"

"How you talk!"

"You are evidently ill with fatigue and require rest. Now I propose that you shall rest here and drink more brandy while I go and perform your duties."

After a little consideration the man consented, and Tomasso started off.

He did not know at first what to do, but when he opened the letter to the King's printer, and found in it instructions to print bills offering a reward for the apprehension of Louise and Can-can, he resolved to have a joke.

Tomasso, therefore, walked into another wine-shop, where he wrote out a bill offering five thousand crowns reward for the apprehension of the notorious criminal Cartouche, who was supposed to be at St. Germains disguised in the likeness of Monsieur Peuchet, and assuming to be the Chief of the Parisian Police.

The printer to whom Tomasso handed the precious document stared a little, but he recognised Peuchet's signature on the letter, so Tomasso was told that if he called again in a few hours he could have some copies of the proclamation to take back to St. Germains.

The Corsican then went back to the place where he had left his friend the policeman and reported progress.

Of course, having been left with a bottle of brandy, the policeman was drunk. But that was part of Tomasso's plan.

"You are getting worse," said the Corsican.

"Don't talk like that," the policeman replied.

"You certainly cannot walk back to St. Germains, so I will finish the business by taking the bills to Peuchet."

"Right you are!" said the policeman, who then stretched himself out on a bench and announced his intention of dying at once. But he only fell asleep.

At the time appointed Tomasso reappeared at the printer's and received the bills, laden with which he travelled out to St. Germains.

"It's rather good fun the notion of my hunting up the Chief of Police. It generally is the other way—he wants me as a rule," said Tomasso, as he trudged along the road.

The fair was at the height of its gaiety when the Corsican reached St. Germains.

Louise and Can-can, with true Parisian vivacity, had joined a dancing party, and were footing it merrily, while Peuchet stood looking on.

"She is much better looking than that coarse, vulgar Madame Bobilet," said he to himself. But whether he meant Louise or her friend is what he could not himself decide at the moment.

The amorous old Chief of Police was in love with both the girls he intended to lock up. He intended to arrest them, claim the reward for doing so, and then allow them to escape, provided they responded favourably to his advances. But he did not know what was in store for him.

Tomasso, as soon as he entered the village, began to stick up the bills, and very soon everyone at the fair understood that Cartouche was there disguised in the likeness of the Chief of Police.

"Well, I could have sworn it was Peuchet himself!" one of the suburban police exclaimed, as he read the bill.

"So could I," replied Tomasso. "But you see how folks may be mistaken. Where is the villain?"

"In the dancing booth. I will go and arrest him."

"Best get some help. He is a desperate fellow."

"True. I will call upon all loyal subjects to aid me."

"That is right. I am anxious to see if he will fight."

"Not he, when he sees me with half a dozen stout fellows to help me," said the policeman, with a proud smile.

Tomasso could scarcely keep from grinning.

Off went the policeman to the dancing booth. Peuchet had contrived to secure Louise as a partner for one dance, and was in the highest state of delight when the officer entered.

"Cease your music!" the fellow exclaimed to the band. "And all good, true, loyal citizens who are present must aid me in apprehending that notorious criminal!"

He pointed at Peuchet, who angrily exclaimed—

"Are you mad or drunk? For whom do you take me?"

"I take you for yourself, Monsieur Cartouche."

"Ass! I am the Chief of Police!"

"We have been warned that you would try and pass yourself off as Monsieur Peuchet. But it won't do—"

"I will have you imprisoned for life!"

"Spare your breath, monsieur. You will be imprisoned for life yourself, that is to say, till the hangman is ready for you."

"This is unpardonable insolence."

"Bah! you are cutting too many airs, Monsieur Cartouche. Seize him, men! here is the bill describing him as being disguised like Monsieur Peuchet, so there can be no doubt about him."

A rush was at once made at the unfortunate Chief of Police, who was roughly handled by the mob.

"Hang him at once!" said a voice in the crowd.

Louise and Can-can extricated themselves from the throng, and eventually got out of the tent.

"Hang him!" was shouted on all sides.

"He will only escape again if the police are to have charge of him," said the voice that first suggested hanging.

"I wish they would hang him!" Louise whispered to her friend. "It is not Cartouche."

"Let us get away as quickly as possible," said Can-can.

Louise, however, was anxious to know how the matter would terminate, and, as it was dark, except where the booths were lighted up with lamps and torches, she easily persuaded Can-can that there would be no danger in remaining, if they only kept out of the crowd.

"Hang him! hang him!" was the cry on all sides.

"Don't let the police interfere," said the voice that commenced the commotion. "Let us do the work thoroughly."

"Gentlemen, hear me!" said Peuchet, who began to feel rather alarmed as he looked round upon the crowd.

"Not a word! silence him."

"I know that voice," said Louise.

"It is Tomasso, I believe," replied Can-can, "but surely they won't hang him, will they, Louise?'

"Likely enough. See, they are taking him away, and the police are afraid to interfere."

The ground on which the fair was held was surrounded by a high fence. At the gate nearest the village was a tall elm tree.

The excited throng hurried the unfortunate man to this point. Peuchet was made to stand upon an empty barrel, while a man nimbly climbed up and fitted a rope to a stout branch. The other end of the cord being tied in a running noose, was passed round Peuchet's neck.

"Gentlemen, gentlemen! spare me!" cried the Chief of Police.

"Why should we? Did you ever spare anyone whose life or money you desired, Monsieur Cartouche?" replied the amateur executioner, giving his victim a buffet on the cheek.

"But I am not Cartouche!" groaned the Chief of Police.

"Liar! we know you only too well!"

"Mercy! let me live—only a couple of hours till I can get men to come here and prove that I am Peuchet."

"Not a minute!" said the man.

And his preparations being completed, he kicked away the barrel, and the Chief of Police was left dangling.

For some few minutes after the execution of M. Peuchet the struggles of the poor wretch were terrible, but at last he relaxed his muscles, and became motionless. The amateur hangman had done his work effectually, if in a somewhat clumsy style, and there could be no doubt whatever that the Parisian police required a new chief.

"Come away now," said Louise.

Can-can was frightened, but Louise had nerves of a much firmer kind.

In going from the fair-ground they had to pass by the body of the unfortunate Peuchet. A circle was formed round it, and a placard affixed to the breast inscribed with the words—

"THIS IS THE END OF THE GREAT ROBBER, CARTOUCHE."

And the men, who had done what they considered an act of justice, began to dance round the corpse.

"Come along," said Tomasso, suddenly emerging from behind the tree. "I will escort you back to Paris—this is no place for either of you."

"I pity that poor man!" said Can-can.

"He tried to hang my lover, so I have no pity for him!" Louise exclaimed fiercely.

"Better not talk about him," Tomasso remarked.

"How shall we manage about getting into the city?"

"The gates are open two hours later than usual during the fair time," said the Corsican. "And as so many people are about the scrutiny is not very strict; we shall not be noticed."

It happened as Tomasso had said—the guard was careless, and the party entered the city without any troublesome questions being put to them.

Louise went back to the catacombs, so did Tomasso, but Can-can retired to her own old humble lodging.

"Tell that rascal Gribichon to come and see me, Louise," said the scent-seller, as she kissed her friend before parting.

"I will tell him as soon as I see him, and that will be soon, I hope and pray."

"Why do you hope and pray that you may soon see my sweetheart, Louise? I shall be jealous of you."

"When he returns I shall see or hear something of my lover; that is why I pray for the speedy return of yours. So good-night, my dear Can-can."

This conversation took place near the entrance to the catacombs. The two girls were not aware that anyone was near except Tomasso, who kept at a discreet distance.

But there was a listener.

On the ground was what in the starlight seemed a shapeless mass of rubbish. If it had been daylight they would have seen that it was the living trunk of a man—a body without feet, hands, eyes, or tongue—the victim of Cartouche's vengeance—Black George.

He heard their conversation, and treasured it in his mind. He intended to be avenged upon Cartouche.

CHAPTER LIV.

MAN OR GHOST.

CARTOUCHE was not satisfied.

He and Gribichon searched with the greatest diligence through all the vaults—at least, all they knew of or could find in the old abbey without being able to discover the hiding-place of that enemy whose shadow had threatened them.

"This is a funny start, captain," said Gribichon.

"Don't be afraid, Gribby."

"I am not—haven't been since you taught me better manners; but still I like to see who is going to hit me."

"Quite right, and we must be on our guard to

see that he doesn't strike when we are not prepared to meet the blow."

"How can we best do that, captain?"

They were standing at some distance from any wall or pillar that might conceal a lurking foe, and Cartouche was thinking which part of the ruin would be the best to use as their lodging for the night. He knew where the most comfortable apartment was to be found, but then safety had to be considered also.

"We will sleep outside, in the graveyard," said Cartouche, speaking in a low whisper.

"But it was beginning to rain when we came in, captain," said Gribichon.

"I know a place where we can keep dry, and at the same time be safe from human interference."

"What do you mean?"

"There is a place in the churchyard where no one who knows the ruin will venture between sunset and sunrise."

"Why not, captain?"

"A horrible ghost is frequently seen there."

"I don't like ghosts—"

Gribichon was going to say more when he began his speech, which he broke off suddenly, whilst with outstretched finger he pointed at something.

Cartouche at an early period in his predatory career learnt the value of quickness both in thought and action.

He turned at once, pistol in hand, and, seeing something black moving between two pillars at the other end of the building, he fired at it.

For a second the smoke of the powder obscured the vision of both, but when that cleared away the black object was no longer to be seen.

"Let us go and look," Cartouche said.

"Perhaps it was the ghost, captain."

"Deuce take the ghost! come along."

Gribichon reluctantly obeyed, and they walked together to the place where they had seen the object at which Cartouche fired.

"Hold the torch a little higher, Gribby."

"There is nothing here," responded the torch-bearer.

"Any way, let us have a good look. Hold the torch in your left hand, so that you can keep a pistol in the right one."

Gribichon did as his chief told him.

"Do you see anything, captain?" he asked.

"No, lad; I must have fired at nothing."

"I see something, though."

"What? Where is it?" Cartouche demanded, as he gave a rapid but comprehensive look round the ruin.

"Here," said Gribichon, pointing down to the floor.

Cartouche stooped and picked up a dagger of exactly the same pattern as that he had seen shadowed on the wall in the vault or crypt.

"Stand still for a minute, Gribby."

"I say, let us get out of this as soon as possible."

"Look here! The roof of this part of the building is still good, and the floor, consequently, is thickly covered with dust; so if anyone has been along here we must see his footmarks."

"It must have been the ghost. There are no footprints here," said Gribichon.

"Ghosts don't carry steel daggers—nor do they wear such hats as this," responded Cartouche, as he picked up a chapeau from the floor.

"The devil!" exclaimed Gribichon.

"Never heard that he wore a hat. It would interfere with his horns. However, if we find the print of cloven hoofs, like those of an ox, upon the floor, I shall certainly think the devil has been about the neighbourhood."

The two friends then looked very carefully about the dusty flag stones with which the place was paved, but could not discern any human footsteps except their own, nor anything at all like the print of a cloven hoof.

"Captain, this hat has a hole in it," said Gribby.

"And it looks very much as if made by a pistol ball," replied Cartouche, after a very brief examination of the defect pointed out by his companion.

"Then it was your bullet, no doubt."

"Can't say for certain. It is about the size."

"If the hat was on any mortal man's head, that bullet must have gone very near his brains."

"Hold the torch a little this way."

Gribichon moved the torch as directed.

"See here," continued Cartouche, "this is the place where my pistol-bullet struck; the hat was lying in a direct line between this spot on the wall and the place where I stood when I fired."

"Here is the bullet, captain."

Gribichon held up a flattened piece of metal which he had found upon the floor about a foot from the wall.

"Then whose hat is this, and where are the footmarks of the owner?"

A question Gribichon could not answer, so he simply replied—

"We had best get out of this."

"I think so too. Stay, what mark is this on the floor?"

Cartouche pointed to a mark on the floor, which Gribichon carefully examined by the light of his torch.

"A dog, or a wolf has been along here."

"Dogs and wolves don't wear cocked hats or carry daggers. Come along, Gribby; put out the torch."

"What do you mean to do, captain?"

"Out with the torch! Come away."

Gribichon put his foot on the flaming brand, and they were at once left in complete darkness, as the moon and stars were obscured by thick clouds, from which a heavy, drizzling rain descended.

Cartouche, however, knew the ruin well, and consequently could do as well without light as with it.

He seized Gribichon by the hand and hurried him away. Both being shod with felt soles to their boots they were able to pass as noiselessly as though they had been a pair of ghosts.

They reached the middle of the extensive graveyard before a word was spoken; then Cartouche paused, and gave a hasty glance round—it was too dark to see or be seen at more than a yard's distance, and the gloom was rather intensified at that spot by the fact that a big yew overshadowed the place.

Gribichon was aware, however, that they were close to a big tomb or monument, which was surrounded by an iron rail.

But Cartouche knew well how to open that rail, and he drew Gribichon inside the enclosure. Then, by manipulating some very artfully-contrived spring, he made the flat slab of the tomb raise itself on its hinges, while one of the ends fell down.

"There are steps here, so take care," Cartouche said.

"Are we going down into the grave, captain?"

"We are; but no corpses are permitted upon the premises except our own. There is not even an empty coffin here, Gribby, my dear boy."

"I don't want an empty one."

"Hiss—ss—who-o-o!" sounded from the yew tree above them. Gribichon looked up, and declared that he could plainly see a white body and a pair of fiery eyes which must belong to Satan himself or one of his principal fiends.

"You fool! it is only an old owl," Cartouche whispered, as he dragged his friend down into the vault, which he then closed by a reverse movement of the machinery which caused the tomb to open.

"Was that an owl?" said Gribichon.

"Yes."

"And the dreadful ghost—what has become of it?"

"That was myself. I used to act the ghost so successfully that the people for miles round would not come near this tomb even in the brightest sunshine."

"But could not a ghost get in here?"

"No; I want to avoid human beings—and wolves. It was the footmark of a wolf you saw in the abbey."

"Yes, but I aint afraid of wolves, you know. I have seen a lot of them lately."

"Well, be quiet. Let us get two or three hours' sleep."

"What, here in a grave?"

"Yes, of course. No one will venture to disturb us, or if they do they cannot break into our bedroom without making more than enough noise to waken us."

With which words Cartouche settled himself down in the narrow vault, resolved to have a good sleep. Gribichon, on the contrary, resolved that he would watch, which he did whilst lying down, and with a pistol in each hand.

As the night wore away and day dawned Gribichon became aware that the vault in which he and Cartouche had lain down had a grating on a level with the surface of the graveyard.

Rising up to look out, Gribby observed that this grating was suddenly obscured by what looked very like a pair of human legs clad in black stockings. He pinched Cartouche's arm, and the captain at once jumped up, pistol in hand.

Not a word passed between them. Gribichon simply pointed to the legs, which seemed not a couple of inches from the little grating, not a foot square, by which the two living inhabitants of the vault had light and air.

The first impulse of Cartouche was to thrust out the barrel of a pistol and shoot; but, checking that impulse, he made a stab at those legs with the dagger which they found in the abbey.

Cartouche passed the blade of the weapon through an opening in the grating, and was about to make a stroke at one of the legs when the weapon was suddenly twitched from his grasp and fell outside the empty tomb.

"What can this mean?" Cartouche muttered. "The dagger has disappeared."

"So have the legs," Gribichon replied.

"Is it a man or a ghost?"

"Not a ghost, but the devil, captain."

Cartouche waited a few minutes till the outside light was clearer, then he once more put in motion the machinery, and the tomb opened to permit their exit.

The soft rain had been falling all night, and the soil round the tomb was moist.

Cartouche could with some difficulty trace the footmarks made by himself and Gribichon the previous night, but in the place where those mysterious legs had been there was no mark whatever, nor any trace of the dagger.

"Look here, captain, it must be the devil. Let us get out of this neighbourhood."

"I will not go till I have solved this mystery. It shall never be said that Cartouche was beaten by a shadow."

"Well, but, captain—"

"It will be well only when I have found out what this affair means. It cannot be anything specially prepared for us, no joke got up for our express amusement, for nobody knew we were likely to be in the abbey."

Just for ten seconds Gribichon stood irresolute, then he said—

"Well, captain, it is getting light now, so d—n the ghost and the devil; let us have a good hunt through the place by the light of day."

They agreed to do so as soon as they had breakfasted on some food and wine Gribichon carried in his wallet.

What came of their search will be seen hereafter.

CHAPTER LV.

CAN-CAN'S UNKNOWN LOVER.

As related in a previous chapter, Louise and Tomasso went back to their respective hiding-places in the catacombs as soon as the hanging of the Chief of Police was over.

Can-can, on the other hand, went back to the lodging she had previously occupied.

For a day or more she did not venture out.

It might be possible, she thought, that some police agent had recognised her as present at the fair of St. Germains when the execution of Peuchet took place, and she did not know how far the vengeance of the Government might proceed against any of those who were there. So Can-can pleaded ill-health and remained within her room, piously wishing all the time that Gribichon would come along to give her advice and consolation.

It was towards the evening of the day after her return from the fair that she was sitting alone, feeling rather melancholy, when the porter knocked at the door of her room.

"Enter!" said Can-can.

"A letter for mademoiselle," the man remarked, holding out a folded paper.

"From whom?" the scent-seller asked.

"How can I say, mademoiselle?" replied the man, speaking and gesticulating rapidly. "It was left at the lodge by a man who would not wait to know if it needed any reply."

This was about the second or third letter Can-can had received during her lifetime, and therefore it was an object of curiosity; so it was to the porter, whose lodgers were not troubled with a great deal of correspondence.

Can-can at first thought it might be from Gribichon—but then, not knowing that he affixed that placard to Peuchet's doorway, she really was not aware that he knew how to write.

The porter waited some minutes, but Can-can did not satisfy his curiosity, although she gratified her own by asking—

"Pray, monsieur, what is the latest news in Paris? Has Monsieur Peuchet succeeded yet in capturing that most daring robber, Cartouche?"

"On the contrary, mademoiselle; Cartouche or some of his desperadoes have succeeded in hanging Monsieur Peuchet."

"Hanging him! surely you are mistaken?"

"Not so. It was done at the fair of St. Germains."

And he related the tragic end of Monsieur Peuchet in words which Can-can knew to be very near the truth.

"But you have not shown that Cartouche or his friends had anything to do with the business," said Can-can.

"It is certain no one else could have done it."

"Do they suspect anyone in particular? Was Cartouche there himself, at St. Germains?"

"He was not, nor was Louise, the flower-girl."

"It is a strange business, monsieur."

"Very strange indeed. The police are completely puzzled."

And then, after a long pause, finding that Can-can was not disposed to be communicative, the porter moved off to his own den at the entrance.

When he had gone Can-can opened the letter. "If this is Gribichon s penmanship, he writes well," was the remark she made, as she looked at the superscription, which, however, gave her no information beyond the fact that the letter was intended for her.

Can-can broke the two seals and had a look at the inside of the letter, which was to this effect :—

"If the young lady, Can-can, who sells in the streets of Paris bottles and packets of scents, which are not half as sweet as her breath, will be at the statue of Diana in the Place Henri IV. at midnight, she will meet with a well-wisher who is able to tell her something about Monsieur Gribichon, and may be able to conduct her to him. This is from   "A FRIEND."

"I like Gribichon, although he eats my supper and borrows my money," said Can-can, when she had perused this very strange epistle. "But I should like to know who is 'A Friend.'"

Not being able to solve this riddle, Can-can decided that she would keep the appointment.

By way of preparation, she fortified herself with a good supper, and then sallied out about an hour before the time mentioned in the letter.

The night was clear, and though the streets of Paris were but poorly provided with public lamps, the square or place was light enough.

There was the statue of the goddess Diana (long since demolished by the revolutionists), and Can-can took a good look round the place.

There was no one stirring so far as she could see, so she took a couple of walks across the square, without meeting anyone.

But, as she was returning to the statue for the third time, someone jumped out from behind it.

Can-can uttered a shriek and drew back.

She saw before her a man, or a figure resembling a man, clad in a long black cloak. With one arm he held this garment up, so as to conceal his face, while with the other he made a grasp at the wrist of the pretty scent-seller, who again started back as her assailant said—

"I have you now safe enough."

Can-can turned, with the desperate intention of making a run to the nearest military guard-room, but before she could do so the fellow clutched her by the arm.

"If you make a sound I will kill you !" said he ; "so you had best come along silently."

Can-can thought so too.

The poor girl knew enough of Parisian life to be aware that outcries, screams of murder, and noises of that sort were so very common that few of the citizens would trouble to look out at their windows if she attempted to make an alarm.

So Can-can, in fear of her life, went along quietly with the man who captured her close by the statue of Diana, and who, from the firm grip he kept on her arm, seemed determined to keep her a prisoner.

They went together through several streets with which Can-can was well acquainted, as, in fact, she was with most of the Parisian thoroughfares.

Several times they met patrols of horse-soldiers and pickets of foot, all searching for Cartouche ; sometimes they met parties of belated roysterers wending their unsteady and devious way homewards ; but when this happened the man in the cloak gave a grip of extra strength at Can-can's wrist, and whispered in her ear—

"If you make a sound you will have a dagger between your ribs."

So poor Can-can kept very quiet indeed, and one might have imagined that she and her unknown captor were husband and wife walking home calmly.

The man who had Can-can did not allow her to see his face, although, when he passed other people, he dropped the cloak from before his face. But at such times he wore his hat so much cocked on one side that his own mother would scarcely have recognised him by such a light as there was in Paris then.

After walking along several of the streets which Can-can knew well enough by daylight, when she was "plying" her usual trade, the man dragged her up two or three narrow courts, of which she had no knowledge, and finally led her into a house which seemed to stand a little apart from the others.

As the door of this gloomy mansion closed behind her Can-can's heart began to fail her, and she uttered a faint cry.

"Ah, you can cry as much as you like now, there is no one within hearing," said her captor.

"Why have you brought me hither ?" she asked.

"You will learn in good time."

"How long must I stay here ?"

"Till you are released."

"If Gribichon only knew of this !"

"He will hear of it soon, I have no doubt. But you need not imagine you are going to see him here."

"You are a villain !" exclaimed Can-can, as she clenched her little fist and struck the man's face.

He had dropped his cloak on entering the house and lighted a candle, so that Can-can could see his countenance. But the scent-seller had no recollection whatever of having seen him before.

"You are a little vixen !' said the man, half angry and half amused at her violence.

He was fairly dressed and of middle age. His features showed him to be a man of resolution ; his general appearance was that of a man who had been a soldier.

"But come, Mademoiselle Can-can, let me show you your apartment, which, though not luxuriously furnished, is fairly comfortable," the man continued, leading her along a passage and down some half-dozen steps into a back room.

It looked gloomy enough for a prison cell ; in

been arranged by which Gribichon could send word when he or Louise—or both—would be leaving the city.

CHAPTER LVII.

A LONG JOURNEY.

LOUISE lived rather a lonely life in the dreary vaults of the catacombs.

Tomasso by degrees ventured out and about the city; The Wolf also was active enough searching for news; but no tidings of Cartouche came till they heard of the robbery of the Lyons passenger boat.

Colonel Leguerre, apparently, was playing some very artful game for the capture of Cartouche, and was not inclined to let anyone know what cards he held. Nobody seemed to know what steps he was taking to catch the great French robber, but there was no doubt in the mind of Louise that some very artful trick was being arranged.

At the first period of her life in the catacombs Louise used occasionally to venture out and spend a few hours in the evening along with Can-can, but after a time they grew risky, and when she went out at all it was late at night, when the darkness hid her well-known face from the prying police.

It was during one of her nocturnal wanderings, escorted by Tomasso, who would not allow her to face the horrors of the French metropolis at night without someone to protect her, that she encountered Gribichon, who that evening had come from Versailles.

Of course Louise was delighted to have news of Cartouche.

She would have started then had the gates been open, but as they were closed she contented herself with declaring her firm intention of being outside Paris five minutes after they were opened.

Gribichon, however, persuaded her to wait till a number of people were astir, and then to go in a hired coach.

"For," said he, "I am not going back for a time."

"What will you do, then?"

"Remain in Paris till I find Can-can. Have you seen anything of her lately?"

"Not for several days," Louise replied.

"Well, you had best go back to the catacombs and rest in preparation for your journey."

"What place is Cartouche going to when he leaves Versailles?"

"I don't know, but I think to the North."

"And how will you and Can-can overtake us?"

"Why, I daresay we shall remain in Paris."

"You and Can-can will remain—that is, if you find her. Now, where will you look for your sweetheart?"

Gribichon had no idea.

Then Louise told him all she knew about the hanging of Peuchet, and how they returned to Paris after that tragic event.

"I shall find her if she is in the town," said Gribichon.

"I hope you will," Louise replied, "for I love Can-can."

"So do I," responded Gribichon, who then kissed the hand of La Belle Louise, and withdrew.

Louise returned to the catacombs, and at an early hour in the morning was dressed, ready to proceed in a hired coach, which Tomasso procured for her, to Versailles.

Her dress was slightly changed, and anyone who looked at her through the window of the coach would have imagined a lady of quality was going out to the suburban palace, where the king was then holding his court.

Winter was coming on, and as her vehicle rolled along the road between Paris and Versailles, Louise wondered how they would be able to get through the inclement season if they were always to be thus flying from the police, with no settled home, and no certainty of being able to rest even a night without having to get up and run.

Great was the joy of Cartouche, and immense the happiness of Louise when they met.

"But we must be off, Louise," said the outlaw.

"Whither, my dearest?"

"I have a notion that I will go up to Strasbourg. The town has not been in the hands of the French for many years. I am not known there, and all the people persist in speaking the German tongue. But I have heard that it is very cold in the winter."

"I don't mind if I am with you."

So it was agreed they should make Strasbourg their home for the winter.

Tomasso was instructed as to the method by which he and Gribichon should communicate, and after a good dinner at one of the best hotels in Versailles the Corsican returned to Paris.

Cartouche and Louise were to go on in the morning by the ordinary stage-coach, as our hero did not think it expedient to draw attention to himself and companion by hiring special horses and carriages, or showing any extraordinary amount of wealth.

It was a long, tiresome journey, and winter came on with rapidity—first a frost, then a snow, and then another frost which seemed to increase in intensity the further they went.

Strasbourg was reached, however, after some days and nights of weary travel.

"Bitter cold!" ejaculated Cartouche as he descended from the vehicle with Louise.

"It would be colder if we were in separate prison cells," Louise replied. "But where are we to lodge?"

It did not take Cartouche long to find a place, humble enough, but still a place where all the sympathies of the inhabitants were antagonistic to the police. Cartouche, in fact, let drop a few hints that he had done things in Calais, Boulogne, and other places on the western coast of France for which he was *wanted*, and the inhabitants of the thieves' quarters at Strasbourg vowed that he should have early intimation of any move made against him by the authorities.

For four or five days they lived in complete seclusion; then Louise, in the costume of a peasant girl and in her wooden shoes, went clattering about the stony streets of the old city. And Cartouche, too, after a time thought he might venture to take his walks abroad.

The outlawed couple had been, perhaps, three weeks in Strasbourg during one of the hardest winters ever known.

Money was plentiful, so they wanted not for food or fire; but Cartouche longed to be at work again.

"Paris is my place!" exclaimed he. "I can always do best in the good old capital."

"Be patient, Dominique, and ere long we may venture to go back once more."

They were out walking in the street when this conversation began. Cartouche was in his usual costume of boots, breeches, and cocked hat. Louise had resumed her wooden shoes, with thick stockings of striped woollen, and a hood to protect her head and shoulders from the bitter cold.

Suddenly, as they walked along the principal street of the town, and were not far from the gate which opens upon the bridge crossing the river, Cartouche halted.

"Villain!" exclaimed an excited person. "It is you that have robbed me on board the Lyons boat."

One or two of the French police came up.

"I have not robbed you, but you look very much like the man who robbed me," replied Cartouche.

The man turned to the police and said—

"I am Herr Adolph Sprenger."

"You lie!" exclaimed Cartouche. "It is I who am Herr Adolph Sprenger. Would you take my name in the same way you took my money, villain?"

The German did not know what to make of it, but spluttered a lot of oaths, while Cartouche quietly turned to the police and remarked—

"The gentleman says his name is Herr Adolph Sprenger; perhaps he has a passport to prove that his words are true."

Of course the police could not help catching at an idea so happily suggested to them, and collared Herr Sprenger.

He had no passport to show—Cartouche carefully deprived him of that on board the boat at the time he took those thousands of livres from him; so Herr Sprenger was told that he would be called upon to account for his being in a frontier city without any document authorising him to travel.

Cartouche, on the other hand, produced the passport that Gribichon obtained for him at Lyons.

"You are invited to attend before the mayor at three o'clock to-day, monsieur," said the polite policeman.

"For what purpose?"

"That it may be decided which of you two gentlemen has the best right to the name and passport of Herr Adolph Sprenger," the official replied.

"I will attend willingly," said Cartouche.

"I suppose I must," Sprenger groaned.

And so they parted. But Louise was in a state of great trepidation, and said—

"Surely, my boy, you do not mean to go before the mayor? Who knows but you may be recognised?"

"I don't intend to do anything so foolish. Come with me, and we will walk out of this town without loss of time."

"We shall be watched and followed."

"Not if we turn about and walk down the town. We were walking towards Germany, now we will point our steps towards our own old France."

"But our luggage?"

"Matters not! We have money enough to buy more."

They walked once more through the town, and out at the gate leading towards Paris.

"Now we will turn off the main road," said Cartouche, and neither knowing nor caring whither he went, he led Louise down a pathway that led to the bank of the mighty river which in those days divided France from Germany.

But they had not gone half a league before Cartouche was aware that they were pursued by soldiers.

"Hurry along, Louise!" said he, catching her by the arm, and forcing her to run.

"But where shall we go?"

"We must leave that to chance—which has been our good friend till now."

As they hurried along by the bank of the river it all at once occurred to Cartouche that the other side of the river was German soil, and if he could cross he might be safe for a time.

The river was full of ice; huge sheets several inches thick were floating down towards the sea with here and there a few feet of clear water between them

"Louise, this is for life and liberty! Come with me across the ice—jump!"

Louise did not hesitate. She was quite willing to go to the bottom of the river with her lover, or any place except a French prison.

She jumped from the bank on to a floating sheet of ice just as two of the foremost of the soldiers sent out in pursuit raised their muskets and fired.

The bullets whistled close to the heads of the fugitives, who, however, did not stop. Cartouche glanced back and saw one man in the act of reloading his piece, while the other seemed to be swearing. It was evident, however, that they did not intend to trust themselves upon the ice.

"One more jump and we are safe!" Cartouche exclaimed. "The cowards dare not follow."

And so it was.

Cartouche and Louise gave not one but two jumps, and then were safe, beyond range of the muskets, on German soil.

CHAPTER LVIII.

SOMETHING MORE ABOUT CAN-CAN.

WHEN Can-can mustered up sufficient courage to have a good look round the prison to which her unknown lover or friend had consigned her, she found it was a place from which it would be very difficult to escape.

The walls were solid enough; there were some bars across the chimney to prevent any exit by that aperture, and the window was closed with strong iron bars. As to the bolts and locks on the door, it is hardly necessary to say anything except that one of the bolts was on the inner side of the door, so that if Can-can could not escape she could, at all events, prevent intrusion.

Can can fastened herself in.

Sitting down to taste the provisions that had been left for her she thought to herself—

"Well, what is the meaning of this? Whose prisoner am I?"

But no immediate solution of the conundrum occurred to her mind, so she drank a glass of wine, and then lay down upon the bed without undressing herself.

It was some time before she could feel sleepy, and during the hours that passed in wakefulness she listened most attentively to find out, if she could, whether there were any other human beings in the house.

Not a sound could be heard except occasionally the wheels of a heavy waggon passing along the distant street, or the noisy shouts of some belated drunkards, who were making their way home.

Can-can slept, and when she awoke there was someone knocking at the door.

In a few seconds she was wide awake.

"Who is there?" she demanded.

"I who brought you here," replied a voice, which the girl very well recognised as that of her captor.

"And what do you want?" Can-can asked.

"To give you some breakfast and then have a chat with you."

Can-can hesitated for a few seconds and then drew the bolt. The man entered with a tray, on which was a jug of coffee and various articles of food.

"Well, young lady, do you find yourself in a more pliant frame of mind this morning?" he asked.

"Not a bit of it," Can-can replied.

"You are a fiery little party, but you are not doing yourself the least bit of good."

"Be pleased to explain yourself, monsieur," was the haughty reply of the scent-seller.

"I mean that you are most likely to obtain liberty when you tell me where I can find your lover, Gribichon."

"What do you know of Gribichon—what do you want with him?"

"I know he is a robber—one of Cartouche's gang—and I want to hang him."

Can-can had secreted in her dress the knife left her to cut her food with. Suddenly drawing this from its hiding-place she commenced a furious attack upon her gaoler.

The man received two or three sharp cuts about his hands before he could succeed in wresting the knife from the furious girl, who, as soon as she was disarmed, sank down upon the bed and began to sob.

"Why should you wish to hang my Gribby?" she asked

"Because it is my duty to see him hanged."

"Who are you, villain?"

"I am Colonel Leguerre, the new Chief of Police."

Can-can started to her feet and stared at the colonel, who quietly went on to say—

"I have caught you because I want Gribichon, and I want him as the means of securing Cartouche."

"I don't know where they are, I assure you, colonel," said the poor girl, and she spoke the truth.

The man looked at Can-can steadfastly for several seconds, and then said—

"I believe you. But Louise is hidden in the catacombs, and I want to get hold of her: you know how to obtain admission to her hiding-place."

"I do not, indeed. I hate those gloomy vaults, and wonder how Louise can stay there."

The man smiled, and said—

"It is pretty certain you know she is there! Well, a few days in this place will, perhaps, make you a little more reasonable, so you must stay. You will have plenty of food, and when you feel inclined to tell me a little more about the hiding-place of Louise, or of Gribichon, or of Cartouche, you need only press that nail in the wall, and a bell will sound which I shall soon answer."

"I know nothing, and if I did I would not tell!"

Can-can was not aware then that the empty house in which she was imprisoned was one of several the new Chief of Police had taken possession of in various quarters of Paris for the purpose of carrying on his plots against malefactors without even his own men being in the secret.

One select man was placed in charge of each building to let the colonel know when that bell was sounded by some prisoner eager to escape.

The colonel rose to depart.

"Well, Mademoiselle Can-can, when you wish to leave this place you may ring the bell. But you must tell me something about one of the three—Cartouche, Louise, or Gribichon—before you can hope to get out, and if you don't give a little information in the course of this week you may find yourself in the Bastile, and you have heard, perhaps, that few people leave that establishment alive. So just reflect."

He passed out of the room and the door was locked.

"I must get out," was Can-can's first thought.

But how was that feat to be accomplished?

Colonel Leguerre had left the knife

When he wrested it from her he carelessly

threw it in a corner; Can-can espied it, and quickly secreted it in her dress.

Another thing Can-can noticed. The key had been turned in the lock, but still the door was not fast; the bolt of the lock was shot, but the door was practically open as the bolt was not thrown into the socket.

"Is this accident or design?" thought Can-can.

She was a very shrewd young person, and thinking that perhaps it was left so intentionally she resolved not to interfere with that door for some hours.

She had received her day's allowance of food before Colonel Leguerre visited her, and, therefore, had little expectation of being visited again by her gaoler that day. So she waited patiently with her ears all attention to catch the least sound of any person moving about the place.

It was some hours before she heard anything, then a footstep passed along the corridor in the direction of the front door, which was opened and then closed, as if someone had gone out.

Can-can hastily gathered up the remains of her food and wine, for she knew not when she would be able to procure another meal. She also took the coverlet from the bed, and, folding it like a shawl, covered her head and shoulders with it.

The little scent-seller then slipped off her shoes, and quietly walked out of her apartment.

The key was in the lock—one of a number—so Can-can quietly locked the door and put all the bunch in her pocket.

Then she decided that before leaving she would have a quiet look at the upper part of the house.

Quite noiselessly she glided up the stairs.

All the doors on the first landing were open, and none had any signs of recent occupation.

A window was open in one of the rooms, which, she guessed, was situated over the entrance. Can-can ventured to look out, and found there was a quiet, narrow street, with no living being stirring in it.

"Now is my time!" she thought.

She descended, and, reaching the hall, slipped on her shoes. The door was locked, so selecting a key she tried it, and finding it fitted, she quickly passed out.

Locking the door again, she took away the keys with her.

But in which direction should she go?

Evidently not back to her old lodging. The Chief of Police would soon hear of her escape, and would send there. Nor was it safe to go to the catacombs, since the colonel suspected Louise to be hidden there, and was watching the place.

She had a little money about her, and her Parisian life had made her acquainted with many places where cheap lodging could be found without any questions being asked.

It was dusk, and being well covered with the shawl Can-can had little fear of being recognised as she hurried along the street. She had to cross one of the bridges, and she took advantage of that circumstance to drop the keys into the river.

"What are you doing, young woman?" said a man, coming close to her.

Can-can turned, and gave a half-suppressed shriek as she found Gribichon close at her elbow.

"Why, Can-can, where have you been?" said he.

And without waiting for an answer he caught her in his arms and kissed her till she boxed his ears, though not so spitefully as she had struck the colonel.

"Well, where have you been, you little beauty?"

"In prison, my dear Gribichon."

"How—why—when—where?"

"Come along, and I will tell you."

"But this is not the way to your lodging."

"I know that; but I dare not go back to the old place, so I must find a new home."

As Can-can hurried Gribichon along she told him all that had happened to her.

"A bad lookout!" said Gribichon. "That colonel means to have the lot of us."

"That colonel is a dangerous man. Do you know him?"

"I have never seen him, but should like to, so that I may avoid him in future. Tell me what he is like, Can-can."

The girl described Colonel Leguerre accurately.

"Then I believe I have seen him, but I suppose he does not know me, or I should have been collared."

"No doubt of that, Gribby. But here is the place where I think I can get a lodging."

Can-can knocked at the door of a house, and was informed that she could rent an apartment there, and enter on immediate occupation by payment of a week's rent.

This was done, and some supper procured, which Gribichon paid for; he also gave his sweetheart a good handful of gold and silver, so that she would not be obliged to go out scent-selling for some time to come.

After supper he bade her adieu, and resolved to walk in the direction of the catacombs, thinking he might meet The Wolf in that neighbourhood.

"But I am not going into the place. I should certainly be seized if I did such a thing," said he to himself.

Sauntering on to the open ground where the entrance to the catacombs was situated, with the air of a man who was having a quiet moonlight ramble before retiring to rest, he soon perceived half a dozen other individuals, whom he recognised as police spies. It was evident that a very strict watch was kept on the supposed hiding-place of Cartouche, who, as the reader is well aware, was many miles away.

Gribichon at once saw that nothing could be gained by loitering about the neighbourhood of the catacombs.

Yet it was necessary that he should see

either The Wolf or Tomasso, so that communication might be made with Cartouche as soon as it was known where that noble captain was.

Gribichon sauntered down to the quay by the Pont Neuf, where he resolved to remain—if he could do so without danger—till The Wolf came.

So Gribby strolled round about for some hours, in fact, daylight was appearing when he espied the youth he was in search of coming down on the quay with Tomasso.

"Why, where have you been?" Gribichon asked.

"Seeing a lady home," The Wolf replied, laughing.

Gribichon looked puzzled, and eventually inquired—

"What lady? Where does she live?"

"The lady is Madame Bobilet, who has been for some time past a prisoner in the private dungeons of the catacombs as a hostage for Cartouche."

"And you have released her?"

"Undoubtedly."

"In what part of the land is he staying now?'

"We have only just heard of his marvellous escape over the icy river at Strasbourg into Germany. But you may be certain he will be back in France—aye, in Paris before long; he won most of his renown in this city, and he will never keep away from it unless very hard pressed indeed."

"Who told you of this?" Gribichon asked.

"It is public news brought from Strasbourg by the mail."

"But last night I went towards the catacombs, and saw that the whole neighbourhood is carefully watched by a number of police spies. How, then, did you get Madame Bobilet past them, and where did you leave her?"

"It may have occurred to you," said Tomasso, "that the French police are asses. At daybreak the night-duty men go away, and for two full hours the place is left unwatched. During that time I brought the lady out—blindfolded, so that she might not be able to show anyone the way in. I placed her, still blindfolded, in a hired carriage which I entered myself, and while the driver was sleepily guiding his horses along the street I stepped out—and I suppose he is still driving Madame about the streets of Paris. Ho! ho! ho! I wonder what will become of her?'

None of them were prepared with an answer to this question, but for the satisfaction of the reader the mystery may as well be solved at once.

The coachman drove away over the rugged streets of Paris for more than an hour after Tomasso quitted the vehicle, and then it occurred to the man that he ought to know where the lady and gentleman wanted to be set down; but to his astonishment he found the gentleman had departed.

So the driver unceremoniously handed Madame Bobilet out of his vehicle, and bade her find her way home as best she could.

Madame tore the bandage from her eyes, and finding that she was no great distance from the police-office, she thought she would go and see Monsieur Peuchet. But she then heard, for the first time, that he was dead.

Colonel Leguerre, however, heard her story of imprisonment, and he became more resolved than ever that those vaults should undergo a thorough search.

Then, having no money, Madame thought she would go to her husband and ask his pardon and protection.

She did so. Monsieur Bobilet, who had resigned his post in the Civic Guard, administered severe chastisement with a stout cane, and then forgave his penitent wife, who, from that time, occupied the second place in their household, and died many years after, respected by all who had forgotten her folly. So exit the Bobilet family.

Tomasso and Gribichon, being outside the catacombs, did not feel inclined to venture back for some days till Colonel Leguerre's activity relaxed a little.

So they took a joint lodging where they could live quite comfortably without having much occasion to go outdoors, when Tomasso generally went to meet The Wolf and hear if he had any news of Cartouche, while Gribichon solaced himself with an hour or two in Can-can's company.

And thus things went on for a time.

CHAPTER LIX.

CARTOUCHE AND LOUISE ON THEIR TRAVELS.

CARTOUCHE and Louise being safe upon German soil, held a consultation as to how they should proceed.

They had plenty of money and jewels, so there was no fear of their wanting the necessaries or comforts of life; besides, if their purses failed, Cartouche could easily replenish them in the old way.

"But where shall we go?" Louise asked.

"We will travel along till we come to Holland."

"I don't think I should like to stay there. I am told that it is nothing but canals and ditches, and everyone who goes there has the ague."

"We will not stay there; as soon as possible we will cross over to England, and eat roast beef."

Louise gave a shudder at the idea, and Cartouche went on.

"We won't stay long in England either—only just while we hear the news from Paris, and consider how to get back there."

"I shall be glad to get back to dear old Paris," said Louise.

Cartouche was thinking whether it would be possible to reside there permanently, even if he succeeded in reaching his native city, as evidently the police would give him no rest.

He did not tell Louise what was in his mind for fear of alarming her, and he knew well enough that she would go with him to any part of the world. So they travelled by easy stages through Holland till they reached Rotterdam, where they remained for some weeks till the water was sufficiently free from ice to enable them to take passage by the first packet that sailed for England. His passport which Gribichon obtained for him was sufficient for both, and in due course of time they landed at Harwich, and proceeded to London.

No need is there to speak of their doings in London. Let it suffice to say that Cartouche carefully abstained from practising his profession in this country; neither did he associate with any of his own countrymen, lest he should be recognised. He waited some three months, during which time he heard that the police of Paris were of opinion that he and Louise must have fallen through an opening in the ice whilst crossing the river, and that they had almost ceased to talk about him. Then he thought he might venture to visit his native place once more.

So Cartouche and Louise sailed one fine day in a packet-boat bound from London to Calais, his passport being duly signed by the English authorities.

"Here we are, on French soil once more!" he exclaimed, as they scrambled on shore at the dirty town of Calais. "Now what shall we do?"

"Have a bottle of wine and something to eat. I am sick of the beer and roast beef."

"You are a little fool!" exclaimed an Englishman, who had crossed the water with them. "We never get tired of beef and beer."

Louise shrugged her shoulders. Cartouche felt inclined to quarrel with the man, but then he reflected that it would hardly be prudent to bring himself into notoriety immediately on landing. On the contrary, if he and Louise were to reach Paris they must travel as quietly as possible.

Cartouche had a scheme in his head, which included a desire to see his father and other relatives before leaving France for ever. But he doubted much how he would be received by them.

It was cold spring time as they travelled by easy stages to Amiens. On reaching that old town they halted for a few days, to hear, if possible, how things were going in Paris.

"How about Cartouche?" he asked in the hotel one evening. "What has been heard of him lately?"

"He escaped from Strasbourg to England, and there our police spies lost him," said the landlord. "It is supposed he contrived to get away to America."

"Likely enough. Have his companions been caught?"

"No, but they are all scattered—dispersed. Paris now laughs at the memory of Cartouche."

"Oh! that is well."

They travelled on two days later, and it must be confessed that both their hearts fluttered a little as they approached the chief city.

Would they be recognised, or had the guard grown careless?

They both had taken some little trouble to disguise themselves, so that unless there was a very close scrutiny of in-coming passengers there was a good chance of their passing without recognition.

At the barrier the carriage stopped.

"Passports, if you please, ladies and gentlemen!" shouted the sentinel on duty.

Papers were at once produced, but the officer whose duty it was to examine them happened to be in a hurry, so seeing that every passenger had a document of some kind he bade the driver of the vehicle hurry on, and make room for other carriages that were approaching.

"Safe!" ejaculated Louise.

"My wife means that we are safe from any attack by robbers now that we are in Paris," said Cartouche.

"Safe enough now that we have a new Prefect of Police," replied one of the passengers.

"Where shall we go now?" Louise asked, when they had alighted.

"You had best remain here. We will have some dinner, and then I will go out for an hour or two, and try to hunt up Gribichon and Tomasso. I daresay I can find them at the catacombs, or they will be promenading the quay, waiting for me."

There was no one within hearing when Cartouche spoke—at least, no one but a beggar, who had a bowl before him into which charitably-disposed persons dropped a few small coins occasionally. This ragged object had a placard on his breast stating that he was both dumb and blind, so Cartouche and Louise each threw a coin into his bowl, Cartouche saying aloud—

"Poor devil, he needs it!"

The blind beggar bowed his head and the two travellers passed into the hotel.

Cartouche little guessed that he had bestowed alms upon Black George, who a few minutes later gathered up his day's gains in his mouth and hobbled off to the police-office, where he was at once taken into the presence of Colonel Leguerre.

They had met once or twice before.

The colonel knew that the poor wretch could neither see nor speak, but had not lost his sense of hearing; also that Black George knew how to write, although, as he had no hands, it was rather a difficult matter.

Colonel Leguerre had, however, constructed a large tray filled with sand, and a long cane being fixed to the stump of the cripple's arm he was able to form a word or two.

"Cartouche and Louise at Golden Lion," he wrote.

"Is that true?" the colonel demanded, when he had repeated the words.

And the sightless being nodded most emphatically.

"Going to look for others at catacombs," was the next piece of information traced upon the sand.

Colonel Leguerre rang a bell, and at once

commanded a strong body of men to be in readiness, intending to go there himself and capture the daring villain who so long had been the terror of Paris.

It took some time to get the men together and in readiness; but at length they were in marching order, and set out, the colonel himself taking six to the Golden Lion, and Lecoq marched the others away to the catacombs.

But the best-laid plans of policemen as well as of other people sometimes go wrong.

The colonel found nobody resembling Cartouche or Louise at the hotel; the catacombs' brigade were equally unsuccessful, although a strong body of them went into the vaults, whilst others stayed outside on the watch.

And the reason was this—Cartouche and Louise were seated at their dinner, when suddenly Louise exclaimed—

"There is Can-can!"

The scent-seller was, indeed, passing along the street, this being almost the first time she had ventured out of her lodging for three months. Louise at once jumped up and ran out of the room to bring the scent-seller in.

And when they had exchanged a few words it was quickly arranged that they should all leave the hotel and go to the house where Can-can resided, and where it was certain Cartouche and Louise could find accommodation.

So they went away quietly some time before Colonel Leguerre and his merry men surrounded the hotel.

And, before many hours had passed, Gribichon, Tomasso, and The Wolf knew where to find their chief.

So things continued for some days, till, as usual, Cartouche began to grow sick of confinement in the house, and resolved to do something to let the Parisians know he was there once more.

"Do they still keep watch at the catacombs?" he asked his three satellites one evening. And they all replied no, for they had nightly watched the watchers, and knew the cordon was withdrawn; also they knew that on three separate occasions the police had gone into those vaults and made careful search without discovering the private apartments, as they may be called.

"Then we will go there to-morrow at midday, especially as you, Wolf, think there will be another house-to house search before long."

"I am certain there will be, captain."

"You are bent on some desperate project, Dominique," said Louise. "Tell me what it is?"

"I will—when we are all safely housed in the catacombs."

So to the catacombs they went—except Gribichon and Can-can.

"Louise," said Cartouche, when they were comfortably housed, "now I will tell you my intentions."

"Good boy! tell me at once."

"I am tired of this life, and have determined to give it up. We will go together to this new world of America, where we can get a farm for very little money, and settle down quietly."

Louise sighed, partly with pleasure and partly with pain, at the idea of leaving France.

"But still we shall be among countrymen," Cartouche continued; "the part I mean going to is called Louisiana, and is inhabited mostly by Frenchmen."

And Louise acquiesced in the proposal at once.

"Gribichon has agreed to go to Bordeaux to inquire when the ships sail, and as soon as he returns we will set out on our long journey, and be quiet and happy."

"You said you would see your father when you got back to Paris."

"He is dead, so is my brother. I have no relative living that I know of, neither have you."

"That is true."

All this being settled Cartouche began to think that he must have a triumphant exit—perform some daring feat before leaving France for ever; but that would be done when Gribichon came back from the port of Bordeaux.

However, he went out every night carefully disguised, and sat in a café while the police were searching the place without being recognised. But all the while he was being tracked steadily.

CHAPTER LX.

THE FINAL FIREWORKS.

CARTOUCHE was good at disguise, so, also, was the man who had vowed vengeance—Black George.

Having once established a method of communicating with Colonel Leguerre they got on well in their schemes for the capture of Cartouche. The colonel had a pair of glass eyes made, and an artificial hand, so that the poor wretch was hardly known as the beggar who had no eyeballs at all. A wig, too, of a lighter colour than his natural hair, made Black George's disguise more effectual.

Still he wore his tattered garb and went every night to the catacombs, as did many other poor houseless wretches.

Black George gradually became so thoroughly acquainted with the vaults that he could grope his way to any part except those private apartments.

And one night he discovered, by accident, the place where Tomasso and The Wolf lodged.

He had laid himself down with his back against what he imagined to be a bit of solid rock. An hour passed, when suddenly that rock gave way, and a man coming out of the side of the corridor swore a great oath.

Black George knew the voice of Tomasso, and by pantomimic action explained that he was both blind and dumb. The Corsican did not recognise him.

Tomasso was not in one of his savage moods that night, so he simply helped the blind man to rise, set him with his face towards the mouth of the cave, and said—

"You will find better lodging a little way on."

Black George shambled along, and heard Tomasso cross the corridor and close what sounded like a door.

The Corsican had, in fact, gone into that part of the cavern inhabited by Louise and Cartouche. Black George knew enough, so he hastened off to the Colonel of Police and told him, by writing on a tray of sand, what he had discovered.

Colonel Leguerre at once ordered out a force which he judged sufficient for the purpose, and told Black George that he would have to accompany the men, who were well armed, and had torches as well as crowbars and other implements for removing any obstacles they might encounter. The colonel himself took command.

Quite unaware of these preparations against his peace and quietness, Cartouche and Tomasso were discussing the last great exploit which should signalise their departure for ever from the gay city of Paris, and this was nothing less than blowing up the police-office with gunpowder, and so giving the Parisians one final astonishment.

They had been collecting powder in small quantities for some time, and had four or five hundredweight stored away in their vaults. They were just arranging how it was to be placed under the police-office when The Wolf came running in, almost breathless from the haste he had used.

"Captain, the police are here."

"They have been here before and done nothing. All we have to do is keep quiet and we shall be safe enough."

And they kept quiet.

But soon there was a sound as of men hammering on the walls to find the hidden entrance.

"Some one has betrayed us, captain!" cried Wolf. "But there is a way out which I never told to anyone. We can get away by that passage."

At that moment came a thump at the door, and a voice was heard to exclaim—

"Ah! this seems hollow."

"It is the Colonel of Police," said The Wolf. "This way, captain."

"Wait a minute!" Cartouche cried. "Tomasso, we may as well blow them up here as in their own house. Let me have that coil of match."

The Corsican handed his chief a roll of matchrope soaked in saltpetre, which Cartouche quickly attached to one of the barrels in which their powder was stored.

Meanwhile the hammering at the door became louder and harder.

"Come along, Louise," said Cartouche, hurrying her along a secret passage which The Wolf had opened, and uncoiling the rope of quickmatch as he went.

They turned an angle, and were just at the bottom of a flight of steps rudely cut in the rock when a crash told Cartouche that the door of their old retreat had given way.

"Wait one moment, and I will give them a surprise."

He stooped down and set fire to the match. There was a hissing sound for about three seconds, and then a tremendous explosion, which shook the vaults.

"Come along, Louise!" he cried.

But the flower-girl had fainted, so Cartouche caught her up, and as the dense, suffocating smoke swept along the passage he bore her up the steps, and, following his companions, soon found a place which the choking vapour did not reach.

Then a spoonful or two of brandy restored Louise, and the whole party hurried along for several minutes in the dark, when they reached what they could tell by feeling was a ladder. Wolf went up first, and cautiously opened a kind of trap-door, which allowed a few rays of light to penetrate to them.

Climbing this ladder one by one they found themselves in an old ruined house, from which they very quickly emerged, Wolf bolting the trap door on the outer side, so as to delay pursuit—if any pursuers remained.

"Now for Bordeaux!" cried Cartouche. "We have no time to lose. You will come with us, Tomasso."

"Yes, as far as Bordeaux, but not to America."

"You come, Wolf."

"Thank you, captain, but I should not be away from Paris, so I will stay, if you please."

Cartouche had plenty of money about him, so he thrust a hand in [. . .] then, with Louise and Tomasso [. . .] can's lodging, where they had left some money, the proceeds of the Lyons boat adventure. Tomasso received his share, Gribichon's was left to the care of Can-can, and Cartouche stowed his in a portmanteau.

Three of them then departed, but, before they left the city, they heard the news—out of fifty policemen only three survived the explosion, one of whom was the colonel. But as fifty-two bodies were found, most of them scorched and mangled beyond recognition, it was proved—to the satisfaction of the Parisians—that Cartouche and four of his men had perished. One of the police swore that a pair of legs, detached from the body, had belonged, during life, to Cartouche; the boots proved that sufficiently.

Colonel Leguerre had an arm broken, and was otherwise injured. Black George's head was identified, but as many of the bodies had lost, not only their limbs, but their clothing, it was impossible to say which was his trunk. However, everyone in Paris rejoiced to think that at last they were rid of that monster, Cartouche.

*   *   *   *   *   *

Well disguised and travelling by easy stages in a hired post-carriage, Monsieur and Madame Cartier (alias Cartouche) and Signor Corsi, as Tomasso chose to style himself, journeyed on towards Bordeaux.

Tomasso intended to take his money to Italy, where he would be able to purchase an estate and live comfortably on the produce of his vineyards and orange groves.

they were to meet with an adventure before their journey came to an end.

The horses were toiling up a steep hill and the travellers were walking a little distance behind the carriage when a horseman rode up and, drawing a pistol, exclaimed—

"Gentlemen, I must have your money."

"Can't spare it, Gribby," replied Cartouche; "but I can give you some good advice. Give up this business."

"Is that you, captain?—ha, ha, ha! But how is it you have left Paris before my return?"

Cartouche told him about the grand final display of fireworks, and Gribichon laughed immensely. Then he told Cartouche the names of three vessels which were expected to sail soon, and also the addresses of the owners.

"Come with us, Gribichon."

"I must have a chat with Can-can first. If she agrees we may, perhaps, follow."

They had a dinner together at the next inn the carriage reached, Gribichon riding back for that purpose. Then they bade each other adieu, Gribby riding on to Paris and the others in due time reaching Bordeaux.

Cartouche, or Cartier as he from this time called himself, put up at a good hotel, and then went out to arrange for the passage of himself and Louise to New Orleans, and Tomasso at the same time bargained with the proprietor of another vessel for conveyance to Naples, and as the vessel was to sail at once he lost no time in getting on board, the others watching till the ship was out of sight.

Next morning Louise was taken by her lover to a church, where she was made his lawful wife, just about the same time that Monsieur Eugene de Gribichon was going through the same ceremony with Can-can at Paris.

Three days later Monsieur and Madame Cartier left France for, and after a long voyage reached, New Orleans.

*   *   *   *   *   *

A year and a half had passed away and Cartier had won the respect of the settlers near New Orleans, when another ship arrived bearing Gribichon and his wife and child, who at once proceeded to Cartier's residence. Madame Cartier by this time had two youngsters.

"Any news of our old associates, Gribby?" Cartier asked.

"Three of them were hanged, the others I had lost sight of—except Wolf, and he is doing very well as proprietor of a comfortable inn twenty leagues from Paris."

"And this is the end of Cartouche's band?" said the late owner of that name.

But Cartier and Gribichon flourished in their new homes.

www.ingramcontent.com/pod-product-compliance
Lightning Source LLC
Chambersburg PA
CBHW080829250626

47160CB00008B/2885